"If you got a battle to fight, you cain't rightfully ask the Lord to help you and not the other fella. Now can you? . . . No, son, you got to fight and hope God likes the way you're using your fists. And that goes for the boy you're fightin'. . . . I hope you won't have to stay here all your life, Newt. It ain't a all-good place and it ain't a all-bad place. But you can learn just as much here about people and things as you can learn any place else. Cherokee Flats is sorta like a fruit tree. Some of the people are good and some of them are bad—just like the fruit on a tree. . . . No matter if you go or stay, think of it like that till the day you die—let it be your learnin' tree."

So spoke Sarah Winger to her son not long before his thirteenth birthday, and this is the story of what happened to Newt Winger during his perilous climb out of childhood.

"THE STORY . . . HAS BEEN TOLD MANY TIMES. BUT NEVER HAS IT BEEN TOLD THE WAY GORDON PARKS TELLS IT . . . WRITTEN WITH POWER, SENSITIVITY AND TIMELINESS"

—ST. PETERSBURG TIMES

THE LEARNING TREE

BY GORDON PARKS

A CREST REPRINT

FAWCETT PUBLICATIONS, INC., GREENWICH, CONN.
MEMBER OF AMERICAN BOOK PUBLISHERS COUNCIL, INC.

A Crest Book published by arrangement with
Harper & Row, Publishers, Inc.

PRINTING HISTORY

First Harper printing, May 1963
Second printing, October 1963
Third printing, November 1963

First Crest printing, September 1964

Crest Books are published by Fawcett World Library,
67 West 44th Street, New York, New York 10036.
Printed in the United States of America.

TO MOMMA AND POPPA

CHAPTER ✤ 1

NEWT WINGER lay belly-flat at the edge of the cornfield, his brown chin close to the ground, his eyes glued to a hill of busy ants. He singled out one struggling with tree bark twice its size, tugging it forward then sideways then backward up the incline. Being a veteran ant-watcher, Newt tracked its course near perfect over the rough and slippery terrain.

For five of his twelve years he had watched these creatures, remembering that his father often spoke of their energy and work habits in contrast to those of the listless blacks and whites in Cherokee Flats. ("Son, the only thing worse than lazy Negroes is lazy white trash—'cause they're born white, with a God-given chance from the start.")

This anthill was a special one, and Newt liked it better than most he'd seen. The sunny side of it glittered like diamonds because a chunk of sandy earth, washed down by the morning rain and held firm by a discarded plow, stuck to this portion of the mound. Newt pressed his chin even flatter, closing one eye, for now the ant with the bark was near the top and he got a clearer view with one eye shut. He moved his blunt nose close to what now seemed a big animal pulling a tree trunk up a mountainside.

As the ant reached the top, the glitter suddenly dimmed and bits of the mound blew into Newt's eye. He blinked and brushed out the dirt, but when he looked again, the whole mound was blowing apart. At the same moment he felt the cool Kansas wind rushing in, stinging his face and throat. Newt's prairie instincts told him this was no ordinary wind. Catlike, he jumped to his naked feet and looked to the sky. A great swirling black cloud was moving toward him from the southwest. It was broad at the top, gradually narrowing to a point at the bottom near the earth—looking every bit like a spinning top. He started to run, but this sight held him transfixed in the biting wind, his bare brown arms shielding his dark face. He leaned into the gale, looking much like a

7

small, wiry, broad-shouldered scarecrow, his tattered shirt and bib overalls flapping from the wind.

"Neewt! Neewt! Where is you? Neewt!" It was Big Mabel's voice somewhere down the cornfield. "Neewt! Neewt—!" As he spun about to answer, his foot struck the remains of the anthill, kicking the insects in every direction.

He jerked his foot up, afraid he had killed; then, falling to his knees, he began cupping the dirt and ants with his hands in an attempt to rebuild the mound. He kept pulling the scatterings together, only to see them blown away. Then frightened and confused, he fell to the ground and placed his body in the path of the wind to protect the rest of the hill. But the wind, mixed now with pouring rain, swept over and beneath him, swirling the loose pile into nothingness.

Big Mabel reached him just before the full front of the storm struck Cherokee Flats. As she yanked him to his feet, the wind-driven rain lashed her naked parts and flattened the wet gingham dress against her body. "What you doin' here, boy? Your maw and paw and all of us was worried 'bout you! Cain't you see the big storm comin'? What's wrong with you, anyhow? What you cryin' for? Come on now, git movin'! We got to hurry, boy! Come ahead!"

Newt pulled loose for a last look at the anthill, but as he did so a gust slammed him hard against Big Mabel and they both tumbled to the ground. As they went down, the girl twisted to break her fall and Newt fell beneath her, striking his leg on the sharp edge of the plow. They struggled to their feet and started off with the wind at their backs, blowing them into a weird slippery trot.

After several yards, Newt screamed in pain and dropped to his knees. "What's the matter, boy?" Big Mabel cried. Newt groaned and lay still. "Come on, boy. We cain't stop here! Come on, I'll help you! . . . My God, boy, where'd you git that slice in your leg? You bleedin' like a hog!"

Newt grimaced. "That old plow back there—shore does hurt, too."

Big Mabel looked about desperately. They were a good mile from the Winger house. Jim Pullens' place was a half mile closer, but still not close enough. She stared at the swirling blackness. "Too far to Jim's or your paw's place from here. Maybe we can make the killin' house to the other side of the field. Come on! Git on my back!"

She squatted in the mud and Newt clasped his arms about her neck, straddling her back, with his legs between her arms. She steadied him and began crawling along the edge of the field, seeking the protection of the cornstalks. But she changed her mind when she saw them bending crazily from their roots. "Cain't make it this way. Hang on, we'll skirt round the end!" She staggered up, balanced Newt's weight, then headed for the slaughterhouse across the field.

The high winds, rotating counter-clockwise, pushed, snatched and twisted them over the violent countryside, and Newt's concern for the ants and his gashed leg gave way to fear of thunder, lightning and screaming wind.

Suddenly Big Mabel yelled, "Dammit to hell, I'm stuck—cain't move!" She was sinking ankle-deep in mud. Freeing one foot then the other, she inched her way to higher and firmer ground.

The wind was behind them again, forcing Big Mabel into a crazy lope, and within a few minutes she was rounding the edge of the cornfield, from where she could make out the blurry image of the slaughterhouse. "We'll git there soon now, Newt! Hold tighter, boy! Hold tighter!" Newt whimpered and dug his face into the back of her neck, trying desperately to keep his wet hands from slipping apart—feeling pain from the cut, and the sticky warmth of blood between his toes.

Thunder rumbled over them and within a split second, in the blinding flash that followed, Newt saw the outline of the house off to their right. "There 'tis, Mabel! There 'tis!" A deafening crash echoed the thunder. He smacked his hands against his ears and lost his balance. "Hold on! Grab—" Big Mabel's warning was late. Newt was already falling.

His head struck first. Pain jolted through his neck to his belly and shimmied out to his toes. Then he was floating on a puffy white cloud fringed with orange and purple raindrops. The wind kept curling the cloud over him like a hot blanket. He tried pushing it off, but it kept covering him, so he kicked it with his foot, which punctured the cloud. He went tumbling through space with a chunk of cloud stuck through his leg. Down . . . down . . . down he fell. . . . "Help! Help! Momma, catch me! I'm fallin'—"

Big Mabel tore a strip from the bottom of her dress, bound it above the wound in his leg and began tightening. "Quiet, boy, you goin' to be all right now. You is safe in the killin' house—this'll stop the bleedin'." She secured the bandage, pulled a butcher knife off a rack, wrung water from her dress onto it, then placed the flat side of the blade against the lump on his forehead. "Why you let loose I don't know —with just a few feet to go." She ripped another piece off her hemline and began cleaning blood from his leg.

9

Newt's hazy awakening assured him of safety. Big Mabel's voice, which at first had seemed far away, was closer now. Slowly he made out the dark broad forehead, high cheek-bones and sullen lips as she moved above him; the bare damp shoulders glistening in the weak light, the full breasts hanging free and swaying with each motion. His eyes caught patches of light in the roof where shingles were ripping away and water splattering through—except where he lay, for directly above him were sheets of tin he and his father had placed in early spring.

"You feelin' better now, boy?"

"My head hurts—and I'm kinda cold."

"Be warmin' you up in a minute. We's lucky to be inside. We's smack in the middle of a cyclone. Everything's gonna blow away if this keeps up."

"How'd my head git hurt?"

"You acted a fool and let loose and busted the ground with that noggin of your'n. That's how." Another patch of shingles tore from the roof. "Damn shore is blowin' to hell out there!"

"What you holdin' that knife on my head for?"

"Quit askin' so many questions, boy! I know what I'm doin'. It's to take swellin' out." She placed his hands on the cracked knife handle. "Here, hold it right there for a minute—gotta find somethin' to cover us up."

She went to an adjoining room used for smoking meat and groped about in the darkness for a moment or so. "Thank God—I know'd this old quilt was here somewheres!" She returned to Newt, took the knife and threw it aside, then spread the musty cover on the floor next to him. "Roll over here, boy." Newt propped himself up on his elbows and eyed the quilt.

"That thing's dirty!"

"You pick a hell of a time to git hinkty, boy. You's cold, ain't you? Well, this'll keep you warm. Git yore little black ass over!"

Newt scooted over on his backside, carefully dragging the injured leg behind the rest of his body. Big Mabel stood with hands on her broad hips looking down on him. "Better git them wet things off, too."

"What for?"

"There you go with questions again. Boy, I'm seven years older'n you, and I know what I'm doin'. Hadn't been for me you'd still be out there blowin' away with them damn ants!"

Newt scowled and began tugging at his overalls. Big Mabel

10

plopped down beside him and pulled them over his feet. Then she yanked the remains of the dress over her head and flung it in a corner.

"You oughta be feelin' better soon now," she said, fixing the quilt over them and, at the same time, pulling Newt hard against her naked body. "Come closer, boy, if you want to git warm." Her voice now was husky and low—so low that he could hardly understand her words.

And soon the warmth of Big Mabel brought a glow to his own body, and a hardness to his groin—one he had never felt before. Big Mabel felt the hardness too. She rolled over on her back, pulled him on top of her.

The killing house shook all over and the shingles kept flying away, but Newt felt even warmer. And the softness of Big Mabel cushioned the shaking; calmed his fears. And though the storm blew on, it was not long before Newt completely forgot its blowing.

Yet, outside over the prairie, groundhogs and skunks, jack rabbits and opossums took flight from the flooding lowlands. And sparrows, robins, bobolinks and swallows alike, trapped in the whirling wind, darted helplessly beneath the ominous sky. In the brush, cud-chewing deer knelt close together protecting their nervous young. And the dark sky drew darker.

Meanwhile, Jack Winger and his son Pete, keeping short distances apart, struggled through wind and rain over the countryside, combed all Candy Hill for Newt. Cutting across the river road, the two powerfully built men saw at the same time a large section of the road wash out and the bobbing headlights of a truck coming toward them. They rushed to the middle of the road, waving frantically at the onrushing vehicle; but the driver spotted the washout too late, and the big truck twisted off the road, jumped a ditch and crashed against a light pole, then slid back down the incline. Jack and his son heard the cracking, saw the upper part of the pole falling away. "Watch out!" Jack shouted. The power line snapped, and at once there was a showering of sparks and a zinging sound, followed by a great splash.

They made their way over to the truck, but the driver was already out of the cab when they reached it. "Damn near killed myself!" he hollered above the screaming wind.

"You hurt?" Jack bellowed.

"Naw—but that damned power line's down over the field there!"

"You betta warn somebody—we gotta keep lookin' for my kid! Didn't see a boy down the road, did you?"

11

"Nope, not a soul!" The two men started off. "Hope you find him!" the trucker shouted as they trudged away.

Bending almost double in the wind, Jack and Pete pushed along the slippery bank of Flynn's River, searching every crevice and cave along the way. Finally they reached the swimming hole.

"Newt! Newt!" Jack cried out. "Newt! Newt!" There was no answer, not even an echo as the wind whipped his voice away. Then Pete was hollering, "Neewt! Neewt!" His cry was all but silenced by a loud thunderclap. Jack shook his head dejectedly. Then they turned their backs to the punishing storm and headed toward home.

They could see the truck still straddling the ditch as they went back across the road, and when they passed beyond the washout, the man stuck his head from the cab. "D'ya see any sign of the boy?"

"No luck!" Pete yelled back, and they kept moving. They were alongside Jake Kiner's ranch now, hearing the hoofs of his frightened livestock pounding in the direction of the downed power line. The two men squinted through the driving rain. A bluish flash lit the prairie and several of the steers lurched grotesquely in sputtering death. The others shied, then plunged on over the tangled wire.

Sarah Winger jumped at the banging on the door. After a quick glance at her fourteen-year-old daughter Prissy, she hastened through the parlor, jerked open the door and watched as the two drenched, exhausted men staggered in.

"Jack?" Her voice was softly urgent and questioning.

He slammed the door, took a deep breath and walked to the corner where Pete was already shedding his wet clothes. For an instant Sarah stood motionless, her heart pumping. "Oh—oh," she moaned softly, "oh, my God." Then quickly she was through the door and into the open, her long black skirt whipping in the wind. But just as swiftly Jack was out beside her, coaxing and pushing her back into the house.

Pete rushed over and pulled them both in, banged the door shut, threw the bolt in place and gently grasped his mother's shoulders. "Ain't no sense in worryin', Momma." His tone was low and positive. "Newt knows this countryside better'n a squirrel."

"Prissy."

"Yessir, Poppa."

"Fix me and your brother some hot coffee."

"Yessir," she answered, and was off to the kitchen.

12

Sarah moved to the window and looked out at the stormy blackness. The clock on the wall showed three, and the wanging of the lead ball against the bell, chiming the hour, sounded incongruous to her ear, as if it were coming from some far-distant place, at some far-removed time. Her husband and son stood watching her, trying to share her thoughts, wanting in some way to banish the fear that held her. Jack took a chair to her and she sat down. And she remained there for an hour and a half more while the house shook under the twisting wind. She silently prayed for the safety of Newt—forgetting all else, peering through the lightning flashes for any sort of image that might miraculously be her son.

Near five o'clock the wind suddenly died, the sky began to pale and the storm was gone.

When Newt and Big Mabel left the smokehouse they could see the heavy clouds being suctioned off by the storm, swirling now into the distant northeast. And as they walked along, frogs leaped into the open and crickets made chirping noises with their wings, rubbing away the wetness. The late sun shimmered in the rivulets snaking through the muddy fields to streams and gullies in the lowland.

"Look'it there!" Newt suddenly shouted. He pointed at what was left of Jim Pullens' house.

"Lordy," Big Mabel blurted, "good thing we didn't try for here." They cut across the field to the crumpled house, seeing that there was no longer a roof and that the wall nearest them had caved in completely. "Lordy, what a mess!"

"Think he's all right?" Newt was tagging behind now, not only because of the pain in his leg but also from a fear of what they might find in the wreckage.

"Who, Jim?"

"Yeah. Don't see nobody stirrin' about."

"Well, come on, let's see." Now Big Mabel was slowing.

"Boy, lucky we didn't git here. We'd a—"

"Shush. What's that whinin' sound?" They stopped and listened.

"I don't hear nothin'."

"Sounded like—"

"It's Collie! It's Collie!" Newt blurted, limping faster toward the sound. "He must be under the roof!" Now he was down on his hands and knees, peeping under the fallen roof. "Here, Collie! Come on, boy! Here, Coll—" Then he recoiled in shock. "Mabel! Mabel! It's him! It's him! He's trapped under the roof."

"What? You shore, boy?"

"Yeh. Come see for yourself." Big Mabel flattened to the muddy ground, squinting beneath the tangled debris. "See?" Newt panted.

"It's Jim all right—he alive?"

"Mister Pullens! Mister Pullens!" Newt hollered. The dog whimpered and began wagging his tail. "Mister Pullens! Mister Pullens!"

" 'Tain't no use, Newt. See all the blood—he's prob'ly dead."

"We better git help. Maybe he's just knocked out."

By the time Newt and Big Mabel reached the Winger house, only a gentle breeze stirred the puddles in the yard. Prissy was skimming the water with her big toe when she saw them running toward her. "Momma! Momma!" she hollered. "Here comes Newt and Big Mabel!"

Sarah heard and ran from the kitchen. Pete, having just returned, disconsolately, from another search with his father, came down the path. "Poppa!" Jack Winger was in the backyard eying his overturned henhouse, and the anxiety in Pete's voice made him wheel around. "Yep, boy! What is it?"

"Here's Newt and Big Mabel!" Pete called back on the run.

Prissy was already pouring questions. "Where was you? How'd you hurt your leg? Where'd you hide out?"

Before Newt could answer, he saw his mother in the doorway. The sight of her was heart-warming, and he wanted to go to her; but instead he turned to his brother. "Pete—Mister Pullens' house blowed down—he's trapped underneath it, and—and—" He was out of breath.

"He hurt bad?" Pete questioned.

"Looks to me he's—"

"Yeh," Mabel interrupted, "blood's all round his head."

Jack Winger was among them now. "What's the matter? Where you been, boy?"

"Jim's trapped under his house!" Pete burst out.

"Jim Pullens?"

"Yessir."

"Well, come on—let's git over there. Come on!" Jack shouted. Then he and Pete trotted off. Newt turned, too, and limped after them.

"Newt!" Sarah called halfheartedly.

He kept running, pretending not to hear his mother. She started to call again but changed her mind. "They may need him for somethin'. It's enough just to have him back! Thank

14

God he's back!" She turned to Big Mabel. "Where'd you find him, Mabel?"

The girl shyly pulled the top of her torn dress together. "Up by the corn patch foolin' round a anthill. We—we made it to the smokehouse 'stead of tryin' to make it here or to Jim's."

"You was right for stoppin', girl. We was worried to death."

"Newt got his leg cut on the ole plow over in the field. I tore up my dress to stop the bleedin', and he's got a knot on his head from a fall, but he'll be all right."

"Well, come on in—you must be hungry," Sarah said calmly. Without waiting, she turned and went back into the house, mumbling and wiping her eyes.

Big Mabel turned to Prissy. "Tell your maw I ain't hungry. See yore henhouse got blowed over." Then she looked at Prissy in a peculiar way. "Tell Newt to—oh, never mind." She went on down the path.

Jim was dead.

"Pore fella didn't have a chance," Jack commented as they pulled him from beneath the house. Newt looked at the crumpled form, the bloody, lifeless face, the sad, beautiful dog still whining at his side. He had seen death for the first time, and a fear set in him—a fear of dying, like this or any other way. As he, his father and brother walked silently homeward, the image of Jim settled firmly in Newt's mind. He tried to erase it by thinking back to his own narrow escape. But this didn't work. He hobbled up closer to Pete.

"Leg hurtin', Newt?"

"Yeh, kinda."

Pete stooped. "Git on," he said, "I'll give you a lift."

Newt climbed on his brother's back, and bouncing along he studied the big, tall frame of his father walking beside them, his large hands stuffed in his faded blue jeans, his wide-brimmed, weather-beaten hat shaped to his head like a turtle's shell; his face with its strong, leathery brown lines curving up from his long, heavy mustache to his high cheekbones. He wondered what his father was thinking, what he would do next.

"What'cha gonna do now, Poppa?"

Jack's head turned toward Newt but he kept walking, his eyes brightening beneath his bushy brows. He was looking at his son as though he had seen him for the first time since the storm. "Where you been, boy? Where was you durin' the storm?"

"Me and Big Mabel hid in the smokehouse over there."

"What's that rag doin' on your leg?"

"Cut it on your old plow in the field."

"I declare, boy—you're born for trouble, born for trouble." Jack sighed. "Gonna be the death of your mother yet."

Newt had expected this type of comment earlier. He knew too that when it finally came it would be brief. Now that it was over, he waited for the answer which he also knew his father had been forming during those few seconds of mild rebuke.

"Ain't much we can do now, boy, 'cept call the undertaker—too bad—too bad."

Newt's mind slid back momentarily to the corpse of Jim Pullens, recalling the bigness and strength of him who lay now without power to open an eye or simply to breathe. Subconsciously he compared it with the live, powerful body of Pete's that carried him so easily over the soggy field. He looked close at his brother's bullish neck, feeling the rippling force of the muscles in the back beneath him. For the first time he realized how much his brother's face resembled his father's—Pete's just looks newer, without a mustache, he decided.

As they jogged along, Newt eyed a big ball of red hanging where the prairie met the sky. The ball cut to a half; a quarter; and then it was gone beneath the earth line, leaving only a glow that shot up through feathery white specks from the dark horizon. He twisted his head, looking northeast. Dusk soaked into the very last of the storm clouds. Behind him, night began settling over Jim Pullens and Collie like a blanket.

Jack Winger was a poor man, but the supper he blessed that night was of things Newt liked best—fried chicken, yams, browned clabber gravy and cornbread. Immediately the talk centered around the big storm and its casualties.

"Jim was a fine fella, one of the best round here."

"How long'd you know him, Poppa?"

"Well on to twenty years, ain't it, Sarah?"

"Closer to twenty-three, if mem'ry serves me right—use your fork, Newt! Seems he came about two years after us."

"Funny thing," Newt said, "old Collie was right 'side him and didn't even git scratched. How you figger that, Poppa?"

"The Lord works in funny ways. Just wasn't the dog's time to go—pass the gravy, Prissy—was Jim's time. Simple as that."

"Anybody hear from Uncle Rob?"

Jack spooned the thick gravy over a piece of cornbread before answering. "Your Uncle Rob's all right. Fact he's blind don't make him no difference. He prob'ly sensed the storm 'fore any the rest of us and got inside in time. The Simpson boy told me he seen him on his front porch right after the storm blowed over."

"How'd Mag take Jim's death?"

"She was plenty broke up when I told her. Her place got smashed up a little bit too. Jim was a good brother to her."

"Prissy," Sarah said, "you go help her git straight in the mornin'."

"Yessem."

"The little Johnson girl got burned real bad, I heard."

"Who told you that, Pete?" Sarah questioned.

"Doc Cravens. He told me they got her over at County Hospital."

"How'd it happen?"

"Her momma dropped a lamp or somethin' like that."

"Drunk, I bet," Jack moaned.

"You shouldn't be sayin' that, Jack. You—"

"You know well as I do, Sarah, that Lucy stays drunk offa canned heat and Chappie's likker."

"That still don't give you right to say it here at the table in front of these kids."

"Well—"

Pete broke in to save his father. "Clint got home yet?"

"Now you talk 'bout drunks—he's the prize one." Jack was back on the firing line. "Tell me him and old Doc Cheney been drunk since way 'fore the storm started."

"Clint's just mixed up, that's all, Jack."

"Yep, but he's your fav'rit mixed-up son-in-law."

"And yours, too."

"Yep, but no fav'rit by any stretch of a sow's tail. If Rende had any sense she wouldn't a even said hello to him, less 'lone marry him. Gits so it's the same every week or so. She comes runnin' here with them kids 'way from him and that ole shotgun."

Sarah was about to answer when Pastor Broadnap appeared at the screen door. "O-ho," he beamed, "caught you sittin' for supper!"

The rotund minister swept into the room, his long black preacher coat flapping at his knees. Little pods of sweat stood out on his forehead at the point where the hairline receded sharply, as if it were shaved. He scanned the table. "Just in time to share the gifts of the Lord," he said.

"Oh my," Newt mumbled, "there goes my chicken legs."

Prissy snickered and Sarah fired a glance at Newt. "Come on in, Reverend," she said, "and have some supper." Newt watched his mother push aside the legs he had hoped for, and he couldn't suppress a groan. "One more grunt out of you, boy, and up you git without any more supper at all," she whispered fiercely.

"Yessem," Newt chirped, his face plumped up in exasperation.

Space was made for the pastor, and Sarah heaped food on his plate and passed it to him. "Got any of your fine apple butter, sister Winger?" he asked.

"Right here in the cupboard," she sang out, reaching through the door behind her for the jar.

"Bless you. Bless you."

"Quite a blow we had today, Reverend."

"Yes 'twas—yes 'twas," he mumbled, reaching for a slice of cornbread with one hand and the gravy dish with the other.

"Any damage to the parsonage at all?"

"No, brother Winger, just the church steeple. Blowed off its base. Don't rightly know what's holdin' it up there. Good thing it stopped blowin' when it did, otherwise it'd shore be on the ground."

"Yep, we're lucky at that, I guess. Could'a been worse, a lot worse. Well, just gotta round up some members for straight'nin' it up, that's all."

"Bless you, Jack. Bless you." He was flooding the cornbread with gravy now. "Well," he continued, chewing, "I attach a very special meanin' to that storm. It's (Newt winced as Broadnap teethed the meat from the bone) a warnin' to the wrongdoin' of all these sinners round here. This place is poppin' with sin—people drinkin', cuttin', fightin' and doin' all sorts of things the Lord don't approve of; nobody comin' to church like they ought'a. Why, I'd say Chappie Logan's place got more drunks in it than we got members on Sunday mornin'."

Sarah Winger looked at the pastor and said, "For some reason it's the good ones who go first."

"Thinkin' 'bout Jim Pullens, huh, sister Winger?" Broadnap said, dipping into the jar of apple butter with his knife. "Well, it's hard to explain—hard to explain. Jim was a fine man. Always come to church and prayer meetin'. Only way I figger it is that the Lord takes the good ones like that so the bad ones'll hafta take more responsibility."

"Old Sam Wong got it too. They ain't found him yet, I hear."

"Naw, and with half that block on top of him they might not find him for a couple of days," Pete said. "And to think he was out safe, then went back for his cat and got killed."

"Well, you find out lots 'bout people in a big wind like that. Some proves weak, some proves strong." Jack Winger wiped his long mustache with his wrist and pulled his pipe from his pocket. "It's a easy time to cut lamb from sheep. Think God does prob'ly send things like this to test us. Wouldn't be surprised if he didn't git tangled up hisself tryin' to figger out these here folks in Cherokee Flats."

"Was you scared, Newt?" Prissy asked.

"Naw. Just sorry I killed the ants. That's all."

"If you'd been home choppin' wood like you was s'posed to, you wouldn't been in such a mess. Them anthills gonna be the death of you yet."

"Keep quiet and eat you supper, girl. You got no right to talk. You was just lucky to be home instead of gallivantin' somewhere."

"Yessem." Newt caught Prissy's eye, grinned impishly, snaked his tongue out at her and resumed his pious demeanor before she could bring his action to their mother's attention.

Broadnap picked up a bone and started gnawing on it. There was one leg and a rump left on the chicken platter, and both he and Newt eyed them. "How about another piece of chicken, Reverend?" Sarah volunteered.

Broadnap chuckled. Newt gritted his teeth and looked blankly at the wall ahead of him, sensing the maliciousness in Prissy's cough. Broadnap chuckled again. "You know one thing, sister Sarah, I think somebody else got their eye on that leg well as me, and I got a little proposition to make with him about who gits it."

"Oh," Sarah cut in, rolling her eyes at Newt, "that ain't a'tall necessary. You're welcome." She put the leg on Broadnap's plate.

"No no no, sister," Broadnap protested. "Now, Newt, you been studyin' your Sunday school lessons lately?"

Newt gulped, "Yessir, I—"

"Fine. Now if you tell me the name of the weapon Samson slew the Philistines with, the leg's yours." Broadnap grinned smugly.

Newt scratched his head in deep thought (Slingshot . . . naw, that was David . . . spear . . . naw . . .). "I got it!" he

19

blurted out. "The jawbone of a—a—" He looked sideways at his mother.

"A what?" Broadnap snapped.

A wry smile wrinkled Newt's face. "Well, I cain't name it right out, but it's the same name as that part left on the platter."

"The ass," Broadnap grunted, dumping the leg on Newt's plate, "the jawbone of an ass."

Everybody laughed.

"Newt," Sarah admonished, "you shouldn't take that leg from Reverend Broadnap. Now—"

"Oh no, sister. The boy won it fair 'n square. I'll take what's left," Broadnap countered, spearing the chicken rump from the platter.

"You been over to see the little Johnson girl, Reverend?"

"Yes, sister Sarah. That child's lucky to be livin'. Hardly any hair or skin left on her. Doc Cravens says we got to ask for some volunteers in church Sunday."

"Volunteers for what?" Jack asked.

"Well, seems like Doc's gonna try to graft new skin on her. That means somebody's gonna have to give some'a theirs."

Sarah looked up in astonishment. "You mean Doc intends to strip skin off somebody else and put it on her?"

"That's what he's sayin', sister Sarah, if she's gonna live any kind'a normal life again."

"Poor child. It's a awful thing—a awful thing," Sarah said, shaking her head.

"Don't worry, sister Sarah, she'll be helped. Some good souls'll come forward."

"Hot coffee, brother Broadnap?"

"No, Jack. Ain't been sleepin' too well lately. Next time round, maybe. Got some more visitin' to do on my way to the parsonage. Sister Pullens and a few others." He got up. Those about the table started to rise, but he spread his arms above them. "Sit, my dear children, and bless you, sister Sarah, for the wonderful repast." He plucked several toothpicks from a bowl and picked up his black "preacher's" hat from the sideboard. As he passed Newt he patted him on the head. "Keep studyin', boy. Givin' the right answer meant that chicken's leg instead of the part that went over the fence last." He chuckled. Then he plopped the hat on his head and left as suddenly as he had come.

After supper the stove was fired, and soon its heat pushed the evening chill away. Pete slumped over a Western saddle, stitching the flaps, while Prissy tended the kitchen. Jack Winger lit his pipe, leaned his chair against the wall and gazed at the ceiling. In the quiet of her bedroom, Sarah rocked back and forth patching overalls.

Newt lay on the dining room floor, swallowed up in the happenings of the day. The ants; the ugly sky; the flight; the fear; the pain; and the impassioned wedding of his body with Big Mabel's was an experience he felt he would never forget. And time and again his mind reached back beneath the warm, dusty blanket to grasp those sensuous moments.

Too, the storm had made him more aware of his family's importance to his existence. He admired certain things about each of them. He couldn't imagine anyone braver than his father; yet there were things about him Newt couldn't understand—why he resented Newt's wanting to play the piano, or why their talks together only dealt with tending chores. Newt thought of when his father was once sick and had sat around moaning, waiting for his mother to give him a teaspoon of medicine. But there he was, Newt recalled, out in that storm lookin' all over for me.

And Jack Winger was thinking it was good to have his youngest home safe and sound. He'd been pretty worried for a while, and he wished he could let the boy know about that. Why did he find it easier to pet a horse or a dog than one of his own kids? And why did he have to be so stupid when they needed help with their lessons? Well, he was glad he had Sarah to give them what he couldn't. Fact was, they'd all be in a bad way without her.

Newt's eyes rolled lazily to Pete's muscular arms and wide shoulders, and he started longing for the time when his own body and strength would match his brother's. Pete, who was twenty-six, had fought overseas in the World War. Newt remembered when he was reported missing during the Battle of the Marne; how his mother had refused to believe he was dead; the way she'd held back tears through the bitter winter, and then cried so hard when the telegram came saying Pete was safe. Now he was back working at odd jobs with his father, happiest when bucking wild broncos or wrestling steers during the local rodeos. He was discontented with Cherokee Flats, but saw little chance of ever leaving it again.

A plate broke on the kitchen floor.

"Save the pieces, Prissy," Newt hollered.

"Shut up," she shot back.

"Boy," Jack growled, "mind your own bizness."

"Yessir, Poppa."

21

Newt had no way of knowing it, but his sister had just been imagining his experience as he had recounted it to his mother before supper. Her subconscious explored his painful cuts and bruises, his fears, and then submitted to a moment of morbidness that fancied her brother lying dead somewhere in the stormy prairie. The apparition frightened her, and she had dropped the plate.

Newt thought of Priscilla as most boys his age thought of older sisters—meddlesome, tattlesome, scary, curious and unsociable. Prissy had once described herself in a letter to a distant cousin as "high brown, tall, gray-eyed, with long red straight hair," when actually she was dark brown, slightly dumpy, brown-eyed, with short curly black hair.

Sarah Winger rocked and sewed in her bedroom with an attitude of thankfulness. Newt's being in danger had shaken her more than she had realized. Her body and mind were spent. She had begun sewing to calm her nerves, gone to the back room in order to hide the anxiety still surging within her bosom. And she thought of her other children away from home. Less than a mile away the eldest child, Rende, no doubt sat fearful in her four-room clapboard, waiting for Clint—realizing that when he did come home drunk, cursing and threatening, she and her two children might have to run for the safety of the Winger homestead. And there was Roy in Chicago, and two other girls, Clara and Lucille, up north in Minnesota.

At fifty-two, Sarah was of unusual looks; smooth dark brown skin, with a sharp-boned face borrowing the high cheek and slanted eye of the Cherokee. A pinkish white scar the size of a quarter marked her left temple, resembling a flower in bloom. And this strange marking, inflicted by a thunderbolt during a long past storm, enriched the tone of her dark skin. A thin layer of curly black hair stretched to a ball at the nape of her longish neck, and her delicate ears, curving gently out from the back, seemed to be shaped of wax. She was short, wiry and quick-moving; and when her long skirt whipped out behind her, she gave an impression of forceful, almost perpetual motion.

Newt thought of his mother now (Wonder why she's back in her room tonight all alone?), and he tried to imagine their life without her. The warmth of the room, the serene images of his father and brother slid into a black void. He was as thankful for her presence as she had been for his safe return.

22

He pushed himself to his feet and limped through the parlor, dragging a finger over the battered piano keys.

" 'Bout time you was in bed, son," Sarah called out.

"Yessem—just comin' to tell you goodnight." He stepped into her room.

"Glad you did, boy—glad you did. How's the leg?"

"Okay, I guess. Well, goodnight, Momma."

"Goodnight. Sleep well."

"Yessem," he said, turning back to the dining room. "Night, Poppa."

"Night, boy."

"Night, Pete."

"G'night, Newt."

He limped quietly to the kitchen door. Prissy was hanging up the last of the cooking pots. "Boooo! Boooo!" he shouted.

Prissy shrieked, "Momma!" and dropped the pot.

Jack Winger jerked the pipe from his mouth. "Boy!" he shouted, "if you don't git to bed, I declare I'll skin your hide!"

Newt limped off to bed with a grin on his face. He was weary and sore, but happy to be home—safe from the storm.

CHAPTER ✿ 2

JACK WINGER climbed the tower ladder to within a few feet of the dangerously tilting spire of the African Methodist Episcopal Church. With trained eye he noted the damage, the angle of tilt, and instantly determined the number of jacks and cabling needed to hoist the structure back into position. From the ladder he swung to the floor of the upper loft. It was caked with a half century of feathers, twigs and bird droppings. He kicked away the top crust for surer footing, then, leaning precariously from the loft window, twirled a lasso in several wide looping motions, aimed it and let go. The circle of rope hit true and he pulled it tight about the two six-by-sixes jutting from the spire's base. He doubled the rope around an oak beam, knotted it, then slapped it for tautness. It shimmied like a tightly strung banjo string. Satisfied, he hollered to the men below. "Bring about ten jacks and all the tackle you got!" Another look and he yelled again, "Rope off a clearin' to the left and front!"

"Okay!" Pete hollered back from below.

The job started, Jack lit his pipe, rested his elbows on the window sill, and looked out over all Cherokee Flats from his perch. As he did, it came to him that contours of the village resembled those of an egg, the broader top half representing where the most well-to-do resided, and the lower half being where the poor and near-poor lived. The Frisco tracks, running north and south across the lower section, drew the social and economic line between the six thousand residents who made up the village. There were no well-to-do blacks, he reasoned, but there were poor whites who shared, to a certain degree, the status of their dark neighbors east of the tracks.

Far away on the north edge he could just see Flynn's River, the sun reflecting on its flat, slow-moving surface, snaking in and out of the craggy rocks and tall trees. Further beyond, where the water cut into the west, he saw the top of

24

County Hospital that perched on a knoll on the very out-skirts of the village. He glanced toward the opposite end of the river where, off to the right of it, he recognized Jake Kiner's red farmhouse—barns, cattle pens and fruit orchards sprawling over the entire shank of the east hill. On up the gentle slopes the bright sun struck the white crosses and mar-ble headstones marking the graves, and still further to the right of that the steep incline of Candy Hill down which the youth of Cherokee Flats raced their wagons and homemade vehicles in the summer, their sleds in the winter. All else outside the village perimeter, as far as he could see, was prairie, cornfield and brush.

He looked back to the center of the village. The stone courthouse and jail (squatting smugly, medieval-castle-like, in the square) stood out strong and unscathed in the bright Saturday morning sun. But the secondary business area, ly-ing a block to the west behind it, had suffered the brunt of the storm. Talbot's harness shop was flat on the ground, its crushed sides jutting out from under the broken roof. Com-stock's store front, peeping from beneath two huge maple trees, sagged, cock-eyed and windowless, against nine two-by-fours. Blake's general store, Davis' bakery, Carson's drugstore, Sam Wong's laundry, Mack's hamburger shack, snuggling together when the storm struck, were now hope-lessly tangled in a half-block pile of crumpled roofs and smashed walls. Sam, the village's only Chinese citizen, was dead somewhere in the rubble of broken bottles, shattered plaster, torn clothes, spoiled hamburger and baking dough, pots, pans, hardware, ladies' accessories and such.

The Regency Theater (featuring William S. Hart this week—this month—this year) and the Mottsy Funeral Par-lor stood together at the north end of the business section on Main Street. And a mile or so behind them Jack could see the two white people's churches and the two red brick schools for white children, all intact and standing relatively short distances apart. Too, in that area, smack in the middle of a terraced block, sat the big multicupolaed, red-shingled Cavanaugh house where Jack's wife worked.

A freight train puffed across toward the river, and he turned to watch its thick smoke curl in and out of the east side houses and shanties. After it cleared he noticed, for the first time, that the colored Shilo Baptist Church, half a block away, was missing several of its blue-purple-red windows, plus about fifty square feet of shingling; that the wooden col-ored grade school was askew on its concrete base. He noted

25

that aside from Jim Pullens' place, Mag Pullens' front porch, Booker Savage's old barn and the Winger henhouse, damage had been mostly in the southwest part of the village.

Jack had mixed feelings about this place. Like all other Kansas towns, Cherokee Flats wallowed in the social complexities of a borderline state. Here, for the black man, freedom loosed one hand while custom restrained the other. The law books stood for equal rights, but the law (a two-pistol-toting, tobacco-chewing, khaki-putteed, leather-legginged cop called Kirky) never bothered to enforce such laws in such books—"mainly 'cause I cain't read," he often bragged.

And though the white and black children were separated in the primary schools and the churches, they played together on the dusty streets, outlying hills and plains. The black boys and girls and the white boys and girls went to the same picture show—the whites downstairs and first balcony, the blacks in the peanut gallery or buzzard's roost. There was no written law against a black man's eating in a white restaurant or drugstore, but there could be trouble, lots of it, if he tried. So seldom, if ever, did he try—especially if he wanted one of the odd jobs that meant his existence.

To Jack Winger, Cherokee Flats and the whole state was a plateau of uncertainty. "Livin' here is like havin' a good lay with a woman you don't quite trust," he had boomed at the superintendent of schools one day. "My boy Pete got high grades in the white high school, and he was the best basketball player in the whole state, but he couldn't play on the school team 'cause his hide was black!"

"I know, Jack," Jess Hicks had sympathized, "but you know my hands are tied."

"And so's a black man's behind,'" Jack had countered.

Now his eyes turned back to the damaged church steeple. He, Pete and several of the other members had volunteered for this job without pay, to protect the church's dwindled funds. But in the rest of the village he calculated a month or more of steady work. He needed it, for his corn crop had done poorly the year before.

Jack could hear the other men making their way up through the tower now. At the same time he saw his son-in-law Clint and old Doc Cheney wobbling arm in arm through the door of Chappie Logan's Restaurant and Pool Hall, just a few steps east of the tracks. He watched them disappear behind the worn clapboard façade and wondered why this "den of hell," as he called it, hadn't perished in the storm.

The workmen were closer now, and the ladder creaked

under their weight. Pete was the first to the top and, though he could see only his father's back, he sensed his deep thought.

"What you lookin' at, Poppa?"

"Aw, nothin'. Just seen Clint and old Doc goin' in Chappie's."

"Rende says he ain't been home yet. She's got Newt out lookin' for him."

"Newt?"

"Yessir."

Jack paused. "It ain't right for that boy to be round Clint when he's drunk."

"He's gonna see a lot worse'n that before he dies, Poppa."

"Well . . . That Clint—Rende ought'a be glad he ain't home. I declare, I don't know what's gonna become of him. Doc and him are so drunk they gotta hold each other up."

Pete didn't bother to answer. He threw the block and tackle from his shoulder to the floor and jumped over it. "It's shore a long time since I was up here." He was changing the subject, for Pastor Broadnap was next up. "This ain't no time for a sermon on Clint's drinkin'," he thought.

A number of things attracted Clint to Chappie's—pool (which he always played with Pee Wee, the rack boy), whiskey (which Chappie made in his cellar) and the tall tales of the porters and waiters who "laid over" between their runs on the railroad. In their business, the railroaders claimed, one talked freely with the Morgans, the Rockefellers, the Vanderbilts and movie stars—even presidents. So Clint often explained to his wife Rende, "the pulse of the nation is at Chappie's more'n it is at the White House."

These men talked of big things, big people and big places, and this left Clint in a daze, for he had never even been outside of Kansas. At forty, he was a lean man of medium height, reddish-brown coloring and prematurely white hair. Half Negro, half Cherokee, he was a smooth blending of both. Despite Jack Winger's feeling, Clint loved his family. That his action now and then belied this fact was because of a weakness that came with his early hatred of Cherokee Flats. He had always had a desperate longing to leave it for good. His marriage to Rende prevented this, and from the day Butsy, the first child, was born, only liquored dreaming replaced the real adventure beckoning him from the bustling big cities. It was during such drunken reveries that he lost control of himself and got the urge to destroy Rende.

And now he dreamed—deep and far—with old Doc Cheney in a stupor at his side. Lenox Avenue ... State Street ... Beale ... Eighteenth and Vine. Chicago whirred past in one searing swallow. Seattle telescoped to St. Louis in less than a gulp. He drifted through New York against the round hot belly of a luscious brown girl. "Set 'em up!" he hollered. "Clint's in town! Set up the whole damn place! Hey, baby—come sit on Clint's knee! I'm loaded! Let 'em roll, fast and hard! Clint fades all fools—sky's the lim—"

"Quiet down, Clint! You want'a git the law on me?" Chappie Logan yelled, twisting his two-hundred-fifty-pound body around.

"—Tell the damn gov'ner to wait—cain't you see Clint's busy? Oh, you fine brown thing—shake—that—thing!"

Newt poked his head through Chappie's door just as Clint tried to stand, his head drooped nearly to his waist. Newt rushed over to steady him, but Clint reeled and crashed sideways to the floor.

"Goddam," Chappie grunted, "hurry up and git him out'a here 'fore he breaks up the joint." Then he helped Newt get Clint to his feet and out the door.

Chappie was surprised to see Rende in the shadow of the buggy canopy when he shoved Clint up into the seat. "Mornin', Rende," he said apologetically.

Rende didn't answer.

"Where'm I? What's this?" Clint mumbled, slumping to the floor of the buggy.

"Come on, Newt. Git goin'," Rende snapped.

Newt jumped up on the seat and popped the reins against the horse's rump. "Gitti'up," he commanded, and the buggy rambled off.

Sarah Winger had worked for Judge Jefferson Cavanaugh nearly twenty years—cooking, washing, cleaning, nursing, advising and generally running things. The Judge, a widower, lived with his two sons—Chauncey, who, at sixteen, had fallen far short of Jeff's hopes, and Rodney, just turned twelve. Sarah had predicted bad days for Chauncey early in his teens, and her prophecy had not gone denied.

Now she pulled back the faded green velvet drapes in the parlor and squinted against the morning sun. After a moment, her eyes conquered the glare and came to focus on the damaged church spire in the distance. She knew Jack and

Pete were beneath its dangerous leaning—and she hoped they would be careful.

Suddenly a groaning came from Chauncey's bedroom. She quickly crossed the hall and stood beside the door, listening. The groaning became louder and steadier, and her hand went to the knob, but she didn't twist it. "Chauncey." Her voice was low but sharp. "Chauncey, you all right?"

The groaning continued, and she gently turned the knob, inched the door open and peeped in. She adjusted her eyes to the dimness (He's stinkin' of corn liquor—) then she gasped, "Good gracious me!"

Chauncey was lying on the floor, and a blond woman (Looks like the Newhall girl—yes, 'tis), her head hanging off the side of the bed, hair streaming to the floor, shared his unconscious drunkenness.

Sarah stepped out hastily and shut the door with a resounding bang.

"Uh—uh—yeh—who's there? Who's—" Chauncey was stirring.

"It's me—Sarah. You better git that girl out'a here 'fore your paw comes for lunch. You hear me, Chauncey? You hear me?"

"What girl—what you—what you saying?"

Sarah's voice rose, and she banged her fist against the door. "Listen, boy! You better come to and git that girl out'a this house 'fore your paw comes!"

"Okay—okay—quit hollerin'—okay. Blanche! Blanche!"

Sarah grabbed the broom and swished down the long hallway. "Good gracious me—good gracious me—what won't that onery boy do next?"

By four-thirty the sun had sucked most of the wetness from the earth, and Newt, having got Clint home and helped him to bed, sat on the ground in the shade of an apple tree, reliving the high moments of the storm. A patch of muslin, soaked with hogfat and camphor, covered the sore lump on his head, and now and then he patted it to determine the decrease in swelling.

A grasshopper lit on his knee. He eyed it for a moment, then his left hand moved above and ahead of the insect. His other hand touched the tail lightly and the insect leaped into the trap. Newt held it between his fingers, his eyes squinting at the narrow forewings and the broad hind ones (no wonder you can jump so far), then, dipping its mouth to his fingers, he noted the tobacco juice (Poppa says you kill the crops), he tightened his grip, winced, smiled, then loosened it. The grasshopper sprang away.

He thought, "What are grasshoppers for anyway, and snakes and mosquitoes and flies and worms, wasps, potato bugs and things? Seems they ain't much good to the world, but God put 'em here. Seems they got as much rights as we have to live. If the grasshoppers didn't eat the crops, they'd starve. No worse'n us killin' hogs and chickens so we don't go hungry. Hogs and chickens and cows and rabbits and squirrels, possums and such must hate us much as we hate mosquitoes and gnats and flies. Dogs and cats and horses are 'bout the luckiest. 'Bout the only ones we don't go round killin' off all the time. The Ten Commandments say we oughtn's kill, then we come home from church and wring a chicken's neck for dinner—and Reverend Broadnap eats more'n anybody else." Newt stretched. "Too much for me to figger out," he said aloud.

Footsteps fell on the path behind him and he swung his head around to the sight of Beansy Fuller. Beansy, twelve, short and fat, shimmied as he walked. And because he was pigeon-toed, his motions resembled (according to Clint) "a pig doin' a foxtrot."

"How'ya, Newt?"

"Hi, Beansy. Sit down."

"Heard about you and Big Mabel gittin' caught in the storm."

Newt's eyes widened. "What'd you hear? Who told you?"

Beansy smiled slyly. "Big Mabel."

"What all'd she tell you?" Newt's eyes flashed to his bandaged leg.

"Aw, you know what she told me." He was grinning now. "She says you ain't got no cherry no more!" Now he doubled over in laughter.

"Shut up. Prissy and them'll hear you." Newt eyed the kitchen screen uneasily.

"Big Mabel got you, huh?" Beansy wiped the tears from his eyes. "How'd it feel, Newt?"

"How'd what feel?"

"Aw, come on—I'm your best friend. I ain't gonna snitch."

Newt glanced toward the kitchen again, then looked Beansy in the eye. "Don't go blabbin' to the rest of the fellas."

"Honest to pete, I won't. Come on, now."

"Come to think of it, I don't know just how it felt. Everything happened so quicklike. I knew I felt somethin' was 'bout to happen that I didn't know anything 'bout."

"Well, how'd it happen?" Beansy squirmed with anticipation.

"I don't know. We was both wrapped up in a quilt together."

"Naked?"

"Well, we didn't have no clothes on. Guess you'd call it naked. I was hard ... so hard it was hurtin' ... and she pulled me over on her ... and I was feelin' warm ... and she was groanin' ... and all at once I had a shivery feelin' ... like a hot chill ... I started tremblin' and shakin' in my toes ... and knees ... and even my head ... and everything was like a dream ... then I went to sleep."

Beansy's knees pressed together tightly and his whole body rocked from side to side. "Boy ... boy ... boy ... what else?"

"Ain't nothin' else. It just kind'a left me feelin' good, mighty good, that's all."

"You gonna do it again with her?"

"Come on. Quit askin' 'bout it. I told you everything."

They were silent, thinking. Newt's mind, awakened to the words of his first sexual experience, began searching for a deeper meaning of it. But his thoughts were no more explicit than his words had been. And his long legs, like Beansy's short fat ones, pressed together tightly; his slender body rocked slowly to the rhythm of his thoughts.

After Beansy left, Newt laid his wide young shoulders on the cool grass and watched the white clouds drift lazily across the sky. As he continued looking, the last of the clouds moved out of sight, leaving only clear, pale space. Still space. His arms came together and rested on his brow, excluding all other things from his vision (and in his mind the space became wider and deeper, easing him up into its mysterious nothingness and all about him was still except the buzzing of a single bee that after a while was joined by the sounds of violins many violins hundreds of violins and horns and drums many horns and drums and voices many thousands of voices freeing him from tasting smelling feeling seeing—no, a sparrow was specking the nothingness and it was coming down—no, a buzzard coming closer—no, a hawk a chicken hawk and the music is fading and the chickens are cackling and the hawk is swooping down)...

Newt jumped to his feet, hobbled to the chicken coops, grabbed a stick as the cackling grew louder. The big hawk started up, a chicken in its claws, but too late. Newt brought the stick down over its head, and it dropped the fat hen to the ground. The hawk fluttered up, claws flying. Newt struck

31

at it again, but the bird jumped backward and up to the top of the henhouse. It wobbled for a moment, regained composure and swooshed off into the sky. Newt watched it disappear, then he cornered the frightened chicken, grabbed it and stroked back its feathers to see if there were any cuts from the claws. Then he released it.

Walking back toward the shade tree, he wondered of the strange music he had heard. He sat down again, tried to recapture the spell. But finally he realized it was one of those moments that would have to come unexpectedly—and without coaxing. And since there was nothing else to do, he felt the joints in his toes, examined the knuckles of his hands and wondered about the power that caused their workings. Ever who makes people is sure mighty smart, he concluded.

Not long afterward, his father and Pete came up the road, their flatbed wagon loaded with cables, jacks and rope. When they reached the alley, the horses slowed; Jack jumped to the ground, and the wagon continued to the barn. Newt noticed in a second glance that his father was coming directly toward him.

"Your momma home yet, boy?"

"Nosir, not yet."

"When she comes, tell her I'm over to the hospital."

"Yessir."

Jack ambled across the yard, and Newt watched him disappear into the pleasant landscape.

That evening Sarah and Newt took the river road to County Hospital. As she walked, her long skirt stirring the dust, Sarah mulled over all the possible reasons for Jack's going there. If he was sick, she reasoned, he would have said so. To her knowledge, no one was there who he would ordinarily choose to visit, and if there was, experience had taught her that he would not have gone without her. Her concern was deeper than she cared to let her young son know, and to hide it she hummed at times—a spirited hymn that gave a nonchalant rhythm to her motion.

Suddenly the humming stopped.

"Newt, you sure your poppa didn't say why he was goin' over here?"

"Yessem, just said to tell you he was goin', that's all."

She thought: "There's somethin' puzzlin' about this. He just wouldn't make off like that without some kind of word—some kind of explanation." And though she stretched her thought, no logic came of it. As they entered the hospital

32

door, her hand went to Newt's arm; then, straining against fear, she spoke to the attendant.

"I'm here to see Mr. Jack Winger."

The attendant, newspaper in hand, looked at her in an unacknowledging way, seeing but not seeing her. "He a patient here?"

"I don't know what he's doin' here. All I know is he's here." Her voice, steeled to a sharpness, brought the newspaper down and the attendant's eyes to focus on her.

"Jack his real name?"

"It's what he's known as. Andrew Jackson Winger is his full name."

"How long's he been here?"

"Came this evenin'." Her voice was losing its agitation.

"Just a minute, I'll check the records. Let's see—Wilson—Williams—yeh, here 'tis— Jack Winger." His forehead clouded. "You shore you didn't know why he was here?"

"Why would I be storyin' to you?" Sharply again.

"No harm. No harm. Just askin' 'cause he's in the operatin' room."

Sarah's heart skipped a beat. Her fingers pressed into Newt's arm. "Operatin' room, for what?"

"I don't know for shore. You better sit down and I'll check. You his wife?"

"Yes, and I want to know what they're operatin' on him for and who's doin' it." The attendant noticed her teeth grinding under her drawn cheeks.

"Take a seat. I'll try and find out. Card says he's Dr. Cravens' patient." A wave of relief swept over Sarah.

"Well, that's good to know," she said.

The attendant picked up the phone. Sarah motioned Newt to the seat, then they both sat staring at the wall. And Newt, sensing trouble, chewed his upper lip. The attendant's voice lowered and the two strained their hearing to it. "Lo . . . lo, Bertha . . . What's the Winger fella's trouble?" There was a long terrible silence. "Oh . . . naw, his wife. . . . Oh, I see (his eyes now no Sarah with a kind of new meaning) . . . yeh . . . yeh . . . okay . . . thanks, Bertha." He placed the receiver on the hook and stood up. "Missus Winger." He coughed. "Your husband's givin' skin to the little Johnson girl who was burned in the storm. He's under ether now and you won't be able to talk to him 'fore mornin', but they told me to tell you everything's gonna be all right, not to worry. Fact is, Dr. Cravens's comin' by to see you tonight to explain things."

A warmth came to Sarah Winger's face and her body relaxed in a certain relief. She thought for a moment, her eyes on the dusty hem of her skirt. "That's all right, that's all right," she said. "I understand."

The attendant remained standing. His voice came soft and unsteady. "Ma'am . . . that was a mighty fine thing for him to do . . . you ought'a feel proud of him . . . she'd a been messed up for life otherwise . . . they been askin' for volunteers all day . . . he's in good hands, ma'am. Doc Cravens'll take good care of him."

Sarah nodded to his words, arose. "I am proud, mister, and so's my son here. Tell Doc Cravens, for me, that I understand and I'll see him later." Pushing Newt ahead of her, she opened the door and they went out.

After walking for a while in silence, she spoke in a near-murmur. "Sure wish your poppa would let folks know what he's doin'."

Newt couldn't remember ever walking alone with his mother, just the two of them sharing moments as they did this evening. And for the first time, subconsciously measuring his gait with hers, he realized that even at twelve he was a little taller than she. He suddenly felt protective toward her, and his mind snatched at an illusion wherein he might defend her against an intruder on this lonely road, this very evening. And he envisaged doing so in the same manner as Hoot Gibson, Tom Mix or maybe William S. Hart. The last eventful forty-eight hours had nudged his imagination to a fertile awakening, and he was full of thoughts, ideas and questions.

Halfway home, he broke into his mother's humming.

"Momma, can I ask you somethin'?"

"Yes, boy. What you want to ask me?"

Newt pondered briefly, and Sarah slowed her pace. "Well, I don't know offhand, just about people and things like that."

Sarah smiled to herself, for she remembered that for the past year she had wanted to talk with Newt about "people and things" but thought him too young to understand the things she wanted to speak of. She had planned especially for him, her youngest, since the day he was born, but in the trials of living and caring for all the others she found it hard to clarify and formulate these plans. Now she welcomed the breakthrough. "Newt, you just ask me anything you want and I'll try to answer you."

"Well, after the storm, Poppa said that the storm and the people killed and everything was the doin' of God. You care if I ask you why he kills some people and not the others?

34

Poppa said hisself that Mister Pullens was a good man. And why did some of the town git torn up and the rest didn't?"

Sarah Winger came to a complete stop, and Newt was instantly afraid he had offended her. He took a step beyond his mother, his face pointed straight ahead, eyes lowered and cast sideways for the reaction. Her lips parted, but she didn't speak immediately; then she started moving again.

"Newt."

"Yessem."

"You know your poppa and me are religious people, don't you?"

"Yessem."

"Well, it would be real easy for me to say, you don't question the ways of God—and I was tempted to—but I know deep in my heart that there's more to it than that. It's true he guides us. But we cain't depend on him for everything. We gotta do things for ourself. Now, maybe if Jim had built himself a storm cellar or a stronger house, he wouldn't a got killed so easy. And if little Fannie Johnson's momma hadn't been drunk, she'd a held onto that lamp and her daughter wouldn't a got burnt. It's like I say, we got to do some things for ourself. If you got a battle to fight, you cain't rightfully ask the Lord to help you and not the other fella. Now can you?"

"No, ma'am."

"No, son, you got to fight and hope God likes the way you're using your fists. And that goes for the boy you're fightin'. Ain't neither one of you got time for prayin' while you're flingin' fists. Too many people, especially some of ours, boy, sit round waitin' when they should be out doin'. You got to always remember that, boy, always."

"Yessem. Are we gonna live here all our life?"

Sarah looked searchingly at him. "Don't you like it here?"

"I don't know, Momma. I ain't never been no place else."

"I hope you won't have to stay here all your life, Newt. It ain't a all-good place and it ain't a all-bad place. But you can learn just as much here about people and things as you can learn any place else. Cherokee Flats is sorta like a fruit tree. Some of the people are good and some of them are bad—just like the fruit on a tree. You know that, don't you, boy?"

"Yessem."

"Well, if you learn to profit from the good and bad these people do to each other, you'll learn a lot 'bout life. And

35

you'll be a better man for that learnin' someday. Understand?"

"Yessem."

"No matter if you go or stay, think of Cherokee Flats like that till the day you die—let it be your learnin' tree."

"Do we all have to die someday?"

"That's one thing we all have to do, boy. No matter who you are. That's why it's so important to be ready when your time comes."

"You mean to be a Christian, like you and Poppa?"

"In a way—in a way. But it's even more than sayin' you're a Christian. It's a matter of givin' more to this world than you take away from it. So when you die you don't owe it anything. It's bein' able to love when you want'a hate—to forgive them that work against you—to tell the truth even when it hurts—to share your bread, no matter how hungry you are yourself. Dyin' comes easy when you know you've done all these things right."

"I'm gonna hate dyin'."

"Won't none of us like it, boy—none of us."

"I hate dyin' so much I wish sometimes that I wasn't even born."

Sarah blurted, "Why, I'm surprised at you sayin' such a thing." When she saw his face she knew he realized that she was stalling for time.

"Is there anybody who has ever come back from death that saw heaven?"

Sarah sighed. (Who's this boy been talkin' to? Where's he gettin' such notions?) "No, boy. Ain't no such thing as that ever happened, to my knowin'."

"Well then, how does anybody know there is such a place?"

Her mind's eye flashed frantically from Matthew to Revelations, criss-crossed ages of praying, of shouting and of preaching. And finally her lips betrayed her teaching, ages of it—made light of the blindness, broke with believers; with the mountains of ever-so-solid faith. "Newt." (And already her expression made him sorry he'd sprung the trap.) "Honestly, I don't know. Maybe there ain't no hell either. Maybe there ain't no gold thrones in the clouds and maybe there ain't no pits of fire tended by a devil with a pitchfork tail. I honestly think God made us and expects us to do some good while we're here on earth. I cain't even say that God's his real name, but it's good as any. It means Almighty."

Confusion disturbed her thoughts. "All my life I've been told there is a better place beyond this one, Newt. And I

36

guess I'll go to my grave believin' it. Such believin' has kept our family goin' when there wasn't much else to go on." She paused for a moment. Swallows, flying low and fast, fluttered the stillness. Then she spoke. "These are the things I was taught. It's awful hard now, this late, not to believe them." They didn't talk after that.

About nine o'clock that night Newt heard Dr. Cravens' Ford pull into the yard. "Doc's here, Momma!" he shouted.

"Well, let him in, boy. Let him in."

Newt swung the door open, and the lanky, bespectacled blond man stepped in. "Hi, Newt. Your mother in?" he asked.

"Come in, Timothy," she called from the kitchen. "Sit down. I'll be right out."

"How's Poppa doin'?" Pete asked from another room.

"Fine, Pete. He's hollerin to come home already."

Sarah came in, wiping her wet hands on a towel. Doc was stretched out on a chair, wearily pushing the fair, graying hair back from his forehead. "Jack's doin' all right, you say?" Sarah questioned.

"Oh, he's goin' to feel a bit of pain for a few days. Then it will ease off and he'll come along fast."

"Just wish he'd tell me when he's goin' to do such a thing."

"He's stuck with his own ways, Momma Winger." Doc Cravens pulled a cob pipe from his pocket and began packing it. "Not much use in our tryin' to change him now."

"You look tired, Timothy."

"You've told me that long as I can remember."

"Marryin' would help you more'n you think. Least you'd eat regular," Sarah said.

Doc Cravens chuckled. "You've been tryin' to marry me off for years now. I'm just thirty-five. Give me a chance."

"You'd better come by here and git a good meal now and then. You look like you ain't ate in a week. You'll be needin' a doctor if you keep goin' like you are."

"That I'll do, Momma Winger, the very first chance I get. It's been a long time since I ate as well as I did here."

Newt's eyes shot to the doctor. "You used to eat here, Doc—"

"None of your meddlin' now, Newt," Sarah cut in. "I want to know how long it'll be 'fore Jack's all right."

"Oh, he'll be up and around in another two weeks. He'll have to take it easy for a little while." He lit his pipe and puffed several times. "It was a great thing he did, Momma Winger."

"Well, yes it was," she agreed, "but he's not the kind to think of it that way."

"That's for sure," Doc Cravens answered, "that's for sure."

"What part of him did you take the skin from, Timothy?"

"His back, legs and arms, but—"

"Oh oh," Sarah grimaced. "Must be awful painful."

"It wasn't an easy thing, not at all. Not at all," Doc Cravens said.

Sarah asked him to have a sandwich and some coffee. He refused the sandwich but took the coffee. After he had finished it he looked at Newt's leg and the bruise on his head. "You had a busy day in the storm, Newt, a real busy day."

"Shore did," Newt replied.

He dressed both wounds, and Sarah poured him another cup of coffee. He gulped it down and got up to leave. He was so tall he had to duck to clear the doorway. "Don't worry about a thing, Momma Winger!" he called back from the car. He stepped on the starter. The motor whirred, caught, and he pulled off the path and into the dark street.

Later Sarah Winger lay in her bed, her arms above her head, her eyes turned sleepily to the blank dark of the ceiling. Cravens had assured her that Jack would be all right, and she believed him. After a while her mind returned to Newt, and a shiver of doubt creased her thoughts. "I wonder," she said aloud, "if I gave him the right answers today." Then her past was brutally before her . . . the dusty Georgia road . . . the three white men rushing in . . . her sister Curtney screaming from the ditch . . . and the fat red face above her, bleeding from the clawing she gave it. And later, her brother Tom's revenge with the rifle . . . and the hounds tracking Tom down . . . and his limp, tar-covered body sprawled in death, a lynch knot about his neck—in the same ditch where Curtney had screamed—and screamed—and screamed.

"I wonder if I told him enough." She sighed. Her question faded into a gentle snore and before long she was fast asleep.

As the first light of Sunday crept over Cherokee Flats, only the delicate chirping of birds tickled the morning stillness. But as the sun climbed, the hens cackled beneath the rooster's crowing, and stirred the pigs into grunting, the cows into mooing, bringing Newt awake.

He sat on the side of the bed, pulling on his overalls, listening to the hogs squeal their hunger, and he knew they wouldn't stop until their noses were deep in the swill. Eyes half closed, fighting sleep, he buckled one bib strap; but before he could fasten the other, his chin dipped to his chest and he dozed again.

Wham! The blast came as he fumbled with the other strap (sounded like a double-barreled shotgun . . .). He got to his feet, leaped over the bed, then, ever so cautiously, peeped out the window. It was Clint, on top the overturned chicken house, reloading the gun and hollering, "I'll git the son-of-a-bitch yet! I'll git him!"

Newt started for his mother's room, but she was already rushing to the kitchen door. Newt followed her. Pete's voice ricocheted against Prissy's. "Who's shootin'? What the matter? Momma! Momma! What's goin' on? Come back here, Newt! Somebody's shootin' out there!"

"It's Clint. He's still drunk!" Newt hollered, slyly enjoying the early excitement. And as he ran out behind his mother, he saw Clint blast away at the sky. Wham! "I'll get the son-of-a-bitch!" Wham!

Sarah Winger didn't stop until she was at the foot of the chicken house. "What you call yourself doin', boy? Who're you shootin' at?" Her tone was in keeping with the Sabbath.

Clint rocked around unsteadily, reloading the gun. "I'm gonna git him! Don't worry. I'm gonna git him!"

"Git who? Who you shootin' at, boy?" she shouted.

Clint wobbled precariously, pushing in the shells. "I'm gonna blow the ass off Jesus Christ, the long-legged white son-of-a-bitch! I burned him a little that last shot. I'll git him for shore this time!"

The others gathered about their mother now. "Put that gun down, boy, and come down from there 'fore you kill your crazy self!" Clint ignored her and started digging in his pockets for more shells. "I mean it, boy. Come down this very minute or I'm comin' up after you!" She fired the command this time.

"But, I'm gonna—"

"Git down, I said! I had enough of your foolishness for one mornin'!" Clint pushed the shells into the chambers, and Sarah motioned for Pete and Newt to boost her up on the house. Pete started to object but realized, soon enough, there was no use. "Quick. Shove me up like I tell you." He lifted her as Clint started to raise the barrels to the sky.

"Clint!"

He hesitated, and she snatched the gun and the flat of her other hand smacked against his jaw. He reeled drunkenly, then tumbled off the side, but Pete caught him and dumped him coldly upon the earth. Then he turned to help his mother down. But first she broke the gun open at the chamber, removed the shells and pitched the gun to Newt; then she swung down in Pete's arms. "You boys take him in the house so's he can sleep that liquor off. I swear, I don't know what's to become of him." She took the gun from Newt, lifted her long nightgown and strode swiftly across the yard to the house, shaking her head as she went.

Clint rolled over on his belly, groaned and broke wind. Prissy tittered. Newt doubled in laughter. Pete, serious and unsmiling, looked down at Clint. "Ain't got a cent of his money left. If he had to pay for takin' a crap, he'd be forced to vomit."

There was tittering and laughter again. Even Pete managed a smile this time. Then he pulled Clint up and dragged him across the yard and into the house.

CHAPTER ✢ 3

NEWT, scrubbed and in his Sunday best, bends forward, elbows resting on his legs, chin saddled between his thumb butts, hearing but not seeing the Reverend Lucius Broadnap racing back and forth across the pulpit dripping sweat, his frock coat flying, spiking his sermon with the text, "What is my life?"

And "Yes, Lord! Yes, Lord!" fervent and wailing, answer the deacons.

"*What's my life?* ... the storm! ... *What's my life?* ... the storm, it came! ... *What's my life?* ... and it left me safe! ... *What's my life?* ..."

"Amen! Amen! Amen!"

"And it came whirlin' over the hills! ... *What's my life?* ... and it twisted through the valleys! ... *oh, God, what's my life?* ... and it tore up the towns and the prairies and the people! ... *yes, what's my life?* ... and it blowed its warnin' smack against the dance halls and the whiskey dens (Broadnap pushes the tempo) ... *what, what, oh, what's my life?* ... um-um-um (and Newt feels the rhythm of the congregation pushing along with the new tempo) ... um-um-um ... and it ripped up time! ... it ripped up space! ... it ripped up our daily life! ... *oh, what's my life?* ..."

"Yes! Yes! Yes! Preach on, brother! Preach on."

"Oh yes! ... *what's my life?* ... it warned us of our sinnin' ... um-um-um ... warned of all your wrongdoin' ... your stayin' away from the church! ... *what's my life?* (lashing now with tearful frenzy) ... and it blowed hard against those short flapper skirts! ... *what's my life?* ... and the devil-red lipstick plasterin' the mouths of our young girls. ..."

"Amen! Amen!" (Newt looks up slyly toward Prissy, who sits biting her painted lips.)

"... deliver us—deliver us—deliver us from this sinnin', troubled world! ... *what's my life?* um-um-um ... *oh, what's my life?* ... oh, stretch-stretch-stretch the bridge over Jordan!"

Emotion strikes the congregation like lightning. Newt feels the floor boards creaking rhythmically beneath him.

"... *what's my life?* ..."

"Have mercy! Have mercy! Have mercy!"

"Give us patience! ... oh yes! ... *what's my life?* ... um-um-um ... help us endure our enemies! ... give us strength to stand against those who want to destroy us! ... cleanse our hearts and our bodies! ... bring home the wayward husbands and the wayward wives." (Berthine Collins geysers up screaming, falls to the floor, the back of her hand plapping against Newt's forehead. Buford Collins, who everybody knows has been sparking lately widowed Emmaline Johnson, catches his wife's action from the corner of his eye.) ... *"Oh, what's my life—my life—my life?* ... um-um-um ... open their hearts to their mates and their little dear ones! ... stop the sufferin', drinkin', cuttin' and fightin' ... oh, tell me—tell me—what's my life?"* (Berthine is flopping like a chicken. "Save us! Save us! Save us!" They are pinning her arms back. And Maggie Pullens rushes over with her stinking camphor bottle. Buford's looking straight ahead. His face and back soaking sweat.) ... *"Oh, what's my life?* ... um-um-um."*

Now from all over the church the shouting comes. Carrie Wells screams, "Go home! Go home!"

Emmaline Johnson: "Oh, my child! Please help my child!"

Martha Thompson, running up and down the aisle, hollering, "Yes! Yes! Yes! Yes! Yes!"

Deacon Henry Fuller moans, "Oh, thanks—thanks—thanks —for your blessin'!"

"What's my life?"

Jenny Crawford, strutting up and down the aisle, hands slapping against her thighs, intoning, "Have mercy! Have mercy! Have mercy!"

"And the storm rushes on, still takin' souls and buildin's! ... and still we sin! ... still we sin! ... oh, what's my life? Oh, Lord, what's my life? ... um-um-um ..." (Now there's stomping all over the place, but Newt stays bent forward, elbows on legs—chin on thumb butts, hoping Berthine won't slap his sore head again.) ... "Every soul here oughta feel blessed for bein' here this day! ... this holy day! ... for not bein' one of those that perished!"

Cornella Wade shouts, "Oh yes, Lord! Oh thank you, Lord!"

"What's my life? ... to do better in the light of this day!

...and to serve God and the church!...um-um-um...
what's my life?"

Beatrice Jones yells, "Amen! Amen! Amen!"

"Now, my good children, look at me. Cast your eyes upon
the servant of the Lord! Look at me." (Newt feels his mother's eyes upon him—and his shoulders lean back to the time-
polished bench, his eyes are stubbornly toward the pulpit.)

Suddenly Broadnap hunches his shoulders, extends his long
arms from his coat sleeves, points his index fingers at the
congregation. His head, hawklike and fierce, juts forward.
His eyes, burning under sweat-drenched brow, search the
upturned, hypnotized faces. "Look at me and tell me, my
dear children, *what's your life?*...think about it in the
bright of day and the black of night!..*what's your life?*
(his fingers recoil into his fists—his arms drop; the tempo
breaks and calm begins to return; the choir is singing, "What
a friend we have in Jesus")....Thank you, dear God who
giveth us life through our Lord, Jesus Christ...bless you, my
children, and lest we forget His kindness to us during this
awful tragedy—let us pray." (The congregation, spent and
still moaning, bows in silent prayer. Newt slumps forward
again and brings his mind to the fried chicken that always
comes with the Sabbath.)

Reverend Broadnap raises his arms again, this time for
sinners and confessioners. Several are going forward—Fred
Jenkins, Clara Brown and Otis Moses. Now everybody's
curiosity is up, because Lester Saunders (he's wearing them
white spats) is raising his head for confession. "What can
God do to make me understand myself?" he asks.

Broadnap, mopping his brow, looks down at him. "What's
troublin' you, son?"

"I don't like women." The church is very still.

"You don't like women?"

"No, I don't like women."

"How long have you been like that, brother Saunders?"

"Ever since I was a man."

Broadnap's thumbing his Bible. "Don't worry or be
ashamed, brother Saunders. God acts in many ways. It may
be your conviction." Now he stops and reads from the Bible
—from Romans, 14th Chapter, " 'One man hath faith to eat
all things; but he that is weak eateth herbs. Let not him that
eateth set at nought him that eateth not; and let not him
that eateth not, judge him that eateth: for God hath received him. Who art thou that judgest the servant of another?
To his own Lord he standeth or falleth.' "

Lester is looking the minister straight in the eye. He turns and looks at the congregation. His left eye is damp. Now he is walking very fast, switching-like, down the aisle. Sadness is on his face. He's pushing through the swinging doors at the rear of the church. They swish back and forth—and he is gone. It is still very quiet. Reverend Broadnap raises his arms above the others and begins to bless them into the church—and again the choir is singing, "What a friend we have in Jesus."

After an early dinner, Newt slipped out to the cow barn and changed into overalls. Knowing his mother's feelings about such a change on Sunday, he hid his other clothes under a bag of grain and, when no one was looking, ducked out the back way to meet the four other members of his gang. As he jogged along, he spotted them sprawled beneath a giant oak at the edge of Logan's Grove.

Besides Beansy Fuller there was Jappy Duncan, a lanky, light-skinned thirteen-year-old, nicknamed for his slanting eyes; Skunk McDowell, also thirteen, dark brown, wiry and blusterous, with a white patch in his hair that resembled the markings of the animal he was named for; and Earl Thompson, thirteen and a half, chestnut brown, stocky, slow-moving, sloe-eyed and sullen, rarely speaking unless he was spoken to first.

"Git the lead out, Winger!" Skunk hollered.

"Take it easy," Newt shot back. "What's your big hurry?"

"Got a probl'm," Beansy said.

"What's wrong?"

"Savage wants to go 'long with us. Think we ought'a take him?"

"How'd he know we was goin'?"

"Skunk here—"

"Don't go blamin' me for it, Fatso," Skunk warned Beansy.

" 'Tain't no use in gettin' all steamed up 'bout it," Jappy cut in. "Nothin' we can do to stop him, anyway."

"What you think, Earl?" Newt asked.

"Don't make me no dif'rence one way t'other," he grunted.

"Aw come on, let's stop by for him," Newt said. And slowly they got up and walked toward the shanty where Marcus Savage lived. The boys weaved through the junk yard off which Marcus' father made his meager living, and as they approached the door they heard the older Savage's voice raised in anger. "You goddam black son-of-a-bitch!" he boomed.

"One more word out'a you and I'll whale you to a inch'a death!"

Then Marcus. "You winehead! You too damned drunk to stand up, less lone fight!" There was a moment of tense silence, then a banging against the wall, scuffling, cursing, and finally the door flew open and Marcus tore through the opening, blood trickling from his nose. "You old bastard! I'll git ya! I'll git ya yet!" he screamed back, ignoring the boys.

Big Booker staggered to the door. He was in his long drawers and held an iron skillet. He aimed and threw, but Marcus ducked it and ran. "Come on!" he yelled to the gang, "let's git the hell out'a here. The old bastard's goin' crazy."

They all moved quickly out of the yard behind him, and without saying anything to each other started toward Jake Kiner's, whose peach orchard they planned to raid.

Marcus Savage was black and tough. Not yet fifteen and motherless since birth, he lived with a father who spent most of his time drinking up what little money his junk gathering brought in. The ruggedness of a tough life added two years to his body, but his intellect barely matched that of any of the younger boys he now walked with. Yet, he was smart in the way that the desperate must be to survive, cunning in the way that the poor must be to cheat their misfortunes. The gang did not like him but tolerated him, and he felt big in their world—a small world that respected his strength and demanded little of his brain.

They were nearing the orchard now, moving stealthily, watching for any sign of life around the Kiner house or barns. Then they were under the barbed-wire fence and into the peach orchard, snatching the fruit from the trees, filling their stomachs and pockets at the same time, unaware of Jake's figure creeping alongside the corral shed, dragging a long buggy whip behind him.

He crept, anger in check, biding his time, making surer his chance to lash one, or maybe more, of the culprits who were stealing his prize fruit. They would get away fast, he knew —so surprise and the whip would have to cut the difference between their youthful speed and his feeble jog. Jake pulled his wide-brimmed hat tight to his wrinkled forehead, kicked off his high-heeled boots and tiptoed the last two yards to the clearing.

Newt was the first to see the raging, whip-waving farmer bearing down on them.

"Run! Run! Run!" he hollered. "It's Jake!"

45

Beansy, a peach in his mouth and his pockets loaded, shimmied off to a fast start. Skunk tripped over Jappy, who had been munching contentedly on the ground, and they both scrambled to their feet, losing half the juicy loot in their getaway. In a few seconds Newt was outdistancing Beansy; and glancing back, he and Earl saw the whip lash Marcus Savage's waist.

"Ouch!" Marcus yelped. "Ouch!" Peaches flew from his arms in all directions as he desperately tried to evade Jake's cutting whip.

"Thievin' dogs!" Jake half grunted, half hollered as he struck again, causing Marcus to stumble to the ground.

"Stop it! Stop it!" Marcus yelled, but Jake kept thrashing him. The others, at a safe distance now, turned in time to see Marcus grab Jake by the heel and spin him to the ground. Then Marcus was on top of him, beating him about the face with the whip handle, and above him kicking him in the face and on the head until Jake lay still on the ground. At last Marcus threw the whip on Jake's prostrate form, filled his pockets with peaches and trotted toward the others. As they started toward Flynn's River, Beansy's scared voice stopped them cold. "Aw-aw, there comes his wife."

"You little heathens! You little heathens!" she screamed, shaking her fist in the air. "We'll git you for this! We'll git you!" Then she knelt over her husband and began shaking him.

No one ate any more of the stolen fruit except Marcus as the six boys made their way toward Flynn's River. And as he chomped viciously, his powerful black muscles flexed a warning to his companions: be with me if trouble comes, or suffer the consequences.

He broke his silence. "The old bastard pushed his damn luck too far. I tried to kill him. Goddam near beat his brains out with his own whip."

"What you think they gonna do?" Beansy asked.

"I don't know," Marcus growled, "and I don't give a shit. All of you saw him beatin' on me with that whip first." Nobody spoke, and this rankled Marcus. He stopped, his hands on his hips, red eyes burning like pools of fire in the blackness of his face. "Well! What about it? You did, didn't you?"

"Yeh"—"Uh huh"—"Shore"—"You're right, Marcus"—"Yeh—yeh," they chorused.

"Well, Winger, what about you? You with me or not?"

46

Newt sensed trouble and he didn't want it. "Yeh, I saw him hit you with the whip." He wanted to say more, and Marcus wasn't exactly satisfied with the tone of his answer.

"Well, anything else? Let's git everything straight now." He glowered at Newt.

"I said all I had to say—only—only I don't think you ought'a of beat that old man the way you did after you got him down, that's all."

"Well now, fellas, ain't that some fine bullshit for ya. He's feelin' sorry for that poor old peckerwood who was beatin' the hell out'a me, one of his own gang."

"We was stealin' from him. Don't forget that, Marcus."

Marcus' voice was foreboding as his mood. "So you gonna stick up for poor white trash. Hear that, fellas? Winger's gonna stick up for a peckerwood who beat up one of his own gang."

Newt bristled, partly from fear, partly from anger. He couldn't whip Marcus and he knew it. And he wasn't quite sure yet where the rest of the gang's sympathy lay. He chose his next words carefully. "I ain't stickin' up for poor white trash, like you say I am. All you fellas know old man Kiner ain't so bad. Jappy's paw works for him and so does Skunk's paw, sometimes. And he give us a whole barrel of cornmeal last winter when—"

Marcus clenched his fist. "I don't give a damn what he gave you last winter or nothin' else." (Newt felt Skunk and Jappy at his side. He knew he could count on Beansy.) "All I want to know is—you with us or not?" (Beansy moved in next to Newt, and Earl, getting the drift of things, half-heartedly followed.) "And I want to know it right now," Marcus went on.

"I'm always with the fellas—here," Newt answered, meeting Marcus' glare straight on, the word "here" spelling out his sudden support.

Marcus' eyes skimmed the opposition. "Okay. Okay. Let's all stick together," he snarled. "Let's stick together."

Newt had won, temporarily at least, and Marcus knew it —but he wasn't forgetting it.

During the next two hours, the slow-moving river cooled their naked bodies, and the impassioned tempers gradually drifted away with the gentle current. Meanwhile, they performed their specialties. Beansy comically portrayed a whale, floating head down in the water, his fat bottom protruding above the water, his feet close together and moving like a fish tail. At short intervals his chunky head popped up and he arched a stream of water from the wide space between his two front teeth, much to the delight of the others. Then Earl and Skunk sank out of sight together. Earl's feet went on Skunk's shoulders and the two shot upward. Near the surface, Earl catapulted from Skunk's shoulders and leaped out of the water like a flying fish. Jappy, swinging out high over the river on a rope knotted to an oak, let go and double-somersaulted, then executed a perfect swan dive, into the water.

Marcus climbed to the top of Rock Ledge and, to the envy of all, sprang his mighty body into space, barely missing the jagged lip below, and spiraled beautifully into the river. Then, adding to the drama, he stayed beneath the water, emerging far downstream. Newt, encouraged by the rest, portrayed a submarine—swimming submerged on his back, a string tied to his pecker, which he sometimes managed to stiffen and pull taut like a periscope skimming the water. When his pecker didn't stand, he substituted his arm, his hand curled into an eye that turned on his wrist, scanning the waterbanks for enemy ships.

When Newt went to dress, his overalls, shirt and socks were expertly tightened into one wet knot. Then he understood, quite clearly, why Marcus had departed earlier than the rest.

Between the river and home, talk went back to Jake Kiner and the beating Marcus had given him. Earl ventured a startling question. "S'pose he dies?"

"Dies?" Beansy squealed.

"You kiddin'?" Skunk grunted, his face screwed into fright at the thought.

Earl hadn't given much thought to the question when he asked it, but now he realized such a possibility and he began justifying it. "He's real old, ain't he? . . . and Marcus beat the hell out'a him, kicked him in the head and everything."

"Well, that's Marcus' tail, not ours," Jappy countered.

"Yeah," Newt said, "but don't forget, we was all stealin'. They'll blame all of us if anything happens to him."

"We'd be crazy to git in a mess over somethin' Marcus did. We all gotta stick together, fellas." Beansy had begun to mop the sweat.

"We just gotta tell it just like it happened, that's all. (Newt was fishing for a response.) Tell it just like—just like it happened." Newt repeated the last sentence as if it were foreign to him, as if he'd never intended saying it. "We just gotta tell the truth, no matter what happens."

And since the truth, in this particular instance, favored their position, they all agreed to tell the truth—knowing within their hearts (but not daring to say it) that no one would really suffer from it but Marcus Savage. They would defend him as far and as long as they could (even to saying old Jake was beating Marcus awfully bad), but after that Marcus would have to be on his own.

They split up at Logan's Grove. Newt slipped into the cowshed by the back way and changed again to his Sunday clothes. When he started toward the house, the sight of the dusty motorcycle leaning against the porch made his heart jump. His mind started racing—Kirky was looking for him. He wondered if he should go in now, or go feed the hogs like nothing had happened. And he backtracked in the direction of the barn.

"Newt." It was Prissy, speaking in a hushed voice from the kitchen window above him. "Boy, are you gonna git it! What you nuts doin' stealin' peaches and beatin' up old man Kiner? Boy, you shore gonna git it. Momma's mad as a wet hen."

"Kirky in there talkin' to her?" Newt whispered.

"Yeh, and he's lookin' for you and Marcus and the rest of them nuts. You better git in here, boy."

"Is that Newt, Prissy?" Newt's heart sank at the sting of his mother's voice. "Tell him I said to git in here, quick!"

Newt was in the room before she could call out again. He stood close to the door, his right toe stabbing the carpet, hands entwined behind him, gazing at the floor.

"Look up, boy!" Newt's eyes shot up at the heated command. "Now, I want you to tell me exactly what happened, every bit of it." She had been cleaning when Kirky had entered, and still clutched a feather duster in her hand. "Come on, boy. Out with it."

Newt avoided looking at Kirky, but his mind's eye saw the smirk on his red craggy face, the tobacco juice caked at the corners of his thin lips, the dirty khaki puttee-type pants and leather leggings strapped about the fat legs, spread now with vulgar authority; the crusty Western hat (off his balding head at Sarah's request) and his big, sweat-smelly torso, draped with two-gun Western holsters, each stuffed with an ugly forty-five revolver.

"We just stole the peaches and run, that's all."

"After you beat ole Jake Kiner damn near to death?" Kirky cut in, tobacco juice gurgling his question.

49

"You watch your tongue in this house, Kirky. We don't use cuss words here!" Sarah admonished.

Newt watched Kirky's lips curl apart, exposing his yellow-brown teeth. "Jake's layin' up in County Hospital, beat to a pulp. I'm just tryin' to git to the bottom of this mess." His voice lowered in a tinge of apology.

"Well, there's a respectable way in goin' about it," Sarah countered. "Now, Newt, tell me. Did you hit Mister Kiner? I want the truth and nothin' but."

"No, ma'am. I swear on the Bible I didn't touch him."

"Well, who did, boy?" Kirky shouted. "Who did?"

Newt was quiet for a moment, reconstructing the facts, weighing the gang's promises against Marcus' threats. "He was beatin' Marcus awful bad with a buggy whip, and he wouldn't stop. He just kept on beatin' him."

"Well, what you sayin' is that Marcus Savage did it. That right, boy?" Kirky urged. Newt looked toward his mother.

"Tell me, son. Was it Marcus?" Sarah's eyes held Newt's, searching them for the real truth.

"Yessem. It was Marcus—but—he was tryin' to keep Mister Kiner from hurtin' him."

Kirky was moving toward the door. "You shore none of the others touched him."

"Yes. I'm shore."

"Who was the others who was stealin' with you?" Kirky bit from a grimy plug of tobacco.

"It was me and Beansy Fuller and Earl Thompson and Skunk McDowell and Jappy Duncan and Marcus."

"Where's all of 'em now?" Kirky was putting on his hat, but by now he was in the doorway.

"Everybody's gone home, I guess."

"Your story betta check with the others', boy, or I'm comin' back for you." Kirky slammed the screen door and went out. He turned just before he mounted his cycle. "The whites round here ain't gonna like what happened to old Jake very much."

Sarah Winger's reply was fast and free of emotion. "We don't expect no trouble, but we can take care of ourselves if it comes."

Kirky grunted, kicked his motor to a start and roared off.

Sarah looked at her son. "Boy," she said, "don't you know it's a sin to steal, 'specially on Sunday?"

"Yessem."

"You gonna git it now, Newt," Prissy warned a moment later. And he knew she was right, for Sarah Winger was

50

already out gathering switches from a small, sturdy elm tree.

"I've knowed them kids all their lives," Jake muttered to Kirky through puffed lips, "so it ain't the derned fruit I'm so mad about. It's that onery Savage boy. He's got bad blood—a born killer—ought'a be put away 'fore he murders somebody."

"I aim to do just that, if Judge Cavanaugh'll sign the necessary papers."

"Where's he now?"

"Locked up over at the jail. Feelin's runnin' kinda high 'mong the whites 'bout his beatin' up on you, Jake." Kirky snorted into a dingy blue handkerchief. "Like you say, the black bastard's born to trouble—broke into Sam Comstock's store last winter—slugged a usher that caught him sneakin' in the picture show the other night—tried to knife Doug Simpson for accident'ly bumpin' him on the street a couple months ago. Yeh, he's a nasty nigga all right. I'll put a slug through his ass one of these days. Wait'n see."

"Ain't he got no parents?"

"If you wanta call that likker-head paw of his such, he has. Ain't never had a maw that I know about."

Jake patted his swollen eye. "Well, no sense in race trouble over the likes of him. He's misery to the colored folks round here too. He's too young for Leavenworth, but there's reform schools that can take him, and—"

"Jake." Doc Cravens ambled through the door. "Got some visitors for you."

Jake's eyes rolled toward the door. "Send 'em in, Doc. Send 'em in."

Doc Cravens motioned in Newt, carrying a pie, warm from his mother's oven; Skunk, Jappy, Beansy (holding a bunch of flowers), Earl and Sarah Winger. The boys stood in awkward silence, petrified in their embarrassment.

"Go ahead, boy." Sarah pinched Newt into action and he thrust the pie forward like a robot.

"Well, what's this?" Jake raised on his elbows for a closer look.

(Another pinch.) Newt began mumbling the planned speech. "We're all here to say how sorry we are 'bout what happened—and—and—and that it won't happen again—" (Another pinch.) "And Momma made this for you—to eat." He put the pie on the old man's night table, and Beansy laid the flowers on the side of his bed.

After a jittery moment, Jake's sour face cracked into a

grin. "If them ain't my peaches in that pie, Sarah, I ain't eatin' it."

Relief swept through the five boys, and Sarah's smile answered Jake's. "Only two in there's yours, Jake. The rest are off the Winger tree, and that's why that pie's gonna taste so good."

"Thank you, Sarah. Thank you lots." Jake's shoulders fell wearily back to the bed. Then, sliding the wire-rimmed spectacles to the end of his bony nose, he peered seriously at the uneasy line of boys. His manner milked shame from each one's heart. "I'm forgivin' you on one condition. The five of you are comin' to help me, for nothin', come peach-pickin' time, and if I catch one of you chawin' my fruit, I'll skin you alive. Hear me?"

"Yessir—yessir—yessir—yessir—yessir."

"You heard that, Sarah." Jake kept his glare on the boys.

"They'll be there, Jake, if I have to pull all of them over by their dirty ears."

After that, Sarah and Newt went to visit Jack in the adjoining ward.

The next day, Kirky got Judge Cavanaugh to sign the "necessary papers" without too much trouble—the hearing lasting hardly thirty minutes. "You're a blight on your race and on society," the Judge scolded Marcus, his white mane trembling over his angry face. He signed the document that would rid Cherokee Flats of Marcus for at least a year.

"What's blight mean, Judge?" Marcus' query rumbled with violent sarcasm.

The skin around Judge Cavanaugh's knuckles tightened as his fist clenched, and he rose above Marcus like a mountain. "I'll tell you what it means, it means you are a disgrace to your people and to our town. And it also means that you're going to rot in Spit's Reformatory unless you rid yourself of the evil that's inside your onery hide."

Marcus smiled an ugly smile. "I ain't got no people and I ain't rottin' no place but in my grave, Judge. And by that time you gonna be long gone."

"Get him out of here, Kirky, before I lose my temper."

Kirky welcomed the order and, grasping his prisoner by the scruff of his neck, applied brute force to his removal from the Judge's chambers. At the cell door he gave Marcus a resounding kick in the behind. Then Kirky slammed the cell door and twisted the key.

Marcus turned and grinned evilly. "One'a these days it's

gonna be just you and me, you dirty, hairy peckerwood. You remember that!"

"I'm shore gonna remember that, boy. I'm shore gonna remember. I'm gonna remember that every day and every night you're in that hole where they're takin' you tomorra. And if you is ever unlucky enough to git out and come back here, I'll be waitin' and rememberin'. Don't you forgit. I'll be rememberin'!" Their eyes burned toward each other for a moment, then Kirky spat on the floor and stomped away.

Sarah Winger made a plea for Marcus while serving the Judge's breakfast the next morning, but to no avail. "The boy's dangerous, Sarah," he argued, wiping oatmeal from his lips, "and he'll be better off over at Spit's where he can learn some discipline." The manner in which he discarded his napkin and rose from the table convinced Sarah of the futility in pleading further.

During the evening of that same day, she had Pete harness a horse to the Winger buggy and the two of them with Newt drove to the hospital to pick up Jack Winger.

Dr. Cravens walked him to the waiting room. Pete and Newt, seeing that their father moved slowly and stiffly, went to assist him. After Jack was comfortably seated, Doc Cravens stepped back and spoke. "Well, Sarah—there he is. Be as good as new in a few weeks."

Sarah didn't answer. She just smiled.

"Okay, Doc," Jack said.

"Okay, Jack."

The reins slapped the horse's rump, and they drove off.

It was Saturday, a week later. Newt, Jappy and Beansy were down on the bank of the swimming hole, but they could hear the crap shooters up the hill behind them.

"That's Clint's voice, ain't it?" Beansy said.

"Sounds like him, all right." Newt knew it was Clint's voice.

"Your roll, Cheney."

"Seven—"

"Seven 'tis—keep rollin'."

"Seven baby—eight—eight's the point. Two I eight."

"It's a bet—got you covered. You takin', Sputter?"

"Two says you don't eight—you covered."

"Roll 'em."

"Eight baby—eight for ole Doc—eight honey, eight—for Doc. Goddam—seven!"

"Your roll, Silas."

"Seven come 'leven. Hit for Silas, baby—hit for ole Silas— 'Leven!"

"I owe you five, Silas—roll."

"Six—not five, Clint. I ain't drunk as you think."

"Okay—six it is—roll."

Down below, Beansy grabbed Newt's shoulder. "Look. It's Kirky. He's sneakin' up on 'em from behind."

"Got his guns out," Jappy whispered.

Newt scooted back out of sight. "I'm gonna try'n warn 'em." He began crawling up through the brush on his knees.

"Careful, Newt. Watch out," Beansy cautioned, "he's liable to start shootin'."

Newt was near the crest of the hill now. "Clint—Clint," he said in a hushed voice, "Clint—look out, Kirky's comin'."

"What? That you, Newt?"

"Yeh. Run—run—it's Kirky."

Clint grabbed up his money. "It's Kirky," he warned the others. The men took off in all directions.

"Halt! Halt! Halt! or I'll shoot!" Kirky's warning came from behind a thicket.

Newt could hear the brush cracking all around him. Then someone hurtled right over his head. He looked back. It was old Doc Cheney, headed for the river.

"Halt! Goddam you—halt!"

Doc scrambled by Beansy and Jappy, drove into the water and started swimming downstream. Kirky ran out into the clearing. He fired a warning shot over Doc's head. Doc ducked under the water.

Beansy and Jappy huddled together in fright, watching Kirky take dead aim at the spot where Doc went under. He fired once—twice—a third time. Then he ran down the side of the river bank, puffing and sweating, watching for Doc to surface. Suddenly there was a big bubble, then some small ones. Doc bobbed up to the surface for a second or two. He wasn't swimming now—just floating.

"He hit?" Newt asked, coming alongside Beansy and Jappy.

"Yeh—shore is."

"He got him."

Doc sank under again, and Kirky stood looking. Doc bobbled up once more for a second, then he was gone for good.

"Damn," Newt said.

"He didn't git a chance." Jappy stood with his mouth open, his naked body trembling with fear.

"Poor ole Doc," Beansy moaned, "poor ole Doc."

54

Kirky holstered his guns and strode back up the incline to where the boys were. They looked away from him to the water where Doc had gone down. Kirky coughed. They kept their eyes on the water, still stunned.

"Well," Kirky said, "now you kin see what happens to crim'nals—'specially ones who don't halt when they're told to halt!"

The boys didn't answer. They just kept looking at the water.

"Shit," Kirky snarled. Then he scrambled back to the top of the hill and disappeared.

"What's gonna happen to Doc?" Beansy asked.

"Kirky's prob'ly gone to get the firemen," Newt said. "They'll have to drag for him."

"You gonna wait around?" Jappy said.

"Maybe we can keep a eye on the spot where he went down," Newt opined. "He's prob'ly trapped this side of the shallows there."

The firemen came back with Kirky and they dragged the bottom of the river from a rowboat for two hours without any luck. A small group of white people had gathered now, and they sat about the banks talking and laughing. The firemen rowed to shore and Kirky went down to talk to them.

Newt, Beansy and Jappy sensed they were the subjects of the conversation. "Prob'ly gonna ask us to dive for Doc," Newt said.

"How much'd he pay Skunk and Earl for haulin' up the guy that killed hisself that time, Newt?" Beansy questioned.

"A lousy quarter. That's all. And they dove a long time 'fore they snagged him."

"Here he comes," Jappy whispered.

Newt was right.

"You fellas want'a make two bits apiece?" Kirky grunted.

"Doin' what?" Newt asked.

"Divin' for Doc like your pals did for Mack Turner."

"Not for no lousy two bits," Newt said coolly.

"Okay, I'll give each of you ten cents extra."

"Nope."

"Well, what you want for doin' it? It's gettin' late."

"We won't do it for no less'n seventy-five cents apiece," Newt said.

"You gettin' real smart, ain't you, Winger? Could run you in for swimmin' naked out here, you know." Kirky was fumbling in his pockets to see if he had the price. He counted

55

for a few seconds. "Okay, you win. Go ahead." He turned to the firemen. "Okay, take 'em out. They'll do it."

Newt was scared. He hadn't thought Kirky would pay that much, and now he was stuck; but he couldn't back out now and save face.

The three boys got into the boat, and the firemen rowed them to a spot about three feet short of the shallows. They jumped into the river one at a time and splashed about for a minute or two. Then the firemen handed each one of them a grappling hook and they sank beneath the water together.

Newt lost sight of the others after he was about six feet down, but he kept pushing closer and closer to the wall of the shallows, thinking Doc might be caught there. He swam slowly, not knowing what he would do if he should see the body. His air gave out and he shot back to the top. Beansy was already up, and Jappy bobbed up right after Newt.

"See anything?" one of the firemen asked.

"Naw," Newt answered. Beansy and Jappy shook their heads. They hooked to the side of the boat for a few minutes and rested.

"Okay—try again!" Kirky hollered from the bank.

They waited another moment or two, then sank out of sight. Newt went straight down this time, and Jappy stayed beside him. They swam around together for a minute or two, then Newt felt Jappy's fingers in his side. Jappy was pointing. It was Doc, floating just off the bottom. Newt jerked his head upward and they swam to the top.

"He's right under the boat!" they called to the firemen.

"Which end?"

"Back end," Newt said, wiping the water from his eyes. Beansy popped up and Newt motioned him to the boat. "We found him," he said nervously.

"You see what he had on?" the fireman asked.

"Overalls."

"Good. That makes it easy. Now listen. I'm gonna push this pole down with these hooks on the bottom of it. You fellas get your hooks in his overalls and float him up over the end of mine. When I feel his weight on it I'll haul him up. Okay?"

They all nodded.

Doc was floating face down when they reached him. Then all together they hooked his overalls and started pulling him up toward the pole. Their air was giving out, but they wanted to get it over with. Jappy motioned and they floated

Doc the last few feet to the pole and placed the hooks under his overall suspenders. Then they quickly swam away.

Newt got a good look at Doc as the pole drew him up through the murkiness. The skin on his face, like bubbly clay, strained against the current. His eyelids, pushed back by the same pressure, left the dead white balls staring blankly in the slow-moving water. The arms and legs, limp as a rag doll's, swayed grotesquely—as if in a ballet of death. The corpse began a twisting motion, as though it were coming to life. A spasm of fear shook Newt and he knifed to the top. He sidestroked over to Jappy and Beansy, and the three of them bobbed about in the water until the head broke the surface.

"Okay! We got him!" a fireman shouted.

Their job done, the three boys started swimming toward shore. They climbed up the bank, collected their money from Kirky and dressed.

They didn't wait for the death wagon. They'd seen enough.

Newt had bad dreams all that night. He kept seeing the wet corpse of Doc Cheney floating all around the room. Fearfully he got up, went into the dining room and lit a lamp. About four o'clock Sarah awoke and saw the light. She too got up and went into the room.

"Why ain't you in bed asleep, son? What you doin' sittin' up here this time of the night?"

Newt sat shaking. "I'm—I'm scared of death, Momma."

She went to him and put her arms about his shoulders. "Why I never heard of such. A big boy like you sayin' he's scared." She was trying to kid him out of it.

"Cain't help it, Momma. I'm just scared of death."

"You have a bad dream?"

"Yessem."

"Bad dreams ain't never real," Sarah said.

"But this one already happened 'fore I dreamed it." Newt was shaking more than ever now.

"Your dream was 'bout death?"

"Yessem."

"Whose death?"

"Doc Cheney's."

Sarah stood for a while, thinking. Then she said, "Death's a long way off from you, son. Doc Cheney's gone. He cain't bother you. His soul's in peace—somewhere."

"But I keep seein' him. He keeps turnin' over and over in my dreams."

"But Doc liked you, always said you was such a nice boy. He wouldn't want to hurt you—even in death."

Newt got up. "Just a minute, Momma."

"Where you goin', boy?"

"I'll be right back."

"All right, son."

Newt went into his bedroom and fished the seventy-five cents from his overall pocket. Then, trancelike, he drifted past his mother and opened the door. After pressing the three quarters firmly together in his hand, he flung them far out into the darkness.

"What was that?" Sarah asked.

"Nothin', Momma, nothin'." He shut the door. "Maybe I can sleep now."

Sarah didn't question him further. She walked with him back to his bed, tucked him in and sat there beside him until he was fast asleep.

CHAPTER ✠ 4

AT FLYNN'S BALLPARK, Newt and his buddies sprawled on the hot bleacher seats, awaiting the first pitch of the game between the Fort Miles Hawkeyes and the Chanute Cornhuskers. One greasy box of popcorn disappeared rapidly among them. The total of the gang's purse (four nickels and five pennies) jangled in Beansy's left hand. This amount had been all they could rake up for a "peep fee" to Captain Tuck, a beefy, fortyish, razor-scarred, dark bully who scouted, for pay, beneath the grandstands for indelicate views of lady fans with wide skirts and no underpants. (" . . . u.p. looks, five cents— b.b. looks, ten cents. Take it or leave it," Tuck's husky voice whispered to his young male clientele.)

The gang had already voted on two b.b.'s (bare bottom) and one u.p. (underpants), which would absorb the purse; and since this arrangement eliminated two of them from any look whatsoever, a lottery, performed with concealed sticks, decided the winners. Earl and Beansy got the b.b.'s and Jappy won the u.p., leaving Skunk and Newt to the ordinary fate of just watching a ballgame.

During the bottom half of the third inning Sputter Duncan, a good hitter, was up, and two Hawkeyes were on base when Tuck came over and nudged Jappy. "One u.p., third row back, five people over—five cents."

"Hold it, Cap'n Tuck. Sputter's up," Jappy pleaded.

"Come on, right now. Cain't wait. Now's the time, while everybody's excited. They close up when things git quiet." Having no choice, Jappy ducked under the stands just as Sputter smacked a base hit, and the crowd roared.

Now Charlie Johnson was at bat with the bases loaded. At such a moment, Tuck motioned for Earl and Beansy; and, torn between both attractions, they noted Tuck's directions after ducking quickly under the grandstand. "A whoppin' b.b., four rows back, nine people over—twenty cents."

"Stee-rike one!" Beansy whirled to scan the field.

"Hurry up, boy. I ain't got all day," Tuck urged. "I got other customers 'sides you."

"Ball one!" (He's right, Beansy. Look, it's a whopper.)

"Stee-rike two!" (Man, she's got more fuzz'n a bear.)

Wham! "It's a homer! It's a homer!" someone yelled. And the b.b. jumped to her feet in the excitement, shutting out the view.

"Wouldn't you know it," Beansy pouted, "she's sittin' back down in a no-good position. Looks like we just gotta wait awhile." And they sat down and waited. Almost ten minutes passed before they got their full money's worth.

The game went two extra innings, giving Tuck an unusually good day, and afterward, as he walked across town to Chappie Logan's, jingling the take in his pockets, the boys followed—listening to Tuck's accounts of his adventures in things dearest to him: drinking, fighting and sex.

"See that!" He knotted his beefy fist. "I kin lick any bastard in the Flats with one hand tied!"

Beansy egged him on. "Where'd you git that long scar on your face, Tuck?"

"Son-of-a-bitch knifed me when I wasn't lookin', but you ought'a seen him when I got through. You'd a thought he'd been through a meat grinder."

Earl fed the next question. "Done any big screwin' lately, Tuck?"

"Haw—haw—haw!" Tuck threw back his thick head and laughed. "I got exactly four hens waitin' for me right now at Chappie's. Four of 'em. What'a you think of that?" He patted his bulging fly. "And you know what? They'll all go home satisfied. And what'a you think of that?"

"You're a helluva man, Tuck," Skunk ventured. "How much'd you make today?

"Damn near five bucks. And what'a you think of that?"

A quarter mile further on, Tuck patted his groin again. "'Member what I said. They're all gonna go home satisfied! Haw—haw—haw!" he roared, bumping open Chappie's door with his massive shoulder. The boys watched as he disappeared into the smoke and noise.

"Boy, Tuck leads a helluva life," Skunk quipped admiringly as they walked away.

"Shore does," Beansy agreed.

"If you ask me," Jappy said, "I'd say he's lucky to be livin', with all the scrapes he's been in."

"Poppa says he's got a charmed life," Newt added.

"He keeps bullyin' round like he does and that charmed stuff ain't gonna do him no good," Earl put in dryly.

Unless Big Mabel could be counted as four, then Tuck's story was untrue, for only she awaited his arrival at Chappie's. By ten o'clock, three of Tuck's five dollars had gone for two bottles of corn, and it was past midnight when they staggered out, arm in arm, and went up the road in the darkness.

They had gotten across the tracks and in front of Silas Newhall's house, where Tuck spotted Chauncey Cavanaugh's Maxwell roadster, idling and empty, at the curb.

"Wait a minit," he burped, rocking back and forth, his red eyes searching the blackness for the car's owner.

"Come on, baby." He pushed Big Mabel into the seat. "Let's you and me go for a little spin." Big Mabel grunted a mild protest, but Tuck shoved her over and slammed the door. Then he squeezed under the wheel and they started off.

Chauncey was slipping out the Newhall side door when he spotted his car rounding the corner. "Stop! Stop!" he hollered. But Tuck just grunted a laugh, jerked back the gas and spark levers—and the Maxwell roared off in a cloud of dust toward Flynn's River.

Chauncey started to holler again, but a light popped on in old Silas Newhall's window. So instead he sprinted the four blocks to the jailhouse and told Kirky what had happened.

"Who was it—what way'd they go?"

"Down the river road! It was too dark to see who it was."

"Come on. Prob'ly a likkered-up nigga. Let's git goin'."

A few seconds later they roared off on Kirky's motorcycle with Chauncey, his coattail straight in the wind, on back clinging to Kirky's Sam Browne belt.

Tuck was just slowing down for the "lover's lane" turn-off when the siren wailed in the distance behind him; and through the rear-view mirror he caught sight of the single headlamp bobbing in the darkness. "Goddam Kirky's chasin' us," he mumbled, nudging Big Mabel to life. "I'm gonna give him the run of his life. Now what'a you think of that?" He began coaxing the motor toward full speed.

"You better stop, Tuck. You just askin' for trouble."

But the dust was already blotting out the single light behind them, and Big Mabel began to sober as the trees from both sides of the road whirred in upon their light and whipped past into the blackness. The siren was closer now and Tuck's face, thrust out above the steering wheel like a gargoyle's, grinned in disdainful joy. "Come on, you son-of-a-bitch! Come on! Let's see how much you can do! Come (a shot rang out, and a crack marked the windshield just above Tuck's head) bastard's shootin' (another shot rang out) git low, way down——"

"Stop, Tuck! Stop! I don't want'a git hurt!" Big Mabel tugged at his arm.

"Just keep down! Keep down—you ain't gonna git (another shot, right behind them now) bastard's gainin' on me—this thing's wide open!"

"Stop, Tuck! Stop! Stop! (again the shot, and this time Tuck's head dropped onto the steering wheel) Help—hel——" Big Mabel felt the car twisting, sliding, hitting, spinning, then somersaulting, and suddenly she was flying free—only to sense, for a split second, the crushing jolt before unconsciousness and quick, merciful death.

Tuck's body, trapped within the hurtling machine, stayed on for the final, brutal crash against a tree, then it settled, from its own dead weight, to the floor of the crumpled wreck.

A peculiar sensation tugged at Newt's innards from the moment he heard of the deaths of Big Mabel and Tuck. It seemed impossible, but everybody was talking about it so it had to be so. He remembered how hot and firm Big Mabel's body had been when he lay against it during the storm. Now that she was broken up (as they were saying), memory of this moment was brought back with frightening clarity. He wondered why he hadn't tried for her again, and regretted not having done so. That evening, his twelve-year-old curiosity impelled him, with Beansy as a companion, to within a few steps of Mottsy's Funeral Parlor—where the bodies of Big Mabel and Captain Tuck lay.

Chris and Orville Mottsy stood talking at the body-receiving door, eying the boys as they approached. "Let's have some fun with those little nigger kids," Chris said in an undertone. Orville grinned at the prospect.

Chris was the first to speak. "Hi there, you-all. Want'a see Captain Tuck and Big Mabel?"

Newt and Beansy stopped dead in their tracks, Beansy a foot or two behind Newt. "Naw," Newt said, "we don't want 'you-all' to show us nothin'."

"Aw, come on. Don't git mad, boy. Captain Tuck'd be awful sore if you didn't pay him proper respects." Chris was inching closer to them as he spoke, but Beansy had already begun backtracking.

"Come on, Newt!" Beansy had sensed the trap and was already running; but Newt was pounced upon before he could follow, and the two pranksters carried him, screaming and kicking, through the entrance.

"Let go! Let go! I don't want'a see Tuck," he wailed.

"Aw, come on. Quit cuttin' up. Cap'n Tuck's gonna be so glad to see you, boy," Orville quipped.

"No! No! No!" Newt pleaded. But the door to the embalming room was being opened now. And quickly they shoved him into the smelly darkness, snapping the door shut behind him. Newt recoiled and scrambled back to the door, pounding, screaming, "Please! Please! Oh, please let me out!"

Chris pushed the light switch, and there before Newt was the naked, bruised gray-black corpse of Captain Tuck on a white slab, lit overhead by a bare fluid-smeared bulb. One eye stared at Newt with a baleful glare. And to his right lay Big Mabel, completely covered with a white sheet, her breasts raising the cloth tentlike above the rest of her broken body. Newt tried to yell out, but cold terror silenced his effort. Things began to swirl and he sank slowly to the floor, hysterically exhausted—and unconscious from an agonizing fear.

The sudden quiet on the other side of the door brought an uneasiness to the Mottsys, and their laughter gave way to apprehensive frowns. Orville opened the door and Newt, having fallen against it in his faint, rolled halfway through the opening.

Chris splashed three cups of cold water in Newt's face before his eyes opened and began focusing on the blurred figures above him. Suddenly reality came to him again and he screamed, "No! No! No!" Then, crawling from beneath his tormentors, he got to his feet and backed through the door. The air helped clear his thinking, slowly gave back his strength. He began running and didn't stop until he was all the way home.

Two days later, the Cherokee *Tribune* carried an item— only five lines long and almost undetectable on the back page—which read: "Chris and Orville Mottsy of Cherokee Flats were attacked and badly beaten last night by another local man, Pete Winger. The latter was given a brief hearing before Judge Cavanaugh but was released when the elder Mottsy, upon advice of his attorney, withdrew all charges."

CHAPTER ❦ 5

IN AUGUST, Newt began riding the Kiner land with Pete—whom Jake had hired as a temporary foreman; and, to Pete's satisfaction, Newt went about learning to mount his father's quarter horse on the run, to ride with his head up and his heels down, to swerve his mount easily in and out of a moving herd.

On Saturdays he peddled brooms with Rob Winger, his blind uncle. During this time he came to marvel at all the philosophies Rob imparted to him on their trips about the village. His uncle talked to him of all the things his father neglected to talk about. It was almost as if Rob, knowing his brother Jack's shortcomings, tried in some way to make up for them. And Newt, already perceptive enough to realize this, looked with regret upon the September morning when they would make their last walk of the year around Cherokee Flats, selling a broom now and then, discussing the ways of man and the universe.

A chill had come to the air and Rob, a sufferer of rheumatism, decided the walks were becoming more harmful than good. Furthermore, school was starting soon, and he felt that Newt should spend his weekends preparing himself, especially since he'd be entering the white high school in another year.

Crossing the Frisco tracks that morning, on his way to meet Rob, Newt saw his uncle, brooms over his shoulder, tapping the ground with his cane and approaching the crossing. Newt broke into a trot, trying to reach him before he got to the drop-off leading down to the tracks.

"Wait up, Uncle Rob!" he hollered. "I'm comin'!"

Rob stopped and stood waiting until Newt came to his side. "Hi there, boy. Thought I'd come to meet you," he said.

"Thought maybe I was late," Newt answered.

"Nope—I'm just a early bird."

"Which way we goin' today?"

"Well, think we'll try the upper west side," Rob said. "Ain't

64

been there in quite a spell." He motioned with his head.
"We'll start over on Mulberry Street."

They moved toward the tracks, Newt holding Rob's hand
just above the nubs where the fingers had been blown off in
an explosion years before. About twenty yards from the crossing Rob stopped, holding his cane to the ground, and Newt
looked up at him, seeing his eyelids blinking rapidly behind the dark glasses.

Then the warning bell started ringing and the red signal
arms started swinging back and forth. They waited a few moments, then heard the whistle, and before long the wheezing
locomotive came pounding around the bend. As it rumbled
by, pulling its eight coaches, Newt saw the images of the
engineer and the passengers blurring past.

"Boy, I shore would like to be on there," Newt said as they
started across the tracks.

"Why?" Rob asked.

"Oh, just to be goin' someplace far away, like them people
are."

"Maybe they're people goin' back home or to places they
don't want to be goin' to." Rob was smiling.

"Well, at least they been some place," Newt said. "Take
me, I ain't never been out'a Cherokee Flats—'cept to Easton
and Fort Miles."

"You're young yet. Got lots of time for that."

"You ever been any place else, Uncle Rob, 'sides here?"

"A trip up to Kansas City once when I was a boy many
years ago. That's the only time."

"Mind if I ask you somethin'?"

"Go ahead."

"It's kind'a hard to say what I mean—what I wonder 'bout
you."

"Try."

"Well, you told me how you got your eyes blowed out in
a explosion. Well, that's been a long time ago—"

"More'n twenty-five years."

"Well, what I want to know is—can you remember what
you used to see before that—can you remember what color
the sky is?—what a bird looks like and things like that?"

They continued along in silence as Rob formed his answer
and Newt waited to hear it. In a little while it came. "Yes,
Newt, I do remember things like they were then. In fact, I
think the colors are brighter in my darkness than they are in
your light. I see blue and red and yellow and green and all
the colors. And sometimes I have a little fun with color in

65

my darkness, like imaginin' you're green with pink ears and a blue nose and purple hair. Sometimes I fill up my dark world with people of all kinds of colors like these."

"Really, Uncle Rob?"

"Yep, boy, it's so. And you know what, Newt? I think sometimes if all the people in the world were made up of colors like that instead of just some black and some white, it would be a happier world. A wonderful world all mixed up with wonderful colored people, nobody bein' the same as anybody else."

Newt closed his eyes for an instant, trying to imagine such a world. Then he opened them again and laughed. "Maybe your world's prettier'n ours."

Rob smiled.

Throughout the rest of the morning they weaved in and out of the streets and alleys, selling their wares to the housewives and small-store merchants. At noon they stopped to rest beneath a shade tree, and Rob pulled some sandwiches from his overall pockets. They ate, rested for an hour, then continued on. By three o'clock they had sold every broom but two, and they turned back toward home.

When, a short time later, they came upon a large white house, Newt said, "Maybe I can sell the last two here." He went up the walk, around to the back door and knocked. A blond boy of about thirteen cracked the door and looked him over. "What you want?" he questioned.

"Your momma want'a buy a broom?"

"A broom?" The boy opened the door wider.

"Yep, a broom," Newt repeated.

"Mother!"

"Who is it, dear? What do they want?" a voice asked from within.

"It's a nigger sellin' brooms! Want any?"

At the sound of the word "nigger," things became tangled for Newt. He threw down the brooms, pushed open the door and cracked his fist against the boy's face. The boy fell back, yelling, "Mother! Mother!" And Newt threw every ounce of his strength into another blow, knocking the frightened boy to the floor.

The woman rushed into the room, staring at Newt in utter disbelief. "What's this? What are you doing? You get out of here before I call the police!"

Newt turned and walked out the door, picking up his brooms. "You better tell your boy to stop callin' people nigger or he's gonna git worse'n that."

66

The woman jerked the door open and spat at him. He ducked, but her spittle caught him in the eye. Enraged, he rushed toward the door, but the woman slammed it and bolted it shut. "You are a nigger!" she shouted from the other side. "Nigger! Nigger! Nigger!"

Newt made his way slowly back to the sidewalk and Rob. He took his uncle's hand and they walked to the corner. "Step down, Uncle Rob."

They crossed the street.

"Step up, Uncle Rob."

They walked another full block in silence. Finally Rob spoke. "What happened back there, Newt?"

"Back where?"

"At the last house."

"Oh—nothin'."

"You're tremblin', boy. Tell me what happened."

"Oh—'twasn't nothin', I suppose—a peckerwood called me a nigger."

"What for?"

"For no reason a'tall—just bein' smart."

"Did you call him a peckerwood?"

"Didn't git the chance."

"What did you do?"

"I—I popped him upside his head, that's what."

"How big was he? Did he have a yellow nose and green hair?"

"A little bigger'n me, and he was white."

"Oh, then it was a fair fight." Rob chuckled.

"He didn't do no fightin'. His maw come runnin' out and she spit on me and called me nigger too."

A frown came to Rob's face. "You didn't hit her, did you?"

"Nope. But I think I would'a if she hadn't jumped back in and slammed the door."

"You satisfied?"

"Cain't exactly say I am. I'd a liked to give him a couple more good pokes."

"You keep goin' around pokin' my customers and I won't have any," Rob said, a smile creeping across his face.

"I'm sorry, Uncle Rob."

"Well, I'd take you right back there and make you apologize if that woman had acted more like a lady. But she didn't, so let's forget it," Rob said. "Take the rest of your anger out on the piano."

"If Poppa's home he won't let me play. Says piano playin's for girls."

"Best thing for you to do, then, is wait till your momma gits home from work. He won't run you up if she's there, will he?"

Newt grinned. "Nope, Uncle Rob. Like Pete says, Momma's got his bath water on."

"You're growin' up fast, boy." Rob was noticing his nephew's touch higher on his arm.

"Be thirteen come November."

"You ever think about what you want to be when you're a man?"

They reached a curb. "Step up, Uncle Rob—well, I ain't made up my mind just yet. Sometimes I think maybe I'd like to be a musician or an artist or somethin' like that—"

"Well?" Rob was smiling again. "Which one do you like best?"

"I like music best, I think. Prissy says the white teachers at high school tell colored kids to stick to bein' a carpenter or bricklayer or somethin' like that."

"So you like music. That razz-ma-tazz stuff?"

Newt laughed softly. "Aw, I know you make fun of jazz music. I kind'a like it, but there's somethin' else—when I'm in the prairie all by myself—when the wind blows a soft kind of sound almost like music, and I think I hear great big orchestras with lots and lots of people playin' all kinds of horns and violins, pianos, drums and things and it goes on for a long time—comin' and goin' with the wind—"

"How often do—"

"And sometimes I try to remember the tune so I can hum it to somebody, but I never do 'cause it's always so diff'rent."

They were quiet for a while after that, walking along with Newt's thoughts rambling and Rob's mind searching the future of his nephew. A quarter mile from the Frisco tracks Newt strained his ears but heard no sound. "She on time today, Uncle Rob?"

His uncle stopped, shutting his eyelids and rubbing the smooth handle of his cane, listening. "Yep. She's comin' right on time. You'll hear her whistle in a minute or two." Then they continued toward the crossing. In less than two minutes the shrill warning came as Rob had predicted, and as usual Newt looked at his uncle in awe.

"How do you do that, Uncle Rob? How do you always know?"

"Well, Newt, it's like this" (the 4:20 express was already upon them, rumbling and blowing through the crossing, and Rob waited its passing). "I know the rumblin' through my cane and feet. They took over where the eyes left off. Simple as that."

Newt looked both ways, then they crossed the tracks, and on the other side Rob continued. "Maybe the teachers think they're tellin' what's best. Maybe they don't understand that a youngster like you has got somethin' else in him that's tryin' to come out. Maybe they don't know you've got your mind set on bigger things. You've got to believe in yourself, Newt —don't let the teachers or anybody else hold you back. Learn all you can, so when bigger things come you'll be ready for them."

"Step up, Uncle Rob."

"You ever talk to your momma about any of this?"

"Just a little—sometimes."

"Well, you ought'a as much as you can. She's a good thinker, and she's got a peculiar kind of faith in you. She talks about you bein' born into the start of a new world. Maybe she's right."

"I git to feelin' like there are things I want'a say or do sometimes, but I don't know how to do it."

"Like what, son?"

"Oh, I don't know for shore. It's like just sort'a bubblin' over, like somethin's inside me tryin' to get out, but I just don't know what."

Talking stopped for a minute or two, and they passed over a wooden bridge and turned down a narrow lane.

"Step way down here, Uncle Rob."

Rob felt first with his cane, then he took the long step to the flat ground. "Well, Newt," he said, "I can make it from here." He fumbled in his pocket for seventy-five cents and put it in Newt's hand.

"Thanks, Uncle Rob."

"Thank you, boy. It's been a nice walk with you today."

"See you next week, maybe."

"Okay, but remember—study hard this year."

"Yessir, I'll try."

Rob Winger tapped on in the familiarity of his dark world, knowing easily the sudden humps and smooth leanings of the earth beneath him. A blue jay cawed and fluttered from tree to tree above his path as if to sound his way, and he smiled. It had been twenty-five years since he last saw this path on which he now walked. The deafening blast and the agonizing hours of near-death were long past. The awakening to blindness and the missing fingers, the slow recovery and painful readjustment—all this was long since over. Now he walked surely in his eternal night.

His cane bumped the first step of his porch and he cleared the other two, unlocked the door and entered. Standing the brooms in a corner, he walked to the window and pulled open the drapes, then sat in his rocking chair, gently pushing to and fro for a reflectful hour. When the tower bell rang in the Baptist church a mile to the east, he rose, ate some cold chicken and pie, closed the drapes and went off to bed.

The September rains came, and from his school windows Newt watched them weight the leaves so that, later, the winds of October easily blew them off and over the ground. By the middle of November frost was on the windowpanes, and the earth was hardening from the cold blasts that swept in from the north.

On the last Saturday of the month Newt awoke a little earlier than usual, because his father had predicted the arrival of a new calf during the night or early morning. With his breath fogging in the chill of the room, he dressed with speed, moving quietly to avoid waking Pete. When he entered the dining room, heat rushed upon him—and this meant his father was already up and out. The potbellied stove glowed, and Newt stepped bearably close to absorb its heat.

His mother had promised to let him accompany her to work, where he would visit with Rodney Cavanaugh, who had a big room to himself with books, microscopes, rifles, framed butterflies, bugs, stuffed animals, a Gramophone, and paintings of Greek statues on the walls. The two boys liked each other, and Newt often returned home wishing that both were either colored or white so they could spend more time exploring these wonders of Rodney's world. And Rodney was usually elated at Newt's coming, for he felt a superior satisfaction explaining the mysterious microscope and the enchanting world its thick lenses revealed.

By the time his mother's petticoats were cinched about her waist, Newt had fed the chickens, horses, and pigs; and he had stacked the firewood neatly behind both stoves. Then he went to the cowshed where his father had been since five, and his eyes lit up when he entered, for Jack Winger was busy pulling a newborn calf from its mother's womb.

"Gee, it's here—it's here!" Newt exclaimed.

"Git me some gunny sack, boy, lots of it," Jack grunted.

Newt raced to the corncrib for the sack, returning just in time to see the glistening calf ease fully into the world.

The mother began licking her baby's steaming body from head to hoof, while Jack gently rubbed it dry.

"Is it gonna be all right, Poppa?"

"Yep, boy, gonna be a fine one." He turned and looked at his eager son. "For a while I didn't think she was gonna git here on time for you. But here she is."

"She for me, Poppa?"

"Yep, son. Happy birthday."

"This my birthday? I forgot. Thanks, Poppa!" And he saw a real smile come to his father's face for the first time in a long while. Then quickly he was down to help rub the calf—but the mother, protective against his sudden move, butted him aside.

"Come easy-like," his father cautioned. "Come easy."

And Newt squatted gently to his father's side, and they rubbed and rubbed until the animal's thin coat was like velvet.

"What you gonna name her, son?"

Newt pondered a moment, trying to think of something that fit the occasion. "Well, I'm thirteen today, Poppa. I think I'll call her Lucky."

Jack lit his pipe and puffed the smoke into the early gray light. "That's good as any, son." He puffed again, and the blue smoke rolled up close to his face and under his broad-brimmed hat, causing him to cough. He repeated, "That's good as any." Then he took another close look at the calf, scratched his stubbly cheek and stood up. "We better be gittin' back. Your momma's prob'ly got breakfast on."

Then the two of them pushed their mackinaw collars up around their ears and went to the house, where Sarah gave them ten pancakes apiece—and presented Newt with a shiny silver dollar for his birthday.

After their breakfast, Jack and Sarah remained at the table while Newt went back to the barn for another look at the calf.

"That boy's growin' up—thirteen today," Sarah began.

"Worries me, sometimes," Jack replied.

"How?"

"Oh, with his daydreamin' and wantin' to play the piano and such things."

"He's different from the rest of the children, Jack. Might as well face it."

"Nothin' wrong with him as I can see. Just don't seem to have his two feet on the ground, that's all. He's all over the place doin' crazy things, dreamin' 'bout music, foolin' round anthills and such 'stead of doin' his work."

"He's a thinkin' boy, Jack. You should'a heard some of the questions he asked me about religion and death. I was hard put for the right answers, I'll tell you."

"Religion and death?"

"That's right, religion and death."

"I declare, he's gittin' crazy notions from someplace."

"His questions wasn't just crazy notions. They made me do a lot of thinkin' afterward. They were about things I used to wonder about when I was a girl, but didn't talk about just because I was scared to, for some reason or another."

"Well, one thing 'bout death, when your time comes you're goin', and that's that. Ain't very hard to answer that."

"It ain't just dyin' he wonders about. It's what comes after."

"He needs to go to church more, maybe."

"We been goin' to church all our lives, and so has he; still hearin' the same things we been hearin' since we was his age. The answers that used to satisfy us ain't goin' to satisfy Newt and the young ones comin' up now. They want proof. Some kind they can see and feel. And they're goin' to want more out of this world than we're gettin' out of it. Time's changin', Jack."

"This is a white man's world, Sarah. Ain't no time goin' to change that."

"No, maybe time won't, but this new crop of colored boys and girls will. You and me prob'ly won't live to see it, but these kids comin' along today are goin' to find a way to change things."

"The white man's got the money and guns—that spells power."

"There's more'n one way to skin a cat, Jack. Schoolin's more powerful than guns or money in the end. I honestly hope someday Newt'll git out of here and go where chances will be better for him. I pray for that."

Jack got up and poured Sarah a cup of coffee, then poured himself one. He gulped his down while standing. "Well," he concluded, "if daydreamin' was the ticket, he'd be gone tomorrow."

"Ain't nothin' wrong with dreamin', Jack. Dreams come true, often as not, if you work on 'em hard enough."

"Maybe so. Maybe so." He filled his pipe and lit it. "See you t'night. I'm gonna be at the smokehouse most of the day —and that's where Newt ought'a be 'stead of at the Cavanaugh's gittin' highfalutin ideas—"

"See you tonight," Sarah said, ignoring his remark. She

72

put on her coat and filled her shopping bag with fresh cleaning rags. "Newt!" she hollered out to the barns. "Come on, time to go!" She banged on Pete's door. "It's eight, Pete—git up! Prissy!"

"Yessem."

"Git up and fix Pete's breakfast. I'm leavin'."

"Yessem."

"Don't 'yessem' me. Git up right now, girl!"

"Yessem."

Later that morning, at the Cavanaugh house, Rodney's hand turned the focusing knob of a microscope and Newt, his eye glued to the eyepiece, watched fascinated as the blobs of brown sharpened to a huge animal-like head.

"Boy, it looks like a dragon or somethin', Rodney."

"That's a worker ant, Newt. They are females, but they don't mate or lay eggs."

"What do they do then?"

Rodney cleared his throat in a professorial manner. "There are several types. Some take care of the younger ants and the queens. Some find food—"

"What kind is this one?"

"He's a worker soldier. See the big strong jaws? This kind defends the colony against its enemies."

"Colony?" Newt looked up at Rodney. "You mean like a city?"

"That's right."

Newt's eye was on the eyepiece again. "How big are their colonies?"

"Oh, as big as an acre of ground sometimes, and as far down as sixteen feet in the ground. Fact is, there are as many of them in a colony as there are people in a big city like Kansas City or New York."

"Gee, really?"

"Yes," Rodney said proudly, "and what's more, there are more ants on this earth than any other insect."

"I guessed somethin' like that. I counted almost two hundred of 'em one time."

"Without a magnifying glass?"

"Yep."

Rodney gave him an admiring grin.

"What's those long things stickin' out of its head?"

"Oh, those," Rodney answered quickly, "are the antennas. Without them they couldn't taste, feel or smell." He removed his eyeglasses, much the same way he had seen Professor Radeaker remove his during science classes. "This particular species finds its way to and from its nest by smell. In fact, it won't even pick up food unless it smells it first."

"Why cain't they use their eyes to see how to git round?"

"Some kind don't even have eyes, Newt. But even those that do can't see much more than light or dark. But let me show you something really fantastic." He nudged Newt aside, lowered the microscope and refocused the lens on the ant's eye. "Now look." He gestured Newt back to the microscope, his thin face glowing with eagerness.

"Looks like a diamond."

"You're right, but actually it's as many as one thousand little eyes."

"—and they still cain't see good?"

"Oh, maybe a bush or a rock or something like that, but not much more."

"Does this spe—kind bite?"

"She sure does bite, and her jaws won't let go even if her body is cut off."

"Poppa told me ants are awful smart and—"

"In some ways they are and in some ways they're a little dumb."

"How so?"

"Well, for instance—"

("All I want from you, Chauncey, is the truth!") Rodney's father's voice boomed from the outer hall. ("Did you or didn't you have that girl in this house?")

("And for the thousandth time I'm telling you, I didn't!") Chauncey's angry voice retorted. Newt's eyes shifted uneasily toward the slightly open door.

Rodney went on, seemingly accustomed to such outbursts, "—well, for instance, they have all kinds of places to store their food and put their trash, and they even have ant cows they milk, but—"

("Silas claims you did!")

("I don't care what he's claiming! I said she wasn't in this house and I'm sticking to it! Can't you take your own son's word for the truth instead of the town's prize bum? He's not pinning something like that on me! And Blanche is a lying so-and-so if she—")

Sarah Winger slammed the door, shutting off the battle from Newt and Rodney. (Blanche—must be Blanche Newhall, Newt thought.)

And Rodney went on, "—but put these ants in a circle, following one another around, and they'll die from exhaustion without having enough sense to get out of it."

After the lecture on ants, Newt heard about Rodney's collection of butterflies in such strange terms as Rhopalocera, Papilionidae and Lepidoptera. Then the two boys had a lunch of peanut-butter sandwiches and lemonade, which Sarah served them. And as Newt chewed and strolled about the room, he noted such book names as Hans Christian Andersen, Thomas Edison, Francis Bacon, Charles Dickens, Edgar Allan Poe, Marc Antony and even James B. "Wild Bill" Hickok. And there were just plain bugs under a glass neatly titled Coleoptera, with such names as *Eyed Elator, Ten Line June Beetle, Purple Tiger, DeGeer's Firefly, Blue Ground,* and a *Fifteen-Spotted Ladybug.* In the corner over Rodney's orderly desk, perched on an oak branch, were three stuffed birds, a *Road Runner,* a *Redheaded Woodpecker,* and a shiny-beaked *Yellow-Hammer.* There was a drawer marked *Chemical Symbols and Formulas;* another marked *Chemical Compounds,* and yet another marked *Inorganic and Organic Compounds.*

Rodney Cavanaugh's room represented a whole new world of knowledge for Newt—a world in which he suddenly longed to dwell; to know in a way that Rodney knew it; to be able to explain it to Beansy, Jappy and the others, in much the same way Rodney explained it to him. As he looked about, he felt that he had been somehow cheated. "After all," he reasoned, "Rodney and me are 'bout the same age, and I like all these books and things too." Then he thought about his home. He didn't even have a room of his own, much less microscopes, books, stuffed animals, pictures and such. And he wondered for a moment whether he would trade places with Rodney if he had the chance—and his decision was an emphatic No.

As he and his mother headed home in the crisp early dusk, tiny flakes of snow were beginning to fall.

Sarah said, "Did you have a good time with Rodney today?"

"Yessem, and he's shore a smart boy. He knows about everything—ants, butterflies, bugs, science and everything."

A strong wind brought the snowflakes in swifter, and Sarah pushed the scarf up close to her nose. "Yes, son, Rodney's very smart. He studies lots, and if you study the way you should, you can be just as smart as him. You'll be goin' to the white high school 'fore too long—there you'll have more things to read and work at."

By the time they reached home, snow covered the earth and trees; and, blowing wet in the strong wind, it smeared the night with its whiteness. Later, Newt sat at the front room window watching it pile up, feeling already the joy of a coming snowbound Sunday. He watched Prissy and Pete play checkers for a while, then started for bed. At the bedroom door he turned thoughtfully. "Pete?"

"Yep."

"Did'ya ever hear the word pap—papa-lon-i-de?"

Pete didn't look up from the move he was pondering. "Pappa what?"

"Papa-lon-nidi."

"Nope," he said, still figuring the move. "Why?"

"Oh, nothin'. Just askin', that's all." When he opened the bedroom door, cold air goose-pimpled his skin, and quickly he was out of his overalls and under the quilts (Pape-lion-i-die . . . pape-lion-i-die . . . is a insect with shingles—with scales —pape-lion-i-die . . . Rodney's prob'ly readin' . . . pape-lion-i-die), and before long he was asleep.

The next morning, as early sunlight cut across the land, the flakes sparkled like jewels in a world of pristine white. Unbroken brilliance lay over the fields, prairies and hills like a colorless blanket—reflecting, here and there, illusive spectral beams of fast-rising light.

Newt rose early, attended to his chores, and with his sled in tow was away to the slopes of Candy Hill before the rest of the family came awake. He met Waldo Newhall where the road bent into Logan's Grove, and they went on together. As usual, Waldo looked a little sad, and Newt often wondered if it was because his father was the town bum. But he liked Waldo, and enjoyed his companionship.

"Where's Beansy and them, Newt?"

"They ought'a be on the hill by now. I had to chop some extra wood for Monday mornin'."

A little further on, Rodney joined them in the final push toward the top of the gleaming hill where the others were already knifing the powdery slopes into fast, hard-packed trails.

Later, racing down with Beansy and Waldo, Newt saw the sled in front of him sideslip, then flip over, throwing its rider directly in his path. Newt's left foot dug quickly into the snow, skidding him sharply about. Then suddenly his sled was tumbling over and over, throwing him free and rolling, until he landed in a powdery heap with the rider who had sprawled before him.

Newt was up first. "Whyn't you look where you're goin'?" He began beating the loose snow from his clothes. "You almost got us both—" Two big brown eyes, set in a tan, dimpled face, stopped him dead. "Oh—I thought you was a boy."

"Well, I'm not, as you can plainly see." She, too, was smacking snow from her heavy woolen sweater.

Newt flustered an apology. "Oh, I can see now, all right. (Boy, she's pretty.) You hurt?"

"Nope. Thanks to you."

"Aw, wasn't nothin'." Six sleds whizzed by. "Just made a quick turn, that's all," he grinned, twisting his toe in a mound of snow. "My name's Newt—Newt Winger."

"I'm Arcella Jefferson."

"You ain't from round here."

"Nope. From Chanute, but I'll be living here for a while, I guess."

Newt's heart skipped a beat. "Well, well, boy, that's real keen news." Then bravely he assured her, "We can shore use some pretty girls round here."

"Use 'em?" Arcella's brow puckered. "What do you mean, use 'em?"

"Well, I—didn't mean it like you're takin' it. I just mean it's gonna be good just havin' you round."

Arcella seemed to know very well what he'd meant, and she smiled at his apparent discomfort before easing up on him. "Do you go to Booker T. Washington Junior High?"

"Yep. I'm in the eighth grade."

"So am I."

"Gee, we'll be in the same classes together."

By now they had retrieved their sleds, and Newt, somehow managing to pull them both, felt a new kind of warmth. And to him the snow they trudged in was no longer snow but just a necessary something to walk on in a world holding only two people, who walked alone in that something with not much to say—simply smiling or coughing without having to cough, wiping noses that needed no wiping. And by the time they reached the peak of Candy Hill, Newt was breathing heavily in the aching flush of first love.

But the crisp beauty of this fine Sunday was not only for Cherokee Flats. Seventy-two miles north, in a valley with postcard charm, the brown brick Spit's School for Wayward Boys rose from the white like a gingerbread cake. At 6 A.M. sharp, three clanging bells (one for each cell hall) broke the calm that lay over the morning.

"Okay! You bunch of fart-heads hit the floor!" Charlie

77

Crapper's voice bounced against the cold gray walls of Cell Hall One and echoed far into the other two sections.

"Shut up, you lousy bastard!" a voice shot back from the second corridor.

"What son-of-a-bitch said that?"

"Me, you stupid brass-ass!" Now a voice came from another direction. "It was me, your mammy's lover!" Laughter filled the halls.

"Cut out that goddam laughing—all you lunkheads! Cut it out and hit the floor—else I'll put my billy to you!"

Then the chorus started. Cell Hall One: "Anybody here seen Charlie's young daughter?" Cell Hall Two: "She can piss a mile and a quarter." Cell Hall Three: "And you cain't see her belly for the steam."

Charlie stalked up and down the halls, outraged into bitter silence, itching for a violator of the slightest demeanor. And the unlucky one was Marcus Savage, for he was the last, out of two hundred and three, to hit the floor.

"You like your rest, eh, Savage?" Charlie's voice was hot for revenge. Marcus, knowing his number was up, didn't answer. "I said, you like your rest, Savage!"

"I'm up, ain't I?" Marcus growled back sleepily.

"Yeh—and since you are, you black monkey, you gonna shovel the front path all the way to the county road—and before you git any breakfast. Now shake the stink out'a them sheets and then go grab a shovel."

Marcus was pulling on his overalls when he suddenly let them drop to the floor and, in a flash, his big fist smacked against Crapper's jaw, sending him crashing to the floor. Crapper struggled up and yanked out his billy club. Then bedlam broke loose. All the boys, as if on cue, swarmed through the corridor in crushing packs between Crapper and Marcus, bumping the guard from one side to the other. They were like bees tormenting a hapless fly. In final desperation, Crapper sounded his distress whistle, and six beefy guards jumped up from their breakfast and rushed in to his rescue; but by the time they came crashing into the area all the boys were standing stiffly, singing, with the most patriotic expressions, the first lines of "The Star-Spangled Banner." The six guards, clubs drawn for action, halted and stood contemptuously at attention as the voices droned painfully slow through the final line, "—o'er the land of the free and the home of the brave."

Standing before the warden, and aching from the private clubbing Crapper finally gave him, Marcus listened unemotionally to the punishment he was to receive: "—dry bread and water the rest of the day, and you git solitary confinement for the next two weeks. But first you're gonna shovel that snow like you was told. Take him away, Crapper."

And Marcus shoveled every back-breaking inch to the county road with Crapper standing over him all the way, avenging his soul with each shovelful. Marcus paused to rest a moment, then his shovel made the final scoop. But instead of throwing the snow aside, he sent it flying into Crapper's red face—and before the startled guard could clear his vision, Marcus slammed the shovel against his head and Crapper started falling; then, just as his big frame settled face down in the snow, the shovel caught him once again and he lay still. Marcus eyed him for a moment, started to strike again; but instead he ran across the road and into the brush.

He scampered through the forest of unbroken snow, fleeing aimlessly. He knew they would be hunting him soon, and, realizing how easy it would be to follow his fresh footprints in the snow, he cut back to a side road, mixing his tracks with others' that had come along before him. After a while the snow began falling again, and when it grew heavier he moved back into the forest, reasoning that the fresh flakes would hide the route of his flight.

At nightfall he was deep into the woods, cold, hungry and lost. He thought of his father and their shack, but no sense of warmth or safety came from those thoughts. So he kept moving along, avoiding the roads and open plains, traveling, without knowing it, in a circle that led toward the school rather than away from it. He saw a farmhouse a half mile off to his right, and his hunger automatically sent him in its direction. He tromped through the snow and crawled beneath a barbed-wire fence, but as he started up the cowpath two large dogs bore down on him, barking and blocking his approach.

"Come, boy. Come, boy," he whispered, trying to stop their barking; but they only barked louder.

He backed away and they followed, coming within a few feet of him. Scooping up some snow, he packed it into a ball and threw it, hitting one of them in the haunches. The dog yelped and ran back toward the house, its mate close on its heels. A shaft of light from the farmhouse blurred through the falling snow, and Marcus could make out the form of a man in the doorway. In his hand was a rifle.

"Who's there!" the man shouted.

Marcus stood silent, watching the man as he stuck two

fingers in his mouth and whistled. The dogs bounded past him into the house and he closed the door. After waiting a few moments, Marcus cautiously moved on to the edge of the forest from where he had come. He was strangely sleepy and chilled to the bone.

He stood freezing in the vast bleary darkness, too weak and hungry to stand straight, impulses welling up within him, bringing him to the point of tears. Even the cold reformatory room would have felt good to him now, and he thought of the other boys chattering away with their rude jokes and wild songs. "Maybe I should try to go back," he thought. "I'm gonna die if I try to stay out here." He rubbed his fingers together roughly, trying to get feeling back into them. His feet felt like painful nubs. He stumbled on from a last desperate will to survive; then his knees buckled under him and he slumped wearily into the deep snow.

Sometime later he heard the barking of the dogs and voices —Crapper's and the others—and felt their pulling him up and carrying him across the field to the farmhouse. The nightmare began to thin out, and he heard the farmer saying, "I had a notion it was the nigger boy missin' from the school my dogs was barkin' at." A half hour later they dumped him in his cell, and he fell into a fitful sleep.

The next morning he was told that the two weeks of solitary confinement had been stretched into three months. He didn't answer, either in protest or acknowledgment of the sentence. He didn't care one way or the other.

CHAPTER ❦ 6

IT WAS ABOUT eight o'clock on the first morning after school let out for Christmas vacation. Newt slipped into the dining room and cautiously opened his mother's fruit cupboard. Spying a Mason jar of apple butter, he lifted it, pulled the rubber collar gently so as not to stretch it, and unscrewed the top. Then, with a dull table knife, he expertly carved a circle an inch in from the edge and the full depth of the jar. This done, he upended the jar and dropped the middle section onto a newspaper, carefully recapped the jar and put it back. Finally he hid the filched preserves in a knapsack—and it was part of the food for a hunting trip he and Beansy had planned for the day. After that he finished his chores and awaited the arrival of his friend.

An hour later the two boys sat on the kitchen floor oiling their raccoon and opossum traps, hungering from the pungent smell of sausages sizzling in a skillet on the stove near them.

"Think we could sneak a couple'a extra sausages for our packs, Newt?" Beansy whispered.

"If Momma gits out'a the kitchen for a minute. They shore smell good. I cain't wait."

Their chance came when Jack Winger called to his wife for a clean pair of overalls. Newt and Beansy were up and over the meat by the time Sarah reached the middle of the dining room. Plucking two of the choicest sputtering patties, they juggled them frantically while Newt simultaneously forked the remaining ones into a position to hide the absence of the others.

Then, before they could know it, Prissy was coming through the door. And as she yawned away her drowsiness, Newt and Beansy shoved the hot sausages into their back pockets and backed against the wall.

Prissy stifled the yawn with the back of her hand and

81

looked at the boys wiggling in discomfort. "What you two nuts actin' so funny about?"

"What'a you talkin' about?" Newt shot back. He was standing the heat better than Beansy, whose plump behind was beginning to smart from the burning.

"You two are up to somethin'—I can tell." Her eyes were beginning to sharpen.

Beansy rocked against the wall, pressing the hot grease down to his tender thigh. "Ouch!" he yelled finally and burst through the door into the open, where he hurriedly slipped down his overalls, grabbed a handful of snow and applied it to his behind. Knowing nothing better to do, Newt rushed out after him. And Prissy, eyes popping, ran back through the dining room.

"Momma! Momma!" she yelled. "Newt and Beansy are pullin' somethin' funny!"

But by the time Sarah returned to the kitchen, Newt and Beansy had grabbed their packs, traps and other paraphernalia and headed for the woods.

They were nearly out of breath when they reached the foot of Candy Hill. And though it was very cold, they sweated beneath their heavy mackinaws.

"That Prissy would have to come buttin' in," Newt grumbled.

" 'Tain't Prissy I'm worryin' 'bout now. My rump feels like I been sittin' on a blow torch."

"Still hurtin' much?"

"Hurtin'? It's killin' me."

"I'll take a look when we git over the top'a the hill. Maybe it's blisterin'."

"Now I know what a steer feels like when they brand his butt."

Newt laughed. "Now we'll be able to tell your rump from the hog's."

" 'Tain't funny a bit."

On the other side of the hill they dropped their traps and packs. Beansy took off his coat and pushed down his pants so Newt could inspect the burn. "How's it look, Newt—red and puffy?"

"What'a you mean, red and puffy? A butt black as yours wouldn't git red if they fried it in red ink."

"Quit horsin' round, Winger. How's it look shore 'nough?"

"You're gonna live, Beansy. Don't git excited. Looks like a scorched ham butt," Newt kidded. Then he reached in his pack for a sausage, pressed some cold grease from it and coated the blister. "That ought'a help it some," he said.

A chilling blast of air swept down the slope, and Beansy jerked up his overalls. "Colder'n a Eskimo turd out here." His voice quivered as he snapped the bib hooks on his overalls and quickly got into his mackinaw. When he was thoroughly buttoned, they trudged through the deep snow to the frozen river, then scrambled up the bank and baited their traps. After setting them, they crawled into Rock Cave for shelter from the cold, got a fire going and settled back to enjoy its warmth.

"Wonder how Savage's doin' up at Spit's School?" Beansy said.

"Marcus?"

"Yeh."

"Funny thing," Newt mused, "I had a dream 'bout him last night, a real strange one." He bent forward, looking deeper into the fire, trying to recollect the details. "Seems like I was walkin' alone in a big forest and all of a sudden a big monster come out of the darkness at me—like a dragon or somethin'—and I had a sword, like the Knights of the Round Table. He had fire comin' out his nose and mouth. Seems like he had a lot of legs and I kept cuttin' 'em off when he come at me—but fast as I'd cut 'em off he'd have new ones. Then —then it wasn't a dragon no more but it was a bull, like they fight in Spain, only he had golden horns, and seems like his skin was made out'a one of them patchwork quilts like Momma makes."

"What's that got to do with Marcus?"

"Well, what's so funny is I was just 'bout to kill the bull with the sword when it began to cry great big tears and I stopped, and a voice kept tellin' me, 'Kill it! Kill it!' but I couldn't, and the voice said, 'Kill it 'fore it gits you!' and I started to run the sword through it but its head had turned to Marcus' head and he was cryin' too, great big tears, so big they turned into a river and he was drownin' 'cause he didn't have no arms, and I tried to save him but he was too heavy and he went under."

"That's all?"

"There was somethin' else—but I cain't remember—it was all so funny and strange-like."

"That wasn't no dream—that was a nightmare," Beansy said.

"I'd forgot all 'bout it till you called his name just now."

"When's he comin' back home?"

"I don't know exactly——'bout spring sometime, if he gits out when he's supposed to."

Beansy leaned back against the cave wall. "It's been kind'a peaceful since he's been gone, don't you think?"

"Yeh, it shore has. No fights or nothin' like that."

"He's gonna be surprised to see how big we all got when he does come back. You're almost tall as he is now, Newt."

"Yeh, but don't forgit he's gittin' bigger too."

"Trouble is, he thinks we didn't stick by him."

"I think it's mostly me he blames," Newt said.

"Maybe the school's gonna make him better. That's what a reform school's s'posed to do."

Newt poked into the fire with a stick, and the flame shot up. He squinted against the heat. "Momma says we all gotta try to help him when he comes out. Says he ain't never had much of a chance to be no better—never havin' a mother or a good home like you and me and the rest of the guys."

"Maybe so. Think the gang ought'a send him a Christmas card or somethin'?"

"Say—that's a good idea, Beansy! I'll ask Momma to git one, then all the guys can sign it 'fore we send it off."

Beansy pushed the conversation in another direction. "Whatcha gonna do next summer?"

"Don't know for shore. Rodney Cavanaugh says a professor at the high school is goin' to give some extra classes in science, free of charge, and he's goin' to ask his poppa to ask the teacher if I can come."

"What you want to go to a science class for in the summer?"

" 'Cause I think it'll help me when I go to the high school next year. You ought'a think 'bout it too."

"Not me. I got other plans for the summer."

"It's only for a week."

"No, thanks—I don't care if it's for a day. I see a'nough of school all year 'stead of foolin' round it in the hot summer."

"Well, to tell you the truth we ain't eli—eligible till we go one year to the white high school. That's why Rodney has to git special permission for me."

"You gittin' some pretty high ideas from that Rodney," Beansy joshed.

"Ain't nothin' wrong with that, is it?" Newt's voice had a bit of pique in it.

"Naw—naw, I guess it ain't."

"Boy like Rodney might be President someday," Newt said profoundly.

"Yeh, and a boy like you might be a dog catcher some-day," Beansy chuckled.

"Ain't nothin' wrong with bein' ready when the big things come," Newt said, quoting his Uncle Rob.

Beansy was quiet for a moment. Then, "Remember the day old Prof Jones got after Earl for not havin' his homework, and Earl said, 'I ain't had no chance to study,' and old Prof said, 'You don't say I ain't had *no* chance to study. You say I ain't had *a* chance to study.'"

Newt laughed. "Boy, do I remember? We all busted out laughin' and he made us stay a whole hour after school writin' f-o-o-l-s on the blackboard over and over again."

"'Nother time he told Skunk that he must'a been sleepin' in the devil's privy when the Lord handed out sense."

They both laughed again. "Boy, we're shore gonna miss old Prof when we go to the other school," Newt said.

After an hour had passed they went back to their traps and found that three of them were still unsprung. Around the fourth was a smudgeon of red and part of a muskrat's tail. Beansy picked up the trap, its jaws still clamped to the flexible, gristly part. "Son-of-a-gun gnawed it off and got away clean as a whistle."

"Can't say as I blame him," Newt said.

"Bet he's got a mighty sore behind right now, though," Beansy countered.

Newt laughed. "Well, that makes two sore asses in these parts today—yours and that muskrat's."

"Yeh, but mine ain't cut off."

"With all you got back there, wouldn't hurt none if you got a little chopped off too."

"Wouldn't talk if I was you—skinny as your ass is." Beansy returned the laugh.

On the way back Newt decided to stop by Arcella Jefferson's house to see if she could go with him to a movie.

After inviting them into the parlor, Arcella said, "Sit down —I'll have to ask Momma," and she went into the kitchen.

"Gosh, she looks scrumptious today!" Newt exclaimed, forgetting Beansy's presence.

"Pretty as a speckled pup," Beansy agreed.

"Huh—oh—oh yeh," Newt answered in embarrassment.

Arcella fluttered into the room, pulling on her two long braids. "Momma said it'll be all right as long as we git home before nine."

"Okay. We'll go at six o'clock. I'll git by here 'bout five-thirty."

The two boys rose and Arcella walked with them to the door. "You coming too, Beansy?" she cooed.

"Well—maybe, I—"

"Nope," Newt cut in quickly, "he's got to patch a tail."

"Tail? What kind of tail?"

Newt giggled. "A blistered tail."

Arcella shook her head and closed the door.

Later, Newt and Arcella sat in the darkness of the "peanut gallery," the flickering light of the movie screen dancing on their faces. Newt took Arcella's hand and squeezed it (William S. Hart is closing in on the villain), then he withdrew his hand and eased it onto her knee, feeling the rolled top of her stocking beneath the gingham skirt. (Hart's lasso is about the villain's waist as their horses reach the crest of the hill.) Newt's other hand slid behind her shoulder (the villain is falling from his galloping mount) and his fingers pressed into the softness of her armpit (Hart jumps from his horse onto the villain), and Arcella pushed his hand down to her waist. (Hart and the villain are fighting at the edge of the cliff.) Newt inched closer (Hart gets it on the chin and goes down) and Arcella moved in closer too (now Hart is up and the villain is down), and Newt's cheek touched her braid (both Hart and the villain are rolling down the cliff) and she pushed her braid aside and touched her cheek to his (down and down go Hart and the villain in flying dust) and his knee squirmed toward hers (Hart and the villain are up fighting on their feet again, and the pretty girl they are fighting over gallops up just in time to see Hart silence the villain with a swift right), then their knees squirmed together (Hart runs back up the hill and embraces the pretty girl) and Newt felt Arcella's long eyelashes batting against his cheek (Hart kisses the pretty girl), then Newt pulled Arcella to him and they kissed (the word "End" is on the screen, the organ blares to a crescendo and the lights go on). Arcella sat up straight and pushed Newt away.

It was below zero when they got outside, so they hurried through the night without saying much. When they reached Arcella's house, her mother let them in and offered Newt some cake and hot chocolate, which he accepted. A half hour later Newt and Arcella were sitting on the davenport in the parlor, and Newt began where he'd left off in the theater, unaware that her father sat looking down on them from the darkness at the top of the stairs.

"Boy!"

Newt and Arcella jumped apart and sat stiffly in embarrassment.

"Seems to me that couch ought to be big enough for you and my daughter to sit on without bein' in each other's laps!"

"Yes—yessir, Mister Jefferson." Then he was up, fidgeting with his hat and coat. "I guess it's 'bout time I was headin' home," he mumbled to the blushing Arcella. "See you in church tomorrow."

"Okay, Newt," she said, scowling up at the darkness, "see you in Sunday school."

"Thanks for the cake and stuff, Missus Jefferson!" Newt called; then he glanced furtively to the top of the dark stairway and was gone.

He walked swiftly in the cold moonlit night, seeing his bulky shadow upon the snow that crunched under his weight. His thoughts turned to summer; to the warm soft breezes playing at Arcella's skirts, and the tender body-close evenings they would steal from the pleasurable months ahead. He drew his mackinaw collar closer about his ears and cut across a field to shorten his journey in the biting cold. He trudged through the deeper unbroken snow of Logan's Grove, leaped a narrow ditch and started into the yard of his home.

"Newt! Newt! That you?" It was his sister Rende—and her two small children, Butsy and Gin-gin—running toward him from the lower path.

He sensed their plight immediately. "Yeh! Yeh! What's the matter, Rende?"

"Clint's after me—with the gun. Momma home?"

"I don't know. She ought'a be—come on!" Newt grabbed Butsy and Gin-gin by their hands, and they all ran up on the porch.

Rende pounded on the door. "Momma! Momma!"

Sarah was darning socks when the shout came. Jack was cleaning his pipe. Prissy and Pete were playing checkers.

"That's Rende, Jack," Sarah said. "Open the door. Clint must be up to his Saturday night foolishness."

Jack got up and opened the door, and the four rushed in. "Momma—Clint's drunk again—he's got that gun!"

Sarah threw the ball of yarn to the floor. "Never seen it fail! Never seen it fail! Every time he gits a little money he tries to drink up half of Chappie Logan's," she said, going for her coat. "Just go on in the bedroom, Rende—nothin's goin' to happen. Quit your snivelin'."

And since this was an old thing to the Wingers, Prissy and Pete hardly stirred. "Your move, Pete."

"Keep your skirt on. I'm doin' a little figgerin' here."

"You want me to go with you, Sarah?" Jack asked, still cleaning his pipe.

"No—I'll handle him. You just gittin' back from the picture show, Newt?"

"Yessem. Missus Jefferson gave me some cake and chocolate."

"Hmm. If I catch you and Beansy stealin' sausage out of my skillet again, I'm gonna give you more'n cake and chocolate." She opened the door to go out.

Newt was at her heels. "Can I come with you, Momma?"

Sarah gave him a look of refusal, then quickly reconsidered, thinking of her son's fondness for Clint. "Yes, come ahead," she said. Then they were out and down the path to meet her son-in-law.

They came upon him shortly. He was stumbling in the deep snow coming toward the house, the shotgun hanging from his hand at the barrel.

Sarah spoke crisply. "Where you goin' with that gun, boy?"

Clint stopped and rocked back and forth, the butt of the gun twisting about in the snow. "Oh—hi there, Momma Winger. Hi, Newt—"

"I said, where you goin' with that gun?"

"I—I'm gonna git Rende—tonight—shore'n hell. I'm—"

Sarah was within reach of him now. "Back, Newt," she said, "back out'a the way." Newt stepped to the side and watched his mother move slowly up to Clint.

"Now look out, Momma Winger—I mean what—I say—look out—" He was slowly raising the gun. "I'll shoo—"

The action was so quick Newt missed it. He heard the smack of his mother's hand against Clint's face and saw him go down; then he saw the dark form of the gun in his mother's hand.

"Help him up, boy. Git him to the house. He's so drunk he can hardly stand up, let alone shoot anybody." Newt bent down and helped Clint to his feet, and the three of them went back to the house.

As they entered, Newt saw Rende peeping at the bedroom door. When she heard her husband groan and collapse to the floor, she crept back into the parlor with Butsy and Gin-gin in time to see her mother hide the gun behind the china cabinet.

Jack threw some more coal in the fire and spat in the scuttle. "Just look at him," he said in a half growl, "his maw and paw shore wasted a night when they made him."

"Git to bed, Newt," Sarah said, ignoring Jack. "Don't forgit, you've got Sunday school in the mornin'."

"Yessem."

Rende went across the room and knelt by her husband. "Clint—Clint," she said, shaking him, "listen to me."

"Yeh—whad—you want—whad—"

"Clint, I'm goin' to have a baby."

The room went silent at her words.

"Me too," Clint mumbled. Then he turned over on his back and began snoring.

Rende wept. "What am I goin' to do, Momma? What am I goin' to do?"

Sarah put her arms about Rende's shoulders. "We've just got to pray over him, that's all. We've got to keep prayin'."

Jack blew out a ring of smoke. "I declare, prayin' ain't gonna do that varmit no good, none a'tall."

"Jack, I want you to stop talkin' like that. You know—"

"I'm tellin' you, Sarah—Clint's lost. God and the devil's both quit strugglin' for him, so it ain't much nobody else can do—I don't care how long and how loud they pray." He knocked his pipe on the coal scuttle and some loose ashes fell out. "He's lucky it's you who handles him. If it's ever me who has to take that gun away from him, he ain't gonna find it so easy. Fact is, he's gonna end up with a cracked skull."

"That's just why I made you stay in the house." She felt Newt's eyes upon her. "Boy, I thought I told you to git to bed!"

"Yessem."

"Don't yessem me. Just git goin'."

"Yessem."

Sarah turned back to Jack. "You've got to understand Clint. He ain't half as bad as you think. We've had some real nice talks together, and—"

"When he was sober."

"—and he's even promised me he's goin' to join the church."

"Well, I guess if anybody can drag him to the pulpit it's you. You got some kind of magic over him, or somethin'."

"Ain't magic at all. It's love, and Clint knows it."

"Well, I hope he don't ever try it when you're not around. He's in for trouble if he does."

Rende started sniffling again.

"You and the kids better stay here tonight," Sarah said. "You can sleep in Prissy's bed. She can make a pallet on the floor."

Jack stood up and stretched. "Got to git up early. Comin' to bed soon, Sarah?"

"Soon as I git Rende and the kids straight."

CHAPTER ✤ 7

"MERRY CHRISTMAS! Merry Christmas!" Newt shouted, rousing all the Wingers from their sleep. He had risen early, made a crackling fire and put on the coffeepot, knowing his father would be less grouchy if his insides were warmed up. By the time everyone was in the front room, bright sunlight was bouncing off the snow through the windows onto the tinsel and colored balls decorating the tree.

And as usual Prissy, with an overpoliteness that irked Newt, handed out the gifts, wearing a new middy blouse over her flannel nightgown as she switched about.

After Newt unwrapped his gifts he noted that they were more practical than ever before. He felt that the overalls, stocking cap, socks, book satchel and dictionary (this last from his mother) reflected his growing up. Proudly, he accepted them in this sense, letting go completely the tin soldier and wind-up car period in which he had found so much joy several Christmases before.

After thanking everyone for his presents, he began thumbing the dictionary (this pleased Sarah mightily) for the word *Papilionidae*. To his great surprise he couldn't find it. But he found *Papilionaceous,* and though he didn't understand one of the explanations for it, he immediately decided to learn the phrasing by heart and spring it on Rodney Cavanaugh when they met again. He jumped up, dashed to his room, grabbed pencil and paper and hurried back to the front room. From the book he scribbled: "Papilionaceous —having an irregular zygomorphic corolla somewhat resembling a butterfly." He copied the words over and over, filling the whole page with the new knowledge. Then he propped himself up on the couch and began memorizing it.

Pete sat on the floor rubbing up a pair of already shiny spurs. Prissy, preening before the mirror, tied and retied the handsome bow on her middy blouse. Jack sat admiring his new rough-grain pipe, and Sarah rocked back and forth fingering and praising the sewing kit that Newt, Prissy and Pete had chipped in to buy her.

"Pete," Newt said suddenly, his head still in the book, "did you or Prissy ever hear the word zy-go—gom, no, zy-go-morp-hic in high school?"

"Not me," Pete said.

"Not me," Prissy said.

Sarah looked up, puzzled. "What do you want to know about the word, son?"

"Just what it means."

"What you think that dictionary's for, lunkhead?" Prissy spouted out.

"That's no way to talk, Prissy," Sarah said. "Git over there and help him find the word and what it means."

"Yessem," Prissy answered, twisting the bow. "Oh, I just look sooo de-vine in this here lo-va-ly middy, so lo-va-ly." She flounced over to Newt. "Now, deah brotha, what is the word that you would have thou sista help you with?"

A common four-letter work beginning with *s* popped into Newt's mind, but his mother's eyes were on him and he answered, "Zy-go-morp-hic."

"Why are you worryin' about a word that you don't know anything about?" Prissy questioned facetiously.

"Prissy," Sarah said, "I'm listenin' to you."

"Yessem. Let's see—w, x, y, z—zy-go-matic bone, arch—oh, here it is. It's zy-go-mor-phic, not zy-go-morp-hic, nut."

"Well, what's the diff'rence, phic or hic. Just 'bout the same," Newt said.

"Oh my," Sarah said impatiently, "just tell him what it means and quit fussin'."

Prissy's cheeks dimpled to a mischievous grin. "It means," she said, "mon-o-sym-metric." She cocked her head at Newt. "That satisfy you, deah brotha?"

Newt was silent, temporarily defeated.

"Prissy, you're bein' smart," Sarah said. "Now, I—"

"No I'm not, Momma. That's all it really says." She took the book to Sarah. "See, look for yourself."

Sarah pushed the book away to a seeing distance. "Well, it must be more to it than that," she said. "Pete, come see if you can't help straighten this thing out."

Pete reluctantly dropped his spurs and moved over to his mother. He took the book and, without speaking, read from zygoma to zymurgy. "Newt," he said finally, "this thing's got me fuddled, but I think mostly it's about bones—cheekbones. It says here to see sym-metrical."

"Zi-go this and zi-go that," Jack growled. "I declare, I wish Prissy'd git out in that kitchen and make some zi-go biscuits. I'm hungry."

"Why ah'd be glad to, Poppa deah," Prissy said, switching across the room.

Jack looked up at her. "That blouse is gonna git you into a mess if you don't watch out, gal," he muttered.

Pete laughed. So did Sarah and Newt. And they were all delighted to let the "zygomorphic" matter drop.

Arcella arrived shortly after breakfast, and when Newt opened the door for her she thrust a package into his hands, pecked him on the cheek and wished him a merry Christmas.

"Merry Christmas to you too," Newt said. "Come on in."

"Can't stay long. Oh, hello, Mr. and Mrs. Winger."

"Hello, Arcella—merry Christmas," they both answered.

"Same to you and to you, Prissy and Pete. I hope all of you have a nice Christmas."

"Very very very," Prissy cooed.

They stood awkwardly for a moment, then Newt motioned Arcella into the front room. "Santa Claus left somethin'—"

"Something," Arcella corrected.

"Sorry—he left something here for you under the tree." He picked up a small, gaily wrapped parcel from the floor and handed it to her. Then he pecked her on the cheek and said, "Merry Christmas, sweetheart."

Prissy started to join them, but Sarah motioned her back. "You just keep out'a there, girl. That's Newt's little party." Prissy shrugged her shoulders and went back to the breakfast dishes.

Arcella and Newt sat in the middle of the floor unwrapping their gifts, and Newt got his open first. It was a book of short stories by Edgar Allen Poe, Newt's favorite author. He flipped the first white page and grinned, for there was an inscription, "A merry merry Christmas to the sweetest person I have ever known. Love, Arcella. December, 1925."

"Thanks. Thanks very much," he said. Then he waited shyly as she opened hers.

"Oh, Newt!" she cried, "it's beautiful, just beautiful." She held the locket out to him, turning her back. "Fasten it. Fasten it. I can't wait to see it on."

Clumsily his fingers pulled the chain with the heart-shaped locket around her neck, and after some trouble he secured the clasp. "There," he said, feeling a warmth all the way to his toes.

Then they were both up before the mirror. "Oh, Newt," she repeated, "it's exactly what I wanted." She kissed him on the lips this time, and he leaned forward for another. There was a quick, breathless embrace, then another kiss, followed by hasty thoughtless chatter. "Got up early this mornin'."

"So did I."

"Then I called everybody and we gave out presents."

"Just about the same over at our place, only not as many people."

"There's five of us here."

"Only three of us. Mother, father and I."

"Well, that's the way it is. Some families are bigger'n others."

"Bigger than. Not bigger'n," she chuckled.

"Momma gave me a dictionary. There's lots of good words in it."

"So now you can stop talking like the rest of that gang of yours."

"They're not so bad."

"If they were as bad as their speech, they would all be in jail, Newt Winger."

"All of them ain—aren't as lucky as I am."

"And what do you mean by that statement?"

"I got you."

Arcella shook her head in playful disgust. " 'I got you,' " she mocked.

"I got you—I have you—I have got you. It all means the same. You're my girl—and that makes me real lucky."

She looked at him for a long nice moment, without saying a word. And he looked back at her, not saying a word. They both felt the need for an early spring, a warm, soft, kiss-luscious spring—each aware of the heat in the other's longing.

"I must go now, Newt."

"See you Saturday for the picture show."

"I hope so."

Arcella bid everyone merry Christmas once more and left. And Newt turned again to the inscription, kissed it and placed the book on top of the dictionary. He stood for a moment in the center of the room. "Momma," he called out, "when I get some more books can I have a shelf in my room like Rodney's?"

"I think that would be fine, son. I'm sure Pete and your poppa will help you make a fine one."

Christmas at Spit's School for Boys wasn't much different from any other day. A few of the exceptionally well-behaved boys were granted trips home for the holidays. The others received a pork chop dinner and a small bag of peppermint candies.

Marcus ate alone in the dimness of his cell. The card from Newt, Beansy, Jappy, Earl and Skunk was propped on the table beside his cot. He glanced at the scribbled names in the weak light, and his mind recalled their faces as they had looked when they stood against him on the road near the river. He thought it was Newt who had betrayed him. Then the face of Jake Kiner mixed with the others, and Kirky's and Judge Cavanaugh's. He began boiling within, and suddenly he took a vicious swipe at the card and it fluttered to the floor. It would be May—with no mishaps—before he could return to Cherokee Flats, and his mind wandered to the river, the open plains and the rolling hills. . . .

He had just settled back on the cot when Crapper hollered, "You got some visitors, Savage! Git up and try lookin' happy."

"Screw you," Marcus growled sullenly.

"Fool with me and you don't see nobody," Crapper warned.

"I don't give a goddam. Ain't nobody I want to see nohow."

But by now the visitors were coming down the corridor.

"Right this way, Rev'rend," Crapper said. He spoke with an exaggerated politeness that forced a grunt of disgust from Marcus. The cell door swung open and through it came Reverend Broadnap, Maggie Pullens—carrying a bag of fruit and candy—and Deacon Henry Fuller. Reverend Broadnap stepped over and touched Marcus on the shoulder. Marcus stiffened. He wanted to tell them all to go, but he held his tongue.

"We come to pray for you and to wish you a merry Christmas, son." He didn't answer, and Broadnap turned to the others and said, "Let's pray."

They knelt on the floor. Marcus' fingernails dug into the palms of his hands and his teeth ground together in an angry embarrassment. He kept his eyes low and straight ahead, as if ignoring their presence.

"Oh Almighty God," Broadnap began, "we come to you on bended knee prayin' for the soul of this young sinner." Marcus' muscles flexed and his gaze shot defiantly to the tops of their heads, then to Crapper, who stood in the doorway with an evil grin on his face. "Wash his black sins away

95

in these white snows of your holy Christmas. Lighten the troubles he has brought to his young dark days. Bring peace to his tormented soul and help him to someday leave this place a cleaner and better young man. Oh God, show him the light. Show——"

"Shut up! Shut up!" Marcus shouted, "and git the hell out'a here!" He was on his feet now. "I don't want'a hear none of your Uncle Tom prayin' over me!" The three people rose, shocked beyond belief.

"You don't know what you're sayin', boy," Broadnap half whispered, trying to quiet him down, reaching again toward his shoulder.

"I know much 'bout what I'm sayin' as you do," he shot back, pulling away.

Maggie put the bag of fruit on his bed. Broadnap took out a Sunday school card with the picture of Christ on it and placed it on the table. "Read the scripture here on the back, son," he said, "and pray to the Savior. He'll hear you."

Marcus snatched the card, tore it in half and threw it at the preacher. "You and your white God git the hell out'a here!" he shouted. "I don't want no part of you soul savers —bendin' down, like Paw says you do, kissin' the feet of a poor white trash God." Tears were in his eyes now. "Look at Crapper there! He's white! Whyn't you git down and start moanin' and groanin' to him, so he can kick the crap out'a you like he does all us 'nigga' boys. Yeh, that's what he calls us—nigga! nigga! nigga! Tell 'em, Crapper. Tell 'em what you gonna do to me when they leave! Tell 'em."

"Son—"

"Don't son me. Just git goin'! So Crapper can tease me 'bout you niggas comin' here to pray over me!"

Broadnap, Maggie and Henry Fuller filed out, their heads shaking. Crapper slammed the door shut and followed them down the corridor. Marcus sat very still awhile, then suddenly he began to feel a deep sense of guilt, deeper than any he had ever felt in his whole life. He was bewildered. These people had come all that way to help him and he had hurt them, said things he didn't realize he could say. But what he'd said was more for Crapper than for them, he realized. If Crapper hadn't stood in the door with that silly grin on his face, things might have been different. But it was too late now. The harm was done. Yet, somehow, he felt he had got a point across to Crapper. He didn't know just what. Maybe he was really defending those people against somebody like Crapper, who had once told him, "All niggas

96

are stupid and crazy." In a way he was telling him that they weren't, that he was on to his kind and their "lily-white God" that his paw damned when he got drunk.

He glanced up. Crapper was back. Marcus said nothing.

"Merry Christmas—nigga," Crapper said disdainfully, and turned back down the corridor.

Marcus was silent. His head fell back in the shadows and he closed his eyes, trying to form the image of a God with black skin, thick lips and coarse hair like his—but he couldn't. The image on the torn card at the foot of his bed had been implanted much too long before. It was difficult to erase that image now, or even substitute another one for it.

CHAPTER ❧ 8

"IT WAS AWFUL the way that Savage boy talked to us—simply awful," Maggie Pullens told Sarah as the two of them sat in the Winger front room that night.

Sarah thought for a while before answering, then she spoke what she knew to be the truth. "It ain't really the boy's fault, Maggie."

"Then whose is it, for the good Lord's sake?"

"That could've been Newt, Beansy, Earl or any of the other young ones around here. If we want to tell the truth about it, then we would say it's our fault—all the Christians, black and white, and teachers and officeholders and everybody who's supposed to have good in them."

"Yes—yes, you're right, Sarah. Guess you're right."

"Our young children's minds here are mixed up. This place with all its drinkin' and fightin' and murderin'—Jim Crow schools, picture shows and eatin' places is too much for these young ones to figure out. They've got bigger ideas about livin' than you and me had at their age, Maggie."

"We're in a rut for shore."

"We was born in a rut, and the reason we've been able to keep goin' is because we always thought someday we're goin' to git out of it. I ain't one to fool myself about my chances any more, but I'm goin' to do all I can to see that my children don't get bogged down here forever."

"It's a big problem, all right."

"Take that Savage boy—nobody's ever done anything big to help him. He should've been taken away from Booker when he was a little boy and put in a good home. There just ain't much good can come of him now."

"The only people tryin' to do anything a'tall is our church missionary society."

"That's true, Maggie, but it's mighty hard tryin' to push out misery and fill empty stomachs with the word of God.

Booker Savage asked me one day if we had a Jim Crow heaven waitin' for our saints."

"That man's awful—just awful."

"Told me Chappie Logan was his god. 'Least he's black like me,' he said."

"Awful—just awful," Maggie moaned. A moment later she got up to leave. "Well, I have to be moseyin' on. Tired after that long trip up there."

"It's good you went, Mag. Don't feel too bad about what happened. I'm sorry I wasn't with you."

"Sarah!" Jack was calling and walking in from the next room. "Did you two see what's on the back page of tonight's paper?"

"No," Sarah answered. "What's in it?"

"Look here." Jack handed her the paper, and he and Maggie bent over her shoulder as she read: "Jess Hicks, district school superintendent, announced today that, beginning next year, Negro students who normally would enter Cherokee Senior High school as freshmen will not be admitted until their sophomore year. These students will be held over at Booker T. Washington school. Mr. Hicks said the action was taken because of overcrowded conditions and shortage of staff at the senior high school. Two substitute colored teachers, Callie Johnson and Fred Simmons, will be put on a full-time basis at Washington school. Asked if this was to be a permanent arrangement, Mr. Hicks replied that it would, unless the State allocated money for expansion at the high school. This, he said, was unlikely."

"Well, I'll be—" Sarah gasped.

"What's it say, Sarah?" Maggie questioned. "I ain't got my glasses."

Sarah sat rigid, biting her lips, her hands crushing the newspaper. "They're pushin' the colored kids—the freshman class—out of the white high school, the one Newt'll be in next year."

"What?" Maggie put both hands on her hips. "You don't mean it? What won't these white people do next? How can they call themselves Christian? Where's their religion?"

"Religion?" Jack scoffed. "A white man don't take his religion out of church. He locks it up there for safekeepin', so it's fresh and clean on Sunday mornin' when he comes to wash his week's sinnin' away."

"Well, I got to be moseyin' on," Maggie repeated. "But that's the best I heard yet. See you tomorrow. Goodnight."

"Goodnight, Mag," they both answered.

"Jack." Sarah was scanning the paper again. "We have to fight this thing. We just cain't let Jess Hicks and that crowd git away with this."

"Fight it—with what?" Jack bellowed.

"With the colored parents and teachers—that's what."

"I'm tired, awful tired," Jack said. "I want to live the rest of my life in some kind of peace."

"There ain't goin' to be no peace for you or none of us unless we make it for ourselves. Newt is—"

"Newt Newt Newt!" Jack was up now, pacing the room. "I declare, Sarah—you think that boy's gonna be President someday—the first black President of the United States?" He shook his head in disgust.

"I ain't worried about him bein' President. All I want for him is a better life than he's got here."

"You already got him thinkin' 'bout things he'll never git, believin' he can do anything Rodney Cavanaugh can do."

"If we give him the chance, he can. That's what the fight's all about," she snapped, "that's exactly what it's all about."

"Well—"

"Well, nothin'." Sarah was angry now. "You and me are goin' to git people together and fight this thing. And we're goin' to git those freshman kids back where they belong, if it's the last thing we do."

Jack turned and looked at her. "She's really got her dander up," he thought. And he said, "Looks like you're gonna stir up some trouble 'spite of my better judgment."

"And you're goin' to help me do it, Jack Winger."

"So be it, so be it," he concluded.

During the rest of January and all of February, Jack and Sarah spent what extra time they had marshaling all the Negro teachers and a sizable number of parents who had shown some sort of interest in "the fight." By the end of March the group, now thirty-five strong, was ready for action, and it met at the colored school. Professor Ebon Jones brought the meeting to order, and Sarah Winger proposed that they call themselves the Negro Parent-Teacher Association.

"That's a good idea, sister Winger," Ebon said, "but it raises a little problem with us teachers here. It's—well, what I'm tryin' to say is that we are sort of responsible to the superintendent's office, and—and—"

"And you're 'fraid to buck him—that it, Ebon?" Jack Winger asked.

"No—let's not get off on the wrong foot, Jack. You got to

100

remember that we teachers get paid by these people—and —and this can develop into a troublesome thing for us if we start snappin' too hard at the hand that's feedin' us."

"That's right," Myrtle Beasly cut in. "We've got a lot more to lose than some of the rest of you. What if—"

"Right, Myrtle." Encouraged by the sudden support, Ebon continued, "I think we better tread lightly and not get too excited about this thing." (Jack felt the restlessness in Sarah. He began squirming in his seat.) "They could cut off our pay just like that." Ebon snapped his fingers for emphasis. "By callin' it the Parents and Teachers Association—"

"Just a minute, Ebon." Sarah was up on her feet, her arms folded determinedly beneath her breast. "There ain't a one of us here in this dilapidated school tonight that don't depend on our bread and butter from the white people. Not a one of us." She defiantly scanned the group. "It ain't the teachers' jobs and it ain't the teachers' troubles that we're here for, so much as it is the problem of our children and what's goin' to happen to 'em in time to come, if they keep gittin' kicked around like they are now from school to school, whenever the white people feel like it. I—"

"Now, sister Winger, you—"

"You just keep quite a minute or two, Ebon. You said your piece. Now listen to mine."

"Go ahead," Ebon apologized.

"The more we let 'em kick us around, the more they're goin' to do it. There ain't no reason under God's sun why that freshman class shouldn't be in the high school where it rightfully belongs. There they can git all the things this school ain't got. Most of you mothers and fathers went to this same school—even you, Ebon. Do you see any changes in it? Same desks, same books, same windows, same old rickety stairs—nothin' changed in it but the kids. Meantime, the whites have built two new schools, gyms and made all kinds of improvements. And they did it off our taxes. But they keep our kids out of these schools and gyms for as long as they can."

Myrtle Beasly spouted, "But what's going to happen to the extra colored teachers, Callie Johnson and Fred Simmons, who were put on here to help teach the freshman class? They have to eat too."

"Like I said before, the children are the main worry. And I'm surprised at you teachers for takin' such a attitude. I had it in my mind you'd be leadin' the fight 'stead of hinderin' it."

"It's like Myrtle said, we got to eat," Callie Johnson spoke from the back of the room.

"You're worried about feedin' your stomachs and us mothers and fathers are worried about feedin' our children's minds. Seems to me it ought'a be the other way around. Ain't no reason why we cain't worry about both, but it's the young ones who're goin' to be facin' the hard years that's comin'— you teachers ought'a know it's goin' to be harder for them than it was for us. The world's goin' to be expectin' more out of 'em, and they're goin' to be expectin' more out of the world."

"We still have to eat, sister Winger," Ebon said.

"Eat! Eat! Eat!" Sarah shouted. "We hardly got enough to feed our own faces at our houses, but I swear if any of you git fired for fightin' for your rights, we'll all put some extra plates on our tables for you. Right, brother Fuller?"

"Right, sister Winger."

"Right, brother Duncan?"

"Amen, sister. Amen."

"Right, sister Pullens?"

"Shore will, Sarah."

"A little order, please!" Ebon said, pounding on the desk. "What do you feel about this, Reverend Broadnap? We haven't heard from you."

Broadnap stood, twisting his hands behind his frock coat. "Well," he said, "I kept quiet so far, 'cause I wanted to hear both sides of the argument. I know how you teachers feel 'bout this matter, but sister Winger's right. It's more to stake than the teachers' jobs, 'cause in the first place the law's against anybody takin' your jobs just like that. On top of that, these kids have got to be educated. That's the law, and we all know it. And we know these white teachers ain't comin' cross those Frisco tracks to teach our black children, so I don't see what you're frettin' 'bout. I think the only fair way is to take a vote on sister Winger's idea on a name for us, and those that's scared, git out—those that ain't, stay in. Just as clear as that."

"Amen, brother Broadnap."

"Well said, brother. Well said."

"I agree. I agree."

The vote was taken, and when it was over the group became the Negro Parent-Teacher Association of Cherokee Flats.

As Jack and Sarah drove Maggie Pullens home, Jack suddenly remarked, "I don't trust that Ebon Jones in this thing."

"I know what you mean," Maggie said. "He shore was pullin' back tonight."

"Well, you cain't blame the teachers altogether for feelin' the way they do," Sarah said. "But comin' down to brass tacks, they ain't no worse off than anybody else. As for Ebon, he'll be all right when the showdown comes."

It was April before the "showdown" came. At the start of the public meeting in Town Hall, Jess Hicks asked everybody to stand and pledge allegiance to the flag. Jack Winger grunted and mumbled to Sarah, "Think we was gettin' ready to throw over the gov'ment."

Jess sat at a table on the platform with Marshall Goodlander, the mayor, and Gordon Blair, the village treasurer, at his right. Miss Tilley Reeves, president of the white parent-teacher association, and Bart Phillips, the fire chief, sat at his left. Only twenty-one of the Negro group showed up. They were bunched near the rear on the left side of the hall. The rest of the room was filled with white parents, teachers and other village folk.

"We're a little outnumbered," Jack whispered to Sarah.

"Makes no difference," Sarah answered.

Jess Hicks rose and introduced his "guests" at the speakers' table; then he looked out over the audience to the blob of black faces to the rear. "My friends, both white and colored," he began, "we're here tonight at the request of a newly formed group"—he cleared his throat—"one involving colored teachers—and parents—that was formed without the knowledge of the school board, his honor the Mayor or myself. Mr. Blair tells me this group does not have a legal charter (Ebon Jones's eyes widened), but I felt it was in the good of the community to air such a protest as the group is about to make, in spite of this illegal procedure on their part."

Jess cleared his throat and paused, letting this information sink into the colored ranks. "Now I'm going to tell you very bluntly what their protest amounts to. They want the Negro freshman class moved back to the already over-crowded high school. Before I ask for their reasons, I'd like to ask Mr. Bart Phillips, our beloved fire chief, to tell us briefly what physical dangers this presents to the students themselves."

Bart, his red face growing redder, got up and said that the high school already held more students than it should, to comply with safety standards. Then Treasurer Blair, at Jess's request, rose and painted a dismal picture of state aid, saying in the end there was no money for building additional rooms at the high school to accommodate the overflow.

"Well," Jess addressed the audience again, "I have stated the protest and you have heard statements from Mr. Phillips and Mr. Blair, who have given much thought to the condition which is the basis of this protest." He cleared his throat and looked squarely at Professor Ebon Jones. "Ebon, are you the spokesman for this group?"

Ebon stirred in his seat, remaining there speechless for a moment or so. Then, feeling the eyes of his association— his illegal association—upon him, he rose slowly. "Well— well, yes—in a way," he stammered, "Mr. Superintendent."

"Fine, Ebon. Now, did your association take the fire chief's findings and the financial situation of the village into consideration when you planned this protest?"

"Well—no sir, we didn't."

"Why not, may I ask?"

"Because—because they didn't know about such conditions, sir."

"They—and you?"

"Yessir."

"Then you would agree"—he was looking toward the Mayor now—"that your group has acted unwisely, wouldn't you, Ebon?"

"Well, sir, in the light of such findings, I suppose. I—I feel maybe we were a little hasty, but the teachers and myself tried to—"

"Just a minute!" Sarah Winger pulled up out of her seat, ignoring Jack's tug on her coat sleeve. "How long ago was it you made these rules about safety and such stuff as you're tellin' us about?"

Jess gazed sternly at Sarah. She stared back.

"I thought Ebon Jones was the speaker for this group," Jess said flatly.

"I thought so too, until just now, but—"

"Well, if he's the spokesman I'd prefer listening to what he has to say."

"And I'd prefer you listenin' to what I've got to say."

Jess continued his bluff. "I'm going to have to ask you to yield the floor to your official spokesman."

There was a stirring in the back of the room. Judge Cavanaugh had risen very quickly to his feet. "Jess," he said rather heatedly, "I think you're being mighty highhanded in this matter, and I for one feel this lady has a right to say her piece."

"I—I have no objections to her speaking, only it's regular procedure to hear—"

"Don't tell me about procedure, Jess. I know a little about that myself, you know." The Judge was unrelenting.

"All right, sir. All right, would the lady give her name and speak up," he said, watching the Judge sink back to his seat.

"I'm Mrs. Winger. You know me."

"All right, Sarah. Speak up. We're listening."

"Mrs. Winger. Mrs. Jack Winger," Sarah repeated.

"All right, Mrs. Winger. We're still listening."

"I'd like to know when those rules were made you're talkin' about."

Jess turned to Bart Phillips. "Can you answer her question?"

"We've always had safety rules at the high school," Bart said.

"I know that," Sarah answered, "but I'm talkin' about the ones dealing with the number of people allowed in the school."

Bart looked up at Jess, then back at Sarah. "Well—during a recent inspection of the premises."

"Just lately then?" Sarah questioned.

"I suppose I'd have to say so."

"Did you inspect the colored school, too, Mister Phillips?"

"We intend to do it this coming week."

Sarah looked down at Ebon, then back to Bart Phillips. "Well, our association can tell you it's a lot more overcrowded than the high school, and that it ain't brick, and it ain't got a gymnasium or indoor toilets. And while I'm at it, I'd like to know why it was just the colored freshmen children who got pushed out and none of the white children."

Now Marshall Goodlander was on his feet. "I'd like the pleasure of answering this woman, if you don't mind, Jess."

"Go right ahead, Mister Mayor," Jess said.

"My good lady," Marshall began, "as mayor of this town, I have gotten to know these people here on this platform very well, and they don't deserve the insinuating remarks you're making against their wise decisions. We care just as much about the welfare of the nig—nigra students as we do the whites. Some of you folks, like Ebon Jones and others, know where my heart is. I know how you feel, my good lady, but you must have patience. You must give us time to rectify whatever wrongs there are in our school system, in our entire community. We love you and we want to help you, but we can't do everything in one day. You just have to—"

105

"Mister Mayor!" Jack was on his feet beside Sarah, holding her trembling arm. "Mister Mayor!"

"Yes—yes, Winger."

"You just said you know how we feel."

"Yes I did, and—"

"Well, let me tell you somethin', Mister Mayor"—Jack was standing at his full six-feet-four-inches now—"there ain't no white man in the world who knows, really knows, how a black man feels—"

"What do you mean?" Goodlander cut in.

"I mean just what I said. If you turned colored right now, they'd have you in a strait jacket up at Osawatomie by this time next week. You say have patience. Well, by God, if we ain't got it I don't know who has. We been waitin' and waitin' and waitin', since way 'fore Lincoln set 'bout tryin' to free us. The proclamation's layin' dusty on the shelves and we still ain't free—"

"Amen, brother," Maggie Pullens murmured.

"You say you love us. Well, it's a funny kind'a love. We pay taxes to you, we do your dirty work, we help fight for that flag you just had us pledgin' to, and you still walk on us—"

"Amen."

"Your young'uns suck the breasts of our womenfolk till they're strong and healthy a'nough to fly on their own— then you start tellin' 'em they're too good to eat by us—"

"That's enough of this, Jack Winger," Goodlander snapped. "I'll not stand here and take this abuse from—"

"Then sit down and take it!" Jack bellowed. "We're here to thrash this thing out once and for all. Did your boy Luke ever have to sit in that dirty peanut gallery at the Regency show house? My boy Pete here ain't gonna ever forget Bert Sampson askin' him to take a sandwich outside his drugstore to eat—the first day he got back from overseas, before he had a chance to shed his fightin' clothes. Did your boy Luke ever have to take such as that?"

"I won't listen to another minute of this!" Marshall Goodlander sat down.

"Winger—" Jess tried to interrupt.

"My wife here and me helped vote you into office. I heard you git up on a platform and talk 'bout how you was gonna do this and that. Now you keep hollerin', 'I won't listen, I won't listen.' Well, next time you're up on one of them stands hollerin' for votes, I won't listen to you either!"

"Amen, brother Winger—amen."

106

Jack sat down. Sarah eased down beside him, her fingers pressing into his thick wrist, expressing her feeling of pride. "Well done, Jack," she whispered. His eyes burned straight ahead.

Jess banged his fist on the table for order. "We aren't getting much accomplished this way," he acknowledged. "I suggest that the school board have time to study this protest, under more favorable circumstances, and that we have another closed meeting before this school year is over."

"With our association?" Reverend Broadnap hollered out the question.

"With your association, sir—your association," Jess answered wryly, "and if there is no more business I'll say that this meeting is adjourned."

Within fifteen minutes the hall was empty and dark.

"Charter or no charter," Sarah told Jack later that night as they undressed for bed, "we've got things stirred up—and everybody thought you did a mighty good job of tellin' Marshall Goodlander off."

"Just got a little hot under the collar, that's all," Jack mumbled.

"Those kids are gittin' back in that school, mind you. You watch what I'm tellin' you." She blew out the lamp and they went to sleep.

May had come. Booker Savage was slinging old automobile tires on his junk heap when a car stopped in front of his shack. He started to throw the last tire, then stopped at the sight of Marcus and a uniformed guard getting out of the car. He dropped the tire and walked toward them.

Marcus spoke first. "Hi, Paw."

"Hi there, boy." Booker pulled a cigar butt from his pocket and lit it. "Didn't know you was comin' today. Nobody told me."

"You his paw?" the guard asked.

"That's right."

"Okay, you gotta sign these papers on this line." He handed Booker a form and a pencil.

"What's this for?"

"To show we turned him over to you. Sign here."

Booker took the paper and marked an X where the guard indicated.

"That ain't no signature," the guard said.

"He cain't write," Marcus explained. "That's his legal way of signin'."

The guard grunted, took the paper and pencil back, got into the car and drove off. Marcus turned and watched the car churning away in a cloud of dust. "Well, I'm glad I won't be lookin' him in the face tomorra mornin'," he said. Then he turned back to his father and they looked at each other without speaking for a moment.

"Well, come on in, boy. Ain't much here to eat, but I'll stir up somethin'." Marcus picked up a small battered bag and they went into the shack.

Booker cooked some oatmeal and poured some molasses over it; then he piled cold biscuits on the table and they began to eat. "How'd they treat you up there, boy?"

"Like a dog."

"I meant to come up to see you, but things got busy."

"Yeh, I know."

"Well—well, you glad to be back, ain'tcha?"

"Anybody'd be glad to git out'a that stinkin' hole."

"They beat up on you?"

Marcus didn't answer. Instead he parted his coarse hair and revealed a long scar, a memento of Charlie Crapper's billy club. Then he turned his head and pulled down his shirt collar. There was an ugly raw scab on his shoulder.

"Them sons-a-bitches," Booker muttered, "I'm gonna kill one of them peckerwoods shore'n hell one of these days."

Marcus remained silent, spooning in the last of the oatmeal. Booker stirred uneasily on his chair, not knowing what more to say. "Goddam dirty bastards—dirty sons-a-bitches."

Suddenly Marcus stopped chewing. His jaws began quivering and he let out a guttural cry, spewing the food from his mouth over the table. Booker saw the tears coursing down his cheeks before he buried his head in his powerful arms—sobbing as if he were an overgrown baby.

"What's the matter, boy? What's the matter?" Booker was up and over him now. "You hurtin' or somethin'? What's the matter?"

Then, as if escaping some unforeseen doom, Marcus jumped up and ran from the house through the junk-strewn paths towards Flynn's River. He didn't stop sobbing until he lay on its banks, watching the river flow slowly past. He was free again, but his homecoming had left him nearly as empty and frustrated as he'd been during his imprisonment. He rolled over and propped himself against a tree. His hand felt the time-worn sides of a pebble. It was smooth and cool and sort of soothing to the touch. He rubbed it over his hot face, up his jaw and stuck the point of it into his right ear. He pushed a finger into his other ear, cutting off all sound. He was deaf to the world. Then he closed his eyes tight against the morning light. At first there was all darkness, then slowly he made out the image of the slow-moving river, still flowing through the blackness of his subconscious void. He remained that way for several minutes. The river image disappeared, then little flecks of white shimmered in the darkness. He opened his eyes and uncovered his ears. The point of the stone had some earwax sticking to it. He rubbed it off on his overall leg, then he stood and threw the stone toward the river. It splapped against the water, skipped twice and sank to the bottom. Marcus stood watching the ripples dissipate, then he turned and walked to the road—and on toward the center of the village.

CHAPTER ❧ 9

"GUESS WHAT, Momma?" Newt said at supper that night. "Guess what happened to me today?"

Sarah raised her head and smiled. "Somethin' good, I hope."

"The class voted for me to make the graduation speech. What you think of that, Poppa?"

Jack's mustache twitched slightly, showing he was pleased, but he grunted, "Uh-hu, uh-hu. Pass me the apple butter."

Sarah beamed. "That's wonderful, just wonderful, Newt."

"Good goin'," Pete said.

"Why'd they pick you? Nobody else want it?" Prissy teased.

Newt was too happy to banter with Prissy. "Goin' to be needin' a suit, Poppa," he said.

"What's wrong with the duds you already got?"

"Don't start that, Jack," Sarah said. "You know he's growin' out of all his clothes."

"Another year'n I'll be almost as tall as Pete."

"I'm six-three, boy. You're gonna have to do some real growin'."

"Polly's comin' soon as school's out," Sarah said.

"I know Polly, Momma?" Newt asked.

"You was very little when she was here the last time."

Prissy laughed. "You ought'a remember her. You went around tellin' everybody your white cousin was here."

"I did not."

"Aw yes you did. Remember, Momma?"

"He didn't know—he was too young," Sarah defended.

"Wasn't much wrong, at that," Pete said. "Polly's 'bout as white as anybody in town."

"Nice girl, good manners and all," Sarah said.

"Whose preserves, Sarah?" Jack was spreading them thick on his cornbread.

"Mary Kiner sent 'em over by Jake the other day."

"Speakin' of Jake—did'ya know Marcus was back, Newt?" Pete took the preserves from his father as he spoke.

"Yeh? You see him?"

"Nope. His old man told me."

"You don't call a boy's father 'old man,' Pete. You know better."

"Sorry, Momma. Didn't mean nothin' by it."

"He back for good, I wonder?" Newt's mood was changing.

"Long as he stays out'a trouble, I guess," Pete said.

Prissy got up and started clearing the table. "Maybe you better study boxin' 'stead of speakin', Newt," she chided. "Marcus don't love you very much."

"I ain't scared of Marcus, and I—"

"—And you don't have no need to be. Prissy, just go on. You're forever startin' somethin'."

"I ain't startin' nothin', Momma. I'm just tellin' him the truth."

"Go on, and quit yappin' so much."

"Yessem."

"High wind blowin' tonight," Jack remarked, getting up.

After Newt finished wiping the dishes, he got a pencil and pad from his room and came back to the kitchen. He waited until Prissy was through cleaning, then he turned up the lamp wick and began writing his speech.

Prissy dried the suds from her hands, hung up the dish rags and started out. Then she tiptoed back and peeped over Newt's shoulder. She read his first seven words, "Ladies and gentlemen, I am here to"—and she finished the sentence aloud—"to louse up this program." Newt sprang up and cocked his fist, but Prissy made off, slamming the door behind her. Sitting down again, Newt penciled out what he had written. Then he settled back and looked through the window into the darkness, trying meanwhile to construct another opening.

The wind had grown higher. It nudged the screen door back and forth, and its wailing sliced away at the quietness of the kitchen. Tree branches bobbed from the blowing, scratched the roof; their shadows suggested human movements at the window. The thought of Marcus Savage popped into Newt's mind, and he began pondering the evils Marcus' presence could bring. He tried to get back to the speech, but no words and thoughts came together in a fitting way. Before long he was slumped over the table, fast asleep—

111

his subconscious tangled in amorphous visions of swirling wind, dust and water; of Marcus; of fighting and death.

"Newt!" Sarah called from another room.

He bolted upright, rubbing his eyes. "Yessem." The lamp wick, bleary to his sight at first, gradually shimmered into focus. He batted his eyelids several times, blinking away the ugly, shapeless dream.

"It's late! Time for bed!"

"Yessem," he said hoarsely. He got up, blew out the flame, and stumbled off to his room with the pencil and pad in his hand.

The next afternoon, on their way home from school, Newt, Beansy and Jappy met Marcus. Having seen them first, he'd hid behind a tree until they were several feet past him.

"Hyee!"

The harsh voice came as familiar to them as a dog's bark. They turned as one in their surprise. "Hi, Marcus." "H'lo." "What'a you say?"

"Thought you guys forgot me."

"Didn't you git our Christmas card we sent you?" Newt asked.

"Yeh," Beansy said, "we all signed it and Newt mailed it. Didn't you, Newt?"

"Sure did," Newt admitted, "sent it two days before Christmas."

"Well, I didn't git no card," Marcus lied.

"Funny," Newt said, "I sure sent it."

"Callin' me a liar, Winger?"

"I ain't callin' you anything. I just said I sent the card. And I did."

"And I'm sayin' I didn't git it. One of us is lyin'." Newt kept still. "I say, one of us is lyin', Winger."

"Okay—okay. So one of us is lyin'."

"You ready to say which?" Marcus was inching in.

"Come on—let's go," Beansy said.

Newt was as eager to go as Beansy, but pride held him to the spot. "I ain't for any trouble, Marcus, but I ain't for runnin' either—that's for sure."

"Here comes Pete," Jappy said almost gleefully.

The words fell on Newt's ears like a blessing, giving him courage. He looked at Marcus squarely for the first time. He thought he still might have to fight him, even if Pete was coming, but he knew Marcus would have to fight fair with Pete around.

112

"I'll see you guys later—'specially you, Winger," Marcus snarled, starting off.

"What's goin' on, fellas?" Pete asked quietly.

"Nothin' much," Newt answered, his eyes still on Marcus.

Pete sensed the situation. "Glad to see you back, Marcus," he said.

"Yeh?" Marcus grunted. He turned and eyed Pete.

"Yep, I am—and I think the fellas here would be too if you'd just let 'em."

"Well, I ain't carin' what none'a you feel."

Pete turned to Newt, Beansy and Jappy. "You guys go on home. I'll see you later, Newt." The three boys slung their books over their shoulders and walked off.

Pete turned back to Marcus. "Goin' my way?"

"Nope."

"Okay," Pete said and started off. After a few steps he stopped and came back. "Marcus, the whole world ain't against you, like you think."

Marcus looked up curiously as Pete continued, "You're back now. Give yourself a chance and try'n forget 'bout what's happened in the past. I—we all know how tough you had it—we know it ain't been easy for you, but if you git into trouble again you're gonna land right back up there, and you know it. Why don't you git a job someplace and make a good start this time?"

Marcus' eyes widened. "A job? Where'm I gonna git a job? Ain't no place in town where they'd let me come in the door 'cept at Chappie's."

"Ain't many doors open to none of us round here, Marcus."

"You niggers is just as bad as the peckerwoods, far as I can see."

Pete chuckled. "I know how you feel." He thought for a moment. "Why don't you ask Chappie for a job?"

"Doin' what?"

"I don't know—washin' dishes, sweepin' or somethin'."

"Why you so anxious to help me?"

"I ain't exactly so happy to help you. I need a job 'bout bad as you—"

"—But you're the son of churchgoin' people and they wouldn't like you workin' there. But it's okay for me, huh?"

"In a way, I guess you're right. But if you want me to, I'll talk to Chappie 'bout you."

"I don't need no help from the likes of you."

Pete looked at him for a moment. "Well, I'm gonna talk to Chappie 'bout givin' you a job. You can go see him if you want. If you don't, it won't be no skin off my hide." He turned and walked across the street and around the corner. Crossing an alley, he entered Chappie Logan's through the back.

Marcus stood looking after him. "Chappie's wouldn't be so bad maybe," he thought. "Better'n nothin'. Least I won't have to eat that garbage Paw slings together." A little later he saw Pete come back around the corner. He kept out of sight until Pete was gone, then he went hesitantly in the direction of Chappie's.

"You come quicker'n I thought," Chappie said, as he waddled around the room with several bottles of corn liquor under his fat arms. "Pete Winger says you want a job. Do you or don't you?"

"Wish he'd tend to his own bus'ness 'stead of mine."

"Pete's a good boy, mighty good boy. Pay you to listen a little bit to him."

"I ain't listenin' to none of his holy talk——"

Chappie set the bottles on a table. "Look, I ain't got a lot'a time. You want a job or not?"

"Doin' what?"

"What I want you to do, that's what."

"What kind'a pay do I git?"

"Five dollars a week and grub when you workin'."

Marcus looked about the empty room. The crooked booths reminded him of cattle stalls, and the murky windows and mirrors hadn't been washed for years. The odor of stale smoke and alcohol hung in the air like an invisible mist. "I'll take it," he said. "When do I start?"

"Right now. You know how to make beds?"

"What you mean, make beds?"

"Change sheets and pilla-cases, stuff like that."

"We ain't never had no sheets and pilla-cases at home, but I had to make the brass-ass's bed up at Spit's."

"Okay." Chappie walked over to a big closet and jerked out eight sheets and eight pillowcases. "Here," he said, shoving the linen into Marcus's arms, "there's eight rooms up on the next floor. There's a broom and scuttle at the top of the stairs. Change all them beds and sweep the floors."

Marcus started up. "What else?"

"You git that done and come back down here and fix my room up." Chappie motioned him up the stairs. Then he turned. "Hold it a minute," he said, opening another closet full of hand towels. "You gotta put two of these under the pillows on each bed. Git me?"

"Yep."

"Okay. Git goin'." Then, "Hey, boy! The railroaders live on the third. Don't go near their rooms till I give you the word."

"Okay," Marcus hollered back.

The rooms were numbered from one to eight, and Marcus started in number one. He was up to room three before he began wondering about the sameness of their appearance. Each one contained a bed and a little stand with an ash tray on it. That was all. "Ever who stays in here don't have no clothes or nothin' else," he mumbled, smoothing out the clean sheets. Then he suddenly laughed out loud. "Goddam, what a dunce I am. This is the whore house Paw's always talkin' 'bout." He laughed again. "I'm a real dunce."

From then on he noticed the condition of the soiled sheets. Their disarrangement and the telltale stains backed up his new-found knowledge.

"Goddam," he chuckled to Chappie later, "ain't this a bitch? I'm workin' in a whore house for a livin'."

Chappie frowned. "Look, don't go spreadin' talk like that round. I told Pete Winger you'd be washin' windows and workin' round the kitchen. You go blabbin' off, and out you go."

"Ain't no need to worry, Chappie. I ain't sayin' nothin' long's I git my pay on time."

Chappie gave him a nasty look, shook his head and ushered him into what Chappie called his "den." The den held wonders the likes of which Marcus never new existed. The bed was canopied, and twice as big as any he'd ever seen. And though the room was very large, the candy-striped paper on the walls could hardly be seen for the great number of pictures plastering it. And what pictures they were, Marcus thought, craning his neck in awe as he awaited Chappie's orders.

"Now, I don't want you to touch nothin' in here but my bed, the floor and that face bowl over there in the corner. Wash that every day. Git me?"

"Yeh."

"Don't fool round with none of the pichures or go in my drawers or fool with none of these papers layin' round here 'less I tell you. Git me?"

"Okay."

After Chappie left, Marcus walked about in this world of strange photographs, circus posters, lurid drawings and sketches. Most of the subjects were nude or close to it, and there

115

were bearded circus ladies, female impersonators, show girls and a motley of others. Almost all of the photographs were autographed to Chappie. One said, "To Chappie, the big daddy with big things. Yours, Poppy." Another, scrawled over the huge breast of a buxom nude, said, "The breast of everything to Chappie. Yours, Cleotopa." And yet another: "To Chappie, from the gal with two beards." Her pose made her meaning clear.

"Damn," Marcus kept saying to himself as he walked about. Finally he came to a corner that was closed in by red velvet draping. He looked cautiously to the door, then peeped behind the drape. There was a makeshift altar, covered by the same velvet, with a crucifix standing on it. Above it hung two ornately framed, tinted photographs. "His maw and paw," Marcus decided. Up in the left corner was a cluster of small half-burned candles. To the far right of the crude altar was a Bible in which were pressed some dried rose petals, sticking from the closed pages like faded parchment. A strong odor of incense clung to the enclosure.

"Paw'd shore be put out to see this in Chappie's own bedroom," Marcus mumbled as he closed the drape. Turning, he drew back at the sight of two pinkish eyes staring from the darkness of the floor at the side of the bed. "What the hell—?" he gasped. It was a huge, moth-eaten bearskin, its bared fangs showing fierce in its massive head, its long claws seeming to dig into the varicolored carpet it lay on.

Now he studied the bedpost with the clusters of cherubs and angels carved into the mahogany. The canopy and the bedspread were made of the same red-wine chintz material. In between the two head posts, and nailed to the wall, was a faded picture of a she-monster with a goat's body and a lion's head that vomited flames. Upon its back rode two unhappy figures clutching one another.

"One hell of a joint," Marcus muttered, "one hell of a joint." He took the broom and swept his way over to a huge oak closet lining the far wall. He peeped into the labyrinthine inner structure. Hanging there seemed to be hundreds of silk shirts, twice as many ties, and almost as many checkered, striped and tweedy suits with caps to match—all lined up neatly, and obviously not worn for years. There was row upon row of sharp-pointed shoes that Chappie couldn't possibly squeeze his big feet into now. "Goddam," Marcus muttered again, "look at all them overcoats. Same color as all the suits."

The room was lit by candles and two red-chimneyed oil

lamps with porcelain peacocks for bases. These sat on an ornate dresser. There were photographs on the dresser too, but they were of Chappie in his younger and thinner days, dressed in some of the finery that now hung neglected in his closet. Too, there was one of him as a baby, sitting in a white lace dress on the lap of the same woman whose portrait hung above the velvet altar. Another one showed him in short pants, a middy blouse, a straw sailor hat, black ribbed stockings and high-button shoes. He wore this outfit as he proudly straddled a white donkey in some long-forgotten backyard.

Marcus inched a drawer open, and there were more silk shirts. As he ran his hand beneath the stack, trying to determine the number, his fingers struck a metal object. His touch curved to the shape of it. It was a pistol. He slipped it out quickly, rubbed the long barrel admiringly, then he heard footsteps. He put the gun back hastily, shut the drawer, grabbed the broom and started sweeping.

"How you comin'?" Chappie asked as he came through the door.

"Okay—okay," Marcus said briskly.

"Told the cook to give you a sandwich and coffee after you git through here." Chappie picked up something from the dresser, and Marcus watched his big hulk move back through the door.

"That bastard must weigh three hundred pounds," Marcus said under his breath.

The following Saturday morning, Pete, without explaining why, got Newt up rather early. "How'd you like to do a little boxin' this mornin'?"

Newt looked surprised. "Boxin'? With you?"

"Yeh, with me."

So right after breakfast Pete took Newt behind the henhouse and gave him his first serious lesson in self-defense—teaching him to lead with the left, feint with the right, double-jab with the left, send home the damaging right and roll away, keeping balance with the left foot forward.

"That's it . . . that's it . . . feint . . . come on . . . two left jabs . . . cock the right . . . feint . . . jab again . . . throw the right."

Newt swung the right—hard.

"Try again . . . you missed . . . come on . . . left, left . . . right . . . feint . . . jab . . . throw it!" Newt aimed for Pete's chin. But the blow never reached its target.

"Uump!" Newt grunted as the wind shot out of his mouth.

Pete's big fist had crashed into his midsection, caving him in. "Ho-hold it a-min—minute—I'm—out of breath."

"Let that be a lesson to you," Pete said. "Don't ever forget to cover your gut. Keep your elbows lower when you come in for the kill."

And the rest of that month Newt worked as hard on the art of self-defense as he did on his speech.

"You comin' along all right," Pete confided about two weeks later. "Keep it up and I'll have to git a few lessons someplace myself."

To Newt, this was like receiving a high school diploma, for Pete, though he wasn't a bully, had gained a lot of respect with his fists through the years. "Pete don't ever pick a fight, but he don't ever lose one either," Jack Winger was quick and proud to tell anyone who misconstrued his son's easygoing manner.

Graduation came on a most beautiful night in June. Sarah Winger took off work that day. "I've got butterflies in my stomach, Judge," she explained to Jeff Cavanaugh the night before. "You'll just have to do without me tomorrow." The Judge understood, predicted that Newt would make a fine speech and begged her not to worry.

Just before the exercises commenced, Ebon Jones stepped from behind the curtain on the stage and, with a broad grin on his face, shouted, "We have been victorious! We have won our fight! This class graduating tonight will enter the high school!"

Applause and shrill whistling shook the auditorium. Sarah pinched Jack in her excitement, and Jack managed a broad smile.

"Well, you made it," he whispered to his wife.

"We made it," she whispered back.

Ebon continued, "The superintendent of schools regrets that he won't be able to be with us tonight. But he sent his greetings along with that good news. I want to thank you all for the courageous effort you put forth. I thank you."

Newt sat proudly, but a little nervous, in the front of the auditorium with the other members of his class. There were in all six girls and six boys—the girls dressed in white, the boys in blue. Newt's father had scraped up enough for a suit two days before.

Arcella sat next to Newt, and every now and then they would accidentally rub each other with a hand, leg or shoulder. After several minutes Professor Ebon Jones stepped again from behind the curtain. This time he spoke to the graduates about the role they would someday play in the world. He droned on about the possibilities that lay ahead for them. Newt hung onto every word he said, binding himself solemnly to their meaning. Then he heard Professor Jones ending with, "and finally I say to you, get as much learning as you possibly can. You will need every bit you can possibly grasp for the long journey ahead."

The class play, with Beansy playing the lead, was Shakespeare's *Comedy of Errors*. And Beansy did justice to the title, bringing the audience to a howl when he accidentally tripped and sprawled in the middle of the stage.

Now it was time for Newt's speech. With a glance at Myrtle Beasly—who had helped him with the construction of it—he walked to the front of the stage, sweat coursing down to his toes. Sarah twisted uncomfortably in her seat until he started:

"Pro—Professor Jones, parents, friends and fellow students, our class's motto has been 'Look back only when you can find something to help push you ahead.' We know that long after we leave Washington Junior High for good we will look back to her, because it is she who has given us the things we need to go forward. She has prepared us for this difficult journey that Professor Jones has told us we must face. (Sarah heaved a sigh of relief.) Our days here have been happy ones, ones we will always remember. They have been days filled with hope—longing for a better world to live in. (Newt fumbled the paper, and Sarah caught her breath.) But we know that we have been sup-supplied with the materials to help us move forward with con-confidence and courage.

"We hope for a better world and we also hope to have a part in making it a better world. Nobody knows better than we do what a country filled with hate and bi-bigotry can do to the people who must live in it. All we have to do is ask our brothers and our fathers who not so long ago faced death overseas. (Pete felt a lump in his throat.) We all hope and pray that those who didn't come back didn't—die in vain. (Newt dropped the paper to his side and spoke from his own heart.) We, our class, never thought we would be going to the high school next year, but we had made up our minds to study all the harder if we didn't. (He read again.) We are all thankful for our parents and teachers who are fighting—who can make you proud of us when we get there.

"As the school year ends, our need for knowledge gets more important. We will be stepping into higher education

119

but also into problems that have faced our people for many years. Our race is not the best liked in the world, and we know it, but our class is de-determined that this will not keep us from going forward. We are proud to be black. And (The applause, something he'd never anticipated, stopped him momentarily; he lost his place then found it again), and we have seen the end of a terrible war. But this is in the past. We look back only to take a lesson from it. What happens in the future will be determined by what we learned from the past. Our class does not expect life to be easy. We only expect it to be better, and we are determined to help make it so by con-trib-uting something to it ourselves. Using some of the words of Abraham Lincoln, I end by saying that our future is piled high with difficulty, and we must rise to this difficulty. As our problems will be new, so we must think anew, and act anew. Thank you." He bowed stiffly and turned about.

It was over, days of rehearsing, nights of fearing he would "flub-de-dub," as Prissy had warned he would. He bounced back to his seat in a hail of applause—hardly knowing what he'd said on that stage that seemed as big as the whole world itself. And Arcella complimented him when he sat down, even squeezed his hand. "Oh, Newt, it was marvelous," she whispered.

Next, they filed up and got their diplomas. They held them on their breasts as the school chorus and orchestra joined in a stanza of "America," then they marched off into the arms of their proud parents, who by now had rushed to the bottom of the steps to meet them.

Later, Newt and Arcella walked home behind their families, and Newt said shyly, "I'd like to take you some place for some ice cream if your momma would let you."

"Let's catch up and see," Arcella said.

They caught up at the next corner and got permission. Pete slipped Newt fifty cents before they took off across the tracks to Sampson's drugstore.

Most of the graduates from the white junior high school were there when they went in. They were jammed around the soda fountain, in the booths and on the floor. Newt made his way to the counter and ordered two banana splits.

"To take out?" the soda jerk asked.

"Two banana splits," Newt repeated.

The soda jerk gave him a distrustful glance, but he turned and dished up the splits—on cardboard plates. "Here you are!" he hollered above the noise. "Thirty cents." Newt gave

120

him three dimes and turned away, his face burning from embarrassment, his whole evening beginning to hint of a bad dream.

"Come on, Arcella—let's go."

"Newt—Newt Winger!" It was Waldo Newhall and his girl. They were sitting at a table, still in cap and gown. "Congratulations on your graduation!" Waldo shouted. "Come sit with us!"

"Like to, Waldo—but we gotta be goin'."

"Aw come on, Winger," he said, nudging Arcella into the seat beside his date. "Kate, this is Arcella Jefferson. You know Newt."

"Yeh, we know each other," Newt said, "but look, Waldo, we can't sit here with you like this——"

Waldo was beside himself with gaiety. "Who says you can't? This is a free country, Winger. Sit down! Come on now."

"Maybe it'll work," Newt thought, "with a white boy invitin' us to sit with them." He decided to try it. "Okay," he said shakily.

Things went well for a few minutes, then Newt saw Bert Sampson, the owner, making his way through the crowd, and his heart sank. Bert came up to the table and tapped Newt on the shoulder. "Okay, buddy, you and your girl'll have to finish eatin' outside. Sorry."

"What you mean?" Waldo said. "These are friends of mine."

"Then go outside and eat with 'em, if they're friends of yourn."

"I ain't goin' anywhere!" Waldo snapped, "and they ain't either! We paid for this slop and we're goin' to eat it here, right here!"

"Forget it, Waldo," Newt said. "We're goin' to a party anyway." The place was dead quiet now. "Come on, Arcella. Goodbye, Kate. So long, Waldo."

Neither of them answered. Kate turned and looked up at Bert Sampson. "You big slob," she said. Bert looked at her sullenly, but he didn't answer. "You big slob," she repeated. Bert turned and walked back to the end of the counter.

Newt jerked the door open and they went out, walking briskly to the corner as if they really had some place to go. They stood there on the curb under the lamp light for a few moments. "Oh, Newt—" Arcella began to cry.

"It's okay," Newt said, putting his arms around her, "it's okay. We'll show 'em someday. We'll show 'em." He

121

threw the remains of his banana split on the sidewalk. Arcella smiled and did the same. Then they walked slowly, arm in arm, to the tracks, across them, and into the darkness of their side of town.

CHAPTER ❦ 10

JULY FOURTH at Peaceful Park was always a big day for Newt. This particular one had special meaning because he was taking Arcella. With Prissy and Pete, he stopped by that morning to pick her up; and after helping her into the buggy, he plopped down beside her in the back seat. Catching a lilac fragrance, he said, "Guess you're wearin' the toilet water I gave you for your birthday."

"That's right," she said, smiling.

He inhaled deeply and moved closer to her—and within a block they were rubbing hands and touching knees.

The sputtering and popping of firecrackers sounded as they neared the park entrance. "They're startin' early," Pete said.

"I don't want those things goin' off around me," Prissy remarked.

"You scared of fireworks?" Newt asked Arcella.

"I don't like setting them off. I think the sparklers are prettiest."

"They'll be shootin' the rockets off over the water after dark."

"That should be lovely," she replied.

"There's Earl, Jappy and Beansy," Prissy said, pointing at Newt's friends walking alongside the lagoon.

"Where's Skunk!" Newt hollered out to them.

"Comin' later!" Beansy hollered back.

"What an awful name," Arcella said, shaking her head. "Why don't you call him by his right name?"

"I did once and he thought I was tryin' to kid him." Newt laughed.

"Oh, well," Arcella remarked gaily, "if he ever gets married, his wife will change that. You won't call her Mrs. Skunk."

"You don't know Skunk. He says he's goin' to stay single all his life and have lots of babes."

"Ha ha," Arcella scoffed. "So you think that's smart?"

"Not me—not me," Newt said, correcting her quickly.

After Skunk arrived, Newt departed with his friends to shoot off cannon crackers, leaving Arcella with Prissy. Though Skunk kidded him about going back after an hour, as he had promised, he returned on time; and then he and Arcella went off in search of wild flowers. They tromped on through the woods, picking a flower here and there, leaving the noises and the voices of the others far behind.

"Oh, look—a cluster of violets," Arcella cooed, "and what a lovely setting—like a garden in the forest." She took Newt's hand and they sidestepped down the incline to the spot. "Oh, they're so beautiful here I hate to pick them."

"Then don't," Newt said softly. "Let's just sit here and look at them for a little while."

"Oh—that would be silly, wouldn't it?"

"But you just got through sayin' it was a beautiful settin', didn't you?"

"Of course, of course, but—"

"Aw, come on. Let's sit just for a little while," Newt said, coaxing her down to the mossy earth.

Then they sat there, still holding hands, gazing at the violets as if they were the only flowers in the world.

"We must always think of this as our garden, Newt—our private garden in the forest."

"We could come and see it every now and then."

"Maybe—who can tell?"

They inched together, joining their warmth. And Arcella's lilac fragrance hung heavily in the fresh damp of their "private garden." Her cheek was suddenly against his. He took her in his arms and gently pressed her back upon the earth. Her lips parted and he instantly leaned over her and covered them with his own. Then they both closed their eyes to the dim-lit woods, their ears to its faint noises—and she began squirming beneath his trembling.

"Arcella—Arcella."

"Don't—don't, Newt, I—"

"Please—please—"

"No—no—no. Let's just lay here like this."

"Oh—Arcella."

"Stop—st—st—stop—I can't—I can't—not now—please—please." She pushed herself free of his body.

"What's the matter? What's the matter, Arcella?"

"I don't know. I want to, but I just can't—not just now. Not now."

"But I love you."

124

"And I love you, but something might happen."

"But I want to marry you someday, Arcella. It—it ain't like I just wanted to have a good time or somethin'."

"I know—I promise, but let's wait."

They sat up. Neither of them looked at the violets now.

"Guess the barbecue's 'bout ready," Newt said.

"Hope so," she answered softly. "I'm awfully hungry."

Newt helped her up and they retrieved the flowers Arcella had dropped earlier. Putting their arms around each other, they kissed again, scrambled up and then strolled off, hand in hand, toward the picnic grounds.

That night, as the two of them sat watching the rockets burst high over the lagoon, Newt began thinking seriously of the day when he would really marry Arcella. They wouldn't live in Cherokee Flats, he thought. And she'd probably insist that he finish college—if he could get the money someplace. His mother and father could never send him, he knew. At that moment he resolved to save every penny he could put his hands on.

A rocket shot up, burst and sprayed its red, white, green and blue over the silvery dusk of the lagoon.

"Arcella."

"Yes."

"Would you marry me if I didn't go to college?"

"Oh, Newt, we've got years to think about such things. Let's watch the rockets."

"But I gotta know now," he insisted.

"You mean you have to know now." She smiled.

"I have to know now—then," he agreed.

"Well, I don't think it would make any difference, but I sure hope you'll try to go just the same." She pinched his arm tenderly.

"I'm sure goin' to try—I—can I say we're sort of engaged now—like—well you know, like we're goin' to get married for sure?"

"One doesn't become engaged with hundreds of people around them shooting off firecrackers, Newt Winger."

"Then I'll ask you again later."

"Prissy tells me your cousin Polly's coming soon, and that she's real pretty. Maybe you'll want to marry her instead."

"Marry my own cousin?"

"Some people do," she said. "Better look out!"

"Don't worry—not me."

Two days later, when Polly Bates stepped off the train, Newt was looking in the opposite direction. "There she is! There she is!" Prissy shouted. "Polly! Polly! Here we are!"

"Where's she?" Newt said, jerking about. Prissy was already running to meet her.

"Come on, Newt," Pete called, "that's her in the red straw hat."

"Golly, she is white," Newt mumbled to himself.

After hugging Prissy, Polly ran and threw her arms around Pete.

"It's so good to see you again," Polly cried out.

Newt hung back. He noticed the whites on the station platform, especially the men, poking one another—saying things he couldn't quite hear.

"Is that Newt?" Polly stretched out her arms. "Boy, how you've grown. Come gimme a kiss."

Newt stepped forward and they embraced and kissed. "Good to see you, cousin Polly," he found himself saying.

"You're almost as big as Pete," she said as the porter handed down her two bags.

"Thanks," Newt replied, not knowing what else to say. He grinned, then he stood back and took a good look at her as she identified her bags. "It's true," he thought, "like Pete said, she's as white as anybody in town." He noticed, too, that her hair was almost blond and that she had a few freckles, and that her eyes were a greenish-blue. "She's downright pretty." He imagined she was about the same age as Prissy. And they were about the same height.

"You gonna stay all summer?" Prissy asked.

"If Aunt Sarah'll let me. I sure hope so. How is she and Uncle Jack?"

"They're just fine," Prissy said. "They're both out workin' now. Otherwise they'd be here too."

Pete and Newt took her bags, and they all got into the buggy and drove off. Newt saw the whites still looking as they pulled away. He held his chin up smugly and ignored them.

The most Newt got to know about Polly's coloring was that she got it from her father. He found this out from little snatches of talk that flitted about the house during the first week Polly was there. ("Your momma used to call your paw 'poor white trash' when she got mad with him.") ("Paw used to get so mad when people took him for white.") ("Your momma Curtney used to kid him. 'Jonas,' she'd say, 'if they ever have a race riot, you're gonna have a hard time provin'

126

you're one of us. Better start paintin' a sign for your back now.' ")

What Newt didn't know—nor, for that matter, did Pete or Prissy—was that Jonas Bates was the offspring of a Negro servant woman and a white Georgia plantation owner. As a boy he had been brought from Georgia to Pennsylvania by his mother—so the story went. When he was a man he had met Sarah's sister, Curtney, who was living in Philadelphia. He fell in love with her and married her after a three-day courtship. Curtney died when Polly was ten, and Sarah had gone to attend the funeral and bring Polly back to Cherokee Flats until Jonas was able to get someone to care for her while he worked.

After a month he had come for Polly, saying he had found someone. A year later he wrote that he had married that someone and that they were moving to Topeka, where he had found a better job. This made Sarah very happy, for again Polly had a mother. But Polly became ill two summers later. And Sarah, having gone to see her, was surprised to find that Jonas had married a white woman. Sarah had no objections to his marriage, but secretly she was upset for a few days. Her brother-in-law was rather matter-of-fact about the whole thing—and honest too. "It makes things easier for me," he had said.

"Bud what about Polly?" Sarah had asked.

"Don't worry, Sarah, she'll adjust to things."

"In other words you're gonna bring her up white."

"That's about it," Jonas replied, "but," he added hastily, "you're always welcome at my house."

"And you at mine," Sarah had replied.

But one day she heard Jonas telling his white neighbor that "Aunt Sarah" used to work in his family back in Georgia, and that he had her up now and then for a visit. And "Aunt Sarah" packed her things that minute and took a train back to Cherokee Flats. She hadn't been in Jonas' house since. And she vowed she would never set foot in it again. Polly never knew about the incident; and Sarah had no intention of ever telling her, for Polly was still as dear to her as she was to Polly.

Polly had never really adjusted to the white life Jonas dumped her into. And it was a relief, she felt, coming to Cherokee Flats where she could be herself. One night she confided to Sarah that if anything ever happened to her father, she would come to the colored side for good.

"Fact is, Paw doesn't know that I'm planning to do just that when I'm twenty-one," she told Sarah.

"Now, Polly, be careful. Don't wind up hurtin' your paw," Sarah had warned.

The circus came to town on its own railroad train during the third week in July. Newt, Earl, Beansy, Jappy and Skunk met it at the outskirts and got jobs watering the elephants, feeding the camels and helping the roustabouts rig up the tents. For this they got free passes to all the shows, free rides on the ferris wheel, merry-go-round and roller coaster.

Newt enjoyed mingling, backstage-fashion, with the clowns, spielers, cowboys, Indians, sword swallowers, fire-eaters, snake charmers, strong men, bearded ladies, midgets and tightrope walkers—feeling himself a part of these people and in tune with their environment. He worked hard through the day—so hard that Spikey, the chief roustabout (a reddish, fat, balding man with little pink ears), offered him a steady job. But Newt refused, saying proudly, "I'm goin' to college and then get married." At night he and Arcella used up the passes in the side shows and the big tent.

On Friday, Beansy got carried away with the art of the sword swallower, and he nearly choked trying to duplicate the trick with a table knife—up-chucking all over the side of the bearded lady's tent. The experience upset Beansy so, he gave Newt and the rest of the gang his free rides for the day and went home. But he was back bright and early the next morning. Newt, Earl and Skunk came across him helping Spikey erect a platform in the middle of the grounds.

"What'cha buildin', Beansy?" Skunk asked.

"A free-for-all-ring," Beansy shot back authoritatively.

"A what?" Newt said.

"Free-fo'-all—free-fo'-all," Spikey cut in. "It's a Missa'sippi spoht. You guys kin make yo'selfs some extra dough today. Whyn't you all sign up?"

"How's it work?" Skunk inquired.

"Simple," Spikey advised, his big shoulders edging a plank into place. "Ten of you in da ring at a buck a head. At da gun shot ever'body starts sluggin' away. Da last two standin' in da ring git a three-minit rest, den go for da big prize. Da winnah gits eight and da losah two—and any extra da crowd throws in da ring."

"Everybody has to git knocked out but the last two?"

"Aw naw—if you git knocked down you gotta stay down—

128

dat's all." Spikey took a slip of paper. "Here, you guys kin sign up fo' da one-fo'ty to one-fifty de'vision."

"You game, Newt?" Beansy said.

"I don't know." Newt looked at the rest of them. "You fellows want to try it?"

Skunk winked at Newt. (He must have a plan, Newt thought.)

"Well, what y'all say?" Spikey had a pencil in hand now.

"It's okay," Skunk cut in, "we'll git Jappy. That'll mean we only have to git five more."

"Dat'll be like duck soup," Spikey said, shrugging away, "here, all y'all sign up right now—even fo' yer buddy Jappsy, or evah what his name is. We'll git da rest out'a da crowd."

They all signed, and Newt signed for Jappy.

"Y'all be heah at three sharp, now. Heah me?"

They all agreed. And Skunk did have a plan. He revealed it to the others after they found Jappy. "Look," he began, "ain't none of us gonna git hurt if we use our heads right—it'll be like takin' candy from a baby."

"What's your plan?" Jappy asked.

"Well, it's like this. There's ten bucks, ain't it? Well, that means two apiece for us with nobody gittin' hurt."

"But—"

"Hold it, Beansy. Listen me out. Well—we gang up on the other five real rough like—I mean really let 'em have it. That'll git the crowd all steamed up. By then they'll think it's a real mean fight. Now here's the twist. Winger, you and Beansy are the best duckers 'cause Pete's been showin' you things. Everybody goes down then but you two. You two put 'em on a good show and one of you go down—then," Skunk shrugged his shoulders in much the same way Spikey had, "then we go off and split the dough."

"Not bad—not bad," Jappy said.

"Okay, fellas?"

"Yeh." "Guess so." "Okay." "All right by me."

At three o'clock the five boys climbed into the ring, all of them stripped to the waist. Spikey strutted about in a striped turtle-neck sweater and a derby, a cigar slanting from his crooked mouth. "Step right up, ladees and genal'mon! See da fight of da yeah. Step in—step in closah—fine-fine!"

Newt and his friends stood around the ring trying to appear tough, their muscles flexed and their chests poked out. Spikey continued, "Now we need jus' five mo' hundred-fo'ty-five to hundred-fifty pounders, da two winnahs take all."

He spied two Mexican boys. "How 'bout you two—yeh—you two wid da young lady dere—fine-fine, come on up! Now we need three mo', jus' three mo' and we's ready fo' da big go 'round—winnahs take all! How 'bout you two fine-lookin' young roosters?"

The two Mexican boys had climbed through the ropes and pulled off their shirts."

"You two a'comin' to join yo' friends? Fine—fine—now folks, we only needin' one mo'—jus' one mo'—how 'bout dat strong young buck 'hind da old man wid da specs. You—you —come on, boy—git some'a dis fine money we givin' out heah!"

The two other Mexican boys climbed in the ring, stripped and stood next to their friends. "They all look puny and skinny," Beansy whispered to Newt.

Spikey went on, "You 'fraid, boy? You 'fraid, a big buck like you? Okay! Okay! Gotta be anotha he-man 'mongst dis crowd—jus' one mo'—jus'—"

"I'll go with 'em—I'll go with 'em!" Marcus Savage was pushing his way through the crowd.

"Oh, shit matittle," Beansy mumbled.

All the flexed muscles began to droop.

"Fine! Fine! Fine! Now we kin staarrt da greeatest fieeght on dis heah earth—da Missa'sippi free-fo'-all!"

Marcus had an evil grin on his face as he climbed through the ropes. He stripped off his shirt and shuffled up close to Newt. "We gonna be the last if I have to hold you up with one hand and beat all the rest with my other," he growled. Fear spread through Newt as if it were injected through his pores. He kept quiet, thinking back to the lessons Pete had given him, trying to fasten them clearly in his mind.

Now Spikey was in the middle of the ring. "Now, dese are da rules. When you fall, scoot off da platform and onto da ground—da last two standin' gits a three-minit rest. Den dey go afta da big swag. Now when ah fire dis pistol ah wants y'all to start swingin'. Heah we go! Ready!"

Newt's skin was stretched as taut as a drum over his knuckles. Beansy was trembling so much his teeth were chattering. He was ready to fall at the first blow. Skunk was ready to fall with him. Earl and Jappy had decided to work on Marcus together—to soften him up for Newt. They inched to either side of Marcus. Newt was scared, but ready to face the test.

Spikey pointed the pistol at the sky.

Bang!

(Newt swung and a Mexican went down with the first blow.)

A roar went up from the crowd.

"Kill those niggers!"

"Bust his gut!"

"Git them niggers!"

(Beansy was being ganged by two Mexicans. Newt spun over to help him.)

"Kill that fat black bastard! Kick him in the balls!"

(Earl and Jappy were banging up Marcus. A Mexican cracked Jappy behind the ear and he went down.)

"Yea! Yea! Yea! Git them greases!"

"Git the big bastard!"

"Bust his gut! Bust his gut!"

(Skunk and his Mexican went down at the same time. Earl's chin caught Marcus' brutal right. He tried to fight back. Another right from somewhere knocked him senseless. He sank to the floor.)

"Watch that grease!"

"Kill him! Kill him!"

"Watch that big black bastard!"

(The last two Mexicans were beaten down by Newt, Beansy and Marcus—all punching desperately together.)

"Yea! Yea!"

"Now git the big nigger! Git 'im!"

"Kick him in the nuts!"

(Newt slammed a right to Marcus' jaw. He reeled, catching Beansy with a light left at the same time. Marcus stayed on his feet but Beansy plopped to the floor.)

"Yellow black bastard! Yellow bastard!"

"Now git that big bastard! Let him have it in the balls!"

(Marcus steadied himself and lunged toward Newt, but Spikey jumped in between them.)

"Hold it! Hold it!" He grabbed their hands and held them above his head. "Da winnahs! Da winnahs, folks!"

The first round was over—in less than two minutes.

Newt and Marcus stood scowling at each other. All the others had rolled from the ring to the ground. Some held their swollen eyes. Some grasped their bloody noses. Above them Spikey was hollering, "Three minits to the main go! Jus' three minits! Make yer bets! Make yer bets!"

Suddenly Newt looked out at all the grinning faces, those that had called them niggers; called the Mexicans greases. He looked below at his fallen comrades and the hapless Mexicans. He wanted to run from there—not from Marcus. He would rather have fought him alone in a quiet alley; rather have been beat to a pulp in some private place than win from Marcus here in front of these people who suddenly reminded him of animals—dirty, white, vicious, grinning animals about to bet on two "nigger boys" who would try to beat each other's brains out.

But he was trapped.

The crowd had grown ugly and boisterous. They were already making their bets. If he quit now no one would understand, and everyone would think he was a coward. If he didn't fight, he might take a worse beating from the crowd than he would from Marcus. He wanted to ask God to help him fight to win, but he suddenly remembered his mother's telling him on the river road, many nights back, that God couldn't favor one fighter against another. He thought next of Pete, wished he were there. The lesson began to come through (cock the right—jab with the left—feint him out of position—jab—throw the right—).

"Alrighty—righty—folks," Spikey said, strutting around the ring, "how 'bout a few nickels and dimes fo' dees gallant fightas who shed blood fo' you. Show 'em you 'preciate it."

Pennies, nickels and dimes began clinking into the center of the ring. Spikey hopped about picking up the money and putting it into his derby.

"Okay, let's git on with the fight!" someone hollered from the crowd.

"Let's go!"

"Three minutes is up! Let's git goin'!"

Marcus had been sizing up Newt in the meanwhile. He was surprised at the hardness of his body and the bulging muscles. "He's growed a lot since I been away," he thought.

"Okay! Okay! Heah we go fo' da main bout, folks. Da winnah gits eight—da losah two. Ah want a clean fight. Da one who goes down first loses. Unnerstan'?"

Marcus and Newt nodded their heads. Spikey lifted his gun.

Bang!

The crowd let out a bigger roar than before.

Newt and Marcus circled cautiously, eyeing each other.

"Hit him, boy!"

"Hit the big bastard!"

They continued to circle. Newt kept his left out, pawing with it as Pete had taught him. He kept his left foot forward—his right cocked—elbows low. Suddenly Marcus lunged with a vicious right. It went over Newt's shoulder, and he sent two hard jabs home to Marcus' jaw and jumped back.

"That's it, Sambo! Kill him! You can do it, Sambo!"

"Git him, Newt!"

"Come on, Winger!"

Newt was feeling more confident. Marcus was fighting off balance. He didn't even have his left foot forward and he was holding his elbows too high. Newt feinted with his right and sent home a couple of stinging lefts, and he saw Marcus blink in surprise.

"Atta boy, Sambo! I got money on you!"

"Good goin', Newt!" Beansy hollered.

"Keep goin', Winger!" Skunk hollered.

Suddenly Marcus rushed him like a gored bull, flinging both fists in uncontrolled rage. Newt felt his jaw sag under the blows. He spun free as Marcus tried to rough him up, tasting the fresh blood in his mouth. The crowd was one big roar now. Marcus lunged again and they rocked each other with hard rights. Newt felt himself losing control. He danced back, trying Pete's method once more. He feinted with a right, slipped in two good left jabs instead; then, taking the big gamble, he followed through with the right. He was so frightened when he threw it he didn't look up. He only remembered seeing Beansy's frightened face. But he felt right at that instant, the way Pete told him he would feel. His left foot was forward and his right shoulder had swung around— and his elbows fortunately were low, for they kept Marcus' terrible right from his stomach. His blow landed. He felt it in his right shoulder and he was still going forward. There seemed to be no one in front of him.

"You got him! You got him!"

"Good, Sambo! We won! We won!"

"Atta boy, Newt! You did it! You did it!"

Marcus was flat.

Newt felt his hand being pushed up in victory. Then he looked down to Marcus. Blood was running from his nose and he was holding his left eye. He suddenly felt ashamed again. He reached down to help Marcus up. Marcus raised his head and let go with a bloody glob of spit. It caught Newt in the face. Then Newt tried to kick Marcus, but Spikey stepped in and pushed him aside.

"Let him at the black son-of-a-bitch!"

"Booo! Boooo! Booo!"

"Kick his balls out, Sambo! Kick his balls out!"

"The black bastard spit in his face!"

Marcus got up, grabbed his shirt and ducked out the back

way, holding his eye with one hand and the two dollars Spikey had given him with the other. Newt and his gang made their way back to the mess tent. Newt clutched the eight dollars as he walked, spitting out blood every now and then. A little white boy about seven years old came running up from behind and patted Newt on his bare back. "I'm glad you won, Sambo," he said, smiling.

Newt whirled and started to hit the boy. "Get out'a here! Get out'a here!" he said through clenched teeth. The boy drew back, surprised. Newt dropped his arms, handed the money to Jappy and started buttoning on his shirt. "Divide it up equally," he said.

"But it's all changed now, Newt. You did all the fightin'."

"A bargain's a bargain," Newt said through puffed lips. "Split it up like I said."

Spikey came up. "Good goin', fellas—y'all put on a good show for 'em."

"What happens to the money they throwed in the ring?" Skunk asked.

"Aw, dat. Dat's fo' da pr'moter. Dat's fo' ole Spikey."

"Bullshit," Earl grumbled. And they all went home. They didn't even go back to use their passes for the rides that night.

By dawn the next morning the circus had packed up and gone.

For several days Newt hated any white face he saw. Time, it seemed, couldn't erase the jeering, inhuman voices that had goaded him to such an indecent victory. They kept coming back, screaming him into bitterness and deep shame. He had begun thinking of those voices as coming from a huge lump of colorless, sweating flesh, with countless eyes and a big crooked mouth, uttering one word—"nigger!" He sat dejectedly on the porch now, wanting to run from this place to some unheard-of-land where such a word didn't exist, wanting to shed the ridicule that cloaked his conscience; wanting to tear the hurt, the puffed eye and the busted lip from his body. He didn't want to see his gang or anyone who might have seen the fight.

"Newt! Newt!" It was Mag Pullens calling from the road. "Yes-mam!"

"Your cousin Polly's on the telephone. Wants you to meet her at Kress's and help her with packages!"

"Yes-mam! Tell her I'll be right there!"

He met Polly soon after.

"You got a lot of stuff," Newt said, looking at the packages.

"Things for Aunt Sarah and the house. Didn't know it was

going to be so much," Polly answered. Then they started off.

They were within a half block of the Frisco tracks when three white boys approached them. Newt recognized Delbert Mottsy but he didn't know the other two. Delbert and his friends kept their eyes on Polly, stopping almost, then single filing as they passed. After a few feet they stopped and looked back.

Newt sensed trouble. It came quickly.

"What'cha doin' walkin' with a nigger, blondy?"

The packages fell from Newt's arms as he swung around.

"Newt—Newt—come on now—"

Polly might as well have remained silent, for Newt was already upon the boys, swinging wildly. Delbert got it first. He was down before he realized what happened. The other two drew back for a second, then came charging in together, knocking Newt to the sidewalk. Then the three of them pounced on him, kicking and beating with all their might.

"Help! Help!" Polly screamed. "Help, somebody!"

Newt fought his way to his feet again, but the others were up with him and he went down under another hail of blows.

"Help! Help!" Polly continued to scream. She ran over and tried to pull the boys off, only to be knocked down herself.

Then suddenly Newt heard Delbert holler, felt one of the other assailants jerked from his back. Someone had come to his rescue. He didn't know who, nor did he have time to find out. A foot was headed for his face. Newt's arm caught the blow of the foot, then he snatched that same foot, upended its owner and pounced on him, flailing him with his fists. The boy scrambled up, pulled loose and ran.

Polly was up, running across the tracks for help.

"Look out, Waldo!" Newt hollered, seeing it was he who had come to help.

Waldo ducked. But not in time. Delbert cracked him across the head with a stick and Waldo went down. Then Delbert and the other boy ran. Newt started after them, but stopped and trotted back to Waldo, who was sitting on the ground, stunned from the blow. Newt helped him to his feet.

"You okay, Waldo?"

"Yeh—guess so." He shook his head. "I'm okay. I'm gonna get that little Mottsy bastard."

Newt began picking up the packages, and Waldo, still a little groggy, helped him. A small group of Negroes had gathered and were coming with Polly to meet Newt and Waldo.

"You really saved me that time," Newt said. "I was havin' a hell of a time for a minute or two."

"What'd it all start over, anyhow?" Waldo asked.

"Over Polly. They thought she was white, I guess. But I sure want to thank you, Waldo. They had me goin'."

"Ain't nothin', Newt. You'd have done the same for me." He blew his nose. "Crazy bastards. I knew she was a nigger all the time."

Newt was ahead of Waldo. He shut his eyes, grimaced and went across the tracks to meet Polly and the others.

Sarah Winger heard about the incident that evening. After supper she had Jack drive her to the Mottsy home on the other side of town, and she gave the elder Mottsy a piece of her mind.

Three nights later, after Polly and Prissy had experienced more trouble on the streets, Sarah called her niece to her room.

"Polly," she said, "I hate to tell you this—but—but I think it's goin' to be better for everybody if you go back home. I—I don't want to do this, but—but—" Sarah stopped abruptly and leaned forward, nearly falling from the chair.

"What's the matter, Aunt Sarah? Uncle Jack! Uncle Jack!"

"What's the trouble—what's the matter?" Jack said, stepping into the room.

"Aunt Sarah's sick or something."

"You sick, Sarah? You—what is it?" He eased her back in the chair. "You want me to call Timothy?"

"No-no Jack. I'm all right. Just had a little dizzy spell—that's all."

"You shore?"

"Just a little dizzy spell," she repeated.

The next morning Polly started packing her suitcases. Prissy sat on the floor watching her. "Sure hate to see you go, Polly. We were just beginnin' to have fun."

"Yeh—I know, Prissy, I know."

"It's a crazy world, Polly."

"It ain't the world, Prissy. It's the people in it."

"Comin' back next summer?"

Polly stood up. She held a calico blouse under her arm. "One of these days I'm coming back for good. I—I—I—oh, Prissy. Oh, Prissy." They embraced and both of them began to cry.

Newt had been listening outside the door. A lump came to his throat and he went out to hitch the horse to the buggy.

Two hours later Polly took the train for Topeka.

CHAPTER ❦ 11

FOR WEEKS after the circus fight Marcus kept out of sight. His feelings had been hurt worse than his body. There was no way he could explain his defeat to the other boys, so he shrank from their presence, feeling more alone than ever. Though he went sullenly about his work at Chappie's, he liked the privacy the job gave him. But he went to bed angry and he got up angry. He was overly sensitive to anything his father said during the few hours they were together. It got to a point where he hardly spoke to anyone—and did not care whether they spoke to him. He cared only about one thing—getting even. But he controlled his impulse to act openly against Newt, being content to store this impulse within the design of hatred that was building stronger and stronger inside him.

The gang welcomed his absence. They had all come to feel the embarrassment of the "Missa'sippi free-fo'-all" and were as eager as Newt to forget it. Only once, undressing at the swimming hole, had they talked about it—and then only briefly.

"That Spikey sure made nuts out'a us," Beansy had said.

"Bastard had more money in that derby for hisself than all of us had together," Earl grumbled.

"Bet right now he's got some other suckers beatin' their brains out someplace," Newt said.

"That damned Mexican shore bopped me upside the ear," Jappy complained.

"What happened to you, Beansy?" Skunk asked slyly.

Beansy got flustered. "I—I slipped, just 'bout the time—"

"Just 'bout the time you saw Savage's fist headin' your way," Skunk cut in.

They all laughed. Then Skunk shouted, "Follow the leader!" and they scrambled over the bank and plunged into the river.

Newt's bitterness gradually lessened as the summer waned.

137

He had lived the experience and now, he told himself, he must forget it. High school was ahead, and he looked forward to the wonders it would offer him. He daydreamed himself into the classrooms with the big windows and roomy desks; the laboratories with the microscopes; the huge gymnasium and auditorium he had heard Prissy talk about.

When opening day arrived, he dressed in the same suit he had worn on the June graduation night. The pants were already too short, but he solved that problem by slipping his belt down over his hips. Then he shined his shoes and slicked his hair back tightly with "Pluko"—a thick, yellow, smelly hair dressing that he and Beansy had obtained from a Chicago mail order house.

He gulped down his breakfast and set out for Arcella's. She was already in front of her house when he arrived, so he took her books and they made off across the tracks—happy as could be on this bright September morning. About a block from the school they met Chauncey and Rodney Cavanaugh, and Newt introduced them to Arcella.

"That Chauncey's kind of cute," Arcella murmured after the two boys had gone ahead of them.

"He's a senior in junior college here," Newt said rather dryly. "He'll be leavin' for the University next year, I suppose—had to make up some work, Rodney says."

"Well, he's sure cute——curly hair and—"

"I heard you the first time," Newt said, a hint of anger in his voice.

Arcella smiled. "Why, Newt Winger," she cooed, "I do believe you're jealous!"

Newt said nothing. They had reached the school door now, so he opened it and followed her into the spacious, clean-smelling hallway.

The first week of school was exciting for Newt. It was a pleasure for him to walk up and down the long corridors flipping hellos to the new friends he was making. He found his teachers generally likable, and he came to like Professor Radeaker the best. He taught science, and at the start of each class he usually had a joke to tell, often at the expense of one of the students.

The white students were friendlier than Newt had expected them to be. One of them, Zack Spears—who sat in front of him in French class—filled him in on lots of things that were not generally known. For instance, Zack and several other sophomore boys had failed French I, not for lack of ability to grasp it, but for a far more impressive reason. Zack said,

"Ever notice Miss Purvelle sits all the boys up front and the girls in the back?"

"That's right, she does," Newt agreed.

"Well, let me tell you somethin'. She don't mind you lookin', if you git what I mean."

The next day Newt borrowed Zack's seat in front, and found the story to be true. And it was also true that the boys with the choice seats were sophomores who had failed the year before. There was one notable exception. Carson Bigelow, who sat dead center, was a junior.

"Hell," Zack said, laughing in his horselike way, "Cars ain't even had a textbook for two years."

Newt's guidance teacher was Miss McClinock, who taught English and American History. She was a large, full-bosomed, red-haired woman with a long nose, who wore black crepe dresses and high-laced shoes. There were no shenanigans in her room, and Newt found out, soon enough, that anyone coming to her class without homework properly done paid rather dearly. For such a misdemeanor she made Newt stay an hour after school three evenings in a row. For those three evenings he missed walking home with Arcella—and this hurt.

"What are your ambitions, Newton?" she asked just before he left on the last day of punishment.

Newt looked up, surprised at the suddenness of the question. "Ambitions?"

"Yes, ambitions," Miss McClinock repeated.

"Well—well, I think I would maybe like to teach English —like you," Newt lied.

"No apple polishing, Newton. Tell me the truth. I'm your guidance teacher."

Newt thought he'd better come clean. "Well, I just don't know, Miss McClinock."

"Haven't you ever thought of what you would like to do when you leave high school?"

"Oh. Yes-mam, of course. I'd like to go to college."

"College?" She spoke as if he'd said an obscene word. "Are you serious?"

"Yes-mam."

"Who put such notions into your head?"

"I—I put them there myself, I guess. I—"

"What does your father do? Where does he work?"

Newt began rubbing his hands nervously. "Oh, odd jobs mostly—and we raise corn every year."

"Your brother Peter attended this school, didn't he?"

"Yes-mam."

"Did he go to college?"

"No-mam."

"Why not?"

"I—I don't really know," Newt said.

"Well, I'll tell you why—for the same reason that ninety-nine percent of the Negro students don't go to college. They aren't college material," she said bluntly. "The few who are—and are lucky enough to get the money—usually wind up as cooks or porters anyway."

Newt felt his anger mounting, but he kept quiet.

"That, I feel," Miss McClinock went on, "is going to a lot of trouble just to become a servant."

"Well, I won't be nobody's servant—college or no college," Newt shot back.

"Don't become angered, Newton. I'm your guidance teacher. I'm here to advise what is best for you. You had best take a general course next year instead of a college preparatory. It will be easier for you, and much wiser."

Newt looked Miss McClinock straight in the eye. He noticed that her long nose was twitching and that there were little beads of sweat on the end of it. "I don't understand you," he said finally.

"You will someday," she said archly.

"Am I excused now?" Newt asked.

"You're excused," she said.

He picked up his books and went out. Closing the glass-paneled door, he saw that Miss McClinock was up and walking toward the window. He went to his locker for his other books. When he passed her room again, on the way out, she was still at the window gazing blankly at the campus.

Newt was confused. He walked slowly toward the front door, his footsteps echoing through the empty corridor. Miss McClinock had given him something to think about.

Newt got a start when he reached home. Doc Cravens' Ford was parked in front of the house. Somebody must be sick, he thought. He walked quietly through the open door and put his books on the dining room table, then he peeped into the front room. His father sat in the rocker moving to and fro. He looked up when Newt's head appeared.

"Somebody sick, Poppa?"

"Nothin' serious. Your momma had a dizzy spell at work and had to come home. Nothin' serious."

"Prissy been home from school yet?"

"She's gone to the drugstore for a pr'scription. You better fetch some wash water from the hydrant."

"Yessir." He went off to get into his overalls and mackinaw.

A moment later, Doc Cravens came out of Sarah's bedroom, and Jack asked. "Well, how's she doin'?"

"All right—but she'd better take the rest of the week off, I think." Cravens was taking a small bottle of pills from his satchel. "Have her take one of these every four hours. It's marked on the bottle. Prissy back with the other medicine?"

"Not yet."

"Those will be pills too. Have her take one each night before goin' to bed." He was moving to the door now, and he motioned Jack out after him. He stopped at the edge of the yard.

Jack was uneasy. "Anything serious?" he asked hesitantly.

"Well—it could be if she doesn't take it easier. It's her heart."

"Her heart?"

"Nothin' to get excited about, Jack. She just needs to take it a little easier, as I said. She should be up and around in a day or so. Nothin' to go gettin' excited about."

"She goes too hard, Tim—too hard."

"I told her about that. Now just follow the instructions. I'll be around again in a couple of days."

Newt approached them with two buckets of water. "Hi, Doc," he said. "How's Momma?"

"Hi, Newt. She's going to be all right. By the way, how do you like your new nephew?"

"New nephew?"

"Didn't you know Rende had her baby this mornin'?"

"Nobody told me," Newt said, looking at his father.

Jack cleared his throat. "Forgot 'bout that," he said.

Doc Cravens smiled, then got into his car and drove off. Jack walked slowly back to the front door. Newt watched him for a moment, then continued on to the kitchen, emptied the buckets in a tub and went back for more. Prissy came through the alleyway as he hurried along. "Miss McClinock told me about you!" she hollered.

"So what?" Newt shouted back.

The next morning Professor Radeaker stood before his class with the usual overly serious expression on his face. "Students," he said, "a certain young man in my class, occupying the third seat from the front on the far right" (all heads turned toward Newt) "is indeed quite a comedian."

141

Newt grinned and squirmed in his seat, realizing that he was about to be honored as the butt of one of the professor's jokes.

Radeaker continued, "Well sir, the other day, after grading one of his papers, I asked this young man if he had taken physics at the last school he attended. What do you think he answered, class? He said, 'Why, nosir, Professor—I never had any trouble with my movements.'"

The class burst into riotous laughter.

"All right. All right. That's enough guffawing for one day," the professor said solemnly. "Let's get down to work." And since it was his custom to ask the victim of his joke the first question of the day, Newt braced himself.

"Newton Winger, you look bright this morning, so you get the first question." Radeaker removed his glasses. "Have you ever heard of a gentleman, notable to science, with the name of Einstein?"

"Yessir."

"His first name, please."

"Albert, sir."

"He presented us with an important theory. Can you tell us what it was concerned with?"

"A—a—"

"A?" Radeaker questioned. A few snickers came from the class. "Quiet, numbskulls!" he shouted. "Well, Winger?"

"A—rel—relativity, sir."

"In what year did he present this theory?"

"Nineteen hundred and—and five, sir."

"Mmmmm. Can you explain it in detail, Winger?"

"No, sir. I don't think I can."

"Well—thank God for that," Radeaker exclaimed. "In case you could, I was going to take a seat and let you teach me. You get an 'A' for honesty. Sit down."

Newt felt very proud of himself and he turned to beam at Arcella across the room. Then his heart sank, for she was gazing out the window, looking as if her thoughts were far away. They met briefly in the hallway after class, and Newt said, "See you for the picture show Saturday."

"Not too sure. I'll let you know later," she answered. He shrugged his shoulders and headed for his French class. When he arrived he found Mr. Faulkner occupying Miss Purvelle's chair. She was out sick, he explained to the class.

Midway through the period, Carson Bigelow became quite ill—so ill, in fact, that Zack Spears had to help him from the room.

"Carson really misses his regular teacher," Mr. Faulkner quipped. Newt guessed from his expression that Mr. Faulkner also knew the score.

As the days went by, the relationship between Newt and Miss McClinock became considerably worse. He got his homework done and it was acceptable, but she never asked questions of him. And though he thought he deserved a B on the midterm test in October, he received a C. He went to see her about this one evening, asking her bluntly why he didn't get a higher mark.

"Are you telling me how to grade, young man?"

"No-mam, I'm not. I just think I should have got a higher mark."

"Well, there seems to be some difference between what you thought and what you got, doesn't there?"

Newt felt the anger rising again. He decided he had better leave and he started for the door.

"You come back here. Don't you dare walk out of here without asking to be excused. Do you hear? Come back here this minute!"

Newt stopped and faced Miss McClinock—and he said what he had been wanting to say to her for a long, long time: "You know one thing. You don't like me or any of the rest of the colored kids. I found out you told my sister and brother the same thing you told me—that we'd wind up porters and maids, and you been tellin' all the other colored kids the same thing for years and years. That's why they always make you their guidance teacher and—"

"You shut your filthy mouth—"

"—and we all hate you—every last one of us!"

"Why, you impudent thing! You're going before Mr. Hall next week. I'll see to that. You wait and see. I'll—"

Newt stormed from the room and slammed the door.

When he got outside, Arcella had already gone, and this added to his disappointment. But he found Beansy waiting for him on the building steps. Newt didn't feel much like talking now and Beansy seemed to understand, so they walked along in silence. Finally they stopped at the athletic field, where the football team was going through a scrimmage.

"Sure wish they'd let us colored kids go out for football," Newt said.

" 'Fraid we'd rub some black off on 'em," Beansy answered jokingly.

"Suppose you're right," Newt agreed. They stood watching a minute or so longer, then walked on.

Beansy said, "One thing, though—you can play on the colored basketball team."

Newt shrugged. "Well, I'm tryin' out for it."

"Aw, you'll make the squad for sure."

"Hope so. It's a lot better, anyhow."

"Yeh."

They lapsed into silence again, walked on to the tracks and crossed over. "Ain't seen you with Arcella lately," Beansy said, failing in his attempt to sound casual.

Newt failed just as badly with his answer. "Oh—old lady long nose has been keepin' me in lately. The old witch's got it in for me."

"Arcella just rode off with Chauncey."

"Yeh?"

"Goin' to the show Saturday?" Beansy was still pushing.

"Guess so—why?"

"Nothin'. Takin' Arcella?"

"Sure. Why not?"

"Nothin'—nothin'. Just thought I'd ask, that's all."

The answer did not completely satisfy Newt, but he was accustomed to Beansy's way of saying and not saying something at the same time.

Newt went by to pick up Arcella on Saturday, but her mother told him she had gone over to Chanute to visit her grandmother for the weekend. So rather than face Beansy and the others at the movie without Arcella, Newt went back home. He stayed close to the house all that weekend— and sadness was upon him like a plague.

"What's the matter, son?" his mother asked him, having noticed his mood.

He wanted to tell her everything—even about Arcella— but he settled for his problems with Miss McClinock, spilling out the whole story almost without stopping. Sarah was thoughtful for a few moments. "You should've told me about this a long time ago," she said finally.

"Poppa said we shouldn't worry you much, so I didn't."

"I'll be goin' to school with you Monday," she said. "You shore you've told me the real truth about this?"

"Yessem—what I told you was the honest truth."

But Sarah Winger wouldn't be able to accompany Newt to school as she had planned, for she took to her bed again Sunday night. It was more than dizziness this time. Newt could tell that by the deep, persistent frown that creased his father's face after Doc Cravens left.

"Your momma won't be goin' back to work for quite a spell," Jack said. "We all better try and help git things in order tomorrow." He moaned despairingly and shook his head. "Rende's goin' to help with the cookin' and washin' for a spell, while you kids are at school. But with that new baby it's goin' to be hard on her—so Prissy, you and Newt start gittin' home soon's you can from now on."

At school Monday morning Newt noticed that Arcella's seat was vacant. He now had reason for double concern, for he had already been told to be in the principal's office during the coming lunch hour. He hardly knew what went on throughout the morning. Though Miss Purvelle was back from her brief illness and the front-and-center boys were happy again, Newt didn't bother to look up. But he did notice, during the English period, that Miss McClinock avoided looking his way.

When the lunch bell sounded, he headed straight for the principal's office—expecting the worst. "I might even be expelled," he thought. When he arrived he was told to wait in the outer office until Mr. Hall could see him. And so he sat fretting, having no planned defense; only a feeling of determination burned within him. Before long Miss McClinock arrived. In somewhat of a flurry she swept into Mr. Hall's office without seeming to even notice Newt.

"Gettin' her story in first," Newt mumbled under his breath.

About five minutes later the secretary's buzzer sounded. She went to the principal's door, then turned to Newt. "You can go in now," she said.

Mr. Hall, a rather youngish, open-faced man wearing steel-rimmed glasses, leaned back in his swivel chair when Newt entered. Miss McClinock sat beside his desk, her fat hands resting firmly on her knees.

"Howdy do, sir," Newt said.

"Hello, Newton. Sit down there," Mr. Hall ordered. Newt sat down, and Mr. Hall twirled his chair in half circles for a few seconds before he spoke again. "Miss McClinock tells me you were rude and impudent last Friday. What have you to say for yourself?"

Newt picked nervously at a scab on his forefinger, looking at the principal. "Well—I guess it's all in the way you look at it, sir."

"What do you mean by that?"

145

"Well—I didn't mean to be rude when I went to see her. It was just because of things that happened between us a long time ago."

"As I distinctly remember, it was about your mark on the midterm test," Miss McClinock snapped. "You felt I had down-graded you."

"That right, Newton?"

"In a way, yessir. But that ain't—wasn't all there was to it."

"What are you trying to say? Out with it."

"It's just that we—Miss McClinock and I—had a little fuss —or I don't know whether you call it fuss or not—but we didn't see things the same way after the first week or so."

"Miss McClinock happens to be your instructor—as well as your guidance teacher."

"I know, sir, but I didn't like the way she wanted to guide me."

Mr. Hall made a few more half turns, scratching his head. "This caused you to tell Miss McClinock that you hated her?"

"I didn't say I—"

"Don't lie, young man," Miss McClinock cut in, her cheeks glowing red. "You know you said it."

"I didn't say I did, alone. I said all the colored kids hated you—and they do."

"Why do you say this, Newton?" Hall asked.

"Because they all say so."

"Do they give reasons?"

"Yessir, they do. They say she tells them all the same thing—that they shouldn't go to college—that they're all goin' to turn out to be porters and cooks and maids. That's sure what she told me."

A frown came on Hall's face. He turned from Newt and Miss McClinock and looked out the window at the tree tops. "This true, Miss McClinock? Do you tell the Negro students such things?"

"Mr. Hall," she began, her nose twitching, "you've been at this school for just two years. I've been class advisor to these colored students for the last twenty years. What I've said to them was what I've been instructed to say to them."

The principal had turned to face her, and his frown was deeper now. "So this accusation of his is true?"

"To a certain extent—yes."

"Who instructed you to say such things?"

"Mr. Hornsby, our former principal. He—"

"Just a moment, Miss McClinock," Mr. Hall said, "just a moment, please. Newton, wait in the outer office until I call you."

Newt got up and went out, then Mr. Hall rose and shut the door behind him.

As he sat there on the bench, Newt began trying to imagine the conversation as it would go between Mr. Hall and Miss McClinock. He had been aware of the principal's surprise when she had confessed to the truth of his accusation, and he felt this was in his favor. His tension had eased somewhat, but he had already taken a pessimistic view of the outcome. He had decided that if he were expelled, he would say even more about what he felt was an injustice. If he won, then nothing more needed to be said. "But any way it goes," he decided, "Miss McClinock's goin' to have it in for me."

He sat there, time going slowly, recalling Washington Junior High, comparing it with this school of big, airy, sun-splashed classrooms, auditoriums and gymnasiums, remembering that there had been no microscopes and no chemical labs, and that their outdoor playground had been no more than a deserted garbage-strewn field adjoining the school property; retaining the memory of the little gym, the way it was used for just about everything, and the odor of stale sweat and smelly tennis shoes that clung to it even on graduation night—despite the thorough airing it was given the afternoon before.

His stomach growled from hunger, and the secretary glanced in his direction.

But he had known some wonderful moments back there too, warm, intimate and gay moments of easy pleasure and unrestrained laughter—moments that had not yet come to him here. He wondered, as he had often done before, what the whites' real reasons were for denying them a part in the school's athletic and social affairs. "Why does our color make such a difference? . . . Didn't God know that we'd have a lot of trouble if he made us black? . . . Since he's white, maybe he don't care either." He smiled wryly. "Never seen black angels . . . even the chariot horses are white."

He gritted his teeth in defiance of the conspiracy he felt Miss McClinock and Mr. Hall must be forming against him; of the scorn he felt she held for his coloring. "If I turned white before they called me back in there, 'twould be a different story altogether. . . ." He knotted his fist and watched the skin lighten under the pressure of the knuckle bones. "Wonder if you tore all the skin off, if it would all come back black? Guess it would...don't think I'd like bein' white, anyway."

He dug into his pocket and brought out three large raisins; after picking lint and pocket dust from them, he popped them into his mouth. Then he got up and started across the room to the water cooler. At that moment, the door to the principal's office opened and Miss McClinock bustled out past Newt and into the hall.

"Come in, Winger," the principal said, and Newt followed him back into his office.

Mr. Hall began very slowly—uncertainly. "I just don't know—well, this is all sort of an unnecessary mistake—or maybe a misunderstanding. I'm speaking of Miss McClinock's attitude toward you and other Negro students—and her advice to you about college and so forth. For an explanation to make sense to you—or me—one would have to go much further back, to a period—a tragic one—before you or I existed." Hall walked to the window and gazed out at the campus, much the same way Newt had seen Miss McClinock do that evening after their argument. "Although she must share the blame for this awful wrong, Miss McClinock is somewhat a victim herself—having been eased into this wrong channel of thought many years ago, not only because she thought it to be right but because it was a truth that existed during those same years."

Hall talked on, seeming to Newt to be addressing some unseen audience. "Mr. Hornsby was more to blame than she—but then, so is my father, my mother, Miss McClinock's father and mother and millions of others who helped shape the ideas that Miss McClinock so unwisely passed on to you—forgetting that time and progress must shake away such ideas." He turned slowly. "Are you following what I am saying? Do you understand, Newt?"

"Yessir—I think I do."

"Frankly, I was shocked at Miss McClinock's confession, but—" He shrugged, then paused for a second. "The valedictorian of my graduating class at college was a Negro, Curtis Mathews. But—do you want to know the ironic thing about this, Newt?" Hall shook his head. "When I came through the New York train station from a New England vacation last summer, there was Curtis Mathews—bearing out Miss McClinock's prophecy—asking me if I would like help with my bags. He was a redcap—a redcap, carrying bags for people who couldn't begin to compare with him in knowledge

148

or social worth. 'What a waste!' I remember thinking when I left him that day."

"Did he know you, Mr. Hall?" Newt asked.

"Oh, yes. Yes indeed. He stopped work and we talked for nearly a half hour." Hall was quiet—remembering again. "He had seven children by then, Newt. I'll never forget it, a man with a master's degree, carrying bags, with seven children—and no hope."

They were both quiet for a moment.

"There are some things here at my own school that I don't like, son. For instance, I feel badly about the school board's keeping you boys off our football and basketball teams. It's a stupid, costly thing. Our white basketball team hasn't made the state championships in the last ten years. The colored team has not only done this, but it's held the championship of Kansas, Oklahoma and Missouri four times during the same period. Believe me—if it were left to me, or Coach Dennison, this would stop, but we are powerless."

"Yessir, I understand."

"I hope you do. And another thing—what I've told you is strictly between us. I had a long talk with Miss McClinock and I'm sure her thinking and attitudes will be different from now on. You continue to work hard. She will do the rest."

"Yessir."

"If you have any more problems, bring them to me. You're excused." As Newt started out, he added, "And you are to show Miss McClinock the highest respect. You understand that, don't you?"

"Yessir. Thanks, Mr. Hall."

"You're welcome."

Newt stopped by Arcella's on the way home from school that same evening. Mrs. Jefferson opened the door for him and said, "Come in, Newt. Arcella's been ailing a bit. I'll call her."

An uneasiness crept over him as he saw Arcella walking slowly down the stairs. She didn't look ill, he thought, but she was puffy around the eyes. He assumed that she'd been crying.

"Sorry you've been sick," he said.

"Oh, it isn't anything—just headaches and head colds," she answered dryly.

"I've sure missed you," he said, taking her hand.

She drew back. "Mustn't get too close—you'll be getting a cold too."

"How long will you be out of school—you know?"

She shook her head wistfully. "Don't know for sure. I hate missing all the classes."

"I can bring your homework to you every evenin'," he volunteered.

"Oh, that would be fine, Newt. If—if I'm not here—downstairs, I mean—you can just hand them to Momma."

She didn't ask him to sit down, as he had expected, so he said, "Anything I can do for you—before I go?"

"Oh, no no. Thanks a lot. I'm going back upstairs and lie down."

Newt touched her hand and looked into her swollen eyes. "What's the matter, Arcella? Tell me what's the matter."

"I told you—I told you. I tol—" She looked as though she were about to cry. Then, turning on her heels, she rushed back up the stairs.

Newt stood looking after her as Mrs. Jefferson came in from the kitchen. She listened to Arcella's door slam, then she turned to Newt. "Did you and Arcella have a falling out, Newt?"

"No-mam." He looked up the stairs. "Why?"

"Well, she's been acting like she was mad with somebody or something. Bad enough tending to the cold she's got, let alone her stubbornness and meanness. Just thought maybe you two had a little spat."

"No-mam, we sure haven't had no spat at all."

"Oh well, she'll get over it soon. Don't worry, son. Women are like that, you know." She was smiling now.

As he walked toward home, Newt had an odd feeling—one of melancholy; of loneliness and futile longing.

Arcella was slipping away from him—and he knew it.

CHAPTER ✤ 12

NEWT MADE the colored basketball squad, traveled with it to Pittsburg, Chanute and Parsons, where they won each of their games. Coach Ebon Jones put him in during the second half of the third game, and he emerged the second highest scorer. When he got home from school the next evening he saw his picture in the paper for the first time in his life. He raced to his mother's bedside with it, bubbling with happiness.

"I'm mighty proud of you, son," she said. "Have Pete pick up some more of these at the newspaper office."

With his spirits thust bolstered, Newt went about his school work more earnestly than ever. And he found that Mr. Hall had been right about Miss McClinock. After the first week she began asking Newt to recite as much as she did the others, and her whole manner became gentler. She even told him that his work was improving. And it was, because he worked extra hard in her class.

As he had promised, he took Arcella's homework to her each day—but he never saw her. She had taken to bed and refused to see anyone. There were rumors that she had tuberculosis; that she had a sleeping sickness. Newt wrote her two notes, but they weren't answered, and his heart became sad again. He wouldn't eat and he couldn't sleep, so finally, in desperation, he went to his mother with his problem.

She was propped in her bed drinking tea when he entered. Sensing that he was troubled, she spoke first. "Somethin' botherin' you, son?"

He nodded gloomily. "Yessem—might as well tell you. It's Arcella. You know she's been sick?"

"Yes. I've been hearin' about it. How is she?"

"That's the trouble. I don't know. I've been to see her several times, but she won't see me. I wrote her twice and she didn't even answer my letters."

"Maybe she's too sick, Newt. Maybe—"

"It's more'n that. Even her mother wouldn't talk to me when I went by there this evenin'."

"Did you do somethin' you shouldn't have?"

"No-mam, nothin' I know about."

"Well, give it time, son. It'll all blow over. Give it time."

But time came and time went, and he got no word.

The Christmas holidays were approaching again, but it was apparent they would not be the same as before. Jack couldn't find much work and neither could Pete. Prissy, who had been working at Judge Cavanaugh's on weekends, took to working full time for the holidays. Newt went about with Beansy and Jappy shoveling snow, or tackling any other odd job they could find.

A few days before Christmas, Newt returned home, cold and low of spirits, to find his father waiting for him outside the door. The scowl on his father's face told him that something was amiss.

"Hi, Poppa."

"Come on in the house, boy," Jack said, "I want to talk to you private. You got some explainin' to do."

What could it be? Newt wondered, following his father into the dining room.

"Boy," Jack started, "that Jefferson girl's father was over here to see me today."

"Yessir."

"Well, don't that mean nothin' to you, boy?"

Newt looked up, surprised at the question and his father's manner. "I don't get what you mean," he said. "Is she worse or somethin'?"

Jack Winger looked long and hard at his son before he spoke again. "Mr. Jefferson says—he says Arcella's gonna have a baby—that's what he says."

Newt felt as if a stick of dynamite had exploded in his stomach. He was stunned beyond speech.

"Well—do you know anything 'bout it?"

He turned away, but Jack spun him back around, whispering fiercely so as not to disturb Sarah. "Tell me—tell me, boy—did you do somethin' to that girl?"

"No, Poppa! No, Poppa!" he cried. "I didn't! I didn't!"

"Quiet. Quiet—"

"Jack!" It was Sarah. "What's goin' on? What's the matter?"

Newt broke from his father's grasp and strode into his mother's bedroom. "Oh, Momma—oh, Momma—" he said.

"What is it, son? What is it? Jack, what's goin' on?" Her hand was about Newt's wrist.

Jack went slowly to her bed. "I didn't want to bother you with this right off—but—but Bob Jefferson was over to see me this afternoon 'bout his daughter."

"Well—what about her?" Sarah asked nervously.

"She's gonna have a baby."

"A baby?" Sarah's grip tightened. "He thinks Newt had somethin' to do with it?"

"Yep—that's what he's thinkin'," Jack moaned.

"Did you, Newt?" Sarah looked into his eyes for the answer. "Did you, son? Tell me the truth. Don't be afraid."

Newt was shaking now—with unutterable hurt. "No, Momma, it wasn't me. But—but—I wish it was."

Sarah looked up at Jack. "He's tellin' the truth," she said, "he's tellin' the truth." They were quiet for a moment. "What does Arcella say?"

Jack shrugged. "She won't say who it was—won't say a'tall."

"Well, Jack, only one thing to do. Take him over there to face the girl and see what she says in front of him. No sense in them thinkin' it's him when it's not."

"Yep. Guess that's the only thing to do. Come on, boy. Come on. I declare, you'll be the death of me yet." Newt turned and followed his father from the room.

A few minutes later, when Newt entered Arcella's room with his father and her parents, she angrily pulled the covers up over her head. But her father snatched the covers back to her shoulders and said, "Now I want you to tell us, here and now, if this boy is responsible. You hear me, girl? Speak up!"

"I told you a thousand times he wasn't!" she shouted. "Why do you keep bothering me with it?"

"Then who is it if it ain't him?" Bob Jefferson hollered back.

"Bob—Bob." Arcella's mother was on the bed beside her. "Tell us, honey. Tell us—and get it over with. Momma'll help you."

The room was extremely quiet for a minute. Mrs. Jefferson wiped the tears from Arcella's eyes with the top of the sheet. Arcella turned over in the bed, then she reached for Newt's hand. "Come sit beside me—you'll try to understand, won't you, Newt?"

"Yes, I'll understand—"

"I'm awfully sorry, Newt—awfully sorry."

"Yes." He was silent after the one word.

153

"You will forgive me, won't you?" Newt nodded his head, and after sniffing a couple of times she said, "Well, Poppa—it's going to shock you, I know—and all the rest of you too. I told you not to go and get Newt mixed up in this, but you wouldn't listen."

Newt had a sudden desire to run from the room, not wanting to hear the rest. He tried to get up, but Arcella pulled him back to her.

"It was Chauncey," she said, "Chauncey Cavanaugh, Poppa—not Newt, like you said."

She released Newt's hand and he got up, walking quickly out of the room. He rushed down the stairs and out into the cold, senseless day. As he walked along, he kept repeating, "Chauncey—Chauncey—" softly to himself.

On Christmas morning Newt got up especially early and made the fire; but he didn't call the others. Instead, he stood beside the dining room door, looking at the tree, remembering the Christmas before when he and Arcella had been so happy. He had a present for her now among the few others under the tree. He picked it up and went out the door. It was snowing heavily, so he turned up the collar of his mackinaw and walked slowly toward Arcella's house. He had decided to place the gift on the porch, and he didn't want to be seen.

As he approached the house he wiped the wet snow from his brows and peered ahead. Then he moved quickly to the porch, pulled back the storm door, and placed the gift on the threshold. Turning to leave, he noticed the window shade was up. He glanced through it, expecting to see the Christmas tree—and caught his breath. The room was bare. Pressing close to the window, he was able to see through most of the house, and there wasn't a stick of furniture anywhere. The Jeffersons must have slipped away in the darkness of Christmas Eve, he concluded.

So Arcella was gone from him—forever. For a moment he stood gazing at the small red and green parcel of lilac water settling in the moist snow between the doors. He started to pick it up, then decided to leave it there. He closed the storm door gently against it, turned and headed for home.

"Wonder why she did it? Must have lost her head for a minute ... thought she could go to the other side of the tracks for good ... Chauncey's big car and his money and big house and everything ... but who knows, maybe she really liked him ... maybe he really liked her ... she was pretty

154

enough for anybody to like . . . only thing wrong for her with Chauncey was her color."

When he arrived the family was still asleep, so he went back to the living room and took another look at the tree. It seemed dull compared to the one of the previous year. The scarcity of presents on the floor spoke of the hard winter. Outside the window the whitened land seemed gray under the thick curtain of tumbling flakes. Newt gritted his teeth, swallowed the lump in his throat, then tromped through the house, shouting, "Merry Christmas! Merry Christmas!" Then, as on other Christmases before, he put on the coffeepot—knowing, as always, his father would be less grouchy if his insides were warmed up.

It snowed on for two days and part of another night. When it stopped, the cattle barns could hardly be seen from the house. The big snow was a blessing for Jack and Pete, for they were hired by the County to help clear the outlying roads. On the last Saturday of the month Newt went along. Sitting between his father and Pete on the big plow truck, he watched the snow churn up and off to the side, where in some places the drifts were higher than the cab of the truck. Halfway between the swimming hole and Jake Kiner's place on the river road, Pete stopped the truck and braced for such a drift; then he revved up the motor and knifed the plow blades into it, sending the snow up over them and in all directions. There was a sudden jolt, and Newt and his father slammed forward into the dashboard. The truck bounced back and stalled.

"What'd you hit?" Jack boomed.

"Don't know!" Pete hollered back. The three of them jumped down and started kicking away the snow from the object buried in their path.

"It's a car!" Newt yelled. "It's a car, Poppa!"

Pete grabbed three shovels off the truck and they began uncovering the car. It was an old Model-T Ford, and it took them five minutes to dig their way to its windshield.

"Careful now," Jack cautioned. "I hope and pray ain't nobody in it."

They dug slower, inching their way.

"Poppa!" Newt hollered, "I hit somethin' on the runnin' board!"

"Git back. Let me see." Jack felt the object with his shovel and carefully scraped away the snow. He stopped suddenly. "Good Lord—it's a man! He's stiff as a board."

"He dead, Poppa?" Newt questioned.

"That you can be shore of," Jack said solemnly.

"Anybody we know?" Pete asked.

"Ain't never seen him before," Jack said.

Newt peeked and said, "Me either."

"It's a Missouri plate," Pete said, brushing the snow off the raised numbers.

Jack turned to Newt. "You better hike back to town and git Kirky. Just tell him what we found. We're gonna keep diggin'. Might find somebody else here too."

When Newt returned with Kirky in Doug Simpson's Ford car, his father and brother had dug the car completely free of the drift. Kirky strode over to the corpse, kneeled down and wiped the loose snow from the face. "Hell," he said, "that's Bats Oliver. He's a bootlegger from K. C." He got up, forced open the back door of the car and yanked a tarpaulin off the back area. "Look here, he's got the whole ass-end loaded with booze!" He inspected the cache more closely. "Hell, must be more'n fifty bottles in there. Want some, Jack?"

"Nope," Jack said, "nothin' I can do with that stuff."

"Well, he shore won't be needin' it," Kirky said. He and Doug loaded the bottles into their car, stepping over and around the body as if it were a log. Then Kirky said, "You all stay here. I'm goin' to git the dead wagon. Be right back." And with that Doug turned the car around and drove off.

On New Year's Day, Sarah had a visit from Judge Cavanaugh. She had expected him for some time, so his coming was no surprise. He brought food packages and a few gifts for everyone, and Rodney had come along to help with these as well as to see Newt.

After a while, in the quiet of Sarah and Jack's bedroom, the Judge told them what he suspected they had known for days. He spoke his regret, and said that Arcella would be taken care of. He didn't say in what way—and Jack and Sarah didn't ask. Of course, Chauncey had denied everything, but to no avail. "He will work this summer—if he has to dig ditches—to pay for all this and more," the Judge said.

He and Rodney ate black-eyed peas and pig's feet with the Wingers for good luck, then they got into their big shiny Maxwell and went off to their big house on the other side of the town.

Five days later Prissy came home and said that Chauncey had packed his clothes and slipped away while the Judge

156

was in court. "All he left was a letter for the poor Judge." Prissy sighed.

January, February and March were equally cold, desolate and hard for Jack Winger and his family. With the feed bins running low and the icebox nearly empty, Jack had to kill off most of his chickens and slaughter two of his best hogs. One cow died, and a horse was crippled from a fall on the ice. Jake Kiner had brought in feed a couple of times when he had needed it desperately. And though Jack couldn't pay for it, he had noted the amount in his soiled account book. "You'll git it back soon's I'm able," he told Kiner.

Yet all was not bad. Jake promised to hire Pete for some spring cattle driving, and Sarah finally got permission from Doc Cravens to return to work on the first of April. In addition, Prissy announced she had a beau—though she never revealed who he was.

Newt, in spite of his loss, had been doing extremely well in school; and he had become a regular on the basketball team, being the third freshman in the history of the school to do so. As the months wore on, the pain of his wound gradually lessened, and every now and then he would completely forget the bittersweet affair. Still, naturally, there were times when, catching the scent of lilac water, or scanning the inscription in Poe's book of stories ("Love, Arcella. December, 1925"), he felt life wasn't worth living. He had inquired of her when his team returned to Chanute after the holidays, but no one he asked knew of the family's whereabouts. It was as if they had disappeared from earth without leaving a trace.

Later, in the early part of April, he dreamed of lying with Arcella on the mossy earth near the violets in Peaceful Park—but he awoke only to a rooster's crowing. And his heart, which had seemed to thump on Arcella's breast, beat only against his lumpy mattress.

CHAPTER ❧ 13

SPRING! Birds darting about—singing in trees and over the prairies. Overhasty flowers popping up from the damp earth. And only two more weeks of school!

Things had got back pretty much to normal for the Wingers. Sarah was at the Cavanaughs again, working hard as ever, and Prissy helped her on Saturdays with the heavy cleaning. Jack was busy in the fields, and every so often he drove a steam-roller for the County. Pete rode the herd for Jake Kiner Monday through Friday. And every day after school Newt joined Beansy, Earl, Jappy and Skunk in the ritual of testing the water at the swimming hole.

On the first Saturday morning in June, Newt went over to the Kiner farm looking for work. He met Jake at the barn door and said humbly, "Mornin', Mister Kiner."

"Mornin', Newt." Jake pushed his spectacles to the end of his bony red nose. "No peaches yet, you young scallywag. What you want?"

Newt grinned and said, "Want some extra work this summer."

Jake grunted. "Extra, huh? None of you young'uns wants anything steady."

"Got to get my swimmin' in, you know that. You was young once."

"I ain't none too happy 'bout it, though. Wasted lots of time—like you're doin' right now. You ought'a be a good hand like your brother Pete,' stead of cavortin' all over the place swimmin' and stealin' peaches and such."

"Oh, them days are over for me, Mister Kiner. I got to make money for college. Only got three more years."

"Sounds good. Prob'ly lotta hot air, though."

"Nosir—I'm goin' for sure. Ask Momma."

"Well, what you want'a do 'sides sleep and eat?"

"Oh, some hoein' and feedin'—helpin' anywhere—maybe ridin' with Pete when he'll let me."

"Just a minute." Jake pushed open the barn door and hollered, "The Harvesta' man bring the plowshares yet, Silas?"

"Said he'd be out this afternoon round three," Silas called back.

"Mister Newhall workin' for you this spring?" Newt asked.

"Well, I'm tryin' him. Don't know how he's gonna work out—quite a boozer." Jake studied Newt for a moment. "Okay, young fella, you come round next Saturday. See if I cain't put you to doin' somethin'."

"Thanks, Mister Kiner, thanks. School'll be out next Friday, so that'll be just fine. I'll be here bright'n early."

On the last day of school, Mr. Hall called Newt to his office. "Newton," he said, "I want to congratulate you on your final marks—and especially on the good report Miss McClinock turned in."

Newt had been nervous when he entered, but now he beamed brightly. "Thanks, Mister Hall. I tried hard."

"Your report card shows you did. See you next fall. Have a good summer."

They shook hands, then Newt made a special trip down the hall to say goodbye to Miss McClinock. She smiled stiffly and told Newt that she appreciated his coming to her. And he felt good as he walked out of the door toward summer and vacation. He joined Beansy, Jappy and Earl on the steps, and they all started across town, comparing marks. As they reached the tracks they met Skunk.

"How'd you git over here so early?" Beansy asked.

"Got a new babe with a big new car," Skunk lied. "You ought to see her. She's got hair down to her ankles and a keester that would make old Rev'rend Broadnap throw his Bible in a privy hole."

They all laughed and continued across the tracks. The rest of the afternoon they wandered aimlessly over Candy Hill and along the road leading to Rock Cave and the river—happy in the freedom of summer that lay ahead.

When Newt entered the house that evening, Prissy handed him a letter—and his heart jumped. "It might be from Arcella," he thought. He tore it open and began reading.

"Who's it from?" Prissy asked, peeping over his shoulder.

Newt kept reading, and a big grin came on his face. "Hot dog! Hot dog!" he shouted.

Prissy was beside herself with curiosity. "What's it say? Who's it from?"

" 'Professor Radeaker invites you to participate in the

special science seminar he will conduct for a week this summer,' it says. Wait'll I tell Momma! Won't Rodney Cavanaugh be surprised? He'll be goin' too."

"Huh—you think you're somethin' great," Prissy said.

"It's a big honor, because he only invites the ten best students every year. They go on field trips and everything." He danced about the room, waving the letter. His summer was shaping up.

The next day Newt went to work on the Kiner farm, and Silas Newhall was four hours late. Jake stormed about the place damning himself for having given Silas a chance. "Should'a known better'n to trust that likker-head!"

"Anything I can do, Mister Kiner?" Newt asked.

"Naw. Just you keep cleanin' up that tack," Jake snapped. Pulling out a bunch of keys, he unlocked a door near the barn entrance. He went in, and a short time later shouted, "Come here, boy!"

Newt dropped the saddle and reins, went over to the door and found Jake stacking bottles on a shelf. He climbed atop a box and motioned to Newt. "Hand me them bottles out'a that tub there," he said. Newt began handing them up as Jake placed them on a higher shelf.

"Look out!" Jake shouted, as one of the bottles toppled from the shelf and broke on the floor. "Hit you?"

"Nope," Newt said.

"Pint'a good peach brandy gone," Jake mumbled. "Okay, keep shovin' 'em up." Newt kicked the broken glass to the side and began handing Jake the bottles again. He was just picking up the last two when Silas staggered into the barn and came over to the brandy closet.

"Mor-mornin', mornin'," he mumbled. "Uh—look'it all the hooch—no wonder you—keep that—big ole lock—on that there door, Jake," he added groggily.

Jake placed the last two bottles and climbed down. A mixture of anger and disgust was on his face as he stood regarding Silas. "What you mean 'mornin' '?" he growled finally. "It's past twelve—and you're soused to the gills!"

Silas giggled. "Jus' a little spir-its, that's all—a little spir-its —" He wobbled closer, and Newt caught the reek of liquor that seemed to come from his clothes.

Jake reached in his pocket and pulled out some money, sorted out several bills and shoved them into Silas' hands. "Here—you're fired," he said. "Now git off my property."

"Now wa-wait a minit, Jake—you cain't do this to me."

"Git out, I say!" Jake started shoving him toward the door.

160

"Okay—okay—" Silas stopped and counted the money. "Lis-sen here, this ain't a'nough—this's a day short." He stood rocking in the middle of the floor.

"That's all you're gittin'. You ain't got a cent comin' for today," Jake said, "not a cent. Now out you go!" Jake pushed him on through the door and into the open. The door banged shut behind them.

Newt went over and started cleaning the tack again. He could hear the two men outside screaming at each other:

"You owe me 'nother day, you ole ba-bastard! I want the money what's comin' to me!"

"Go on, git out! Git out!"

A few minutes later Newt went outside for lunch, and he could see Silas far across the field, stumbling toward the village. "Poor Waldo," he thought. "What a guy to have for a father." He took a paper sack from his overall bib, unwrapped a ham sandwich and began eating. After a while Jake came out with a cup of milk. "Somethin' to wash it down with," he said, then walked back toward the house.

Later that evening, at the Winger supper table, Newt remarked about Silas' being fired. "Jake was plenty mad too," he said. "He just shoved some money at Silas and told him to get goin'."

"Silas drunk?" Pete asked.

"He sure was. Couldn't hardly stand up."

"Shame," Sarah said. "I feel so bad for Waldo. He's such a nice boy at heart."

"Cain't say the same for Blanche, though," Jack put in.

"Well, Silas shore ain't set no great pattern for neither one of them to go by," Sarah retorted.

A knock came on the screen door. "Newt—can you go?" It was Beansy and Skunk.

"Just a minute," Newt answered, and looked at Sarah. "Momma, you care if I go to the early show with Beansy and Skunk?"

"Long's you git home before nine, it's all right. No later."

"Yessem." Jumping up from the table, he grabbed his cap and joined his friends.

On their way to the Regency Theater they passed Chappie Logan's place, and Newt spotted Silas Newhall coming out the door. He was still drunk, leaning on the arm of Booker Savage. Newt tried to hurry past without being seen, but he wasn't fast enough. "Hey, boy!" Silas hollered. "You tell that ole goat Jake I'm comin' for my money. You tell'm now, hear me?"

"Yeh—yeh," Newt answered, still moving.

"An' tell'm he better put more'n one lock on that booze he's hidin' in that barn, too. You tell'm, hear?"

"Yeh—yeh," Newt repeated.

As the boys went on down the block, Skunk quipped, "Them two are the ass-ends of nothin'."

"What's Silas talkin' about, Newt?" Beansy asked.

"Jake Kiner fired him today for bein' late and drunk."

"Su-prised me he hired him in the first place," Skunk said. "I wouldn't trust him behind a mosquito's pecker."

They walked on to the tracks, where a freight train stood blocking their path. "Come on, let's go over the top," Skunk urged, "else we'll be late for the show." He jumped on the bottom step and began scaling the metal rungs of the box-car. Newt and Beansy hesitated a moment, then followed. They had just reached the top of the car when the brakeman spied them.

"Git off there, you bastards!" he shouted.

"Screw you, red balls!" Skunk hollered back.

They scurried down the other side, leaped to the ground and made off toward the Regency.

CHAPTER ✤ 14

NEWT ARRIVED at the Kiner farm early the next Saturday morning. There was a note from Jake tacked to the barn door saying that he and his wife would be away until afternoon. Newt stuffed the note in his pocket, wishing now he had gone to see Pete ride in the rodeo at Parsons.

He cleaned tack for the first hour, then swept the floor and went out to the fields, hoeing weeds until nearly twelve o'clock. Finally, tired from the half day's work, he swung the hoe to his shoulder and looked about for shelter from the burning sun. There was a tree close by, but he found it too skimpy for shade; so he walked back to the barn—figuring to get a good hour's rest before Jake returned.

He entered the barn, stood the hoe against a wall, and settled on a box. Then, changing his mind, he climbed the wooden ladder to the loft and stretched out in the hay. It took him several minutes to devour two sandwiches, then he rolled over on his back and gazed idly at the ceiling until his eyelids got heavy. Before long he was fast asleep.

More than two hours had passed when he sprang awake to a squeaking noise down on the floor beneath him. He scooted quietly to the edge of the loft and peeped below, fearing that Jake had discovered his absence. Then his breath caught in his throat. It wasn't Jake. It was Booker Savage— and he was ripping the lock off the door to the room where Jake stored his applejack and peach brandy.

Afraid of what Booker might do if he saw him, Newt just lay quiet and watched. The bottom hinge was loose now, and Booker wedged the crowbar under the top screws. With one powerful jerk he wrenched the lock and hinges off and they clattered to the floor. Then, hooking the crowbar on the back pocket of his overalls, he placed a gunny sack on the floor and slipped into the dark room. Within seconds Newt saw him loading pint bottles in the sack.

Booker stopped at the sound of Jake's angry voice coming

from the barn door. "You ain't gittin' one penny more out'a me, Silas! Now git out'a here, you drunken bum, 'fore I throw you out!"

Silas Newhall staggered in after him. "I ain't leavin' here till you pay me what's comin' to me, you goddam old pinch-penny!"

Jake's face screwed up in anger, and he reached to the wall for his bull whip. "I'm warnin' you for the last time to git out!" he hollered, threatening the reeling Silas with the heavy end of the whip.

"You don't scare me, you old son-of-a-bitch!" Silas grabbed Newt's hoe as he yelled back, but before he could swing it Jake stepped to one side and clouted him on the temple with the butt-end of the whip. Silas fell unconscious to the floor.

Jake had stumbled on the sack of bottles as he swung, and now, as he steadied himself, he saw the awesome figure of Booker Savage peering from the dark of the doorway. Bewildered, he paused a moment with his mouth open—then he snapped the whip and struck. Booker flinched and raised the crowbar. Jake drew back again, but before he could swing, the crowbar smashed against his head. He went down without uttering a sound. With the first blow the beast seemed to have been loosed in Booker, and he smashed the crowbar time and again into Jake's bloody head.

Finally Booker stood over the two forms on the floor, looking about, breathing heavily. Silas moaned. Booker stooped, pulled the whip from beneath Jake's arm, and beat the moan to a stillness. He dropped the whip by Silas' head and started away; then he turned back, picked up the crowbar and placed it in Silas' limp left hand. After that he lifted the sack of bottles, stepped warily through the door and fled across the field.

Newt hadn't moved during the swift, brutal assault, and when he did it was in a maze of nightmarish thought. It was as if he'd had a bad dream and, not yet fully awake, believed he was still dreaming. He crawled to the back of the loft and pinned his eye to a crack in the wallboards, watching Booker make off into the nearby woods.

Suddenly he knew he had to get out of there himself. He started for the ladder, then stopped and crouched back, for Mary Kiner had appeared at the barn door. Catching sight of the forms lying in the shadows beyond the doorway, she stepped in further, an apprehensive look on her face. Then she threw up her hands and ran screaming toward the house. "Oh my Lord! Oh! Help! Help!"

When she was gone, Newt clambered down the ladder, crept toward the door, glancing timorously at the two men sprawled like ragamuffins on the floor. He peeped out the door, then burst through it and loped over the furrowed earth toward home. He slowed down as he approached Logan's Grove. He was shaking now, so instead of going to the house he cut across to the cowshed, staying there until the shaking stopped.

Though fatigue was upon Newt like an opiate this night, he couldn't sleep. He had slipped off to bed at nightfall, dinnerless and faking an upset stomach. Jack Winger sensed more worry than ailment in his son's complaining, but he was wrong about the source. "That boy's heart shore must be heavy if he goes off to bed without eatin'," he confided to Sarah, slapping a fly on his forehead. "Must still be thinkin' 'bout that girl."

"Well, it was a pretty hard blow for him to take at his age," Sarah said. And then they had dropped the subject.

Twice during the night the harrowing scene ran through Newt's mind and flushed him to a fearful awakening. He lay in what seemed like never-ending darkness, wondering whether he should tell . . .

By church time Sunday morning the news of Jake Kiner's death and Silas Newhall's arrest had swept across languid Cherokee Flats like a storm. Every minister in town sparked his sermon on the tragedy, but the Reverend Lucius Broadnap preached a half hour overtime, ending finally by shouting, "—the devil got in here yesterd'y afternoon and undone all the good the word of Jesus been spreadin' among us for years! Bless the sorrowful widow of this poor man whose life's blood lays cold this minute on the floor of his barn. Bless us all, dear Jesus—amen."

Later, an uneasy calm lay over the Winger household while Sarah and Prissy spread the Sunday table. Uncle Rob, heavy eyelids batting behind dark glasses, sat in the shadow of the chimney pipe. Pete stood at a window, gazing into the distance, watching the slow turn of the weather vane atop the Kiner barn. Newt sat on the floor, his back propped against the sideboard, staring into space. And Jack leaned against the wall in a straight-back chair, smoking his pipe. He was the first to break the silence. "Powerful sermon Broadnap preached today, Rob."

Rob's head lifted and his lids blinked even faster. "Yes, it was. Yes, it was." His right little finger was nervously rubbing the nubs on his other hand. "And his words about Jake sure touched the heart." He paused, then went on, "Jake was a good sort—a little cranky maybe, but he did lots of good things too—like the time he donated the stain-glass window for the church."

The talk about Jake brought a new agitation to Newt, and he began rocking back and forth in little inconsistent rhythms, glancing furtively at his father, uncle and brother. And before he could halt the words, they were flowing from his mouth: "You know, Poppa, I did some hoein' for Mr. Kiner yesterday."

Jack was coughing out smoke and Newt thought his father hadn't heard, so he added, "I left his place early, though."

Rob inclined his head toward Newt. "What did you say, boy?"

"Oh, I just said I'd done a little work for Mr. Kiner lately, a little hoein'."

"Oh, you did."

Pete eyed Newt curiously, and Newt had the feeling that his brother was aware of his cover-up.

Sarah entered the room and placed a platter of chicken on the table, and Prissy followed with hot bread and vegetables. Jack took his brother Rob by the arm and led him to his seat at the table. After they were all in place, Sarah called on Newt for the blessing.

"Lord, make us thankful for what we are about to receive, for the nouris-nourishment of our bodies. Amen."

Sarah heaped food on Rob's plate and sat it before him. "There you are, Rob," she said.

"Thanks, Sarah."

"Leg, Newt?"

"Yessem, guess so."

"Prissy?"

"Same, please."

"Pete, you and your poppa help yourselves."

Jack stuffed a napkin in the collar of his white shirt. "I declare, I cain't for the life of me understand how Silas Newhall could do such a thing."

"Whiskey'll make a man do lots of crazy things," Rob said.

"Got Silas over at the jail?" Sarah asked.

"From what I hear he's at the hospital—pretty well banged up himself."

"Heard they'd been fussin' about a week over some money Silas claimed Jake owed him."

"Who told you that, Pete?" Jake asked.

"Talk about town."

"Coffee, Rob?"

Rob dropped his fork. Newt picked it up, wiped it on his napkin and placed it in his uncle's hand. "No thanks, Sarah."

Jack chomped the white off a scallion. "Well, I'm shore glad 'twasn't a colored man who done it," he said. "It'd be trouble shore enough."

"Yep. We can all be thankful for that," Pete agreed.

"Poor old Jake," Sarah sighed, "he had enough trouble in the last couple years."

"Yeh," Jack replied, "with the beatin' the Savage boy gave him and all."

"What about Mary?"

"They say she's been out'a her mind ever since it happened."

"Where's she, home by herself, Sarah?"

"Nope. She's—eat, Newt—she's over at the hospital under Timothy's care."

"Well, it's a shame—downright dirty shame. Who'd ever thought it could happen right here under our very noses?"

"Sin's got no respect for time or place, Jack. You know that."

"Silas'll prob'ly git life, won't he, Poppa?" Pete said.

"Don't see how he can 'scape it. Seems to me they got him dead to rights. Found him layin' right 'longside of Jake, drunk as a loon."

Rob's face lifted before he spoke, and Newt could see the whole table reflected in the black lenses. "They still have to prove he's guilty first. Never can tell. Silas's liable to plead self-defense or somethin'. Never can tell till it's all over."

"Ain't you hungry, Newt?" Sarah questioned. "Whyn't you eat your chicken?"

Newt shot a side glance at Pete, then picked up the leg and began chewing listlessly. Pete looked away. "Got any more coffee, Prissy?"

"What does it mean, 'gettin' life,' Poppa?" Newt popped the question while Jack had his mouth full of food.

Rob sensed his brother's long delay and cut in, "Means he'll go to prison for the rest of his life, Newt."

"Till he dies?"

"Till he dies," Jack finally answered.

"Lucky he ain't in Missouri—he'd git death," Pete said, shaking his head.

"Don't mention such a thing, Pete," Sarah said, getting up. "It's awful just to think about such a thing."

Sarah served hot mince pie and poured the grownups more coffee. And after everyone was finished, several minutes of quiet fell over the table. Newt was apprehensive. Things were worse than he'd thought.

Then his mother was up, taking the dirty dishes off the table. "Come on, Prissy," she sighed, "let's clean off the table."

At three o'clock Rob asked for his hat and cane. Jack, who had been dozing on the front porch, called Newt to walk his uncle home, and it was a welcome duty for Newt. Sarah wrapped some cold chicken and pie in a grocery sack and gave it to Rob. "You might git hungry this evenin'," she warned.

Rob took the package and smiled. "I might, at that," he said, "I might, at that. Thanks, Sarah." Newt gently took his wrist, helped him off the porch, and they went on their way.

A half hour later, as Newt sauntered back across town, he wrestled with his harsh dilemma (If I tell on Booker, there could be lots of trouble . . . and all the colored people might call me a snitch . . . and I'd sure have trouble with Marcus all the rest of my life . . . but it ain't right for Silas Newhall to go to prison for somethin' he didn't do either . . . still, Silas is white and he might get off easy . . . if I tell on Booker, lots more people might get killed . . .).

As he drifted down the quiet road he suddenly envisioned the blacks and whites of Cherokee Flats fighting each other—Pete and his father swinging clubs at the Mottsys and Simpsons and Stocktons, and all the houses burning and people screaming and fighting with guns and knives and himself fighting Waldo hitting and hitting his head with a rock and Kirky and some others dragging Booker through the streets with a rope around his neck and Booker screaming for help and Marcus trying to get him loose and being knocked down and his mother rushing in trying to stop all the fighting and yelling stop it! stop it! and Prissy hiding in the bedroom with Rende and Butsy and Gin-gin—and Rodney Cavanaugh hiding and crying in his big house on the hill with the blacks burning it down. . . .

"Hi, Newt." ,

He looked up, surprised. It was Waldo Newhall on his bicycle. "Hi—hi—how you doin', Waldo?"

"Want a lift home? Get on."

Newt thought Waldo looked very sad. He straddled the seat. Waldo shoved off, stood up on the pedals and pumped the last blocks to the Winger house. Newt got off, thanked him and started into the yard, wanting to leave Waldo as quickly as possible.

"Guess you heard about all the trouble Paw's in, huh?" Newt paused and turned back, wide-eyed. "Yeh—oh yeh—what's gonna happen?"

"Don't know—don't know."

"I'm awful sorry, Waldo."

"Think your maw'd let you drive me and Blanche over to the hospital to see Paw in a little while? Blanche ain't got no way to get over there."

"Why—why sure. I—I can ask her—for you, Waldo. I—"

"Okay, I'll go in with you now so Blanche'll know for sure."

Sarah was glad to help, so she told Newt to hitch up the horse to the buggy and drive them over. And in less than an hour Newt found himself standing with Blanche and Waldo outside Silas' room. Blanche had cried on the way over and Waldo had wanted Newt to go in with him.

"Not in the room," Newt had said.

"You can wait outside the door."

Blanche knocked and a nurse peeped out the door and said. "Yes?"

"I'm here to see my father," Blanche said tearfully.

"Oh," the nurse said. "He's just now come to, and I don't think you—hold on just a minute." She turned back into the room, leaving the door cracked.

"What you gittin' at, Kirky?" It was Silas' voice.

"You know what I'm gittin' at. You know well's I do—Jake's dead. And you kilt him!"

"You must be out'a your head. Why'd I do such a thing?"

The nurse came back with Doc Cravens, who stepped outside and closed the door behind him. "You're the Newhall children?"

"Yes," Blanche sniffled.

"Hello, Newt. What you doin' here?"

"He drove us over," Waldo answered quickly.

"Well, your father's been under sedatives most of the day. He's comin' around now. You wait out here for a few minutes and I'll take you in to see him." He opened the door and went back in. Kirky's voice came through the opening: "—and you done too much blabbin' 'fore you pulled it off. That's your trouble, Si—" Cravens shut the door behind him.

Blanche started crying again, and Waldo, not knowing what

169

to do, spread out his hands in a helpless gesture and looked at Newt.

It was nearly twenty-five minutes before Doc Cravens called in Blanche and Waldo. While they were inside, Newt sat on the floor and propped himself against the wall. This thing was growing too big for him. Twice in the buggy he'd been inclined to blurt out the truth, to relieve Blanche and Waldo of their anxiety. But confusion, more than anything else, stopped him. Now his thoughts were becoming even more jumbled, and suddenly he didn't trust himself on the ride back. He got to his feet and started toward the exit.

He was about to go through the hall door when he heard Blanche crying again as she and Waldo came toward him. "Kirky's stayin'," Newt thought.

It was pitch dark when they got back to the buggy, so Newt and Waldo lit the side lamps. As they rode along in the country darkness, Newt glued his mind to the sound of crickets in an effort to shut out any other thoughts whatsoever. The three of them were quiet all the way to the New-hall house, and then it was only after Blanche had gone in that Waldo spoke. "You know one thing, Winger?"

"What?" Newt asked nervously.

"I don't believe Paw killed anybody."

"Did he say he didn't?"

"Yeh. And I can tell when he's tellin' the truth, 'cause he lies so damned much."

"What'd he say?"

"Not much. He's still kind of dizzy from those drugs they been givin' him for pain. But he kept sayin' he thought he saw somebody else there besides Jake—thinks for sure he did."

Newt began chewing his lips. "Did he say what he looked like?"

"Said he looked colored."

"He said that sure enough?"

"Yeh, he said it, all right. But I don't think anybody much is gonna believe him. He's in a tough spot—a real tough spot."

"Maybe somethin'll happen, Waldo."

"Can't tell."

"Can't tell," Newt repeated.

Waldo jumped to the ground and thanked Newt, then moved on toward the house. Newt gazed after him a moment, then drove off. As he rode along he looked up at the sky. The moon was out. It was full, and the man in it was smiling.

Later that Sunday evening Marcus Savage was at the stove, heating leftover beef stew, when he heard Kirky's motorcycle screech to a halt at the front of the shack. He kept on stirring the greasy chunks in the bubbling gravy. (Wonder what that son-of-a-bitch wants here—somethin' to do with the killin', I bet.) A knock came on the door. "Yeh! What'a you want?"

The knob creaked, then Kirky was in the room. "Well, well—look who's cookin' Sunday dinner—Mista Savage's little innicent chile."

Without turning, Marcus spat in the coal bucket and kept on stirring. "What the hell you want here, brass-ass?" He spat again. "You come to give me a ride to church?"

"Watch your goddam trap, boy," Kirky snarled, "or you might have to dig my foot out'a your black ass!"

"You ain't got no biz'ness here, so git out! I had enough trouble out'a you."

"Well, you gonna have a lot more if you ain't got the right answers to some questions I'm gonna ask you."

"Yeh?"

"Yeh. Where was you b'tween one and four o'clock yestidy aftanoon?"

Marcus pulled two tin pans from the shelf above him. A cockroach jumped from the top one onto his arm. He shook it to the floor and squashed it with his foot before it could get away. He planked the tins on a nearby table, scraped the boiling stew equally into each one, pushed back a curtain and called out, "Come on to dinner, Paw!" Then, kicking a small barrel in place, he sat on it and began to eat.

"You hear my question, boy?" Kirky asked.

Marcus chewed out his retort. "How old you have to be in this stinkin' town 'fore white trash quit callin' you 'boy'?"

"Oh, ah begs yo pardon, Mista Savage, suh. Now would you mind tellin' this po, humble white trash where your sweet, noble black ass was yestidy b'tween one and four, please, suh—and what you did with all them green bottles'a peach brandy and applejack you stole out'a Jake's."

Marcus shot up like an uncoiling spring. "I was at your mammy's, you—" Kirky cocked his fist and moved forward.

"What's goin' on in here? What's all this fuss?" Booker Savage's big menacing frame, naked from the waist up, ambled through the doorway.

Kirky's arm dropped to his side. "I'm just tryin' to clear

171

your hotheaded son here from some trouble that's brewin', that's all. I'm tryin' to find out where he was when Jake Kiner was killed."

"Jake Kiner? Jake Kiner's dead? You kiddin'!"

"You ain't heard?"

"Naw—I been here all day, sleepin'."

"Well, he was killed yestidy in his barn."

Booker shook his head. "Ain't that somethin'." Then he turned on Marcus. "Well, where was you, boy? Where was you?"

Marcus grumbled. "I cleaned at Chappie's in the mornin', then I went to Blanche Newhall's and helped Waldo clean out her basement from 'bout twelve to five. That's where I was at. If you don't believe me, go and ask her yourself." He pulled a silver dollar from his pocket. "Right here's the money she give me for doin' it. Every goddamn bit of it."

"All right, boy, I'll ask her," Kirky scowled. "I'll sure ask her." He went out the door and banged it shut.

Marcus was still eating when, a few minutes later, Booker left the kitchen, went into the bedroom and returned with a blue shirt. Dark stains were on the lower sleeves. Booker lifted the stove lid and shoved the shirt in the fire. "Goddam chicken got blood all over me."

"What chicken?" Marcus asked.

"One I killed for Mag Pullens t'other day."

"Oh—"

Booker got drunker as the evening wore on, and eventually he stumbled to the other room and flopped down on the soggy pallet that he shared with his son. Before long he was snoring, groaning and cursing. Marcus couldn't stomach the racket, so he pulled two chairs together for a bed in the kitchen. They didn't suit him. Then he lay upon the floor for a few minutes, rolling from side to side, straining for comfort. Finally he remembered an old mattress he'd seen in the coal shed; he lit a lantern and went outside for it. He had already lifted the mattress and was turning back when his light struck the green bottles sticking up from the gunny sack (Where in hell'd the ole man git all that booze, I wonder ... must'a stole it someplace ...). He pulled the door to and started up the path, then he turned quickly and re-entered the shed, holding the light close to the bottles (Goddam ... Kirky said somethin' 'bout green bottles ... wonder if the ole man ... goddam, this is somethin' ... I cain't believe it ... goddam ...). He tossed an old quilt over the

172

bottles, shut the door and headed back toward the shack (Ain't this a bitch . . . ain't this a bitch . . .).

He was breathing heavily by the time he reached the kitchen door. Pushing it open with his shoulder, he closed it quietly behind him and dumped the mattress on the floor; then he put the lantern on the table and sat on a chair listening to the fitful snoring in the next room. Finally he jacked up the lantern chimney and blew out the flame, then leaned on the table, his arms crossed beneath his head. . . .

"O! O! O! loog out! loog out! Naw! Naw! Naw! . . . lemme go . . . lemme go . . . Aaaaw . . ." Marcus' head lifted to Booker's hollering, then dropped back wearily on his arms. He couldn't sleep—and he didn't try. He just closed his eyes and tried not to think.

The next morning, as Marcus peeped into the icebox, Booker staggered in holding a half-empty bottle of peach brandy. "You ain't gonna find nothin' to chaw on in that thing—ain't even no ice in it."

Marcus spoke without looking at his father. "I'm so hungry I could eat the bark off a tree."

Booker grunted, lifted the bottle to his mouth, took two hefty swallows and wiped his lips with the back of his wrist. "Well, 'less you spend that dollar you was showin' off when Kirky was here, you betta start skinnin' that big cottonwood 'side the house. It's got plenty bark." He grunted again and turned back toward the bedroom.

"Paw—where'd you git all that booze you got hid out in the shed?"

"What booze you talkin' 'bout, boy?" His red eyes were glowing with meanness as he wheeled drunkenly to face Marcus. "What booze you talkin' 'bout?"

"That booze in them green bottles in the gunny sack that was under this mattress, like the bottle you got in your hand now."

"What you been snoopin' round like a filthy black cat for? Spyin' on me or somethin'?"

"I wasn't snoopin'. I wanted the mattress to sleep on. You was hollerin' and fartin' all night, so I went out to the shed to git it—and come across all them bottles."

"Ain't none of your biz'ness where I got it. Keep your goddam trap shut or I'll put my fist in it." His body trembled under the fury of his threat.

Marcus eyed the bottle in his father's grasp. "Okay, Paw. Guess you know what you're doin', but if you don't, you betta ask somebody. And you know well as I do, ain't too many round here hankerin' for your askin'."

"What you gittin' at, boy?"

"I'm tryin' to say that if you got some kind of trouble, you ought'a tell me 'bout it. I'm your son, ain't I?"

"I had to take your maw's word for that, boy."

Marcus bristled. "Why, you—" He weighed his chances against the burly two hundred and fifty pounds, decided against finishing the sentence. Instead, he stood looking at Booker, feeling a hatred that even he thought himself incapable of possessing. All at once he shuddered, burst into a frantic sob and lunged toward his father with both fists flying—expecting to go down under a hail of blows and really not caring. But Booker just grabbed him about the waist and held him as if he were in a vise.

"Simmer down, boy. Simmer down—" He had become unexpectedly contrite. "Your ole man's sorry for sayin' such a thing. Honest, boy, I'm sorry." Gradually he released his hold and Marcus stood free, stunned at the first kind words he could ever remember his father speaking to him. And the tough shell that for years had shut him off from tender emotion gave way for an unusual moment—and Marcus gave himself to this rare instant in a flood of tears.

"You think I killed ole Jake, don't you, boy?" Marcus was silent. "Well, boy—I—I did kill him. I didn't mean to, but he caught me breakin' in his place and it was my only way out—and he hit me with that damn whip, same as he did you. You believe me, boy?"

"Yeh."

"It's our secret, ain't it, boy? Don't be forgittin' I'm your ole man. It could git us both in lots of trouble round here. You know that, don't you?"

"Yeh."

"Then I kin depend on you, huh?"

"Yeh."

"Good boy. Good boy." His hand went toward his son's shoulder, but Marcus avoided it and went out the door.

"Where you goin', boy?"

"Over to the bak'ry for some stale buns."

"Atta boy—atta boy. Uh—Marcus."

"Yeh?"

"Git a little coffee on your way back."

"Okay—okay."

Booker watched his son turn from the front path into the road. He rubbed his stubbly chin in a moment of thought, gulped another mouthful of brandy and returned to his greasy pallet.

That same morning Newt was scraping down the hog troughs when he heard Pete's voice at the barn door. "Must'a been workin' extra hard on Lucky. Coat's smooth as silk."

"She's a good girl—be two this fall."

Pete asked the question more directly than Newt had anticipated. "You know anything 'bout that killin'?"

"The killin'?" His mind was racing.

"Yep, the killin'."

"Naw—naw, I just said that—"

"Remember, I'm your brother—your own flesh and blood. You gotta tell me the honest-to-god truth."

Newt had thought at first he might be able to confide in his older brother. Now he felt it would be impossible to compromise Pete's honesty. "He'd tell Momma for sure," he thought. "What makes you think I ain't goin' to tell the truth? You ain't givin' me the chance to answer you."

"Okay, now you got the chance. Go ahead."

"Okay then." He feigned anger, stalling for time. "Let me say what I want to say."

"Go ahead. I'm listenin'."

"All I said before was I'd been doin' some hoein' for Jake lately."

"Not lately, Newt. Saturday. Ain't that right?"

"Yeh, that's right—but I left real early in the afternoon, 'cause I didn't think Jake would get back before five or six. And since Silas was fired and Missus Kiner was away, I sort of took off."

"Well, why'd you git so shaky yesterday when you told Poppa and then tried to back out of it the next minute?"

"I thought you caught on to what I was doin'—I got to thinkin', real quick, that Poppa would give me hell for sneakin' off the job like that. You know how he is, Pete. And you know as well as I do that it's crazy to get messed up in somethin' like this if you don't have to."

"Then you don't know anything 'bout the killin'?"

Newt's look of innocence contrived his answer. "You know doggone well I don't. I was just scared stiff 'cause I knew how close I was to it."

"Okay—okay—I see your point now. But if you're gonna go round tellin' people you was there on the day of the killin', you're gonna find yourself right in the middle of it."

Relief swept over Newt. "You're right there, Pete. I'm

keepin' my mouth shut from now on." He watched Pete stroll back toward the house. The matter was closed—and he felt that he'd given the right answers.

A few minutes later he had finished his chore. He went to the house, got his books and went off to school.

CHAPTER ✤ 15

A GRAND JURY indicted Silas Newhall for the murder of Jacob Elijah Kiner, and he spent the rest of June and all of July in the county jail at Fort Miles. During the first week of August he was brought back to Cherokee Flats to stand trial.

The prosecuting attorney was Stewart McCormack, a flamboyant, portly, white-maned lawyer from Fort Miles. McCormack had senatorial ambitions, and a conviction in such a case as this could further those ambitions. The defense was to be carried by Harley Davis, a red-haired young man from Cherryvale. He had finally accepted the unfavored case after Blanche Newhall traveled to his office twice in one week to persuade him. A need for money and experience, and his belief in Silas' innocence—after a three-hour talk with him—influenced his decision.

It was Tuesday, a very hot day, and the townspeople milled about the square, mopping sweat and talking about the trial. The jury had been picked and court was due to reconvene within an hour. Silas lay on his back watching a fly buzz about the top of his cell, darting in curving patterns from one wall to another. It started down, spun into a looping dive and struck his forehead. He swatted at it. The insect buzzed away, and Silas watched it sail between the iron bars to the outer room. He covered his eyes with his hands and lay waiting.

And while Silas lay there, Newt Winger was squirming in his seat during the science seminar, his mind wandering in a world of death, guilt and fear, with Professor Radeaker's voice puncturing his thoughts: "... the sciences include mathematics and logic, the physical sciences, such as physics and chemistry ... then there are the biological sciences, such as botany and zoology ... fourth, there are the social sciences, such as sociology and anthropology. Now, scientific study may be divided into these different categories ... and pure science summarizes and explains the facts and principles discovered about the universe and its inhabitants. Applied science uses these facts and principles to make experiments ... so both pure and applied science are necessary to bring the benefits of scientific research to—Newton Winger!"

"Yessir."

"Are you observing something of scientific nature out that window?"

"Aaa—yessir—I mean, nosir—"

"Well, in that case it might do you well to make notes, same as the rest of the class!"

"Yessir."

"Let's see now, where were we? Oh yes—we were on the necessity of both applied and pure science—"

Just about that time, Silas Newhall's cell door opened and Kirky entered with Harley Davis and a tray of food. Silas sat up.

"Here's your lawyer, and some victuals," Kirky drawled. "Looks to me you need 'em both purty bad."

Silas reached for the tray without answering, and nodded for Harley to sit beside him on the cot. The two didn't speak until Kirky left.

Harley placed his hand on Silas' knee. His tone was low and friendly. "Silas," he began, "I'm going to ask you a few questions—some I have asked you several times before. Answer them truthfully. I want to know exactly what I'm fighting out there this morning—the truth or a lie."

"Go ahead," Silas said, still chewing.

"Did you kill Jake Kiner?"

Silas lowered his eyes and stopped chewing. "It's like I told you before—I just don't know."

"Do you honestly feel that you didn't?"

"Yep. I feel that all right. I shore feel that."

"Why?" The question was fast and sharp.

"Well—"

"Why?"

"Well, I just wouldn't ever kill anybody, 'specially over a day's pay. I just wouldn't—that's all."

"But you went after him with the hoe."

"That was only to pr'tect myself 'gainst his whip."

"Would you swear you saw someone else there, besides Jake?"

"No—I don't s'pose I could swear to it."

"But you honestly think you did see someone else?"

"Yep."

178

"Do you remember what this someone looked like?"

"Nope. It just seemed like a dark form."

"You're sure now, Silas—you're sure?"

"Shore as I can be, since I was half out and drunk."

Harley rose to his feet and began walking slowly back and forth. "Eat, Silas. We don't have too much time." He continued pacing. "You know one thing, Silas?"

Silas looked up. "Yeh, Mister Davis?"

"Call me Harley—I believe you, Silas. I believe you're innocent. Now you've got to start believing in yourself. Do you understand?"

"Yep."

"You've got to believe that you didn't do this thing, and I've got to prove that you didn't do it. Do you understand?"

Before Silas could answer, a shattering sound came at the window and glass showered over the cell floor. Someone had thrown a rock through the bars from the street. Silas started to get up, but Harley motioned him back on the cot and inched toward the window.

"What bastard did that?" Silas asked nervously.

Harley was peering into the street from behind the wall now. "It's some young—" He ducked, and another rock banged against the bars and dropped back to the ground. "It's some young dudes whooping it up down in—"

"We gonna git you! You killin' bastard! We gonna git your ass! You ain't gonna git off with life, you bum!" someone shouted from below.

Harley grabbed Silas' spoon and banged it against the bars of the door for five minutes before Kirky finally came. "You still got another twenty minutes 'fore trial time," Kirky protested as Harley bounded past him toward the outer door. "Where you goin' in such a hurry?"

"To the Judge's chambers," Harley snapped back, "that's where I'm going."

Twenty minutes later, Jeff Cavanaugh was standing high on the flat base of Thomas Jefferson's statue in the center of the town square, and a crowd had closed in to hear what he had to say. Kirky and the two lawyers were directly beneath him and Mary Kiner stood just in front of them. Jeff remained erect and unruffled, looking very much like the man with whose image he now shared the marble platform. After a considerable wait, he raised his long arms above the crowd for silence.

A stillness came over the crowd as Jeff began:

"Fellow townsmen, I am going to speak to you—not as a

179

judge or as a member of the legal body of our State—but as a friend. A few minutes ago some irresponsible persons threw stones through a prisoner's window from the street. You all know who the prisoner is, and why he is in there. In case you don't, let me inform you. He is Silas Newhall, a citizen of our town, who is about to go on trial for his life. A reliable jury of twelve people has been picked from amongst you." (Jeff wiped the sweat from his face.) "If he is found guilty, I will, in the name of our State, pronounce sentence to fit his crime. Not a soul here would be denied the same chance we are about to give Silas Newhall. The widow of Jacob Kiner, for whose death the charges in question were brought, stands here below me. She is a woman who is as anxious as anyone —even more so, I should say—to see that justice is done. But she asks that there be no violence of any sort and that you leave it in the hands of your courts to decide the fate of the man there in that cell. This woman has suffered more than any one of us here. Let none of us do her or our country the disservice of denying her that simple request. We here must yield to the right that is within us. There is none here who hasn't erred. And all of us, at one time or another, have been wrongly accused when we were innocent. Such injustice leaves a terrible scar. If we were not to give Silas Newhall an unbiased trial, our crime would be far greater than the one we are about to explore—one which I promise to preside over in all conscience, in all fairness and without favor or fear of anyone. I have the power to bring in U. S. troops, if necessary, to carry out Mary Kiner's request, but my faith in you is as solid as this base on which I stand. Please, I beg you, do not destroy that faith." He stood for a minute looking into the faces of the crowd that stretched out to the street, then he said, "That is all," and got down.

A few minutes later, Kirky returned to Silas' cell with Harley. He unlocked the door and said, "Silas."

"Yeh."

"Time to go." He opened the door, motioned Silas out and shackled his wrist. Then the three of them started down the corridor toward the courtroom.

"Well," Harley smiled, "here we go. Are you okay?"

"Reckon so, Harley. Reckon so."

"Don't get excited now."

"Too late for that now, Harley. Too late for that."

"There's going to be a lot of people in there. Keep your head up and face them. Don't start off looking guilty."

"Hope Waldo ain't there."

"Be better if he is."

"Why?"

"Don't worry over things like that. That's my job."

"Okay, in this way," Kirky grunted.

Silas' heart beat faster. "I feel licked already."

"Remember your promise—"

They were through the door now and in the courtroom. The spectators turned as one toward Silas, their voices building up all around him. He kept his head high, as he had been told, but his eyes shifted all over the courtroom. Blanche and Waldo were near the front to the left. Silas glanced at them, then at Mary Kiner, who sat on the far side of the room. She was dressed in black and wore a veil over her head. The seats were filled and a number of people stood around the walls. Most of the Negroes sat on the left side and near the rear.

"Sit down here." Kirky removed the handcuffs and sat behind Harley and Silas on the same bench with Blanche and Waldo.

Someone banged on the wooden table up front. "Everybody rise!"

Harley touched Silas and they rose with the crowd. Jeff Cavanaugh came in from a side door dressed in a long black robe.

"Hear ye, hear ye, the court is now in session!" the bailiff bawled out.

"... the Honorable Justice Jefferson Cavanaugh presiding..."

Harley touched Silas again and they sat down.

There was a moment of silence, and Jeff motioned for Harley Davis and Stewart McCormack. The two lawyers approached the Judge's bench, and the three of them talked quietly for a few seconds, then the lawyers returned to their seats. Jeff's gavel banged for silence. The jury was asked to stand and was sworn in by the droning bailiff.

Jeff's gavel sounded again. "Ladies and gentlemen of the jury, the State of Kansas has charged the defendant, Silas Newhall, with the first-degree murder of Jacob Kiner. During this trial the prosecuting attorney will make statements about what he intends to prove and about the way he feels the crime was committed. Likewise, the attorney for the defense will make statements on what he intends to prove and will attempt to show the defendant innocent of the charges that have been lodged against him. I must caution you that state-

181

ments by either of the counsels is not to be considered as evidence by you. The evidence comes solely from witnesses, documents, articles, utensils or any other items used as an exhibit toward proof in this case. You are to appraise this evidence by the manner in which it is given, by the motives for which it is given and the vantage points from which the witnesses were able to observe the facts to which they testify —and from all these facts it is your sworn duty to determine what consideration, if any, is to be given their testimony. Do not discuss testimony or any other aspects of the trial amongst yourselves, with your family or your friends. Unless you are instructed to do so by the court, do not visit the scene of the murder. Above all, keep an open mind. This crime and these charges are serious ones indeed! Now, did each of you understand me clearly?"

All nodded affirmatively.

"Then let us proceed." Jeff cleared his throat. "Mr. District Attorney, you may now present State evidence and witnesses."

Stewart McCormack rose, his hands grasping the lapels of his coat, his pince-nez glasses shaking on the bridge of his fat nose. He began, "May it please Your Honor, Mr. Foreman and ladies and gentlemen of the jury. My opening statement seems hardly necessary in the true light of this atrocity, but I make it because the law states that I must. Actually it is a good thing, because the details of this dastardly crime must lie fresh before you if you are to understand the serious business we are about. The charge against this defendant, Silas Newhall, is murder in the first degree. The indictment is not in itself any proof, but a charge made by the grand jury which the defendant is called upon to meet— and which the people must prove beyond a reasonable doubt.

"It reads: 'The grand jury of the County of Becker by this indictment accuses Silas Newhall of the crime of murder in the first degree, committed as follows: That the said Silas Newhall, of Cherokee Flats, in the County of Becker and the State of Kansas, on the fourteenth day of June in the year 1926, on the farm of the deceased, in the county aforesaid, with a blunt instrument, with force, willfully, feloniously, and with malice aforethought, beat and killed one Jacob Kiner with a certain blunt instrument, contrary to the form of the statute in such case made and provided, and against the peace of the people of the State of Kansas and their dignity.' The witnesses and this brutal evidence will bring home to you, more than any statement of mine, the vileness of this offense against heaven and humanity."

Silas' head lifted and he saw the crowbar on the table for the first time. He stirred nervously and Harley's hand pressed against his leg.

During his pause, McCormack's eyes swept the courtroom in hypnotic glare, falling at last on Silas. "—And there, ladies and gentlemen, sits the beast who—"

Harley was on his feet. "I object, Your Honor, to such reference to this defendant."

"Objection sustained. Watch your language, counsel."

"I'm sorry, Your Honor. We intend to prove that he (his left hand pointed at Silas) did with premeditation and willfulness, murder the deceased with (his right hand reached for the crowbar and he waved it through the air) this instrument—in cold blood!" Silas winced and shut his eyes against the outburst. "We will prove that he even boasted publicly of his intentions before actually committing the crime! We will prove that he attempted to steal from the premises of the deceased, after being befriended and hired by this very same man he so heartlessly bludgeoned with this iron (he smacked the crowbar against the table) instrument of death." He paused again and looked about the hushed room.

"But I didn't steal nothin' from—"

"Quiet, Silas—take it easy. We'll have our turn."

McCormack wiped the sweat from the creases in his neck and continued. "I am here, as your servant, to emphasize the meaning of this indictment against one whose guilt is as clear as the charge. It would indeed be difficult for the State to produce a more damaging piece of evidence than this iron crowbar, used for intended burglary and eventually murder, found, mind you, in the defendant's hand—only a few feet from the man who had been beaten to death with it. Jake Kiner's blood is still on it and so are the fingerprints of the accused. This too we will prove in due time. In fact, during his arraignment, the defendant readily admitted boasting to half of Cherokee Flats that he was going to 'git'—yes, that's the very word he used, 'git'—Jake Kiner. Unfortunately, he made good his boast, and it is up to the State to see that he pays the ultimate penalty."

McCormack clasped his hands together beneath his chest. His head dropped forward and his voice was very low and wavering. "I would have liked to spare this woman and you, ladies and gentlemen of the jury, the gory details of this vile crime, but duty prevails upon me, in the interest of our society, to lay the facts, cruel though they are, before you. And it is better that I did. For when at last the penalty is extracted, we can all say and know that justice was indeed triumphal."

Silas watched as McCormack's face swept the jury. The back of his white linen suit was soaked with sweat. "It is my intention, as Prosecuting Attorney for this State, to prove, beyond a reasonable doubt, the charges we have brought—we are going to show that when the body of Jake Kiner was found there was evidence of considerable bleeding and severe wounds; that the man was a victim of burglary and robbery; also that this death was not only committed in a brutal manner—repeated beating over the head, showing deliberate intent to kill—but also that it was committed with unwarranted vengefulness.

"Ladies and gentlemen, you will hear about Silas Newhall. You will hear reliable people testify to statements he made, and we ask you to pay particular attention to these witnesses, to all of the evidence, and we know you will withhold your judgment until the entire case is concluded and then render a verdict according to your conscience and good common sense, and according to the evidence in this case. I thank you."

A rumbling of the crowd began. Silas stole a side glance at Waldo, who sat next to Blanche. Waldo was biting his fingernails. The Judge's banging gavel snapped Silas' head around. "The attorney for the defense may now address the jury if he so wishes," Cavanaugh said.

Harley rose.

"Your Honor, Mr. Foreman, ladies and gentlemen of the jury. On behalf of the defendant, Silas Newhall, I want to let you know we are cognizant of the sacrifices that you are making to be here, and the deprivations of your own families, but it is our jury system that is the bulwark of our judicial order in this country, and without it our system of equality and justice would suffer; so I am sure that this morning each of you is aware of your responsibility in this case. As the Honorable Justice has informed you, both Mr. McCormack and myself will attempt to prove certain things to you. We will make statements contradictory to one another's, I am sure, but in the end it must be you who will decide the truth.

"We, the defense, do not come here this morning seeking pity or sympathy. We simply ask that you give us your open minds, and our evidence your considerate appraisal. We will show that on the day in question, this defendant, unarmed,

184

at some hour in the afternoon of June fourteenth, went to the farm of the deceased with no intent to burglarize or kill, but solely for the purpose of business—namely, to collect monies that were owed him by the deceased.

"We will show further that when the defendant did not leave as quickly as the deceased thought he should have, the deceased attempted to forcibly evict him, that it was at this point that he, the deceased, attacked the defendant and repeatedly beat him about his face and head; that it was therefore after this defendant was attacked, while he was in fear of his own safety and when he had no other alternative, that the defendant picked up a hoe, not the instrument exhibited, and attempted to defend himself; but that before he had a chance to use it he was knocked down by the deceased, then beaten to unconsciousness while he was on the floor, not regaining consciousness until he was in the Fort Miles County Hospital, where he found himself handcuffed to a bed.

"We indicated in our questioning of you that our defense is and will be based on a plea of not guilty of any of the charges made in the indictment. We intend to show you that the wounds and abrasions on this defendant were inflicted by the deceased in a fit of violent temper. We intend to show you that the deceased, not the defendant, was the aggressor.

"We intend to show you that the wounds inflicted on the deceased, causing his death, were not inflicted by the defendant's but by another's hand.

"I say in conclusion that the defense feels confident, from the questions propounded to you and the forthright answers you made to questions, that you intend to be fair in this case, and that is all that we ask. We do beg you to listen to the evidence carefully and judge this defendant's guilt or innocence solely upon the events as presented in this case—and with that, we leave the fate of this defendant in your hands. Thank you."

Harley returned to his seat.

Cavanaugh spoke now. "Due to the late start, the court will be adjourned until one o'clock. Can we begin hearing testimony from the State witnesses at that time, counsel?"

"Yes, Your Honor. We will be ready," McCormack answered forthrightly, as he popped to his feet.

Back in his cell, Silas tried eating a piece of ham and some string beans which had been brought to him. But the ham was too tough and the beans too raw, so he pushed them aside and gulped a couple of swallows of steaming black coffee. Then he sat there, staring at the wall, seemingly defeated. He had already confided his fears to Harley after what he considered a "damagin'" speech by Stewart McCormack.

The hour passed swiftly, and he was taken back into the courtroom. During the first few minutes there was a conference, in secretive tones, among the lawyers and the Judge. When Harley was back beside him, Silas asked, "How's it goin'?"

"Okay—okay," Harley answered.

"The State will now call its witnesses!"

McCormack was up, a look of confidence on his face. "Yes, Your Honor. Will Officer Jason Kirky please take the stand?"

"Yessuh," Kirky drawled. He got up gingerly and strode toward the witness stand. As he stepped up, he stumbled— and faint laughter flitted through the courtroom. He stood up straight, raised his hand and was sworn in.

"Officer Kirky, you visited the scene of the crime immediately after it was committed, didn't you?"

"Yessuh, I did."

"What did you find when you arrived?"

"Jake and Silas was both out on the floor."

"Would you please elaborate—or describe more fully the situation as you found it?"

"Well, Jake was layin' in a pool'a blood—"

"Was he dead yet?"

"Aw, yessuh. Dead as a door nail."

"Go ahead, Officer Kirky."

"Well, Silas there was sprawled out and moanin' somethin' crazy-like. I shook him but he didn't make no sense a'tall— jest kept moanin'."

"Did he have anything in his hand or close to his person resembling the weapon we have there on the table before the court?"

"I object, Your Honor!" Harley said. "Mr. McCormack is leading the witness."

"Sustained. Counsel, please rephrase your question."

"Sorry, Your Honor." McCormack paused. "What did you see other than the deceased and the defendant on the floor?"

"That crowbar that's layin' there. It was layin' under Silas' hand when I got there."

"Did you find anything else irregular?"

"Irreg'lar?"

"On the prem—in the barn. Near the dead man."

"Oh—oh, yessuh. The door to the little room where ole Jake kept his peach brandy and stuff was yanked off the hinges."

"In other words, it appeared as though the defendant used the crowbar to rip the door off its hinges and—"

"I object, Your Honor. The prosecuting attorney is putting words in the witness's mouth. The witness is being questioned for facts and not what appears to be fact," Harley protested.

"But, Your Honor," McCormack intoned, "I'm trying to establish a likely situation developing out of an additional motive here—"

"Objection sustained. Defense counsel is correct. Personal conjecture is not expected of the witness here."

"Very well, Your Honor, I am indeed sorry. I will phrase my question differently." McCormack patted his wet brow with a handkerchief, then continued, "Officer Kirky, was the crowbar used for breaking into the room the same as the one used as a murder weapon?"

"Well, the grooves in the wood that was smashed, they fit the same size crowbar. I found out that much."

"That's all for now, Officer Kirky. Thank you."

Judge Cavanaugh pulled off his glasses and looked down. "Would the defense care to cross-examine?"

"I would, Your Honor." Harley got up, approached the stand and said promptly, "Officer Kirky, what was the condition of the defendant when you found him?"

"He was layin' out on the floor like I said, and he was groanin'."

"You say he was groaning. Was he bleeding from any parts of his body or face?"

"Well, not so much when I got there, but you could see where the blood had been runnin' out his nose and down over his lips and chin."

"What condition was his face in?"

"All black and blue-like."

"Would you say he had been beaten rather severely about the head and face?"

"Yessuh, he took quite a wallopin', all right."

"Did the defendant smell of alcohol at the time?"

"Yessuh. He smelled like he'd been dunked in a keg of it."

"You testified that the crowbar was laying under the defendant's hand. Which hand was it?"

"Let me see—uh—the left hand. That's right, the left hand."

"Did you later inspect it for fingerprints?"

"Not me. We had a expert do that—Mr. Wiggins from Fort Miles, there in the second row."

"Did you find the article which the defendant had been beaten with?"

"Yessuh."

"Where?"

"By Jake's body."

"What was it?"

"A whip."

"Are you saying that a whip could inflict the kind of bruises that were on the defendant's head and face?"

"It was the heavy handle part, so Doc Cravens said."

"Were there indications of a violent struggle—that is, apart from the condition of the deceased and the defendant?"

"Not so much. There was a hoe on the floor and a few scuffle marks showin' on the boards."

"Thank you, Officer Kirky. That will be all for now."

McCormack's next witness was Clarence Wiggins, the fingerprint and blood expert. His testimony was brief, establishing the fact that Silas' fingerprints were on the weapon and that the blood on the crowbar was that of Jake. Then Harley faced him. "Mr. Wiggins, you say you inspected the crowbar in question and found the fingerprints of the defendant on it."

"Yes, sir, I did."

"Which hand?"

"The prints of the left hand were the only ones found on the instrument."

"Only the left hand?"

"Yes, sir."

"Did you find other fingerprints on the same crowbar?"

"Yes, there were some weaker impressions that I believe to have been those of the deceased. I also found a stronger impression of two other hands."

"Two others?"

"Yes, sir."

"Did you find out who they—these other two hands—belonged to?"

"No, sir, I haven't."

"Have you tried?"

"Yes, sir."

"Would you say the two foreign sets of fingerprints belonged to the same person?"

"Yes, I would say they did."

188

A murmur came from the crowd, and Harley said, "Thank you, Mr. Wiggins, that will be all."

During the remainder of the afternoon McCormack brought several witnesses to the stand. Silas knew all of them but two—a shaggy-haired, unshaven man named Dilly Case, who claimed he had heard Silas threatening to "git" Jake for not paying him the money he had coming; and a Mrs. Betty Link, a blond woman, who said she had only moved to Cherokee Flats three days before the murder, but that she had seen Silas drunk the night preceding the slaying and had also heard him make threats against Jake's life.

"Now, Mrs. Link. It is Mrs., isn't it?" Harley cross-examined.

"Yes 'tis. My husband ain't livin' here—but I'm still married to him."

"Fine. Now, Mrs. Link, you said you heard the defendant making threats against the life of the deceased."

"Shore did."

"Just exactly what did he say, word for word?"

Betty Link sat up straight as though she was starched from the middle upward. Pursing her highly rouged lips, she pulled her tight skirt down over her knees before answering. "He said somethin' like—"

"Not something like, Mrs. Link. We want to know exactly what he said. Try hard now. Stop and think."

She was silent for a second or two, then she said, "First off, he was drunk and his words was kind of slurry—"

"Slurry?"

"Yeah, sorta runnin' into each other, but I heard him say, 'I'm gonna git my money from that old skinflint or die tryin'.' Yeah, that's exactly what he said—and somethin' about 'over my dead body.'"

"Mrs. Link, can you remember ever having said such a thing as 'I'll die trying' or 'over my dead body' when you were very determined to accomplish or prevent something you felt strongly about?"

McCormack was up. "Your Honor, I object. The inference is irrelevant and of no consequence in this case."

"Your Honor, I intend to establish that common use is made of such a statement by many of us in normal everyday conversations."

"I see no harm in this question, Mr. McCormack."

Harley turned back to the witness. "Do you remember ever having made such remarks as these, Mrs. Link?"

"'Course. When Charley—my husband—told me he was

gonna git a divorce from me, the first thing I said was 'over my dead body.' " Laughter filled the courtroom.

Jeff's gavel banged for quiet. "If quiet isn't maintained here, this room will be emptied of all spectators. Proceed, counsel."

"To whom was the defendant speaking when he made these remarks?"

"I don't know who the man was. All I know was that he was colored and that he was drunk too."

"Where did all this take place, Mrs. Link?"

Betty Link's face turned noticeably pink. "Well—well— I'd heard about this late-hour place called Chappie's and thought I'd drop in to see what it was like."

"Chappie Logan's?"

"Yeah. That's what they call the joint—place—or—"

"What time was this, Mrs. Link?"

"Oh, about two-thirty in the mornin' or a little later."

"Did your escort hear the threat also?"

"Escort?"

"Yes. Didn't someone accompany you there?"

"Nope. I was just sorta driftin' round by myself that night."

"One more question. Did you hear the defendant call the name of the deceased at any time?"

"He just kept callin' him an old skinflint."

"Then how do you know he was referring to the deceased?"

"Well, it all came back to me when I heard about the murder and saw his picture on the front page of the paper."

"Whose picture?"

"His. The Newhall man."

"Thank you, Mrs. Link. That will be all."

"Can I git down now, Judge?" she cooed.

"You may, Mrs. Link."

After the evening adjournment, Harley went along with Silas and Kirky to the prisoner's cell. Kirky said, "Your dinner'll be comin' in soon's I git mine. Take it easy. You stayin', Mister Counsel?"

"For just a little while. Come back in about ten or fifteen minutes, Kirky."

Rain was beginning to fall outside, and Silas moved to the broken window and peered out at the square. He could see people ducking in and out of buildings. And as the humid warmth of evening drifted through the window he wiped the sweat from his bony face. "I'll be glad when all this is over." He plopped down on his cot. "How long do we have to listen to that flour-headed old goat paradin' that bunch of lyin' dogs up to that witness chair? Why don't they just go on and give me life like they're gonna do anyhow?"

"That's no way to feel, Silas." Harley's answer was given without much feeling. His mind was groping for something more important.

"I don't much care how I feel right now."

Suddenly Harley reached into his satchel and pulled out some loose papers. "Here, hold these a minute, Silas. I figured out something a while ago."

Silas' hand went out for the papers. "What's these for?" Harley closed his satchel. "Now hold this for a second."

"What's all this for?" Silas asked, shifting the papers to his other hand and taking the satchel.

"Are you left-handed or right-handed, Silas?"

"Why, I'm right-handed. Why?"

"That's just what I thought. We've got a little something working for us, old boy. Just a little something."

The trial droned on, and on Thursday night of the second week Newt tossed about in his bed, trying to fight off the secret weighing so heavily upon him. At the dinner table he'd heard his father size up Silas Newhall's chances. "He's goin' up for life shore as I'm sittin' here. He's got 'bout as much of a chance as a feather in a wind storm."

"Too bad—too bad all the way round—for Mary, for Blanche and Waldo—and Silas. I'll never understand why he did such an awful thing," Sarah said.

Three o'clock came, and though Newt closed his eyes against the night his thoughts boiled on. "A man's whole life is at stake. But if I tell the truth, a lot more people might git killed, even some of us right here in this house."

He continued rolling and thinking. It was four-thirty by the time he decided to lift the weight from his shoulders, and he went through the darkness to his mother's room.

He touched her gently on the shoulder. "Momma." She stirred slightly and rolled over toward Jack, who snored like a fog horn. The next moment Newt was against telling her, but as he started toward the door a board creaked under his weight and Sarah came awake.

"Who's that?"

"It's me, Newt, Momma."

"What's the matter, boy? Havin' bad dreams?"

"It's lot worse'n that."

Sarah was sitting upright now. "Come here and sit down by me," she whispered. "What's troublin' you, son?"

Newt sank to the bed and started telling his story. "Wait a minute," his mother said. "We'd better go out in the livin' room. We don't want to wake your poppa." She rose and wrapped a blanket about her, and they went in and sat together on the divan.

Newt, his mind unraveling like a ball of yarn, poured out the nightmare hurriedly, as if he couldn't wait to rid himself of it. When he was finished, the two of them just sat there until dawn without saying any more to each other. Toward six o'clock the room gradually filled with a soft light. Sarah was still awake, but Newt was sleeping peacefully now, his head against his mother's shoulder, his mind free for the first time in two months.

When Jack awoke later, Sarah told him Newt's story and the three of them decided that nothing further was to be said until Sarah talked with Judge Cavanaugh.

She told Jeff just before he sat down to breakfast, and then he slumped down to his chair, rubbing the mahogany arms. "This is fantastic, Sarah! Do you think the boy is really telling the truth?"

"I know he is. I know he is," she sighed.

"Does anyone besides you and Jack know about this?"

"No, no one."

"Good—good. Now Sarah, this is a ticklish situation. As a judge trying this case, it would be highly improper for me to divulge this information. You must do it. And the proper person to receive such information is the Prosecuting Attorney. You'd better prepare to come to court today with Newt and Jack. I'll call for a two-hour recess so you'll have sufficient time with Mr. McCormack. I would rather he didn't know you told me. In case he asks if you told me, I would advise you to say that you did. But don't volunteer it. Do you understand?"

Sarah said she did and that she would get Newt and her husband and appear at the trial. "Do you think he—Mr. McCormack—will listen to me, Judge?" she asked.

"You just hand him a sealed note when I call for a recess and tell him you are supposed to wait for an answer. Just write that you have some very important information concerning the case and that you would like to talk with him in his office during lunchtime. He'll listen to you. Don't worry."

"You'd better tell me just what to write, Judge. I may not say just the right things."

Jeff dictated the note. Sarah sealed it in a plain envelope and stuffed it in her apron pocket. "Another thing," Jeff added, "try not to let anyone see you hand him the note. Come through the side door. I'll have the bailiff save seats for you."

After that, Justice Jefferson Cavanaugh had his breakfast and then went off to open the morning session of the trial.

After serving Silas a breakfast of lumpy, lukewarm oatmeal, cold biscuits and black coffee, Kirky said, "You look pale, Silas. Somethin' gittin' your spirits down?"

"Naw, but this slop you feed me is ruinin' my insides."

"Well now, ain't that somethin'! Our celebrity's complainin' 'bout his victuals." Kirky chuckled. "It's a lot worse at the big house, a lot worse. You take my word for it."

Later, when court reconvened, Harley noticed the dark rings under Silas' eyes and he attempted to cheer him up. "Blanche and Waldo told me to tell you that they are pulling for you, Silas."

"I got a feelin' they'll need a twenty-mule team to help pull me out'a this."

"We're all doing the best we can. Keep up your faith."

"I'd be glad to if I had any left, Harley. I know you're tryin', but there just ain't much to go on."

"It'll work out. Don't worry."

All that morning the witnesses kept coming. And in spite of Harley's frequent objections, a picture of Silas emerged, portraying what the town had known him to be over the years, when he wobbled up and down the streets and alleyways of Cherokee Flats, swearing to himself in his drunkenness. An official of the welfare agency told of his children being shunted from one house to another after their mother's death. And the black picture grew blacker.

Sarah, Jack and Newt Winger arrived in the middle of the morning session, and the three of them squeezed into a spot the bailiff had reserved upon instruction of the Judge.

Jack Winger leaned close to Newt, whispering, "You all set?"

"Yessir." Newt was looking away as he answered, his face gone ashen, his heart constricted at the sight of Booker and Marcus Savage sitting unperturbed in the middle of the room.

"What's the matter, boy?" Jack noticed Newt's tenseness.

"Booker and Marcus are here."

"You shore?"

"Yessir, right in the center there."

"Well, I declare," Jack muttered to himself.

When the noon recess was called, Sarah felt the Judge's eyes upon her and her hand automatically squeezed the envelope in her pocket.

Quickly Sarah was at the lawyer's side, the note held close and low to her side. "Mister McCormack."

"Yes—yes. What can I do for you?"

"Here is a note for you."

McCormack took the envelope and slipped it in his pocket. "Well, thank you, lady. Thank you." He started to move away.

"I'm supposed to wait for a answer."

"An answer? For whom?" The courtroom was emptying now. Only a few stragglers, lagging behind in gossip, approached the exit. Newt and his father stood by the wall on the far side of the courtroom.

"You'd better read it now, sir," Sarah said. "It's awful important."

McCormack looked at her, then glanced at Jack and Newt waiting on the side. "Those two waiting for you?"

"It's my husband and son."

He tore open the envelope and read the note. "What's this all about, lady?"

"About this case—and it's awful important."

McCormack pulled out his watch and checked the time. His impatience was mounting. "Well, hurry—come on in this side room over here."

"I'll need my son and husband, too."

"Okay, but let's hurry. It's lunchtime."

McCormack listened impatiently for a half hour, then he grumbled, "Why didn't you volunteer this information earlier, boy?"

"He was scared of race trouble," Jack cut in.

"That's no excuse—no excuse whatsoever. I hope, for your sake, you haven't told anyone about this except your parents."

"Nosir, I didn't."

"Good—good, because, whether you know it or not, you could be seriously implicated yourself. You might even wind up behind bars too."

"What you think I should do?"

"Only one thing. Since you've waited this late—keep your mouth shut and let me handle it from here."

"But—"

"No buts, boy. You're lucky you came to me instead of someone else. Now don't, under any circumstances, reveal this to anyone else . . . Understand?"

"Yessir—I understand."

"Fine. Now I must be off to lunch." Then McCormack was through the door and gone. Sarah, Jack and Newt moved slowly into the corridor. Silently and nervously they ate some sandwiches Sarah had prepared.

Meanwhile, Booker and Marcus devoured two bowls of chili in the backroom at Chappie Logan's. Later, heading back toward the courthouse, Booker told Marcus the trial would probably be over in less than a week.

"Yeh," Marcus agreed. "Looks like old Silas's gonna git it."

"Yeh, shore does."

Ten minutes later they mixed into the crowd that was flowing back into the courtroom.

Stewart McCormack called Sam Stockton to the witness chair, and he told of seeing Silas, in a drunken condition, going in the direction of the Kiner farm that fatal afternoon. Two other witnesses testified to about the same and Harley declined to cross-examine them.

The rain had stopped. The late sun was splashing against the drab courtroom walls, and Newt sat nervously awaiting the moment when he would be called to give the testimony that would perhaps free Silas and maybe at the same time set off a racial explosion worse than he dared imagine. Then, unexpectedly, McCormack turned in the direction of Mary Kiner.

"My dear Mrs. Kiner, if it isn't too much for you, the State would like for you to take the witness chair." There was a stir in the room as Jake's widow rose slowly and made her way to the chair.

"Now, Mrs. Kiner, we won't hold you long or ask you many questions. God in heaven knows you have suffered enough. But it is my duty as the State's Attorney, to leave no stones unturned in our relentless search for the truth. Now, Mrs. Kiner, will you please tell the court why your husband hired the defendant, knowing too well that he was an habitual drunk and of unsavory character?"

"I object!"

"Objection sustained."

"Sorry, Your Honor. I will rephrase the question. Now Mrs. Kiner, why did your husband hire Silas Newhall?"

"Well—Jake was like that. He believed in givin' everybody a chance. Silas asked him for such a chance because everybody else turned him down, and Jake gave it to him."

"How long did he work for your husband before he—uh—this unfortunate thing happened?"

"Oh, 'bout two months, I guess. I don't recall the exact day he hired him."

"Did he do his job well?"

"Well, yes he did till up near the end when he started drinkin' again."

"You and Mr. Kiner were very happy together, weren't you?"

"Oh my, yes. We had our little fusses now and then, but I loved—" Tears welled in her eyes.

"Do you wish to stop for a while, Mrs. Kiner?"

She reached beneath the veil and dabbed at her eyes. "No —no—I'm sorry—I can go on now."

"Do you feel, or know rather, whether or not your husband owed the defendant any more money—that is, after he had fired him?"

"I just don't know 'bout that part of it. But I cain't imagine Jake not payin' anybody he owed. He just wasn't like that. And everybody round these parts knows that."

"Where were you when this awful thing happened?"

"I'd come into town for shoppin' in the mornin' with Jake, then later in the day I went to have his glasses fixed. He had busted the ear-piece on one side of them. Silas was at the gate when we got back and he started arguing with Jake—and I went on in the house to fix some lunch. Then I went to the barn to call Jake to eat."

"Now, Mrs. Kiner, we are just about through with the questions. I sincerely hope this will be the last of this, but it is very important to tell the court what you saw when you went to the barn to call your husband in for lunch. Just take it easy and tell us as simply as possible."

She paused for a moment, wiped at her nose, braced herself by placing her elbows on the arms of the chair and brought her hands together in a firm grip. "Well, I came across the field—the barn door was hangin' open—and I first caught sight of Silas, on the floor. I first thought maybe he was just drunk—but then I saw Jake's hand—I was afraid to look in—but I did and—"

"Go on, Mrs. Kiner."

"—and there he was—all bloody and everything—"

"Yes?"

"I could tell from the looks of him—that he was dead—"

"What did you do then?"

"I—I—I—"

"Easy, Mrs. Kiner. Easy now."

"I just run back across the field to the house and called

the operator—and told her—my husband—oh oh oh—" She had lost complete control now, and McCormack whipped out his silk handkerchief and put it in her trembling hands.

"That will be all now, Mrs. Kiner—unless the defense wishes to cross-examine." Harley motioned negatively. Then McCormack walked slowly back to the front of the courtroom. He stepped squarely in front of the jury and stood looking at them for a few seconds, as if trying to gauge their compassion, their sorrow, their hatred for this man upon whom they would soon be called to pass judgment. Then he turned toward the bench and said, "Your Honor, the State closes its case."

Jeff Cavanaugh's eyebrows raised and he stared at McCormack as though in disbelief.

There was silence. Since it was late, both counsel awaited the familiar words of adjournment as Jeff continued staring at McCormack. Finally, he asked, "Will the defense present witnesses tomorrow?"

"Yes, Your Honor."

"Then court is adjourned until eleven o'clock tomorrow morning." Jeff then closed his notebooks and stood up.

On the way out Sarah whispered to Jack that she was surprised that Mr. McCormack hadn't called Newt to the stand. "Oh, he's prob'ly got somethin' up his sleeve. He'll prob'ly call him tomorra sometime."

"But you don't understand, Jack. He said that the State rested its case. That means he's through prosecutin'."

"Aw, you must be wrong, Sarah," Jack said. "These legal doin's ain't easy to understand. The Judge'll explain it all to you tonight."

Newt didn't venture an opinion. He was relieved at not having been called to the witness stand. He and his father walked Sarah to within a block of the Cavanaugh house. Then they turned back toward home.

Sarah had just come through the door and was putting on her apron when the Judge called from his study, "Sarah! Sarah! That you?"

"Be there in a minute, Judge!" She scurried along the hall, sensing urgency in his voice.

He met her halfway. "Didn't you tell Mr. McCormack what you were supposed to tell him?"

"Yessir, I did."

"Everything?"

"Yessir, we talked to him for—"

Rodney came through the front door loaded down with

school books. "Hello, Dad—Sarah. Why wasn't Newt at the seminar today?"

"Hello, Rodney."

"H'lo, Rodney."

"H'lo, Rodney. He had to stay home today," Sarah said.

Rodney continued on to his room. Sarah and Jeff moved into the study. "As I was sayin', we talked to him for over a half hour."

"What did he say after you told him?"

"Well, he just thanked us and told us not to say anything to anybody else about it."

"Well, so help me—this thing's really got me puzzled."

"His closin' the case without callin' Newt to the stand?"

"Exactly. Exactly. Well, you are going to tell somebody else. You're going over to Mr. Davis, the defense lawyer, and take Newt with you. And you're to tell him the same thing you told Mr. McCormack." Jeff was red with fury. "By the way, does Mr. McCormack realize that I know about this information?"

"No, your name wasn't called at all, Judge."

"Fine. Now you be on your way. Go pick up Newt. Rodney and I will make out for supper."

"Where's he stayin', Judge?"

"Oh—over at Jennie Brighten's place. You'd better call and make an appointment with him before going there. His number's in my book there." He picked it up and thumbed through some pages. "Let's see—here it is—4437. Better call him right away."

Sarah telephoned Harley and he asked her to come to his place at eight. Later, the attorney sat facing her, Newt and Jack, finding it difficult to believe what he was hearing. During the full twenty minutes of Newt's story, he took notes and asked Newt to repeat now and then. When Newt had finished, he took him over the same ground, step by step, trying to find some discrepancy or weakness in the fabric of his astounding story. But the words were too solidly stated, the events too logically placed. Harley was convinced he was telling the truth.

"Why didn't you come forth with this information before now, Newt?" Harley asked softly.

"I was afraid—afraid that there might be a lot of trouble between the colored and white people if they found out Mister Savage did it."

"I understand," Harley said. "I think I know how you felt." He looked at the boy long and hard. "Newt, how do you feel now about the possibility of such trouble?"

"I don't know—I just don't know—"

"Are you afraid?"

"A little." Newt looked Harley square in the eye. "Are you, Mr. Davis?"

"One truth deserves another, Newt. I'm a little afraid too, but not so afraid that I won't do what I know to be right."

"Well—you're white. You ain't got much to worry about—"

"Newt," Sarah interrupted, "I—I don't—I don't think Mr. Davis feels no different than we do 'bout this." Her eyes were upon Harley. He knew they expected a truthful answer.

"Thanks, Mrs. Winger. Naturally, I'm interested in seeing justice done in this case, and—as much as it is possible for a white man—I understand Newt's concern for what his testimony could do to racial relations in this town. Feelings have run rather high around here. I was with Silas the other day when those rocks came smashing through his window." He paused. "And it wasn't a very comfortable situation for a while—but I think Judge Cavanaugh's plea for calm was well taken by the townspeople."

Jack Winger spoke now. "I hope so, but if they can give a threat to a white man like that, what won't they do when they find out it's a colored man?"

"We have to have faith in the people," Sarah cut in, "that's all that's left to do."

"That's my feeling too, Mr. and Mrs. Winger. However, Newt here is the one the burden is on. Will you be willing to repeat what you have told me in court tomorrow morning?"

Newt looked toward his mother and she answered for him, "He'll be there tomorrow mornin', and so will my husband and me."

"Fine. Fine. Fine." Harley was on his feet. "This is going to make all the difference—all the difference." He walked up and down the room, banging his fist in the palm of his hand. Sarah, Jack and Newt rose and prepared to leave.

"Mrs. Winger."

"Yes, Mr. Davis?"

"Pardon me for asking again, but you did say you spoke to Mr. McCormack about this?"

"Yes, I did," Sarah assured him.

"Incredible—incredible," Harley repeated. "One other thing —who told you to come to me?"

"Do we have to say that, Mr. Davis?" Jack asked.

"Not if you don't want. Believe me, that's unimportant, so unimportant."

"Well, we'd rather not, if you don't mind," Sarah added.

Long after the Wingers' departure, Harley was busy taking notes and checking Newt's statements. It was well past midnight when he finally went to bed.

The moment Newt made his appearance in the courtroom the next morning, Harley beamed. Silas sat gloomily beside him, unaware of the turn of events.

Harley nudged the defendant, but Silas barely reacted. "Yeh?"

"Perk up, Silas, things look good—very good."

"Yeh?" Silas moaned.

"Lot of colored people here today again, Silas."

"Yeh."

"You know most of them?"

"Yeh."

"Do you know Booker Savage?"

"Yeh, that's him sittin' over there in the middle. He ain't hardly missed a day."

"You mean the big husky fellow with the red shirt?"

"Yeh, and that's his boy alongside him. Why you askin'?"

"Oh, I just heard some talk about them last night."

"Stay 'way from 'em if you don't want'a git hurt. They're bad actors," Silas warned.

Court convened at eleven sharp. And, after what seemed like an eternity to Newt, Jeff called out, "The counsel for the defense may now present evidence and witnesses."

Getting up, Harley whispered, "I may have to call you to the stand today, Silas. In case I do, give the same answers in the same way—exactly as you have in the past—and don't be nervous." Then, he walked up front.

Harley pulled out his watch and noted the time. There was less than an hour before noon recess. The trap would have to be sprung before then.

"Would Officer Jason Kirky take the stand," Harley said. Kirky strode forward and plopped down in the chair.

"Officer Kirky, would you tell us, in which hand did you find the crowbar?"

McCormack jumped to his feet. "I object, Your Honor. Officer Kirky did not say that the crowbar was found in the defendant's hand. He stated that the crowbar was found beneath one of his hands."

"Correction, Officer Kirky. Under which hand did you find the crowbar?"

"The left hand."

"Officer Kirky, did you know the defendant was right-handed?"

"Nosuh, I didn't."

"Now you heard Mr. Wiggins testify that only one set of the defendant's fingerprints were found on the crowbar—the left ones."

"Yessuh, I did, suh."

"Now, in the light of this disclosure, and taking into consideration the slight build of the defendant, do you think it was possible for this defendant to bludgeon the deceased, to the extent that you testified he was bludgeoned, with his left hand and still show only one set of weak fingerprints?"

McCormack was up again.

"Your Honor, I object strenuously to Mr. Davis' question! The witness has not professed to know the limits of the defendant's physical prowess."

"Objection sustained."

"One more question, Officer Kirky," Harley said. "Did you find any of Mr. Kiner's bottles of brandy in the defendant's possession?" Marcus shivered a little at this question.

"No."

"That's all," Harley said.

A low buzzing filled the courtroom. Harley, a look of confidence on his face, noticed that McCormack was mopping sweat from his brow. And Silas, seemingly encouraged by this last bit of testimony, took a more dignified posture. A slight smile even came to his lips. Blanche and Waldo whispered to each other, and the Wingers exchanged confidential glances.

Now Harley was ready. "Your Honor," he said. "I would like to request a short consultation with the bench."

"Request granted. Will both attorneys please come forward?"

The buzzing grew louder as McCormack rose with a quizzical expression on his face and joined Harley in front of the bench. The consultation was very brief, and when it was over McCormack looked unhappy as he went back to his seat.

The Judge then called Kirky and the bailiff to the bench and whispered something to them. The two men nodded and went in opposite directions, the bailiff to the side door on the right, Kirky to the one in the rear. They locked these doors —and the buzzing now turned to excited talk, which rose higher until Jeff's gavel banged for silence.

Jeff spoke first. "Ladies and gentlemen of the jury, the

court has found it necessary to undertake a rather unusual procedure at this time. Due to the nature of the next witness's testimony, no one will be allowed to leave the room unless he is accompanied by a court officer. I hope this is thoroughly understood so that there will be no trouble. The court sincerely hopes that no one is inconvenienced by the action—which it deems highly necessary. You may call your witness now, Mr. Davis."

"Thank you, Your Honor," Harley said. "Will Newton Winger please take the stand?"

For Newt the moment of truth had arrived, and with a belly of nerves he drifted across the front of the courtroom and mounted the platform, feeling the crowd leaning toward him, sensing their stares—especially those of Silas, Booker, Marcus, Stewart McCormack and Mary Kiner. A wave of murmuring rose, then died, and everything was quiet.

Newt found himself repeating after the bailiff, "—to tell the truth and nothing but the truth, so help me God." He asked strength of something, be it God or whatever, to carry him, his family and the rest of the colored people safely through the trouble he now imagined his testimony would bring.

Stewart McCormack twisted in his seat again, mopping his brow, as Harley began his questioning. "Would you give the court your full name?"

"Newt—Newton Buchanan Winger."

"How old are you, Newton?"

"Fifteen in November."

"Did you know Jacob Kiner, the deceased?"

"Yessir, I did."

"How long?"

"All my life, I guess."

"Did you ever work for him?"

"Yessir."

"What kind of work did you do for him?"

"Hoein', weedin', pickin' fruit and stuff like that."

"When did you last work for him?"

"On June fourteenth."

"Of this year?"

"Yessir."

"Then you worked there the day Mr. Kiner was killed?"

"Yessir."

"How long did you work that day?"

"Well, I was supposed to work from eight to five, but I didn't."

"Why didn't you work out your full time?"

"I got tired and sleepy."

"What did you do then?"

"I sat under a tree to rest, but it was too hot so I went inside the barn and went to sleep."

"Where in the barn did you sleep?"

"In the hayloft."

Booker Savage flinched.

"What time was this, Newton?"

"About twelve noon."

"How long did you sleep?"

"About two hours."

"Did you wake naturally, or did someone wake you?"

"Nosir. I woke up when I heard some noise downstairs."

"Noise? What kind of noise?"

"Somebody was rippin' off the door to where Mr. Kiner kept his peach brandy and cider and stuff."

Booker stiffened and nudged Marcus, who screwed his right fist in the palm of his left hand, squinting his eyes in burning contempt toward Newt.

"What was this person using to break into the room?"

"A crowbar."

"Like the one here on this table?"

"Yessir. Just like that."

"Did you say anything to this person?"

"Nosir."

"Why not?"

" 'Cause I was scared. I didn't know what he might do to me."

Silas was now leaning forward in his seat, his mouth agape, following every word.

"What happened then?" Harley asked.

"Mr. Kiner and Mr. Newhall came through the door, fussin' at each other."

"What were they fussing about?"

"Well, Mr. Newhall was claimin' Mr. Kiner owed him some money and Mr. Kiner claimed he didn't, and he told Mr. Newhall if he didn't get out he would throw him out, or somethin' like that."

"Go on. What happened then?"

"Well, then Mr. Kiner got real mad and hit Mr. Newhall over the head with his whip handle—and Mr. Newhall grabbed a hoe, but Mr. Kiner hit him and he went down before he could get a blow in."

"Mr. Newhall went down?"

"Yessir."

"Did Mr. Newhall appear drunk?"

"Yessir, he was pretty tipsy."

"What was the person who broke into the room doing all this time? Or had he left?"

"Nosir, he hadn't left. He was hidin' in the dark."

"Then?"

"Well, when Mr. Kiner stepped back, after hittin' Mr. Newhall, he saw this other man and started hittin' him with the whip too, but the man raised the crowbar and got him across the head—and he kept hittin' Mr. Kiner on the head after he fell down."

Mary Kiner started crying, and Sarah moved over quickly and put her arms about Mary's shoulders. "Poor Jake, poor Jake," she cried. Silas sat as if in a trance, showing no sign of emotion. Booker looked about nervously, and Marcus whispered, "Take it easy, Paw. Take it easy."

"Go on, Newton. What happened after that?"

"Mr. Newhall started groanin', like he was comin' to—and the man took Mr. Kiner's whip and beat Mr. Newhall over the head with it till he stopped groanin', then he put the crowbar in Mr. Newhall's hand—"

"Which hand?"

"I don't exactly remember. Then he picked up this gunny sack full of bottles and left."

"So this man beat both Mr. Kiner and Mr. Newhall?"

"Yessir, he did."

"What did you do when it was all over?"

"I started to get down and run, but Mrs. Kiner came to the door and looked in—"

"Yes—go on."

"Well, she started screamin' real loud and ran back toward the house."

"What did you do then?"

"I got down from the loft after I was sure she was gone. Then I went home."

"Now, Newt, I want you to tell the court why you didn't come forth with this information before now."

"I—I was scared—that's all."

"Scared of what?"

"Well—I don't know—I guess I was scared of what the people might do—"

"You mean—well, what do you mean by that?"

Newt hesitated. "I—I thought it might bring on some kind of race trouble."

"I see. Now, Newton, I want you to look carefully around this room and tell the court if you see this man—the one who broke into the room and then beat Mr. Kiner and Mr. Newhall."

Newt saw his mother's eyes on him now, demanding the truth. His own eyes shifted, and every head in the room turned and followed his gaze until it rested on Booker Savage.

"That's the man. There in the red shirt. It's him—Mr. Booker Savage."

"He's lyin'! He's lyin'! He's lyin'!" Booker sprang up, shouting above the mumbling crowd. And Newt closed his eyes, trying to shut out the scene from his mind. All things he had seen before him, the faces, walls, floor, ceiling—all floated in a jumble of gray nothing. He was limp with fear. But he was free now, free to meet violence if need be, as he had met the truth—without guilt smothering his conscience.

"Git the nigger killer!" someone shouted in the back.

"Order! Order!" Jeff pounded his gavel until it was quiet. Then he said, "Proceed, counsel."

"That's all, Newton."

McCormack waived cross-examination and Newt was told to step down. He opened his eyes, stepped off the stand and rejoined his mother and father on the other side of the courtroom.

"Your Honor," Harley said quietly, "the defense requests that this man Booker Savage take the stand."

"Officer Kirky, escort Mr. Savage to the stand," the Judge commanded.

Kirky stepped gingerly into the aisle where Booker sat and motioned for him. Booker got up, patted Marcus on the knee and moved his big frame into the aisle. Then he lumbered up toward the front, towering over Kirky by a head.

"Lynch that black bastard!" someone shouted. "Kill him!" the echo came from the opposite side of the room. Booker flinched at the shouts and whirled around. Newt gritted his teeth and shut his eyes again.

"Order! Order!" Jeff shouted, banging his gavel. "I want the persons who said that to——" He didn't have a chance to finish his words, for just in front of him Kirky was sinking to the floor from a swift, powerful left-handed punch that Booker had shot at his chin; and somehow Booker had grabbed the gun from Kirky's right holster.

There were screams, and Booker shouted, "I'll kill anybody who tries touchin' me! I'm gittin' out'a here, Judge—right through your chambas!" He swung his legs over the railing, brandishing the weapon nervously toward the spectators. Kirky rose to one knee, his right hand inching toward his remaining gun. "Flatten out, you bastard!" Booker bellowed. "Keep your hands free and flatten out to the floor!" Kirky plopped down and Booker backed quickly past the bench, motioning Jeff Cavanaugh to one side.

"You won't get away with it, Savage!" Jeff hollered. "Put the gun down—nothing's going to happen to you!"

"Git back! I'll plug you too!" Booker threatened. Then he leaped through the door and slammed it behind him.

The crowd was on its feet. Then Kirky jumped up, whipped out his other gun and a bunch of keys and leaped over the railing. Now a bunch of whites was pressing forward.

"Lynch him!"

"Kill him!"

"String the black bastard up!"

"It's started—it's started," Newt said to himself. "I knew it would happen."

Kirky fished about for a key on the ring. Finding the right one, he twisted it in the lock, then holstered his gun and started waving the angry crowd back. "Hold it! Hold it!" he shouted. "He's trapped—the door to the outside's locked too! Hold it!"

"Naw—let's git the bastard!"

"Quiet! Quiet! Quiet!" Jeff hollered, beating a tattoo with his gavel. "Back to your seats! Order! Order!—"

A shot rang out from inside the Judge's chambers.

Several women screamed. Kirky, gun still drawn, slowly twisted the key in the lock. "Stand back," he cautioned. Then, standing sideways, the gun pointed, he eased the door open and peeped in. After a moment he holstered his gun and pushed the door fully open. He motioned for the Judge, and Cavanaugh stepped down from the bench, went forward and looked into his quarters. Booker Savage lay mortally wounded—a bullet hole in his temple. In a few moments he was dead.

Marcus rushed up, pushed by the Judge and went in. For a while he stood looking down on his father, then he began sobbing. Jeff Cavanaugh shook his head and closed the door. When he was back on the bench he waited until everyone was seated, then he rapped his gavel several times. Quiet was finally restored, and he said, "Stay with him, Officer Kirky." Then he turned to McCormack. "I think it's your move, counsel," he remarked dryly.

Stewart McCormack rose and in an extremely low voice said, "Your Honor, in view of what has taken place—here before us—I think it no more than proper to—to withdraw all charges against the defendant, Silas Newhall—if the court will permit."

"The court will permit," Jeff answered sternly. "And the court wishes to thank the jury for its patience, unselfishness and admirable duty to the people of this state. I now order the defendant released. The case is closed—but let me say this—" He turned to face the spectators and went on. "A man lies dead at the feet of his son in this room behind us, and you who hollered out for his life a few minutes ago have your wish. You are as much—or more—responsible for his death as he himself. In less than five incredible minutes you judged him and screamed for his black life, because you assumed he had killed a white man—forgetting, in your senseless moment, that a black boy had just saved a white man's life—right here before you. It took courage, a lot more than those of you who shouted have, for him to do it. It was what this boy feared of you that kept him from divulging earlier the information that might well have prevented this second tragedy."

Jeff Cavanaugh paused and looked about the room. "We have a judicial system in this country which gives any man the right to a fair trial when accused. You who yelled so barbarously frightened him out of that right. You pulled the trigger. You sent the bullet tearing through his brain. This moment should haunt your minds forever. Go home—and pray to Almighty God that you be forgiven for your sin."

The doors were unlocked and the crowd rose quietly, turned and headed out. Marcus Savage emerged from the Judge's chambers and stood stiffly by the door; then he moved away, walking slowly toward the exit. Newt intercepted him and said, "I'm sorry, Marcus."

"Yeh?" Marcus answered surlily. They stood eying each other in cold silence for a few moments, as Jack and Sarah stood off to the side watching with Waldo, Blanche, Silas and Harley Davis.

"Come on, son," Jack said finally, and Newt turned away.

Marcus walked on with his head down, muttering to himself, "I'm gonna kill that Winger son-of-a-bitch if it's the last thing I do."

When Newt rejoined the group, Jack said, "You did the most you could, boy."

"You certainly did, Newton," Harley agreed, "and all the Newhalls are grateful to you—and so am I."

"You can bet'cha life on that," Silas said, pumping his hand.

"I'm sorry you had to go through so much, Mr. Newhall—but I was in a spot—didn't know what to do. I hope you understand."

"He understands," Harley cut in quickly. Both Blanche and Waldo patted him on the arm reassuringly.

"Jack—Jack—"

"What is it, Sarah?"

"We'd better—we'd better—" She couldn't finish the sentence, and she was slumping toward the floor. Jack caught her in time, lifted her up and laid her on a bench.

"Run git Doc Cravens, Newt—fast as you can! She's fainted."

Sarah had lapsed into a complete coma by the time they finally got her home to bed. Doc Cravens stayed in the bedroom with her for more than an hour. When he came out he took Jack aside. "I hate tellin' you this, Jack," he said, "but I don't think she's goin' to make it this time. You'd better notify the rest of the children."

Jack's voice trembled when he asked, "Any—chance a'tall?"

"As long as she's breathin' there's a chance, Jack. But I don't want to get your hopes up. I have to give you the truth—it's a severe heart attack. She never should've attended that trial."

"With that boy on the stand, you couldn't'a kept her away. You know that, Timothy."

"I know, Jack."

"Well, what do we do now?"

"Just wait—that's about all we can do." Doc Cravens closed his valise and started toward the door. "I'll be at the hospital in case you need me. Otherwise, expect me about nine o'clock. Just keep things very quiet around her."

That evening Prissy sent telegrams to her brother and sisters and cousin Polly.

CHAPTER ❦ 16

THERE WERE some Negroes in Cherokee Flats who criticized what Newt had done, but the majority felt he had done the right thing—and they said so openly. Some outside newspapers called his testimony sensational, courageous—even heroic.

"I was just scared," Newt told a reporter from Kansas City, but his statement was glibly translated by his interviewer as an expression of great modesty. "Surprise Witness, Modest Hero," the sub-headline read in bold print in the following Sunday edition.

Newt, still shaken by the trial and aware of the talk that was making the rounds, stayed close to home for the first few days. Beansy, Jappy, Earl and Skunk hung around the Winger yard, sensing Newt's reluctance to go out. After the third day they tried coaxing him off to the swimming hole, but he refused. "Got to stay around the house," he said. "Momma's awful low."

"Maybe he's scared of meetin' Savage," Skunk suggested to the others, as they headed toward the river.

"He's just all upset," Beansy defended.

"Winger ain't yellow," Jappy said, "you ought'a know that, Skunk."

"Didn't say he was, did I?"

"I wouldn't've wanted to be in his spot," Earl said grumpily. "Bet you wouldn't either."

"And to think he knew it all the time," Beansy remarked, scratching his backsides. "Boy, I'd'a been scared to death."

"He's had a tough time," Jappy said, "Arcella and everything."

"He says he forgot all about her," Beansy cut in.

"He ain't forgot—that's a lotta crap," Skunk said. "He'd take her back if she showed up tomorrow."

"You wouldn't run from her yourself," Earl said.

"She ain't done nothin' to me," Skunk said flippantly.

" 'Tain't your fault." Earl's retort was loaded with sarcasm.

By now they were at the river, and they started undressing on the run. "Last one in's a donkey turd!" Skunk hollered. And one by one they plunged into the water.

Bitterness, fed by frustration and loneliness, ate deeper into the soul of Marcus Savage. Two days after his father's death, he had stood by himself as they lowered the body into a pauper's grave on the far side of Candy Hill. Mag Pullens, Deacon Fuller, Chappie Logan and Reverend Broadnap stood in the background watching. Broadnap had offered to say some last words, but Marcus had told the undertaker, "I don't want nobody prayin' over my old man—nobody." And Broadnap, respecting his wishes, did his praying silently as the cheap box disappeared beneath the earth.

"Okay, Chappie, let's git goin'," Marcus said, after taking a final look. He brushed by the others as if they weren't there and made for Chappie's big Dodge.

Chappie turned and waddled behind him. "Don't you think you ought'a say somethin' to those people who was kind a'nough to come?" Chappie asked softly.

"I didn't ask 'em to come, did I?" Marcus snarled.

"But, boy, you—"

"Hell with 'em. If you don't want to ride me home, I'll walk."

"Git in," Chappie said.

As the others made their way to the undertaker's car, Mag Pullens moaned, "What can you do for a boy like that?" No one had an answer.

Chappie and Marcus drove along without speaking. "I'm all by myself now," Marcus was thinking. "Ain't a soul carin' if I live or die." Then he said aloud, "I know one thing—I'm gonna git that Winger bastard."

Chappie gave him a quick glance. "Aw, come on—you're doin' all right now. Don't go foolin' around and git yourself in a lot of trouble."

"He's the cause of my old man bein' in that grave right now."

"Take my advice and stay out'a trouble," Chappie said. "Want to stay at my place tonight?" They had turned off the highway.

"Naw—reckon not."

"You're welcome, you know."

"Want to git home. Got lot'a thinkin' to do for myself."

Chappie was quiet after that. They drove on the last few

blocks and stopped in front of the Savage shack. "Want tomorrow off?" Chappie asked.

"Naw—be in early." Marcus got out of the car, slammed the door and walked off. Chappie sat watching him. Suddenly Marcus stopped and turned around. "Thanks," he said gruffly.

"It's okay, boy." Chappie shifted the gears and the car rattled off.

Marcus took off his coat as he walked down the path between rows of rusting junk. He pushed open the door of the shack, threw his coat to the floor, then stripped off the shirt and tie Chappie had given him for the burial. "The old man died without friends and he got buried without 'em—that's prob'ly the way he wanted it," Marcus mumbled. He threw the shirt and tie on the table and stood in the middle of the room for several minutes—a great loneliness seeping into him. There was nothing—no today, no tomorrow, not even a cursing, drunken father any more. It was as though he were an abandoned piece of charcoal, dropped dead-center of an empty, slow-turning world—one without people, air, light, dark or sound. He wanted to cry but couldn't. Instead he began laughing, and he laughed and laughed until tears rolled down his rough cheeks and his hot neck, and his arms crossed and his fingernails cut into his skin until it bled and he felt the blood and the punctured flesh at his fingertips.

He began, at last, to cry.

On Friday of that same week, Earl drove his father's car up to the Winger yard. Newt was sitting on the front porch, and Earl got out and came over to him. "Gotta drive over to Fulton to pick up a saddle for Paw. Want to go along for the ride?"

"Comin' right back?"

"Yeh—right back. Come on."

Newt climbed in and they took off in the Model-T Ford. They reached their destination by eleven o'clock, picked up the saddle and headed back toward Cherokee Flats before noon.

"Damn!" Earl said suddenly. "I'm 'bout out of gas!" They had been riding quite a while now.

"Ain't no station between here and home!" Newt hollered above the popping motor.

"I know it." Earl looked at the little white needle that indicated his supply. "Guess we can just 'bout make it!" he shouted.

They putted on through the outskirts of Easton, churning up dust from the dry road. And as they bumped along, Newt slumped in his seat, watching the parched corn stalks moving lazily in the gentle wind. They stretched ahead on both sides as far as the eye could reach.

"Summer's goin' fast!" Newt hollered.

"Summer, hell!" Earl bellowed. "More worried 'bout this damn empty tank! We still got more'n three miles to go yet!"

"Aw, we could walk from here."

"You could—not me!" The motor coughed once, and Earl shot a quick glance at the trembling needle. "Don't stop here, baby! Git me home!" Then he quit talking—as though conversation, itself, might drink up the gasoline.

Newt welcomed Earl's quietness, for now he was thinking back four years to Big Mabel and the storm. His mind wandered over the corn and across the prairie to her grave on the slopes of Candy Hill and reshaped the dust of her remains into the firm, rounded figure it once was. The image held for a moment, then faded—she was only dust again. "What a waste," he thought. "Big, good-feeling Mabel is just a pile of dust."

The Flats were growing dull to him now, and within him stirred the possibility of leaving them for good. The thought caused him to open his eyes and look down the road. He could see that they were approaching the Easton railroad tracks. Then, in the distance, he saw the warning arms swinging—and above the sound of the motor he could hear the clanging bell. About a hundred yards from the crossing, Earl slowed down and looked to the curve at his left, then to his right.

"I don't see no damn train! Do you, Newt?"

Newt popped up, his ears straining for the familiar sound. "Seems like I hear rumblin'. May be a slow freight, but no tellin' what's around that curve. You better slow down!"

Earl pressed in the clutch and braked the car to a near-stop. The tiny white needle trembled wildly. He eyed it quickly, then once more shot looks in both directions. "Must be a freight! Curve or no curve, I can beat a freight here. Always done it before." Suddenly he jerked down the gas lever and the car shot ahead. "Damn, I cain't run out'a gas here!" he yelled.

Fear gripped Newt as they roared over the last few yards to the crossing. Then both of them froze at the frightening sound of the engine whistling in from the left.

"Damn!" Earl yelled.

It was the Katy Express, not a freight, and it was blowing hard as it came barreling down on them. Earl slammed the brake and clutch in together just before the engine reached the crossing. The car shuddered to a stop, but the nose of it was just touching the track.

"Jump! Jump!" Earl screamed. Newt was already rolling in the weeds when he heard the crunching sound and saw the car somersaulting alongside the speeding train. At the same instant he saw Earl in a flying plunge just ahead of it. By the time the Express screeched to a halt, a half mile away, the car was aflame. Newt jumped up and ran over to drag Earl away from it.

"You hurt, Earl? You all right?"

"Yeh—just shook up a little. Help me up." Newt bent over to help him—then drew back and screamed.

"Your foot's gone, Earl! Your foot's gone!"

Earl kept his eyes on Newt. "You're crazy—you're crazy, Newt! I don't feel nothin'!" Then slowly he turned his head and looked down at the chalk-white splintered bone sticking through his bloody pants leg. "Oh no no no! Good God no! No no no—"

Newt looked beyond the burning car and he could see people running toward them. "Help! Help! Over here!" he shouted, cupping his hands around his mouth. "Help! Help!"

The big fireman arrived first. His red puffy face was streaked with coal dust and he was sweating. "What you two niggas tryin' to do—kill us all?" he raged.

Newt stood and bristled.

"My Lord! His foot's off!" It was the engineer. He brushed the fireman aside and bent over Earl. "Git the first aid kit, Rufus! Hurry! I'll try a tourniquet. Gimme your shirt, sonny." Newt ripped off his shirt, handed it to him. "Now git me a good strong stick, boy!"

"How big, mister?"

"About so-so—" he said, spacing his bony hands apart. "Hurry, boy! Hurry!"

Newt returned with a stick, and the engineer broke it across his knee. After tying a loop in the shirt, he thrust the stick through and began twisting it above Earl's knee. Earl was quiet now.

The engineer said, "Here, sonny, hold this in place. Hold it tight, now."

Newt took the stick, then looked down at Earl. "Does it hurt much?"

"Not too much," Earl said.

"Didn't you boys hear the bell ringing?" the engineer asked.

"Thought we could make it. Thought you was a slow freight."

"You ought never try beatin' a train," the engineer said, "freight or whatever."

Newt was aware of more people around them. They were passengers from the train. A conductor began asking questions. "What's your name, boy?"

"Newt Winger."

"And his?"

"Earl Thompson."

"Where you live?"

"Cherokee Flats."

"Him too?"

"Yep."

"Whose car was it?"

"His—his paw's."

"You hurt any?"

"Naw."

A short fat man in a checkered suit, wearing rimless glasses without ear-bars, looked down at Earl's leg. He just kept looking, with his mouth open. A tall, birdlike woman peeped over the fat man's shoulder, turned white and grabbed him by the arm. "Come, Gerald," she said. "How can you bear to look?" They left, and others closed in.

"You people have to stand back now," the engineer said. "Give us some air." He turned to Newt. "There a doctor close by, sonny?"

"Over at the Flats. Doc Cravens is about a mile and a half from here. He's got a ambulance."

"Well, you better run for him. I'll take the tourniquet now. Hurry on!"

The better part of an hour passed before Newt and Doc Cravens pulled up in the makeshift Model-T ambulance. Newt watched Doc fill a glass tube with liquid, attach a needle to it and stick it in above Earl's knee.

"That's a good tourniquet you tied there," Doc said, and he and the engineer nodded to each other. Then they lifted Earl into the ambulance. Newt got in beside him and closed the door.

They were a good half mile down the road before Earl spoke—and to Newt's surprise, he was grinning. "Anybody back there ever bother to look for my damn foot?" he asked.

214

Newt managed a weak smile and, looking through the back window as they bounced down the road, he could see the Express picking up speed. Then suddenly it was out of sight. The warning arms stopped swinging, and he saw only smoke from the gutted Ford in the distance—curling slowly over the cornstalks and the desolate crossing.

While Doc Cravens was operating, Newt sat in the waiting room, wrapped in a wrinkled intern's jacket, explaining the accident to Earl's parents. He mumbled the details in much the same way he had once related a bad dream to his mother, after running to her bedside in the dark of a wintry night. Throughout his disordered narration he listened to Martha Thompson's soft crying, interspersed with the consoling voice of her husband, Fred.

After a long wait, Doc Cravens came. "Earl's sleepin' now," he said. "His condition's serious—but he's goin' to be all right." He looked to Martha Thompson. "I saved as much of the limb as possible, Martha. No sense in any of you worryin'. What's done is done." His eyes moved to Fred. "He's alive. Be thankful for that much."

"We are. Believe me, we are."

"He should sleep through the night, so you'd better come back in the mornin'." He turned again to Martha. "Remember—no worryin'."

They were leaving the hospital now. "You takin' Newt home?" Fred asked.

"Yep," Doc said. "Got to call on Sarah. Haven't seen her since this mornin'."

"How's she doin'?" Fred asked.

"Seems to be holdin' her own. Well, goodnight. Come round in the mornin' after eight."

"After eight."

"It'll be that late before I can tell you anything."

Fred put his arm about Martha's shoulder and they walked slowly to their buckboard. He helped her in, untethered the horse and climbed in beside her. As they rode off, Doc put his hand on Newt's shoulder. They watched the wagon as it disappeared in the darkness—and listened to the clomp, clomp of the horse's hoofs and the creaking of the dried-out wheels.

"Momma any better, Doc?" Newt asked.

They looked at each other for a moment, then Doc said, "Your mother's in bad shape, Newt—you might as well know."

215

"She'll be all right sometime, though, won't she?"

"Only time will tell, Newt."

They went on to Doc's car, got in and drove off. As they rode along, Newt wanted to ask more about his mother but he didn't know how to form the questions. Too, there was an inner fear of facing the fact that she might be dying. So he contented himself with what little he had been told, and he watched the road come up blurry and whitish from the edges of the country darkness.

His mind shot back to Earl. It seemed ages since they had started out that morning. Poor Earl! No more basketball for him—no swimming at Flynn's River—no more races over Candy Hill. If only he'd listened! That chalk-white bone sticking from his bloody pants leg, a white person's bone couldn't be any whiter.

The car slowed. Two deer, caught in the gleam of the head-lamps, stood transfixed, readying their leap toward the sudden brightness. Doc Cravens quickly switched off the lights. A moment later he turned them on again. The deer had fled into the brush, and the car picked up speed.

They were halfway to the Winger house when Doc finally spoke again. "Newt."

"Yessir."

"My father died when I was just about your age. You're fifteen, aren't you?"

"Almost."

"Well, soon after he died, my mother ran off to St. Louis with a fellow from Kansas City." Newt turned and looked hard at him. "Surprised, huh?" Doc said.

"Well—"

"I was alone, so your mother took me in and cared for me like I was one of her own."

"You mean you used to live at my house?"

"Before you were born. Durin' that time I came to know the way people could really live on this earth if they only tried." He twisted the steering wheel and they turned the corner into Logan's Grove. "It wasn't easy for her, either. Folks, black and white, did some talkin' against her takin' in Sadie Cravens' white son, but their complaints fell on deaf ears. I didn't miss a day of school or go without eatin'—for two years, mind you."

Newt was quiet.

Doc Cravens reflected for a moment or so. "Early in the third year my mother died, and your mother paid my way to her funeral in St. Louis. I stayed there and went to school on money my mother managed to leave me. I don't know where she got it."

"Why'd you ever come back here?"

Doc pulled up alongside the Winger yard and stopped. "I can't exactly say why, Newt. It's as good a place as any to help people who really need helpin'.... Let's go in. Oh, by the way—your sisters and brother came after you left this mornin'."

Newt followed him into the house, and Doc went on into Sarah's room. Clara, Lou and Roy got up smiling as Newt crossed the hushed parlor to greet them. He hugged and kissed his two sisters and shook hands with Roy. Lou looked about the same, but Clara—who Jack called "the marryin' one"—had changed. She looked skinnier to Newt, and she was dressed in fancier clothes than when he had seen her several years before. Roy looked the way Newt felt all sharp Chicagoans should look—hair parted to the side, striped suit, striped tie, white spats and needle-nosed shoes. "He'll be tellin' us some wild tales about Chicago," Newt thought as he pumped his hand.

The next day Newt, Clint and Roy were lying in the yard beneath the big apple tree. It was hot, and Roy lay face down in a clump of cool grass, the other two flat on their backs. Newt held a string tied to the leg of a huge June bug that spun lazily about their heads. Clint said, "What's that June bug doin' hangin' round here in August?"

"I've seen 'em later'n this," Newt said.

They were silent for a while, then Clint said, "Tell us 'bout the Windy City, Roy. Anything happen to you lately?"

"Not much. Got robbed last week—that's about all."

Clint and Newt raised to their elbows in simultaneous motion, and Clint's eyes popped. "Robbed? Hell, man! Tell us 'bout it! What happened?"

"Wasn't nothin' out of the ordinary, Clint. Guy just stuck a big forty-five at the back of my head and told me to fork over."

Clint cocked his head to one side. "Well, come on—what'd you do?"

"What'd I do? I gave him the dough. What else could I do?" Roy chomped off the end of a blade of grass, winked slyly at Newt and suppressed a grin. "I was lucky he didn't slug me. He had me in the clutch, and I wasn't about to give him no back talk."

"Didn't you say nothin' to him, at all?"

"Sure. I said, 'Here you are, sir—have a pleasant journey.'"

Clint shook his head, chuckled and fell back on the ground. "Boy! You shore lead a hell-of-a-wonderful life, Roy."

"Wonderful? What's so wonderful about a gun pointin' at the back of your head. Naw, you're lucky to be here away from all the crap you have to take in a big city. Right, Newt?"

Newt sensed the whole tale was a lie, but he was flattered by the confidence. He winked at Roy. "Right you are, Roy. Right you are."

"Just the same," Clint said dreamily, "it must be terrific. Action and dames and everything. Nice—nice dames. Boy—"

"You kiddin'? A bunch of money-grabbin' chicks lookin' to take you for everything you got. Nice dames. Boy, some of them would steal the white off rice. Naw, Clint, you better be thankful you're here in the Flats."

"What else happened you ain't told us 'bout?"

"Couple other things. Ain't got time now. Maybe tomorrow." Roy jumped to his feet and walked away.

The June bug lit on Newt's nose. He watched with crossed eyes as it crawled up the bridge of his nose to his forehead, dragging the dirty string over his lips. Suddenly the bug took off with a jerk, leaving its leg on the string.

Clint propped himself up on his elbows, watching the insect's crazy flight to freedom. Then he said, "If I was that goddam bug I'd fly straight to Chicago without stoppin'!" He got to his feet, brushed the dirt from his behind and moved over to the porch where Jack Winger sat smoking. "How's Momma Winger doin', Poppa?"

Jack puffed a couple of times, removed the pipe and spat. "Seems to be holdin' her own." Then he went on puffing.

Clint pushed his hands deep into his overall pockets, kicked the side of the porch, looked to the sky and spat. "Rain for shore way back there, Poppa Winger."

"Yep—does look like it."

Clint's hands jumped from his pockets to the shoulder straps near the bib. "It's hot," he complained. Then he turned abruptly, his mouth twitching nervously, and hurried down the path toward his shack. When Jack turned in puzzlement to look after him, he had already disappeared below the hill.

Newt remained in the shade of the tree, squinting toward the mirages of shimmering heat that hung over the cornfields and plains beyond. The small talk had relaxed him and left

218

a warm and special feeling. But now a sense of guilt crept over him, so he got up and called, "Poppa, I'm goin' to the hospital to see Earl!"

"All right, boy. Tell him I'll be to see him 'fore long."

Clint was right about the rain. It started around six that evening, and by seven-thirty the creeks and rivers were reaching their watersides. Marcus Savage had been rummaging through the junk in the yard when the first downpour came. He scurried into the shack, leaving the door cracked to let in fresh air. Then, sitting on the floor with his back to the wall, he watched the silver rain coming down in sheets beyond the opening.

He pondered his circumstances. "Ain't got nobody now. All on account'a that Winger son-of-a-bitch—couldn't keep his trap shut—helpin' white trash 'stead of his own kind. 'Course Paw killed Jake—the dirty bastard had it comin'— I spent a year in hell on account'a him." He plucked a small ant crawling over his knee, held it for a moment, watching it wiggle helplessly; then his powerful black fingers rubbed it into nothingness.

He took a raw turnip from his pocket and pulled a knife from his overall bib; pressed a tiny metal button at the end of it and a huge blade popped from the groove. He peeled the skin, tossed it aside and sank his teeth into the starchy white meat, chewing viciously. "But I'll git Winger. He's been stickin' close to home. Sooner or later he'll come down to the river and—" He sensed a movement at the door. It was a big field rat, seeking shelter. As it slithered through the opening, Marcus sprang up. "Git! You son-of-a-bitch!" The frightened rat bared its yellow fangs and backed off cautiously, then whirled and fled back into the wetness.

CHAPTER ❦ 17

NEWT SAT on a barrel in the corner of the kitchen, listening to the downpour vibrate the tin roof above him and watching Lou and Clara ready the evening meal. Realizing that if his mother died he might have to live with one or the other sister, he observed them closely—trying to decide which one he would rather be with. He liked them both, so he sat mentally sifting their habits and dispositions, applying them to his own simple, yet important, personal plans and desires. "Clara's a little bossy," he thought. "She'd prob'ly want me to stay in all the time—want to pick all my friends, too, but she likes to dress fancy—prob'ly help me get some keen things to wear. Lou's easygoin' and easy to fool. I like the way she fries potatoes, but she'd prob'ly want me to go to church all the time. Sure had enough religion to last me a long time."

"Newt, put some wood on the fire. Hurry up, now!"

(Yeh—Clara's mighty bossy, all right. . . .) "Okay, okay." He went to the outer shed adjoining the kitchen, came with the wood and stoked it in above the glowing grate. Then he returned to his perch on the flour barrel. Glancing into the dining room, he saw Maggie Pullens rise and walk toward the front of the house. When she came back she said to Jack, "Sarah's breathin' easy."

"Doc Cravens seems to think she's gainin'," Jack said.

"Glad to hear it," Maggie sighed, " 'cause I don't mind tellin' you that a white dove come and set on my window sill this mornin'—you know what that means—I thought the worst had come. Well, I dressed and grabbed this camphor bottle and got here fast as I could."

"Supper's about ready, Poppa."

"Git me some buttermilk, Prissy."

"Yessir." Prissy switched back to the kitchen. "You want some buttermilk, Newt?"

"Huh?"

220

"Whyn't you wash out your ears? I said do you want some buttermilk?"

"Sure I want some buttermilk—and I wash my ears more'n you wash your a—"

"Newt!" It was Clara. "Don't you dare use such language with your momma on her dyin' bed!"

"Aw, I ain't said anything, yet." He slid from the barrel and started for the dining room. Reaching the doorway, he turned to Prissy. "You know one thing, twitchy pants, one of these fine days you're goin' to turn up missin'."

"Save your bluff for Marcus Savage, big boy. You don't scare Prissy none."

"All right. You two cut it out and get to dinner!" Clara whisked past them, carrying a big platter of chicken. "Come on, Poppa. Come on, Miss Maggie. There's plenty here for everybody. Pete—Roy—come on!"

A short time later Jack began blessing the table. "Lord, make us truly thankful for—"

"Help! Help!"

Newt sprang to his feet. "It's Rende, Poppa."

"Sit back down, boy!" Jack ordered. Then he got up and went to the door. "I'll handle this." He jerked open the door and peered into the darkness, the rain needling his face and arms. "Rende!" Rende!"

He could see her vaguely in the pouring black waterscape, carrying the baby, coaxing Butsy and shoving Gin-gin up the slippery path. He rushed out to meet them. "What's the matter, girl? What you screamin' 'bout now?"

"It's Clint, Poppa! He's got the shotgun!"

"I declare! Where's he at now?"

"Followin' us up the path," Rende gasped.

"Git in out'a the rain!" Jack said, ushering them into the room. He looked back toward the dark path. "Why'd he pick a time like this to booze up?"

Everyone was standing when Rende and the children scrambled through the door, soaked to their skins. Jack came in behind them and quietly forced the door shut. Lou took the baby, and the two small children stood there big-eyed, shining in their wetness, until Clara moved over and began wiping their faces with her apron.

"Now don't start that bawlin', girl," Jack said to Rende. "Git your momma excited."

Prissy stayed close to the older women, while Newt, Pete and Roy stood watching their father. Suddenly Jack seemed to realize that he was confronted with Clint for the first time.

221

He turned to his sons. "I don't want your momma hearin' a fuss and gittin' upset, so you boys stay out'a this. Git my hat and raincoat, Newt. Rende, you and the kids go in Prissy's bedroom—and stay there. Rest of you sit down and finish your supper. Now, everybody do as I say. Hurry up, Newt!"

Newt bounded across the floor with his father's hat and black rubber raincoat. He helped him into it, then grabbed his own overall jumper and started putting it on.

"Take that jumper off, boy," Jack snapped.

"Yessir." Newt dropped the jumper and moved to the table.

Jack watched Rende hustle the children into Prissy's room, then he finished buttoning his coat and started for the door.

"Better be careful, Poppa," Pete cautioned.

"Don't worry, boy." Then he was out the door. He was pulling it shut when he felt the double barrels of the gun push firmly against his belly.

"Where's Rende?" Clint drawled menacingly.

Jack's voice was steady and low. "Boy, this ain't no time for trouble and you know it, no matter how drunk you are." The gun pushed harder, and Jack backed off the pressure. But quickly it was upon him again, forcing him into the room where the others watched, horrified.

"There won't be no trouble if you just git me Rende, Poppa Winger." A grin was set on Clint's face. "Where's she hidin'?"

"Close the door, boy. It's rainin' in here."

"We'll just leave it open. I aim to be goin' pretty quick." The gun moved up and down. "I ain't foolin'. Both these barrels is loaded—and there's plenty for reloadin'. Where's she, in the bedroom?"

Maggie Pullens dashed out the kitchen door. "I'm callin' Kirky," she cried.

"Git back here!" Clint shouted, his eyes shifting toward her. But she was gone. His eyes were on Jack again and he pushed him on toward the bedroom ahead of the gun. Pete, Roy and Newt stood by the table, tensed for action.

"Clint, you oughta be 'shamed of yourself," Clara scolded, "you know Momma's breathin' her last."

"Keep your fancy mouth shut, Clara, or you might git it too!" The gun raised to Jack's chest. "All right, Poppa Winger—move away from the door."

"You gonna have to kill me first, boy." Jack's right hand inched toward a flatiron on the pressing board nearby.

"Okay! Hands up high!" Clint barked. The gun was against

222

Jack's forehead now, fuzzing his view of all except the long black steel barrels through which the blast would come. They seemed to spread across his entire forehead. He could see Clint's wet knuckles, shining and trembling beneath the finger on the trigger.

"Okay, Poppa, I'm countin' to five," Clint said, "if you ain't out'a the way by then, off goes the top of your head! One—"

Pete had motioned everyone back, and they were all on Clint's right now.

"Two—"

Pete grabbed a plate from the table and threw it at the door. It struck with a startling crash. As Clint wheeled toward the noise, Jack felt the barrel rims tearing across his forehead —heard the blast, the splintering door and the screams.

Everyone had fallen to the floor except Jack. He grabbed the flatiron and threw it just as Clint bounded out through the door. The iron missed Clint and sailed into the open. Clint sprinted for the cornfield, emptying the smoking shell chambers as he ran. He continued several yards in among the stalks, then stopped to reload.

Sarah had awakened with the blast and Jack had rushed to her bedside, sopping blood from his gashed forehead with a dish towel.

"Oh my—he's been doin' fine till now," Sarah said. "Wonder what got into him?"

"The devil—what else?" Jack answered.

"Where's Rende and the kids now?"

"In the bedroom till Kirky comes."

"Kirky?"

"Yeh. Maggie ran out and phoned him."

"No more shootin', I hope."

He patted her arm. "Don't you go gittin' excited, Sarah. Everything's gonna turn out all right."

"Where's Newt?"

"In with his brothers guardin' the doors."

"Keep him out of the way, Jack. He might try somethin' foolish."

"I'm watchin' him. Don't worry." He pulled the cover up under her chin. "There's Kirky's 'cycle. I better git out there."

Kirky came stalking through the rain with two pistols drawn. Doug Simpson and Bull Terry, his hastily formed posse, flanked him, each of them carrying a high-powered rifle.

These two had come in Doug's Ford. The rain had slackened, but they were all wearing slickers.

Jack and his sons met them in the yard.

"Where's Clint hidin', Jack?" Kirky's tone was brusque and mean.

"Don't know for shore. He made for the cornfield there."

Thunder rumbled in from the west, and lightning streaked across the black sky.

"I'll bring him out—if I have to drag him out by his goddam heels!" Kirky growled. He turned toward the field, "Come on, men. Keep low and be careful. This bastard's crazy when he's boozed up. We'll go in 'bout ten feet apart. I'll take the middle. Doug, you take the left—and, Bull, you cover from the right. When we spot his position, blast in his direction—not to the side. We'll go in ten steps at a time and stop. Wait till you hear me 'fore goin' any further. Got it straight?"

"Yeh, we understand."

"Okay, let's go."

Jack touched Kirky's arm. "Lemme call him first. Maybe he'll give up."

Kirky shook his head. "I'm callin' signals now, Jack. You and your boys better git out'a the way now—" He motioned them aside with his guns.

Jack ordered the boys into the house, and Newt said, "If only Momma wasn't sick. Kirky won't give him a chance, Poppa."

"Ain't much we can do now, boy. It's all Clint's doin'."

Kirky and his men were at the edge of the cornfield. "All right, Clint! It's Kirky!" he bellowed. "You comin' out or do I hafta come in and drag you out?"

Except for a low rumble of thunder, and rain beating on the cornstalks, there was silence. Kirky motioned toward the ground with his guns, and he and his deputies crouched low, took ten steps into the field, then stopped.

"Okay, Clint! You better yell out your position so we don't shoot!" Silence. "Okay, men. Ten more." He was speaking softly now. They had just taken the third step when thunder and lightning cracked above their heads—and at the same time Clint let go with a blast, shearing the corn tops above them. The three men dropped to their bellies and returned the fire—crack—bam—bam—crack. Then there was silence again.

Suddenly Clint's voice chided from another part of the

field. "What you waitin' on, Kirky? You red-neck son-of-a-bitch! You scared?"

The posse crawled ten paces toward the direction of the voice. Boom! Clint blasted again. The three flopped to their bellies, and their guns fired back into the wet, swaying corn. "All right, men," Kirky said, "crawl out to where we started. We gotta track from another position." They scooted back to the edge of the clearing.

"This ain't the jazzy little party you told us it'd be, Kirky," Bull said, wiping the mud from his face. "That black bastard's shrewd as a fox."

"Don't worry. We'll git him. Don't worry." Kirky was wiping his gun.

A light had appeared in the doorway, and through it came Pete and Roy, carrying their mother into the yard. She was heavily wrapped in quilted blankets. Clara and Lou held umbrellas over her head and body.

"What's this?" Doug motioned toward the house. Kirky and Bull turned to look, and Kirky dropped his guns to his sides.

"Who's that they're carryin'?" Bull asked.

"Jack's wife. Must be out'a their minds. She's half dead." Kirky started waving them back, but they kept coming.

Jack walked over to Kirky and said, "He'll come out if he knows she's out here."

"You're crazy, Jack! Git her back to bed. Clint's gone loco. He'd kill anybody now!"

"Try it her way," Jack said.

"Naw—"

"Call out to him," Sarah said, and Newt cupped his hands around his mouth. "Clint! Momma Winger's out here! She wants you to come in! Can you hear me, Clint?"

After a moment, Clint's voice came from a new direction. "You're lyin', Newt! She's in bed! You git back out'a the way!"

"Honest, Clint—she's here! We'll turn the car lights on her so you can see for yourself!"

"Naw—don't you turn them lights on!" Kirky shouted.

"Maybe we ought'a let her give it a try," Doug urged. Kirky shrugged, and Doug rushed to the car, started it, and switched on the headlamps. Then he drove up the path and stopped, with the lights flooding the group.

"Here she is, Clint!" Newt hollered. "See for yourself!"

There was a slight rustling in the field, and Kirky's hands tightened on his guns. Everyone else stood rigid and quiet.

"Don't try no monkey business!" Clint called out. "If it ain't her, I'll shoot! Turn her to the light!"

Roy and Pete turned their mother into the beams of light. "Come on, before Momma gets soaked!" Pete yelled.

Clint was on his belly now, snaking his way in, the gun barrels parting the stalks before him. He halted a moment, then continued in a crawl, stopping finally within a few feet of the clearing.

"That you, Momma Winger?" The question was almost whispered.

"Yes—Clint. Come ahead. Nobody's goin' to harm you."

"You shore?"

"I'm sure. Come on."

Clint wriggled quickly to the edge, then jumped up and burst from the cornfield toward Sarah.

"Drop that gun!" Kirky bellowed.

Clint ran for the refuge of the group, dropping the gun in the mud—and Jack's fist cracked against his jaw, sending him to the earth. He got up groggily.

"Git in the house—you lunatic," Jack said heatedly, grabbing him by the scruff of his neck. "I declare—I ought'a—" He shoved Clint into the house.

They carried Sarah back into her room, where Lou and Clara removed the wet blankets and covered her with dry ones. Clint came in, dropped to his knees and started praying. Rende observed him a moment or two, then she moved over and knelt beside him. But Kirky stepped up and grabbed Clint's shoulder. "Come on, Clint—you're goin' in."

"Leave him—to me—Kirky," Sarah said. "You didn't git him—I did."

Kirky looked at her, then at Jack. "Okay," he grunted. He motioned Bull and Doug from the room, and they stomped out of the house without looking back. "I'll git that bastard yet," Kirky growled as they crossed the yard.

Doc Cravens met them near the end of the walk. "What's goin' on?" he asked.

"When you find out, tell me, Doc. I'd like to know too," Kirky snorted as he mounted his motorcycle.

Newt was undressing for bed when Pete called, "Momma wants you, Newt."

"Somethin' wrong?"

"She's askin' for you—better come right away."

Newt walked slowly to the bedside. He sensed the others in the room, but he looked only at his mother—noting the sunken cheeks, the pallor lying like silk over her deep brown skin, the dullness of her eyes beneath the half-closed lids.

"Come close, son." Her face twitched to a faint smile as she spoke.

Newt dropped to his knees and touched his lips to her cheeks; and through his hands, resting on her thin arms, he realized the full extent of her suffering. "How are you feelin', Momma?"

She looked at him for a moment before answering. "I'm goin', son—just wanted a few words with you."

Newt's eyes began to water.

"Now don't go puckerin' up," Sarah said, smiling. "I'm ready—I'm happy and I don't want cryin' from any of you."

She was silent for a few moments, seemingly gathering strength. Doc Cravens pressed a damp cloth against her forehead, propped an extra pillow behind her neck, and took her pulse. Rende, Lou, Clara, Prissy, Roy and Pete stood off to the side. Jack was in front of them, his smokeless pipe hanging from his lips. The rims of his eyes were swollen and red.

Sarah went on. "Your sisters are takin' you back north with them. Promise me you'll mind them—and keep out of trouble."

"I promise."

"It's another kind of world up there, Newt—hope and more promisin' things. Put—put somethin' into it—and you'll git somethin' out—simple as that."

"Yessem."

"Make a good man of yourself up there. It's a dream of mine—for you—make it come true."

"I'll try."

"You'll do it."

"Yessem, I will."

"Do the ri—right thing—not always the easiest—"

Her eyes were closing and Doc Cravens touched Newt's shoulder. He started to move away, but stopped as his mother spoke once again. "Believe in somethin' and live up to it. Be good, son. Be—" Her hand dropped to the side of the bed.

Doc Cravens lifted Newt up. "She's sleepin' now," he said. "You better get to bed."

At the parlor door Newt turned for one more look, then went off to his room.

Lying in the darkness of his room, he began absorbing the full measure of the tragedy now facing the Winger family. For the first time in his life he realized it was his mother

227

who had really kept things together; who performed the miracles—such as she had done with Clint this very same night —that insured their existence; who calmed the fears that came with the trials of long, bitter winters. His father, though he would be willing, could never shoulder the burden. Newt knew it, Jack Winger knew it, and so did everyone else.

It had already been decided that Prissy would go with either Lou or Clara, as he would. He began thinking of his family as a shrinking tree. His mother, part of the trunk, was withering away. His brothers and sisters, like leaves, would soon scatter in all directions. Now his mind wandered to the faraway place up north—where his mother expected him to bring flowering to her dream. He couldn't conjure up a clear image of it, but his heart, he knew, was already racing there. Soon he would join it and go in search of the "promisin' things" she had just spoken of, just a few minutes before.

He tossed and turned in his bed, got up twice for water, and made a trip to the outhouse. It was nearly three when he finally slept—and his dreams were as frightful as his day had been. One dealt with a huge chunk of peanut brittle he was trying to keep from sinking to the bottom of Flynn's River. After a couple of violent twists in the water, it was no longer peanut brittle, but Marcus Savage. Marcus had only one leg, and when Newt grabbed it to pull him ashore, he was horrified to find his hand wrapped around a hot, double-barreled shotgun.

His dreams were of such substance when he stirred to a hand on his cheek. "Newt. Newt. Wake up."

"Who is it? What you want?" He could just make out Clara's dark form above him.

"It's me. Clara."

"Yeh. What's the matter?"

"Newt—" she said softly.

"Yeh?"

"Momma's dead."

CHAPTER ✣ 18

DAWN ARRIVED painfully slow, and Newt, as if in a trance, lay gazing out the window through the dank lace curtains. He watched the sky pale as the sun climbed to the foggy horizon and brightened the upper reaches. His mind, with unaccountable calm, explored the reality of this hour over the deep, uneven snoring of Roy and Pete, sleeping beside him.

Their mother was dead, he knew, but it was hard to believe. Suddenly he wondered if, somewhere up there in the pale blue nothingness, her soul—free of tortured body and earthly things—was already floating silently about, knowing at last the real purpose of its sojourn on a complex and troubled earth. What if she had found that all the praying and religious rites were just a lot of folly; that her soul floated with no more righteousness or dignity than that of Doc Cheney, Big Mabel, or even Captain Tuck? What a shock it would be to her!

He now thought uneasily of such a possibility, and he couldn't help but feel that this was more than likely the case —and the feeling shamed him. Then he softened his shame with the reasoning that if such were true, she would never begrudge anyone such equality. Whatever judgment settled upon her, he thought, would surely be the best that eternity could possibly extend.

As Newt dressed quietly, the sun burned through the fog, warming the wet rooftops, drying the leaves and grass. And the moist cool earth took in the heat and in return gave forth little curlings of cloud that quickly disappeared in the clean morning air.

He entered the dining room and looked around. Everything was just about the same, except the door which the shot had blasted. Stepping to it, he ran his fingers over the splintered surface. Daylight leaked through it now, and a sudden fright gripped him, for he realized that this destruction was actually meant for Rende. Remembering the gun against his father's head, he shivered and stepped back involuntarily (this could've been Poppa's skull), then he moved warily across to his mother's room. They had already taken her to the undertaker's.

The odor of camphor and medicine still hung in the air, and a bouquet of withered posies lay on the rocking chair in the corner of the room. The sheets had been removed, and the mattress was doubled upon the sagging springs. Above the antique dresser hung an oval-shaped photograph of his father and mother, framed in a polished, worn wood. It had been taken their wedding day, and both stared straight ahead—unmindful of this faraway moment when their last child would stand silent, alone and uncertain in this room of death.

Almost in every sense, Newt had come to link death with violence. Even his mother's passing, he thought, couldn't escape a brush with it. Nearly everyone he had known intimately, and who had ceased to live, met their demise in bloodshed. And it was probably for this reason that he feared death so much—and this fear, he reasoned, was childish. His mother's easy, tranquil and unflinching acceptance of death enhanced his respect for her. Now, this morning, it was creating within him a near-fanatical desire to rid himself of this stigma that had dogged his soul since the day of Doc Cheney's death.

Turning from the room, he channeled his thoughts into an imaginary rectangular hole that someday would be his grave. And his whole being reacted against the eternal blackness, the unending airlessness, the unchangeable recumbent position of his body—never to eat, taste, feel, speak or hear again. He shuddered. Now he envisaged the others reposing about him, acre after acre; worm-bored coffin sides, everlasting decay, dust piling forever upon eternal dust—entombed in the still, suffocating blackness.

Why, then, was life given, and for no logically explained reason taken away again? He recalled the rolling, wearisome voice of Pastor Broadnap. "—From dust you came and to dust you must returneth!" Newt remembered his authoritatively hollering such things over Big Mabel's coffin. He remembered, too, his swing about the pulpit, frock coat flying, sweat dripping, screaming of immortality—"of the spirit, of the soul"—not the good, solid body.

Newt opened the front door and stepped out on the porch. As his bare feet moved over the clammy boards, he heard the creaking beneath them and noted that they would soon have to be replaced. Sunlight bathed the edge of the porch, so he went to stand there, warming his body in the brilliant glow.

Morning eased into afternoon, evening, night, restless sleep—then there was morning again. The gray, simple casket arrived in the early afternoon. It was placed in the parlor by the window, resting on six silver wheels, and by late evening the room had become filled with flowers.

Twice during the day Newt went to look at his mother, once with his father and then with Prissy and Pete. Prissy cried, but he didn't; and as the three of them walked from the coffin, he placed his arms consolingly about her shoulders—this for the very first time in his life. And she cuddled to his touch. It gave him a good feeling, a good, big-brother and close-family feeling; one that demanded swift growing up, in mind and body alike. His entire body and his mind reacted to this demand, and he seemed to grow on the spot, feeling the expansion in his muscles, his thighs and belly—and heart. On impulse, he said to himself, "I've got to prove somethin'—to myself."

"What'd you say?"

"Nothin'. Just thinkin', Prissy. Just thinkin'."

Later, walking through the backyard toward the hog pens, he had a certain notion, and as he worked this notion grew. He would sleep this night on the floor beside his mother's coffin, in the very presence of death. If during the night his fear left forever, the purpose would be served. If it remained ... His thoughts juggled the possibility for a few seconds, then he shrugged it off. "Mornin' holds the answer," his voice sighed to the crimson evening, "mornin' holds the answer."

As night raced upon him, all else—funeral plans, mourning, telegrams, arriving kinfolk—passed as would trifling scenes in a powerful drama. He was caught in an impulse that denied significance to anything but that impulse. And though he existed in the land of the living, his mind was unrelated to it.

By one-thirty in the morning he was lying in his bed hearing nothing but the deep, unrhythmed sleep of the household; his heart pounding, the finger of fear touching it, the challenge calling from the dark room where his mother's body lay. The reality of the moment grasped him like steel claws. Dreamlike, he rose as if pulled from the bed and draped a blanket about his shoulders. The immense underground of death took its place in his mind, but he moved on toward the room through the ever-so-quiet darkness. Reaching the parlor door, he stopped, breathing heavily. He felt that he had awaited this moment all his life, and now that it had arrived, he could not fail it. He pushed the door open gently, paused, then stepped in—leaving the door ajar behind him. In the dimness he could see the shape of the coffin. His heart sank, and he wanted to run from the room; but he realized he had to go through with it after coming this far. Sweat dripped from his armpits, and he could feel the moisture in the palms of his hands. He made another small step toward the coffin (the lid's down), one more step— driplets of sweat coursed down the sides of his face. He gently eased up the lid, shivered, trembled, looked. The dark form of his mother lay deep in the cushion of crinkly white. (I made it, Momma—I made it—give me strength to stay on—give me strength.) Bracing himself, he took a final steady, muscle-taut, teeth-grinding look, dropped the blanket to the floor, spread it, lay upon it, jerked it about him, closed his eyes tightly—sealing off all blackness except that of his own inner being. After a while the heartbeat slowed, the trembling eased. He commenced the struggle with sleep. Though his eyes were closed, all the counterparts of fear tried forcing their way into his vision; but he helped his mind form the image of his mother as it had existed in reality, before death—and he held onto that image with great tenacity. (. . . I ain't afraid . . . I ain't afraid . . .) An owl hooted in the nearby woods; crickets chirped in brittle unending chorus; and in this hour Newt heard the forlorn cry of the whippoorwill. (I ain't afraid no more, Momma . . . I ain't afraid. . . .) He was easing into weariness now. (I ain't afraid. . . .) At last, as if in answer to his courage, sleep came. Before long, he was snoring softly. His dreams, unafraid.

Here, Jack Winger found his son in early morning. At first, the sight of Newt curled up on the floor alongside the open coffin shook him. But he quickly understood. He knew his son better than his son thought. And the look of peace on the boy's face signified something more important than his just sleeping there. He started to rouse him and put out his hand, then suddenly drew it back, tiptoed out and softly closed the door. Then he went through the foggy morning to appease the hunger of his squealing hogs.

". . . Ashes to ashes . . . dust to dust . . . from dust we came and to dust we returneth." The petals of the broken rose fell from Pastor Broadnap's fingers, twisted and dipped in blurred confusion before Newt's tear-filled eyes, then came to rest on Sarah Winger's coffin. ". . . may this beloved mother and wife rest, forever, in peace. May God have mercy on this family . . . amen."

Newt felt his Uncle Rob's hand ease to his shoulder, pressing home the end of the rites. Grief engulfed him as he stood staring into his mother's open grave. (Goodbye, Momma—I won't forget your dream.)

"Come on, son—let's go," Rob said.

"Okay, Uncle Rob, I just want to stay a little longer."

"It's all right, boy. Take your time." Rob waited as the others started filing out toward the waiting cars.

Newt's eyes swept the grave for the last time, continued on to two chalk-white headstones, lined up stiffly to the left of his mother's final resting place. Time and weather had worn the once crisp lettering:

Clarinda Winger	Miller Winger
Born May 12, 1901	Born December 16, 1897
Died May 12, 1901	Died June 14, 1909

A warm gentle breeze licked his ear. He turned at its touch and took Rob's hand and they walked away. As he neared the car, he noticed two workmen sitting beneath a giant oak tree. Picks and shovels lay at their sides, and they were eating from tin lunch pails. (. . . grave diggers . . . they'll be coverin' Momma soon's we leave. . . .) The thought began overpowering him, and he screamed inside. He hurried Rob the last few yards to the car, helped him in beside his father and slammed the door.

"Everything all right, boy?" Jack asked.

"Yessir, Poppa. Everything's all right now."

The big black funeral limousine moved slowly through the huge wrought-iron gate, turned onto the highway and rolled smoothly into high gear. Newt heard its tires singing on the hot macadam, drowning out the stifling silence of anguish and sorrow. He closed his eyes and his thoughts, slumped down into the seat and completely surrendered his body to the car's gentle, surging motion.

The following day Newt began packing for his trip north. As he neatly arranged his meager belongings, Beansy sat on the dining room floor, his back to the wall, harboring a regret at Newt's leaving.

"Hate to see you go, Newt. Won't be the same round here without you. But it's prob'ly best this way."

"Maybe yes. Maybe no." Newt paused and gazed blankly at the candy-striped pajamas in his hand. "Who can say—I'll miss you and the fellas—but I'll be comin' back for visits—and who knows, maybe you can come see me before long. It ain't really like we won't never see each other again." He pressed and held his weight upon some wrinkled overalls.

"Wonder what it's like up where you're goin', Newt?"

Newt folded his gray bell-bottomed pants on top of the overalls. "I don't know for sure. Clara and Lou say you don't have to sit in the buzzard's roost at the picture shows, and you can even eat in some of the white places and play on white school teams like everybody else."

"You think that's just a lotta talk?"

"Don't know."

A grin stretched Beansy's rubbery, fat face. "What about the white girls, Newt?"

"I ain't worried about *them* none. I ain't for kickin' 'em out if they get in bed with me. But like Roy says, 'All behinds feel the same in the dark.'"

Clara strutted in and stood above them, her hands wet with washing suds. "Newt, you ain't takin' those bell-bottom pants nowhere."

"What's wrong with 'em?"

"You just ain't takin' 'em, that's all." She picked up the end of one of the spreading legs. "Why, that cold air'd git up under them things and freeze your tail off. You're goin' north, boy—not south." She wiped the suds off on her dress. "Take 'em out now, like I say." She switched off to the kitchen.

"Crapmafittle," Newt said under his breath, exchanging grins with Beansy. He glanced toward the kitchen, took the pants, hid them in brown wrapping paper and squeezed the package in at the very bottom of the pasteboard suitcase.

"She's gonna be bossy, Newt."

"Her growl's worse'n her bite. Anyway, I'll be on my own soon's I get myself a job." Roy had given him two shirts and a tie. He cocked his head to one side and proudly observed the presents and placed them on top of the pile. He exhaled deeply, then pushed the bag into the corner. "That's about all I can do now—finish the rest in the mornin'."

"Prissy gonna live with you?"

"No. She's gonna be with Lou, but we'll be in the same neighborhood. Poppa and Pete are gonna stay here for a while. They may come up later."

"What time we meetin' the gang over at the river?"

"About four," Newt said, "I went over to the hospital to say goodbye to Earl this mornin'."

Aware now of their possibly never seeing each other again, Newt and Beansy casually ambled into the open, and for the next half hour they sat quietly on the edge of the porch, swatting flies, pitching rocks, whittling sticks—their thoughts saddened by the waning hours of comradeship.

" 'Bout time to meet Jappy. He'll be at Logan's Grove at a quarter to four," Newt said.

"Where's Skunk?"

"Cuttin' grass—be over later."

Marcus had an armful of dirty sheets when he saw Newt and Beansy from the second story window at Chappie's. "Must be headin' for the river," he thought. "Now's my chance."

He dropped the sheets and walked casually, but swiftly, down the stairs. He saw the back of Chappie, who was sprawled in a big chair talking to the cook. He moved quietly past the big bar, entered Chappie's room and opened the drawer in which the gun was hidden. He broke it open and eyed the breech. It held one bullet. He shoved the revolver into his pocket and, feeling for more ammunition, upended the shirts. Finally, his hand struck one bullet lying on the very bottom. He dropped it in beside the gun and kept hunting—to no avail. As he attempted to straighten out the shirts, a stack of loose bills slid out of one of the sleeves.

"Damn," Marcus whispered. He fingered the money quickly. "Must be two hundred bucks here—'nough to git anyplace on." As he crammed the bills into his back pocket one peeled off and fluttered to the floor. He closed the drawer and crept into the barroom, then slipped out the front door and headed toward the river.

Chappie got up and looked through the door. "Seems like I heard somebody come in," he said to the cook. He looked around the room and up the stairway. "Savage!" he shouted. "You up there?" He wobbled over to the foot of the stairs. "Savage—you workin'?" Chappie wearily climbed the stairs, the boards creaking under his tremendous weight. "Savage!" he called out angrily, seeing the sheets lying on the floor. He went back downstairs and crossed to his room. "Savage!" He saw the ten-dollar bill on the floor, and his eyes shifted to the drawer. He pulled it open, seeing the ruffled shirts. His hand felt for the money, then the gun. "That bastard!" He

235

grabbed his hat and started out the door, then he called to the cook, "Potsy, I'm goin' over to the jail!"

"What's up!" the cook hollered back.

"That goddamned monkey's stole my money and gun! Watch out till I git back!" He piled into the car and shot off over the tracks. He met Kirky coming out of the door and told him about the theft.

"Where's he now?" Kirky asked.

"How'd I know?" Chappie said heatedly. "Prob'ly gonna try'n shoot that Winger kid 'fore he skips out!"

"Prob'ly right," Kirky agreed. "See if you kin round up Bull and Doug for me—tell 'em to meet me over to the Winger place."

"Okay," Chappie said, and Kirky hopped onto his motorcycle and bolted across the tracks. Two blocks away he spotted Skunk pushing a lawn mower down the street. Kirky skidded to a stop.

"Seen the Winger boy?" he shouted.

"Naw," Skunk answered.

"Betta tell the truth, boy. It's for his own good."

"Somethin' wrong?" Skunk asked casually.

" 'Twill be plenty wrong if I don't git to him 'fore that Savage boy does. Come on now—where's he at?"

"At the river—goin' swimmin'. I'm meetin' 'em soon's I put this mower up."

"You stay 'way from there!" Kirky shouted as he roared off.

Newt, Beansy and Jappy had crossed the river road now and they were trooping through the brush toward Rock Cave. Jappy carried a heavy stick, and now and then he would stop and swing at a stone, bottle or tin can in a golfer's manner. The river was in full view now, and Newt subconsciously noted the pinkish-gray coloring upon it in the distance where the watersides curved again into the forest. "It'll prob'ly be the last time I'll see this place—be on the train this time tomorrow," he was thinking. They were passing the cave now and heading down toward the bank. Beansy walked over and knelt beside the water and pushed his hand against the current.

"Gittin' colder," he observed.

"Yeh, won't be long now before you guys'll be trappin' down here again." Newt was remembering his and Beansy's last trapping expedition, when he stole the hot sausage from his mother's frying pan. It seemed like years had passed since then.

"You guys goin' in?" Beansy hollered.

"Let's wait up for Skunk," Jappy said.

"Okay by me," Beansy answered, "he ought'a be comin' soon."

They continued along the bank, filling their last hours with small talk. Three sparrows darted about in hot pursuit of a crow. The boys watched the big bird wheel, rise, drop, rise again and shoot into the tall trees, the sparrows still on its tail.

"Nest robber," Newt said.

There wasn't much left for them to say. The world had suddenly grown quiet. The sun was lowering into a pink haze. A cracking of brush came from about twenty yards behind them. Beansy turned. "Skunk must be com—" The rest of the word froze in his mouth.

"Winger!" Marcus hollered.

"He's got a gun!" Beansy yelled.

Newt, Jappy and Beansy scrambled into the woods between the road and the river. Marcus aimed toward Newt and fired.

"Ow!" Jappy screamed. He had caught the bullet in the leg. Marcus was running toward them. "My leg! My leg!" Jappy hollered, as he kept stumbling toward the road. Newt and Beansy looked back, horrified.

"He's after me! Help Jappy, Beansy! Help Jappy!" Newt fell to the ground and grabbed the stick Jappy had dropped; then, terror-stricken, he rolled behind a thicket, got to his feet and ran off in another direction with Marcus close on his heels. Beansy pulled Jappy up and helped him out to the road. "Oh God—oh God," Beansy kept saying.

"Run for help, Beansy! Hurry! Hurry!" Jappy shouted. "I can make it from here! It's just my leg!"

"You shore?"

"Yeh—hurry!"

Marcus was closing in fast, and Newt, feeling it useless to run any more, stopped—the stick clutched tightly in his hand. He stood against a tree; will shattered; body tensed; wanting to cry out for mercy; for help; ready to fall whenever the bullet came ripping through.

Marcus aimed and pulled the trigger.

Click—click—click—click—

Spasms of fear shot through Newt's body.

Click—click—click—click—

"You bastard!" Marcus shouted. Then, inflamed at the misfire, he threw the gun at Newt with all his might. Newt

237

ducked. The gun smacked against the tree and bounced off his shoulder to the ground. Looking back to Marcus, he saw him pull his knife, flinched as the blade popped out. Newt backed toward the road as Marcus circled to the right. Marcus lunged. Newt swung the stick. The blow aimed for Marcus' head, caught him on the shoulder, knocking him off balance; but the momentum of the charge brought them into contact, and the knife, aimed for Newt's heart, sliced his left shoulder instead. Newt felt the blade tear through his skin. He hollered, jumped back and frantically swung again. The stick found its mark this time, and Marcus dropped to his knees. But quickly he was up—blood running from his nose to his chin—stalking Newt like a wild animal. "You son-of-a-bitch! You gonna die! You gonna die!"

Newt felt the warm blood at his elbow, but his eyes stayed on Marcus and the glistening blade. He circled backward, being careful not to stumble, his fear mixed with a great desire to survive. Marcus crouched, sprang again, low this time, and Newt swung—but missed him—jumped to the side as the blade slashed through the denim of his overalls just above the knee. Marcus plunged onto the ground. Newt started in, hesitated; then Marcus was on his feet again, cussing, circling, cussing. "You son-of-a-bitch! You black bastard! I'm gonna cut your fuckin' heart out!" The blood rolled thick over his lips now.

"Come on! Come on! I'm ready for you!"

The courage in Newt's voice enraged Marcus. He spat a gob of blood, stuck out the knife and charged. Newt's aim was true, and as the blow smashed against Marcus' skull he went down with a howl and a thud, the knife flying from his hand. Newt dropped the stick and dived for the knife, beating his dazed assailant to the weapon. But Marcus was not finished, and his hand coiled Newt's wrist in a powerful effort to shake the knife from his hand. But Newt held on, and they wrestled to the side of the road, their bodies rolling as one in the dust, the knife extended beyond their heads. Finally they landed in a ditch with Newt on top, and with a last burst of strength he yanked his wrist from Marcus' grasp. Then the blade was up, the hand trembling, the arm tensed for a downward thrust. But the look of helplessness and fear beneath the bloody mask that was Marcus' face stopped Newt's arm cold. For a split second their eyes burned into each other's.

"I ought'a kill you, Marcus." Newt breathed heavily, the knife still up. "I ought'a kill—"

A siren sounded, and they both started. "It's Kirky, Newt! Gimme a chance! He'll shoot me to pieces!"

Newt glanced up the road, then back at his frightened enemy. "Okay, git goin', and don't never come back." He released his hold, and Marcus staggered up and started running toward the rocky ledge. Newt pushed the dirty wet blade into the groove, felt his arm. It wasn't as bad as he had thought. The next minute he was secretly hoping, even praying, for Marcus' escape.

Kirky's motorcycle skidded to a stop in a cloud of dust. He jumped off, eyed Newt quickly and drew his guns. "Where's he at? You hurt?"

Newt looked toward the opposite direction from which Marcus ran. "He went into the woods."

"Which way?" Newt didn't have to answer. Kirky suddenly spotted Marcus loping toward the rocky ledge. He fired and shouted, "Halt! Halt!" Then he started running, firing and shouting at the same time. "Halt! Halt!"

Newt pocketed the knife and followed. (Run, Marcus, run, run, run . . .).

"Stop, you black bastard! Stop, goddam you!" He was firing both pistols now, and Marcus was trying to reach a safe diving position from the ledge. It was obvious he was going to attempt the river—under water, downstream. Kirky fired again, and the bullet chipped the stone above Marcus' head.

Suddenly Newt yelled, "Look out! Oh God! Oh God!" Marcus had slipped and was falling down toward the stone apron, screaming as he plummeted through space. Kirky's mouth flew open and he held his fire. Newt slapped his hands over his eyes as Marcus' body smashed and crumpled against the jagged lip, stayed for a moment, then began a grotesque end-over-end plunge downward. When it splashed into the calm river, great ripples swelled from the entry point, then began wasting themselves in their own motion. The head bobbed up a couple of times, the body rolled over like a slow-moving fish, then spiraled to the bottom of the river.

Kirky holstered his guns, mopped his brow with the back of his hairy hand and spat. "Well, Winger, you kin rest easy. You won't be bothered with him no more."

Newt stood gazing into the easy-moving water. "Ain't we goin' to try and get him out?"

"Not now. Pull him out tomorra mornin'. Be dark soon. It's a cinch he ain't goin' nowhere tonight." He took a plug of tobacco from his puttees and bit off a chunk. "He cut you deep?"

"Not too bad."

"Git on. I'll give you a lift home."

"Nope. I can make it by myself."

"Okay by me, boy," Kirky grunted. He mounted the machine and stomped the pedal with his foot. The motorcycle pop-popped to a start and belched off in a cloudy roar.

The last of the sunlight was gone now, and the crickets had already begun rubbing at the evening dampness. Newt started off then stopped, his mind jumping back and forth between home and Marcus' body, wallowing now somewhere at the bottom. For an instant he thought of going back, not knowing why; then he reasoned against it.

Newt turned for a last look at the river. The pink coloring was gone, and the gray was edging into blackness. Marcus was just a memory. He felt his arm, shivered, then slowly turned homeward over the dusty road.

"I haven't seen her all day," Vance said.

The brothers grew serious and shared a glance.

"We'd better go check on her," Lars said.

"So, are you really worried about her?" Vance hurried after them. "You don't think something could have happened, do you? Her sister called. She was supposed to pick her up."

Vance joined them on the elevator.

"There are a couple of places that a person wouldn't want to fall into."

"What?" Vance's gut tightened as he looked from one brother to the other. "What places?"

"No point in borrowing trouble." Karl shrugged.

"Yeah, she's probably looking around by herself like she always does after we leave."

"Looking around? For what?" How did they know she looked around after they left if they were gone? Odd.

Neither brother answered, but Vance didn't miss their shared glance.

While they waited for the doors to open, the thought that Andi could be hurt somewhere on the missile launch center crept over Vance. He shoved it away. Like Karl said. No point in borrowing trouble. But if something had happened to her. . .

His concerns over his job and the tricky game he played with the algorithm meant nothing to him. He had to find Andi, make sure she was all right. She already meant way too much to him. Never mind that she'd built a barrier he couldn't seem to scale. Never mind that it was obvious she and God weren't on good terms.

At the moment, he cared about nothing except finding her.

ELIZABETH GODDARD is a seventh-generation Texan transplanted in Southern Oregon near the Rogue River. She loves to write and read inspirational fiction in several genres, including thriller, suspense, historical, and speculative fiction. When she's not writing, she's busy homeschooling her four children and serving with her husband as he pastors a local church. She enjoys hiking in the Redwoods and camping on the Oregon coast with her family. Find out more about Beth at www.elizabethgoddard.com.

Books by Elizabeth Goddard

HEARTSONG PRESENTS
HP777—Seasons of Love

Disarming Andi

Elizabeth Goddard

Heartsong Presents

Dedicated to my husband, who always encourages me, and my children who understand when Mom has to write. A special dedication goes to the missileers—America's "Underground Air Force" who guarded our country during the Cold War—and those who continue protecting us today. Thanks to Ed Peden of Twentieth Century Castles and Gina Shipman of Shipman Construction, who shared their expertise and advice. And to Julie Neidlinger whose family owns the Echo-0 launch control facility, thanks for allowing me to draw from your experiences.

A note from the Author:
I love to hear from my readers! You may correspond with me by writing:

Elizabeth Goddard
Author Relations
PO Box 721
Uhrichsville, OH 44683

ISBN 978-1-60260-756-9

DISARMING ANDI

Our mission is to publish and distribute inspirational products offering exceptional value and biblical encouragement to the masses.

PRINTED IN THE U.S.A.

prologue

Fargo, North Dakota

"Show your face here and you're dead."

The words, though said in jest, came rushing back to Vance Young as he returned to work late that night, plodding through the revolving doors.

Vance ran a hand down his face. He should have left for vacation earlier in the day. He'd been delayed, but it worked in his favor because in the middle of the night, no one would see him at the office, hence he was in total compliance with CEO Peter Lundgren's wishes. No one would see his face.

Well, except for Tom, who stood tall and intimidating at the granite-topped security counter. Behind him, chrome letters formed the words ANND Systems. *Artificial Neural Network Defense.* Everyone pronounced it Andee.

The name seemed to leap at Vance from the backdrop of azure marble. He inserted his laminated ID card through the thin slot, then pressed his thumb into the fingerprint reader, hating the jump through security hoops every day. Wouldn't it be nice if Scotty could just beam him up?

Accustomed to seeing Vance working all hours of the night, Tom nodded and offered his usual friendly smile. "Evening, Mr. Young."

Vance made his way to the elevators, his steps across the marble floors echoing, and stared at his reflection while he waited for the metallic doors to open. He'd be long gone now if he hadn't forgotten his telescope. Somewhere on the North Dakota prairie was a house his great-uncle had bequeathed him. On a beautiful night in the middle of July, the stars would be easy to see in the country away from light pollution.

5

Vance was looking forward to some quiet time.

"Mr. Young?" Tom blurted from the foyer.

What now?

Tom stood behind him, staring at him in the reflection.

"Mr. Young."

Vance turned to face the security guard, who'd never followed him before now. "Hey Tom, what's up?"

"Thought you were leaving for your vacation today."

"I forgot my telescope." The elevator doors swooshed open. "Hope it doesn't take too long. I'm ready to be outta here."

"I hear you." Tom nodded.

Vance stepped into the elevator, grateful for the speedy precision with which the doors closed. On most mornings, he cursed their slowness as he struggled to gain access with a score of others shuffling to their jobs in the morning rush.

Alone in the elevator, he allowed himself to lean against the flimsy wall for support as the undersized box rushed to the top floor. The small bead of sweat that usually formed on his temple spread across his forehead.

Finally, the doors slid open and he stepped into the software development department. He took another step forward and began to relax as he strolled past a score of gray, empty cubicles on his way to his office.

Vance passed the dinosaur pen—the glassed-in halo-protected processing room—where the data-crunching mainframe he called Cindy resided. Oddly, the humming sound created by the processing of massive amounts of data soothed him.

Peter preferred using mainframe computers because of the sheer volume of data, approaching petabytes, or one quadrillion bytes. Eh. All they needed was what amounted to a bunch of PlayStation 3s clustered together.

Once in his office, Vance didn't bother switching on the lights. He took a deep, peaceful breath. Late at night he had a stellar view of the stars.

Over on his desk, Vance noticed something out of place, so he flipped on the lights. A woman stared back at him from a picture frame. It should have been face down, exactly where he thought he'd put it several days ago when Peter had said the only thing better than a computer was a girlfriend. Yeah, well, Vance had a girlfriend once. But then Janice only wanted him for his brains. What a joke. She'd used him to help her through some of her more difficult college classes this past school year. Though he'd graduated five years ago, he knew computer science.

Vance had pulled her picture out of the frame, only to see the photo of a gorgeous blond model that had come with it. With hair cascading a bit past her shoulders and soft, delicate features, she held her chin just so, giving her a feisty air of defiance. Big blue eyes and oh. . .that smile. Well, no wonder he'd left her photograph in the frame. Over time she'd become his dream girl. She was out there. Somewhere. . .

Vance began packing up his telescope.

"Mr. Young." Tom's voice boomed from behind, startling Vance.

He turned to face the security guard, stifling his irritation. "What's up?"

"Sorry to bother you again. Just got off the phone with Mr. Lundgren. He said I was to escort you out of the building since, well, you're *supposed* to be on vacation."

"What is he? The keymaster?" He clamped his lips tight to keep from spewing what Tom could take back to Peter. It wasn't Tom's fault. That was some way for Peter to treat him, though. He had no right. "Well, did you tell him I forgot my telescope?"

"He said you need a vacation and he would kick you out if he had to." Tom's grin was teasing. "If you ask me, you do look kind of pale, could use some sun."

"It's hard to get ultraviolet radiation when you're hidden away like a Morlock." Vance grinned, hoping to disarm Tom.

The security guard smiled back. "Morlock, sir?"

"You know, from H. G. Wells's *The Time Machine*."

Tom gave him a funny look.

"You see there's this guy who invents. . ." What was he doing besides wasting time? "Oh forget it."

Tom laughed.

"Let me finish packing. There's no need for you to wait."

Tom stiffened. "Just doing my job, Mr. Young. You don't want me to get fired, do you?"

"Not at all." Peter wanted Vance to be at his best when he returned, but in order to do that, he had to actually leave. If only he could shake the sense that Peter *needed* him gone.

Peter had enticed him from his job in Texas with talk of a classified government contract and the promise of promotion to vice president of. . .something. Vance knew data mining and thought it would be stellarific to have a shot at stopping the bad guys. Like a simple Boolean equation, the answer was obvious and he hadn't thought twice about saying yes. Working for Peter, he'd labored for months on the software to find specific patterns in data to identify terrorist activities.

It had been like a dream come true, except Vance was miserable and should write the entire experience off as a loss. At twenty-seven, he thought he knew what he wanted. But North Dakota winters weren't to his liking. Dad had warned him, telling him that sometimes a person thought he knew what he wanted and when he got it, discovered how wrong he was.

Telescope packed, Vance walked with Tom to the elevators. They discussed the weather on the way down. Once in the foyer, Vance left Tom and strode to the revolving door.

"You dropped something."

Vance turned to see Tom standing there, holding out a small disk.

Vance searched his memory. "I didn't—"

"Must have fallen out of your pocket."

Vance mechanically reached for the small storage media. "Thanks."

Tom held on to the memory card for a split second longer than necessary while he stared at Vance. Then the security guard nodded and returned to his station.

Vance examined the disk. It wasn't his. But then again, at two in the morning maybe it was.

જ

He should have waited until morning to leave, but he was packed and ready to go, anxious to get away. Later, after three and a half hours of driving through the early morning along lonely dark highways and county roads, Vance was all the more bleary-eyed. The sooner he found his uncle's house the faster he could sleep for a few days.

An unpleasant thought occurred to him. What if his uncle's house was completely vacant of furniture and amenities? How could he have overlooked that possibility? In that case he'd have to stay in a hotel and make a quick decision on the house. Then he could go to Cancun ahead of schedule.

He came to a small town named Herndon. His uncle's house was somewhere nearby. According to Vance's GPS all he had to do was drive through the town and go another five miles, take a left on a side road for another two. As the sky lightened, his spirits rose and so did his hopes of finding the place.

Vance pulled on to a paved road in the middle of a wheat field that seemed to go nowhere, and then turned onto a gravel road, which ended up at a tall chain-link gate. He climbed out of his car. The fence surrounded a large area that included a metal building and. . . Was that a helicopter pad? Even though he was sleep-deprived, the sun brought a dawning with it that hit him like a bomb.

He was standing at an old missile site—a product of the Cold War.

"You've got to be kidding." His words spoken to no one seemed to magnify the seclusion.

What was going on? There had to be some mistake.

A padlock secured the gate. There was one way to find out if he was at the right place. He found the keys he'd been given to his uncle's property. To his disappointment, one of them looked like it belonged to a padlock. Warily, he inserted it.

The lock opened.

Stellarific.

one

Andi Nielsen hit the brakes of her old rusty Dodge pickup. The vehicle ground to a standstill a mere inch from the gated entrance to Vance Erickson's property.

"Um, sis, when are you going to get those fixed?" Her teen-age sister, Elisa, gripped the door handle with white knuckles.

"Good gravy. You know we can't afford that right now." Andi jumped out of Dad's old truck. If there was one thing she hated it was squealing old brakes.

Could things get any worse? She'd secured a contract with Vance Erickson months ago to renovate an old decommissioned launch control facility into a lavish home. But he'd died just before they were to begin work on the next section. The major portion of her fee wasn't due until she'd completed the entire project, and there was no chance of that now. This job should have kept her busy for a long time.

She'd been outbid on everything else. Either that or people were listening to talk from subcontractors who wouldn't work for a woman, and in this small town in North Dakota, there were plenty of men who thought taking orders from a woman was demeaning.

From those who didn't care, she had other problems like quality work for the right price. She refused to use subs that cut corners with cheap materials.

Finishing the missile site would go a long way toward giving her construction company respect in the community. With respect would come the referrals she desperately needed. Sure, people remembered her contractor father, but he died a few years ago. His daughter had to prove she had the nails for the business—and at only twenty-one, she had some large shoes to fill.

Oh, Daddy...

She kicked the tire, then pulled the keys to the missile launch control facility from her bag. She'd never returned them. No one had shown up to claim them either. She grabbed a flashlight from behind the seat.

"Um, Andi. I don't know about this." Elisa clipped at a nail, then stuck the clippers she always carried into her back pocket. "Mr. Erickson is dead now. You can't just waltz in there. You got no right."

Andi glowered at Elisa, wanting to ask what she knew about it, if anything. Elisa had gone out of her way to cause Andi more than her share of trouble. "Look, this is all I have left."

She might not ever finish renovations or see the money, but at least she could look for what her grandfather had stashed inside years before when he'd worked at the missile site. Stomping over to the gate, she jangled the keys, searching for the right one.

Before Andi found the key, Elisa shoved the gate open. "You still think that letter you found means something, like it's a treasure map?"

Andi stared at the chain-link fence. "Hey, I could swear I locked—"

"You're not listening. But what's new?"

"I heard you. Yes, I think it's worth a look." In fact, Andi believed it could be the very reason Mr. E had hired her.

Elisa stepped through the gate. "I should have stayed in bed."

"Wait a minute. I need to make sure it's safe."

"From what?"

Andi swallowed her frustration with her sister, wishing it were a school day and not a Saturday so she could have peace from the constant arguing. After pushing through the gate, she walked up the short drive and cautiously to the right side of the only building Mr. E had left standing on the site. Most of it had burned last year, but they'd managed to salvage part of it.

"You mean who."

Elisa followed Andi and stood next to her. "Huh?"

"Someone's here. I don't recognize the vehicle," Andi said.

"Nice. A brand-spanking-new red Jetta." Sarcasm dripped from Elisa. "It's probably someone who'll want those keys back."

"Whoever it is, I need to look around."

If only one last time.

⁂

This is crazy. Vance had taken the access stairs rather than risk the elevator, but now that he'd gone down several flights, descending a good fifty feet underground, he wasn't sure he'd made the right decision. Did the stairs go anywhere? He'd assumed they did considering there wasn't much left of the building above ground. Most of that had been destroyed except a small section that appeared to house the entrance to the underground. . .what. . .dwelling? Had his uncle actually lived here?

Difficult to believe, that's what he'd been told, though he'd missed the part where someone had referred to nuclear bombs and launch facilities, either that or he'd had a random access memory leak. Or had that information been purposefully left out? Either way, he'd committed to getting this off his smart phone reminders list.

What must Uncle Vance—his namesake—have been thinking to give this to him? Had he known of his nephew's aversion to closed places? No way. Vance wasn't sure his mother even knew. In his estimate, by the time he stepped in front of what looked like a blast door, he'd descended another twenty feet for a total of seventy. The door appeared to be part of the elevator shaft.

To his right was a tunnel. He strolled through the long cylinder and stopped at a convex blast door, shaped like the exterior of a sphere. Another one? He chuckled to calm himself. That and to let the bears know someone was coming. It was best to alert rather than startle. Boy Scouts 101. This would have been a great field trip when he was a kid. As it was, he felt like he was in a science fiction movie.

The door read STAND CLEAR OF BLAST DOOR. CAUTION. DO NOT SPIN WHEEL. TURN WHEEL APPROXIMATELY THREE TURNS TO OPEN OR CLOSE.

He touched the wheel, then paused, feeling the sweat trickle down his back. The surroundings were getting to him. He tugged his shirt collar, even though it was loose to begin with. The site had been decommissioned years ago, he reassured himself, or else he would never have been allowed into the facility. Air Force guards would have been everywhere. Vance took a couple of deep breaths, surprised the air wasn't stale, but rather smelled like vanilla air freshener.

Would he be able to open the door? Shoving aside his growing anxiety, he turned the wheel three times and pulled. The door swung open. Vance fully expected to be required to offer his identity at this juncture. But to whom, he didn't know. He held his breath and stepped into a room. Lights automatically flickered on.

Sweet fractured motherboards! He stood in what looked like the decadent inside of a mansion, rather than the sterile drabness he'd expected.

He stepped down into a large open room that housed, among other things, a beautiful modern kitchen with granite counters and stainless steel appliances.

Suddenly, his stomach grumbled. He hoped the fridge was loaded, but that was probably asking too much. Opposite the kitchen was a living area, sufficient for a gathering of at least twenty people, along with comfortable furniture and a large screen television.

Jazzy, but no windows. He wouldn't be able to look at the stars. Sure it was spacious, but he didn't know if he could tolerate the sense of confinement.

"Why couldn't this have been above ground?"

"Because it was used to house the launch control center of a nuclear missile site," a woman's voice answered for him. "It's called Ground Zero."

Startled, Vance swung around to see...

...the gorgeous blond from the picture in his office. She stood there, one hand behind her back. Her blond hair was pulled back into a tight ponytail, but it was her.

Vance rubbed his eyes. The light must be doing something to him. Or his anxiety from being boxed-in was giving him hallucinations. Thank goodness it wasn't a complete phobia, or maybe he'd see her standing next to a red Lamborghini, too. He was already tired before he'd started the trip, now he was dreaming.

He took a few steps closer, peering at her.

"What are you doing here? This is private property belonging to Vance Erickson." She placed her free hand on her hip.

"I...uh..." Vance took a step toward where she stood in the kitchen. "Have you ever done any modeling?"

two

As the stranger approached, Andi stood her ground, gripping the mallet she'd brought with her. A girl couldn't be too careful. Besides, he didn't look local. Most folks around here were farmers and ranchers. He was dressed in a suit, well, white shirt and suit pants, but she bet he'd been wearing a tie and coat earlier. The last person she'd seen dressed like that around here was—a knot suddenly rose in her throat—Jorgen.

The man moved closer and she gripped even tighter, lifting the mallet so he could see she had it.

He adjusted his glasses and squinted at her.

What did he think? She was an apparition? "Whoa. I'm packing here. No need to come any closer. I'll ask you again—"

"You all right, sis?" Elisa spoke from behind.

"I told you to stay up top." Andi brushed off her sister and waited for his answer

The man stepped forward. "I'm being rude. Let me introduce myself." He grinned and offered his hand.

"That would be nice." Andi didn't budge. This guy wasn't going to charm his way out of trouble. She doubted he could if he tried. If she had to size him up, she'd say geek, though she did like his dimples. But she and smart guys—well, they never got along too well.

"I'm Vance Young. My uncle left this place to me."

Andi stepped back, feeling like he'd thrown her a box of bricks and she'd caught it. Resentment crashed down on her. She'd had to work hard for every morsel. If there was one thing she hated it was people like this man who received things without earning them. If anything, Mr. E should have given the place to her. He owed her, didn't he? This character

15

didn't care one scrap about this home or the surrounding community. He'd inherit the place and would probably never realize its value.

Composing her emotions, she finally shook his hand. "It's nice to meet you."

"Now it's my turn. This is private property. What are you doing here?"

Andi had prepared to be challenged at some point. But not like this. "I'm Andi Nielsen of Nielsen Construction and Remodeling, and this is my sister, Elisa."

"Andi?" The man frowned, releasing an odd laugh. "Is this some sort of joke?"

"Excuse me?"

"Uh. . .it's just that. . .nothing. So *you're* in construction?"

Andi bristled at what sounded like skepticism but kept her composure. She'd learned to deal with that sort of chauvinistic reaction. She motioned to the setting around them. "Yes, my company is responsible for this room. Do you like what you see?"

The man's eyes subtly glanced over her, then to the room. "Yes, very much so."

Unwelcome warmth flitted through her. Had he referred to her or the room?

"So, you remodeled this place. What are you doing here now? Did you forget something?"

Andi moved around the large granite-laden island to the refrigerator and set the mallet down. She opened the fridge and retrieved a bottle of water. "Actually, it's complicated."

The young Vance crossed his arms, waiting.

She took a swig, giving herself time to think. This was her chance. She had to convince him. Elisa moseyed to the sofa and plopped down, announcing her impatience.

"You say your uncle gave this to you. Probably put it in the will, expecting it to be of value. But it's worth nothing until it's complete."

He cocked a brow. She could see he wouldn't be so easily

convinced. Definitely not bad looking, but with his black-framed glasses and thick brown hair shagging well past time for a haircut, he had the look of what?—an astrophysics professor? She was beginning to feel intimidated. Not good. She reminded herself she had a year of college toward her business degree.

She raised her chin. "I'm not finished with the remodel. You'll never be able to sell it until the renovations are complete."

"And after the renovations? How much would it be worth?"

"In the hundreds of thousands. Maybe millions. Your uncle had big plans."

She'd grown a soft spot for the old man, and at the thought of him, pain filled her. As she stared back at Mr. Young, she noticed he was really a younger version of his uncle.

"It looks pretty good already. I'm not sure it needs anything else."

"Why don't you let me show you around before you decide."

"It hardly matters. I don't plan to stay."

Andi hoped her smile would hide her sinking hopes. "You can't expect to make an informed decision until you've seen what needs work."

Vance looked thoughtful. "All right, on one condition."

"What's that?"

"There's another bottle of water in the fridge, though I'd prefer something that's sugary and fizzes."

Andi laughed and peered inside the appliance. "You're in luck. There are two sodas my sister left from when we were remodeling. And if your luck holds, you should find the food storage room stocked. I'll be happy to show you around."

"That would be cool." He took the soda from her. "And I like that the place comes with its own tour guide."

Andi hoped she could be more than a tour guide by the time they finished the tour. "Do you know anything about its history, Mr. Young?"

"Nothing at all, I'm afraid. And call me Vance."

"All right, then. Vance." Andi held Vance's gaze. Remove the glasses and put some meat on his bones and he'd definitely look like his uncle might have looked thirty or more years ago.

"I came here expecting to see a mansion. Not this missile silo. Talk about random."

"This is not a silo. It's a launch control facility that's been decommissioned. The room you're standing in now, the LCC, or launch control center. Of course, everything the Air Force used here, especially what they used to launch missiles, was removed during the decommissioning. Of the missile sites that were decommissioned in North Dakota, all the silos were filled in, completely destroyed."

Vance cleared his throat. "And the blast doors?"

"Oh, those. Mr. Erickson wanted to keep them for nostalgic reasons."

"Nostalgia, huh. So, can you tell me why he chose a missile launch facility? He must have been eccentric."

So the young Vance didn't know his uncle very well, and yet, he'd inherited all this. A knot of resentment grew in her throat.

While Andi agreed with him on the eccentric point, she had her suspicions of why his uncle had purchased this particular site. But she couldn't share those with his nephew. Not yet, if ever.

"Don't kid yourself. Plenty of people have purchased decommissioned missile sites like the Atlas, Titan, and Nike all over the country for conversion into homes or other uses. By the way, this is an old Minuteman facility."

"I know that much. It was part of Grand Forks Air Force Base. I heard a joke about North Dakota being the world's third strongest nuclear power."

Andi sighed. "Yeah, I'm sure after a few missiles were deployed, nobody would be counting anymore."

She had to steer the conversation back to remodeling. This morbid talk was likely to scare him off, and she intended to find out what her grandfather hid here. But to do that, she had to convince Vance to let her finish the work, which would also be money in her pocket—something she desperately needed if she were going to pay the bills. Eating would be good, too.

⋆

"Well, enough on the history." He grinned. "Give me the tour."

He tugged his glasses off and bit the end of the earpiece so they hung from his mouth. Everything there was to know about missile sites and the people who lived in them was available for perusal on the Internet later. Right now he needed to know what to do with this one.

"Oh, an important question for you. Is this place wired?" Vance could connect through his mobile networking system from anywhere, except maybe seventy feet underground. To think there was something he hadn't explored. He'd have to seriously reconsider his goals in life.

"You mean for Internet and other communications? Sure. The military already had communications in place, of course, but your uncle made sure everything was up-to-date with satellite communications, the works. I hired an independent contractor if you'd like to talk to him. It's not my expertise."

Thank you, Uncle Vance. "Not necessary. As long as it works, I'm good."

"Let's step out of the living quarters through the blast doors." Andi went first.

After a glance back at her sister reclining on the sofa, he stepped through the blast door while shoving his glasses back on.

"We'd planned to begin work on what was once the equipment building. Much of the unusable materials have already been cleared out. We put in new environmental control systems that are much quieter than what the military had in place."

Vance followed Andi through the cylindrical tunnel into the area where the elevator waited. "Does that work?"

"The elevator? Yes." She tilted her head, looking at him. "You took the stairs?"

The way she said it made him feel like he should be embarrassed. He snorted. "Look, I had no way of knowing if it was safe, okay?"

She nodded. "I guess you're right about that. But still, those stairs. . ."

"Yeah, they're brutal."

"Your uncle had us put those in. They didn't come with the original site. He just had a quirky fear of elevators. Was afraid he wouldn't be able to get out, say if the electricity were to go off. But then he was afraid he couldn't make it up the stairs so he suffered through the elevator." She smiled softly, a distant look in her eyes.

Ah. So his uncle had an almost-phobia as well, not too dissimilar from his own. "Makes you wonder why he wanted to live underground, then, doesn't it?"

She laughed. He could get used to that laugh.

Then she looked thoughtful for a moment. "I don't think being underground bothered him as much as smaller spaces."

They continued on to see another blast door. "Allow me."

She stepped back. "Be my guest."

Vance stared at the door, which was different from the other one. He scratched his head.

"You have to pump open the steel lock pins just there."

He nodded. Maybe it was some macho thing that had inspired him to show off his amazing talent to open blast doors—though he was sorely lacking in experience—but after three minutes of pumping, he glanced her way.

She smirked. "Give it two more minutes."

"Shutting and opening these things every time is taking the nostalgia a little too far, don't you think?"

"You're the new owner. You get to decide." Her smile radiated warmth.

Stellar. Vance was in some sort of competition. What was it? More importantly, what were the winnings?

Click. Finally, he unlatched the lever and pushed. The door didn't budge.

"This is where you really have to show some muscle."

Ah. She knew how to work the men. Challenging their manhood would produce results. Something she probably learned in construction.

He shoved his shoulder against the door.

"No, like this." She put her back to the door. "Help me."

He joined her and together they slowly pushed the monster door open. Breathing too hard for the cool composure he liked to portray, Vance hissed at the door, "Fiend."

Andi threw her hands up. "See, no one wants to open that all the time. Imagine trying to sell this place with that door."

Vance tried to envision living in a place where reminders of imminent nuclear conflict were everywhere.

Stepping into the room, darkness greeted them. That—and the sound of water dripping in the distance, echoing off empty walls—made the room seem like a large cavern. "Now that you've piqued my curiosity, I'm expecting to see stalactites and stalagmites."

Her laugh resonated through the room. "No, nothing so exotic."

Vance shuffled forward into the darkness, brushing her shoulder. She had nice shoulders.

Andi flipped on her flashlight. "You can see this entire section needs to be remodeled. Your uncle died before we began working in here. We'd need to strip it down first, leaving only the superstructure in place, then build on top of that."

Vance noticed the sadness in her eyes. Was she sad because she wasn't able to finish the job? Or had she cared about his uncle?

"If you're not going to stay, I'm assuming you're going to sell."

Vance took a deep breath. He hated admitting it, but he didn't have the brain circuitry available to process all of it at the moment. He stepped back through the blast door and waited on Andi.

Once safely beyond the grip of the ogre door, she took up a get-down-to-business stance. The way she morphed from a mallet-holding property protector to businesswoman-closing-a-deal intrigued him.

"Mr. Young, allow me to finish what I started here, and we can both walk away with a lot of money."

"It's Vance, remember?" He rubbed his chin and the back of his neck, then caught her staring at him with a funny look on her face.

"You look exhausted."

"That bad, huh?"

"I'm sorry, I didn't mean it that way."

"I'm wounded nonetheless." He grinned to ease her concern. "I'm sure I look like something that crawled out of a grave. I haven't slept in too long."

Maybe that's why he had the crazy urge to touch the lone strand of hair that loosened from her tight do.

As if hearing his thoughts, she pushed the hair from her face. "You've got a comfortable place to rest. And even though there's a lot of renovation to be done, you can stay here while we work. Your uncle did. There is part of your living space that needs to be finished, but I can show that to you later. You just look. . ."

"Like I'm about to collapse."

"Yeah."

"He must have been some paranoid old fool to buy this place."

Andi smiled. "Okay, I wasn't going to say it, but I'll agree with you, after all."

"Let me sleep on it. I'd be crazy to make any decisions just now."

"Here's my card." She held it out between two fingers.

Taking it, Vance studied her reaction. Her wide, beautiful smile didn't hide the disappointment behind her intense blue eyes. Somehow, he felt disappointed, too, and wished he could give her an answer. The one that she wanted. But he already carried the burden of bad decisions made in haste.

He wouldn't make another one.

three

Back in the bodacious remodeled section, Vance watched Andi and her sister exit through the blast doors, leaving him alone in the space pod floating through the universe. Considering his love of astronomy, that was probably the best way for him to think about it—a sort of virtual reality of the mind. How else was a guy who hated close quarters to tolerate living in a small underground capsule?

With some serious mind control.

Plopping on the still-warm sofa where Elisa had lounged, he chuckled, thinking of the great impression he must have made looking like a sleep-deprived zombie. No wonder Andi'd brandished the mallet.

He flipped his cell open but, of course, got no signal. *The landline it is.*

He dialed his parents' number and absorbed his surroundings while waiting for an answer.

"Hello?"

"Dad, hey."

"Son, we've been wondering about you."

"I'm at Uncle Vance's house, if you can call it that. Did you know about this?"

Dad chuckled. "You mean you didn't know that it's a refurbished missile site? What planet are you on?"

Dad knew him too well. "I'll admit, the construction company has done some amazing stuff."

He pictured Andi showing off her work. Even though she'd put on a good show as a professional, her veneer of confidence was a little too thick in his opinion. He'd seen a crack and, underneath, she seemed desperate to finish the rest. Maybe business wasn't too good in Herndon, North Dakota. Or, maybe she wanted to focus on a niche market.

"Son? You seem distracted."

Too late Vance realized his thoughts weren't on the conversation. What had Dad been saying? "Sorry. This whole thing threw me, that's all."

"Well, what do you think you'll do?"

"I'm not sure. I think the woman who owns the construction company wants to finish the work she started for Uncle Vance. I think she needs this job."

"You know you can't make a decision based on her need for a job."

Couldn't he? "Right."

"The quicker you decide, the better. But we can talk about it when you get here."

Great hacking malware. He'd forgotten to tell them he wasn't coming to Texas until *after* Cancun. God created procrastination for a reason, and Vance was willing to give it a chance. But Mom would be. . .well, he didn't have a good euphemism for her at the moment.

"I'm not sure when that will be, but I'll let you know when I know."

"Good enough."

Vance ended the conversation. His father wasn't one for long talks anyway, preferring to get to the point.

Except for the humming of the refrigerator, complete silence surrounded Vance. Once the lights were off, total darkness would envelop him as well. What was he supposed to do with a missile site—all underground? Although all evidence of a nuclear arsenal poised for war had long been removed, the place unsettled him. Thankfully, he would be leaving in a few days, heading to Cancun.

He'd done what he said he'd do. His parents had urged him to look at it, stay a few days, see if he could figure out why Uncle Vance had given it to him. Decide if he wanted to keep it. But after seeing it, he knew there was no way he could live here, so he'd definitely sell.

Could Andi be right when she said finishing the remodel could mean a lot more money when he sold? Made sense. But could it be enough for him to start his own company? Forget about working for Peter?

The thought wormed its way deeper, but even that couldn't combat the heavy fatigue that crashed over him. He needed sleep. A fluffy blue pillow, compliments of Uncle Vance, rested next to him on the sofa, so he grabbed it and, after reclining, pressed it over his eyes.

The pillow was a partial lunar eclipse, leaving just enough light to prevent sleep. He found the light switch, hoping the lights that came on automatically when the blast door opened could be shut off again when inside. He flipped the switch. Complete and utter darkness engulfed him, magnified by the fact he was in a box. Underground.

He grappled for the switch and flipped it on like a little kid afraid of the dark. Except this darkness would alarm even the biggest tough guys. Without infrared or night vision goggles, he couldn't see his hand in front of his face. If he woke up in the middle of the night and stumbled for the bathroom, he could end up falling down a dark shaft somewhere.

What he needed for comfortable sleep was soft dark. If he hired Andi the builder, he'd make that his first request—a dimmer that would create soft dark. Eh, he'd buy a few nightlights next time he was in town.

A large window in the ceiling so he could gaze at the stars would be good, too. Not only was that impossible, it was unnecessary. He wasn't staying.

Then why did he have to keep reminding himself?

With the lights remaining on for now, Vance lay on the sofa and once again tugged the pillow over his head, willing himself to rest. This time, images of the missile site remodeler kept sleep at bay. If only she didn't so closely resemble the photograph in the frame at his office, which he'd dubbed his dream girl. Though Andi had pulled her hair into a tight ponytail, he imagined the gorgeous blond strands lying across her shoulders or blowing in the breeze like in an overdramatized shampoo commercial. Her blue eyes soft and receptive, rather than guarded and secretive.

He smashed the pillow against his face. If he pressed long and hard enough, he'd pass out before he suffocated, getting some sleep.

Hours later, Vance woke up to a growling stomach and the feeling he'd been run over by a military tank. He rose from the couch and walked to the fridge. In addition to food, he could use an energy drink to take the edge off his fatigue. Once his brain got going, it'd forget that the rest of him was still tired.

What were the chances the fridge was stocked with anything he would want to eat? Nope. Nothing there except one last soda and a few bottles of water. Andi hadn't shown him the food storage room before she left, so he made his way through the rest of the refurbished area, noting the bedroom, then a small bathroom, which he quickly took advantage of.

Though he would have appreciated seeing food in the fridge, he wouldn't want to see anything left over from his uncle's time at the house either. He couldn't call it a house, or his home. He settled on what Andi had called it.

Ground Zero.

What sort of person wanted his home underground in a place protected from everything but a direct hit from a nuclear bomb? He'd have to call Mom to find out more about his great-uncle. She'd known him much better because he was really *her* uncle.

A set of double doors beckoned him at the end of the narrow corridor. Vance opened the right door and came face to face with the food storage room. One glance and his hopes sank. He wondered if food set aside for long-term storage was really fit to eat. A seemingly limitless supply of freeze-dried meals stared back at him, featuring everything from chicken teriyaki, spaghetti with sauce, lasagna, and beef stew to more chicken and beef and noodles. It was all the same stuff, just prepared differently.

Yum.

A voracious hunger tearing at his gut, Vance made the trip to Herndon, only a few miles away, and stocked up on real food—stuff a normal person could survive on like Ding Dongs, chips and burritos, pizza, limeade and energy drinks, and a bag of broccoli crowns with ranch dip for good measure. Every guy needed his vitamin A.

While at Gary's Grocery Store, Vance noticed Andi's business card, along with those of other area businesses, pinned up on a small bulletin board, proclaiming her skills. She looked professional. He'd hire her if he were hiring.

For some reason, Cancun didn't sound as interesting as staying in town and watching Andi transform the rest of Ground Zero. If he hired her to finish the site after all, he'd cancel his plans. Cancun had been Peter's idea to begin with. Not his. The more he thought about it, the more jazzed he became about Andi's completing the work, then his selling for a huge profit. Afterward, if God directed, he could start his own company.

While he stared at the bulletin board, an elderly woman approached him. "You looking for a church?" She touched her finger to a brochure pinned to the board.

"Well, that depends on how long I stay." Vance explained the reason for his visit to town.

She nodded her understanding, welcomed him to town, and continued into the store to shop.

Back at Ground Zero he explored Uncle Vance's office just off the living area. Vance opened his laptop and while it booted he assembled his telescope. As evening neared, he grew antsy, feeling like a caged animal. Now would be a great time to contact Andi and offer her the work. She hadn't left his mind all day. Maybe that was God's nudging him to give her the job. Finding her card, he opened his cell but there was no signal. Instead, he used the landline.

"Hello?"

"Andi, this is—"

"This is Elisa, I'm on the other line. Can I take a message?"

Vance paused, surprised at the girl's rude tone. "Sure. This is Vance Young. Please let her know that I called and—"

"Okay." *Click.*

Vance stared at the phone, disappointed he couldn't talk to Andi. He'd been looking forward to hearing her voice. Or was it simply human contact he needed? At least in an apartment or house the normal sounds of life surrounded a person. He usually tuned it all out, but now that he was holed up underground, he noticed the quiet. He put in a call to Dad and let him know of his decision to hire the contractor after all, and that his plans didn't include Texas at the moment.

After placing a pizza in the oven, he popped the top of an energy drink, then took a sip. He positioned himself on the sofa with his laptop and, after chugging the drink, crushed the can and tossed it at the garbage, missing. He'd have to change that habit if Andi would be stopping by, though she never said how involved she would be in the remodel. For all Vance knew, she might work from her office, allowing her subs to do all the grunt work.

In the meantime—the sugar had done its job. An image of Tom handing him a small disk came to mind. He'd completely forgotten and found it in his pocket. He loaded it. No password was required, allowing him instant access.

Incredulous, he stared.

"What. . . .is this?"

Who had dropped it, and why had Tom given it to him?

Regardless, only one thing ran through Vance's mind as he stared at the data spilling onto his computer screen.

This is just. . .stellar.

❧

The smell of bacon lingered in the air, and if there was one thing Andi hated, it was walking into a house that smelled like stale bacon. That or fish. She grabbed the air freshener and started to spray, then eyed the last piece of bacon on the plate. Elisa wouldn't appreciate tasting Cool Caribbean Breeze on her bacon.

"Come on, Elisa!" She'd have to eat her breakfast running out the door.

Andi scraped the stack of bills and late notices into a box, then grabbed her large leather bag of a purse, cell phone, and organizer from the kitchen table. "You're going to be late for school and you're going to make me late, too."

If Elisa had even heard her, it wasn't likely she cared about Andi's schedule. Even though there wasn't much business to speak of right now, Andi never quit trying. Plus, she planned to stop by Freya Emerson's this morning. Take her some cookies. Freya had been one of her grandmother's long-time friends, and since Grandma's death, Andi had neglected to have Freya over. Though Andi missed the visits, life seemed to get in the way anymore.

Thank goodness only a few more weeks of summer school remained. Andi wasn't about to allow Elisa to take the bus today. In the fall Elisa would enter her sophomore year. Andi intended to make sure her sister made it to the high school even if it took until Elisa graduated. Despair overshadowed the aggravation she felt that she couldn't trust her sister to walk into the school, sit in her seat, and do her work.

And she hated starting every day with the yelling, but she couldn't get a response any other way. "Eli—"

"Okay, okay." Elisa rounded the corner from the hall. "You don't have to yell."

"Don't I?"

Elisa downed her orange juice, then tugged on her backpack before heading out the door without another word.

"Guess you don't want your bacon." Andi grabbed the crispy piece and stuck it in her mouth, then rushed through the door, spraying the air freshener behind her. She set it on the counter just before closing the door.

Juggling everything, she locked up. She climbed into the driver's side of the truck and slid in next to Elisa, who had already tuned her out with an MP3 player and ear buds. She nudged her sister, who responded with the look. "Turn it down. I shouldn't be able to hear it."

"What?" Utter disrespect dripped from her lips.

Andi fought to stifle her anger. Oh, how she hated starting her day like this. *Lord, if You're there, please help me.* But then, she knew He wasn't. She sighed long and hard. "Look, those things can damage your ears. I shouldn't be able to hear the music."

"Whatever." Elisa tucked them back into her ears and stared out the passenger side window.

Andi deserved Elisa. Especially after all the trouble she'd given their father when she was a teen and then their grandmother who raised them. She'd died a year ago. It made Andi wonder what her grandmother or father had done to deserve *her*? Where did the cycle begin? Regardless, she was sorry for every time she'd given people a hard time when she was growing up.

She started the truck and backed from the drive, taking solace in the fact that Elisa had turned the music down. Even so, Andi didn't think God had answered the silent prayer she'd sent up. He stopped caring a long time ago. Out of nowhere, tears formed.

Gut it up, this is life. One long sniff through her nose and she was good to go. She wouldn't give up. Not now. Not ever. Never mind that Mom left Dad when Andi was a girl and Elisa a baby. That Dad had died four years ago. That Grandma had left them with scarce funds when she'd died last year. That Andi had had to leave college to take care of Elisa.

The house Dad had left them still had a mortgage on it. She'd had to think fast to keep it, so she ended up following in his footsteps, starting her own business. She'd obtained her license to become a contractor. It was all she knew to do. College could have changed that, but it was out of the question now. Still, she'd had a tough time winning any bids.

Then Vance Erickson had come to the rescue, hiring her to remodel the missile site. She couldn't have asked for a better job. Now he was gone, she had no new jobs, and what little money was left wouldn't hold up long against the mounting bills.

His namesake had shown up two days ago—a little strange like his uncle and cute in a nerdy sort of way. A whisper inside her said God had sent him. That He was listening after all. But she shoveled and buried the thought. Life had been too hard on her, and Vance Young didn't deserve to inherit a property like that—he hadn't even known his uncle. She had.

Mr. E had loved her grandmother, wanted to marry her when they were younger, before Grandpa. Andi liked to think if they had both lived, they would have married.

Waiting at a red light, she glanced at her cell phone resting on the seat. Still no call from Vance Young. She shook her head. Why hadn't the guy called? Surely he could see that work on the missile site had to be finished.

Plain and simple, she was desperate.

She pulled up to the curb at the school.

Elisa went frantic. "No! Park *away* from the school. I can't be seen in this." She slunk down into the seat.

Andi drove past the school and stopped. "Okay. I'm going to sit here and watch. If I don't see you walk into that building, I'll park in front and walk you in myself next time. You hear me?"

Elisa stepped from the truck, then stuck her head back in, smiling. "Thanks, sis. Oh, I forgot. That missile base guy called." She slammed the door, then took off toward the school.

"What? Wait. When?" Andi stuck her head out the window. "What did he say? Elisa?" But she'd been talking to the street. Elisa hadn't heard.

Andi ground her teeth. *That girl.* She watched until she saw her sister meet up with friends and walk into the building. What more could Andi do than that? The truancy had to stop. She shifted the truck into gear. Maybe she needed to get her sister counseling or therapy. Or maybe Elisa needed to get a grip like Andi had.

She looked at her cell phone but found no messages there. Why hadn't he called her on her cell? Likely Elisa told him she'd pass on the message.

Andi growled. "Teenagers!"

Without his number she couldn't call him back. She'd have to remember that little trick in the future—ask for a cell phone number!

If his answer wasn't positive, she sure didn't want to drive all the way out. She wasn't in the state of mind to persuade him otherwise. If she found a number on caller ID, it might be Vance Junior's. Except if he'd called her on his cell and now he was down under, he'd never get her return call. How could such a simple thing be so complicated? What was the matter with her?

Elisa is the matter. While Andi was trying to keep both their heads above water, Elisa was determined to drown them both.

Andi placed her palm against her forehead. *Get a grip.* Was the phone that rang directly into the base still working? She dialed Vance Erickson's old number to the missile base and allowed it to ring twenty-five times without an answer. Her spirits sagging, she hung up.

A visit to Freya would do her good at the moment, then she'd try Vance Young again. After she swung by the local grocery store to grab the cookies—white chocolate and macadamia nuts—Andi headed to Freya's, wishing she had baked them fresh. Didn't Freya deserve that much? Andi turned off a street onto a bumpy dirt road. The older woman lived a few miles outside of town near the railroad tracks in the same house where she grew up. Freya's Oldsmobile of twenty years was parked in the driveway. Good. Andi hadn't made the drive out for nothing.

Before Andi climbed from her truck, Freya stood on the porch, holding the screen door open for her. "Well, aren't you a sight for sore eyes?" she called out to Andi.

Andi smiled, grabbed the cookies, and shut the truck door.

Once on the porch, she said, "I brought you something."

Freya patted her back as she entered the house. "Thank you. You rest on the davenport over there, I'll get us some tea. Chamomile?"

"Sounds good." Andi breathed in the smell of the old home. Memories flooded in on her. Because Freya and Andi's grandmother had been close friends, Andi and Elisa had spent time here, eating pot roast on Sundays, playing cards in the evenings, and running around in the fenced-in backyard.

Freya approached, offering a teacup on a saucer. "What's bothering you?"

Gently taking the cup and saucer, Andi sighed. She didn't want a trip down memory lane right now. A big smile would throw the woman off. "Nothing at all. So how've you been?"

Freya proceeded to share long-drawn-out tales of her two dogs—they had taken to barking incessantly. There must be a wild animal nearby. Then on to the local gossip.

"I hear there's a new tenant at the old missile site." Sipping her tea, Freya lifted a questioning brow.

Andi almost spewed her tea. "What? How did you hear that?"

"Someone talked to a fellow at the grocery store. Said he was staying there."

"Mr. Erickson's great-nephew. His name is Vance Young."

Freya winked. "Thought you might know of him. Have you met him yet? Is he anything of a looker like his uncle?"

"I guess you could say that." She glanced at her watch. "More tea?"

As much as she adored Freya, Andi felt sure the woman wanted her to stay so she could pry more news from her. But Andi really had nothing to share. At least not yet. "No, thank you. That reminds me. I'm working on a bid, so I have to go now."

"That's my Andi. Your business is going to take off. Just you wait and see."

After a quick peck on Freya's cheek, Andi wished her well

and left. Back in her truck, she tried to call Vance again.

"Hello?"

Sweet potatoes. He'd answered. Relief was quickly replaced with panic. What if he turned her down? "Mr. Young. . .uh, Vance, this is—"

"Hi, Andi."

Andi liked the sound of his voice. "My sister informed me this morning that you called."

"I told you I'd get back to you."

"Yeah, you did. Have you made a decision, then?"

"I have."

Andi's breath hitched. "And?"

"Let's do this."

Trembling, she almost dropped the phone. Maybe, just maybe, God was listening after all.

There was only one problem—by now the subs she had used were probably working on other jobs.

four

The next day, Andi drove on the stretch of highway that passed through the North Dakota prairie and farmland to her revived worksite—the old missile launch control center. A coyote darted across the highway, causing Andi to slow up. Clear blue skies promised a beautiful day, though that wouldn't matter since the bulk of their work was done underground. Still, some of the messier jobs—like cutting tile or granite with a wet saw—were best done outside.

She'd spent yesterday lining up subs, relieved that she'd have her old standbys, brothers Lars and Karl Handley. They'd both known her dad years before and had been more than happy to give her a chance when she started the business.

They'd worked at Ground Zero and knew how to do almost everything in construction. They worked well together, which was good because she didn't want to give the new owner any reason to doubt her ability to finish the job. He'd sounded doubtful when she informed him she was a contractor. Still, he'd seemed impressed with the work.

How could he not be impressed? It was beautiful.

Only one problem tried to dampen her mood. Elisa moaned from the passenger seat as though she could read Andi's thoughts.

Andi pounded the steering wheel. "What am I going to do with you?"

"Just leave me alone," Elisa mumbled, leaning her head against the window.

Andi pursed her lips. She wanted nothing more than to give Elisa a good tongue-lashing, but she figured Elisa had had her fill of lectures. Andi knew from experience there came a point when a person wouldn't listen anymore. What

Andi had to figure out was how to reach her younger sister.

Teenage years were never easy, but Elisa had pushed Andi to the edge. She'd stayed out all night last night—a school night, no less—and come dragging in during the early morning hours. Andi had thought she'd been asleep in her bed all night.

Not only did Andi have to watch the girl walk into the school building—"Do I have to check up on you every five minutes now?"

Only a grunt came in response. Any response at all was a surprise.

Andi pressed her lips together again, wanting to say more, oh so much more. She pulled up to a stop sign and slumped against the seat. After the lone car passed, Andi drove across the intersection.

"What am I going to do?" she asked, for her own benefit. She didn't expect a coherent answer from her hung-over sister. She couldn't send her to school because she was too sick to function. Nor would Andi dare leave Elisa at home alone.

If there was one thing she hated, it was feeling like she had no control over a situation, and the situation with Elisa had definitely spiraled out of control.

"If you're bent on skipping school, then you can just work with me." Andi still had a job to do and a secret to discover within the walls of Ground Zero.

"Could you stop talking?" Elisa leaned forward and put her head in her lap.

Andi shook her head, giving up for the moment, and focused on the drive ahead. Dealing with Elisa had put her behind this morning. Again. Though the missile site wasn't too far now, she'd be lucky if she made it there before Lars and Karl. She drove into the parking area where the brothers were unloading their trucks.

She stepped from the cab of hers. "Hey, boys. Thanks for coming to my rescue."

Between the three of them, they should be able to handle the bulk of the remodel. Andi and Vance had agreed that the quickest path to completion would be for him to foot the costs of materials and subs—he had a decent savings—but she'd have to wait on a good portion of her contractor's fee, again, until Ground Zero sold. Selling a lavish underground home could take awhile. Until another job opportunity came through, it was the best prospect she had.

Remodeling would also mean she'd get to see more of the younger Vance.

Why had that thought dropped from the sky? *Get a grip.* She pressed the intercom to announce their arrival to Vance below ground and waited for his response, which, if nothing else, should prompt the elevator door to open—all designed for the older Vance. When Vance Junior didn't respond, Andi used her key to unlock the elevator lock-down button, figuring he hadn't heard the intercom for some reason. It occurred to her that she hadn't shown him how to use the system. At the time, he'd seemed eager to get some rest, and she wasn't sure he'd be staying for even one night.

The men followed her into the elevator, loaded down with ladders and tools. It was a tight fit. Today they'd trim out the portion of the launch control center that served as an extra bedroom. She'd have to get the electrician in before they could do anything on the equipment building. That, and pump any excess water out.

She didn't bother to rouse Elisa. When it grew warm enough, she'd come inside. Andi glanced at her watch, glad they were getting started bright and early. Though she'd called to remind Vance to expect her crew today, since he'd not answered, she hoped they wouldn't be stumbling into anything. . . embarrassing.

The elevator doors swooshed open and they hiked through the tunnel. Lars opened the blast door for them, then Andi cautiously stepped through into the well-lit living room.

"Hello?" She crept slowly, hoping not to startle Vance, Lars and Karl behind her. Even if he were the type of person to sleep in, their clanking gear would have woken him by now.

They'd have to agree on a plan for her entry every day. Most mornings, his uncle would greet her crew with bacon and eggs. Not a requirement, but it made a great start to the day. Oh, how she missed that. Missed him. Why had Grandma not fallen for him back in her day?

Another step and Andi froze. Vance slept on the couch in his sweats, one arm over his eyes. No wonder he hadn't answered the intercom. He was sound asleep.

Andi stared for longer than necessary, but she couldn't pull her eyes away from his sleeping form, his physique like that of a tennis player rather than some muscular brute who played defense on a high school football team. Completely unlike. . .Jorgen.

Good-night pajamas. When would she stop thinking about Jorgen? What was she doing comparing Vance to him? Or Vance to anyone for that matter? Besides, a guy like him—good-looking, smart, and with a bank account—had to have a girlfriend.

A laptop along with electronic equipment she didn't recognize lay scattered around the room, as well as an expensive-looking telescope.

Make that a *smart* girlfriend.

"Uh, Andi." Lars snickered. "We should just get moving and let *you* take care of *him*."

Her cheeks were over-heated pipes, full of steam and ready to explode. How long had she been standing there lost in her ridiculous thoughts? *Get a grip.* She couldn't think of a client as anything other than just that. Lars and Karl shuffled past her to the room they'd left incomplete a couple of months ago. They made plenty of noise passing Vance.

He moved his arm and opened one eye, looking right into hers.

If she thought she couldn't be any more embarrassed, she was wrong. Her face felt like a rocket had just blasted off, using it for a launch pad. Why had she let her guard down, allowing herself to admire him?

She sucked in a deep breath. "Hi. . uh. . .Mr. Young. I mean, Vance." She shrugged with a smile. "Sorry, I didn't mean to surprise you. I hoped you'd be expecting us."

"No problem." Vance sat up and rubbed his eyes, then wiped a hand down his unshaven face. "What am I saying? I did expect you. I obviously overslept. The apology should be all mine."

"Yeah, looks like you were up and waiting but fell back asleep."

He glanced around the room and laughed. "Looks that way, doesn't it?"

Vance stood and stretched, appearing like he hadn't gotten much sleep. Unfortunately, to Andi, he still looked good. Especially when he grinned. She loved his accent. Was he a Texan?

She walked over to where he'd set up his telescope. "So, you like to look at the stars, then?"

"Yeah, I'm a stargazer."

"It's amazing." She moved to touch it.

"Don't—"

In a flash he was next to her, gently taking her hand into his, sending a surge of heat up her arm.

"What was that?" she asked, and snatched her hand back. Oh no, had she spoken that out loud?

"Sorry. I'm way too obsessive about my stuff, especially when it's new and expensive."

She'd meant the electrical current he'd sent up her arm, but she could hardly tell him that.

"Just ignore me. I'm a complete idiot on most days." He found his glasses and put them on, transforming him from ruggedly handsome to seriously smart.

"And on days when you're not?" She smiled and put some distance between them. He might be cute but he'd nailed it when he called himself obsessive.

"Afraid there's not too many of those."

"It's too bad you won't see stars down here."

Vance stared at her and cracked the grin she liked. She *liked*? How had he managed to chip away at her defenses in no time at all? She straightened her back, resolving to be impervious to his charm. She had a job to do, and he was her client. Nothing more. She'd never liked women who fell too easily for men who eventually trampled over them, leaving them behind.

Hurting them.

"I like wide open spaces. That's why it didn't take me long to decide to sell the place. I was expecting something much different."

"I see. You wanted a big view of the night sky." Now, there was a *big* difference between Vance and his uncle. Mr. E seemed to enjoy his underground dwelling. "Something like that." He tugged his glasses off and stuck the end of the earpiece in his mouth, studying her.

"Listen, let me say I'm sorry again. I shouldn't have panicked when you touched the telescope. I guess you could say it's a little quirk of mine."

"Okay, I'll say it. It's a little quirk of yours."

When he laughed unexpectedly, it warmed her insides—a clear warning that she had better get to work and keep her mind off Vance Young.

He moved around the kitchen island, then leaned against it. "Would you like a cup of coffee?"

Without waiting for an answer he reached into the cabinet and grabbed the same two cups from the cupboard that Mr. E would grab when he shared with her.

"Thanks, but no. I'd better get busy." She'd already downed a large mug at home, which was probably the equivalent of three cups. "We can't make our money until we complete this job."

"You mean until I sell it."

"Right." She smiled, despite the discouragement seeping in. At least she had the job and the opportunity to find the secret that lay within.

After pouring himself a cup, Vance took a long gulp of black coffee and squeezed his eyes as though he hated the stuff—the mannerism reminding her of his uncle. She looked down at the granite counter, a smile creeping onto her lips.

So, they had some similarities after all.

Vance's uncle had often said to her he wished he were a lot younger, then he would have tried to win her heart. She'd laughed with him at the sweet comment, not knowing at the time of his affection for her grandmother when he was young. But with a much younger version of him standing on the other side of the counter right now, she wondered how far the similarities went.

And the differences.

&

Andi the builder glanced at the junk he'd strewn around the living area. "We're going to work on the extra room today and maybe the rest of this week. I don't plan to start on the equipment building until we get the power on there. I hope we don't disturb you."

"You won't bother me at all." Vance watched her walk away. Nothing unfamiliar about watching a gorgeous woman walking away.

He hung his head over the counter. A laugh escaped. Vance dumped the rest of his coffee. She'd taken an interest in his telescope and what did he do?

Idiot.

He'd practically yelled at her. He could still see the look of shock on her face. When would he ever learn?

In his few encounters with her, she always acted wary, untrusting, but like she wanted to open up, like she needed a friend. It was weird, but not in a science fiction sort of way. Stomach growling again, he grabbed a muffin and stuffed his face. A hot shower would clear his mind.

When he'd arrived at Ground Zero, his trip to Cancun was just a few days away. Now he'd dug himself in deep—deciding to finish what Uncle Vance had started. But whether his uncle's intentions were to finish the missile site or help Andi or both, Vance wasn't sure. Honestly, he wasn't even sure of his own intentions. But the arrangement could benefit them both.

Add to that, something was out of place at ANND Systems. After seeing the anomalies on the disk, call it a gut feeling or a sixth sense, he had a strong niggling feeling he was involved—that it would all somehow come back to him. In that case, he could be in big trouble. Unless what he'd seen was nothing more than the product of a sleep-deprived brain drawing the last of the juice from an alternate power source.

But what exactly had he seen? He'd have to figure it out, turning this into a working vacation. Fun and rest seemed about as accessible as the moon right now. After looking at the disk Saturday night, he'd tried to focus, even drank several of his usual energy drinks, but going for weeks without sleep in order to make the project deadline had worked against him. When he crashed, he typically crashed for days, but now he didn't have the luxury of that much time even on a vacation. Until he figured out how to get a real snooze in this temporary underground home, he couldn't be at his best.

He was heading for the shower when Andi stepped out of a room to the left and walked right into him.

He grabbed her arm to steady her. "Sorry about that."

"I should watch where I'm going." Appearing flustered, she continued about her business.

"No problem." Vance waved, then scowled. Why had he just waved at her?

He blew out a breath. The remodeling would be a distraction for him, especially with Andi here. How much of the work did she actually do herself? It seemed odd—her in construction. She appeared dainty compared to his idea of someone in that line of work. He wondered how she got into the business. Had she dreamed about managing a construction site or remodeling homes all her life? Or was it more about surviving? She was attractive and interesting and. . .

What are you doing? Any interest in her would lead him

the same place it always did—nowhere. It didn't help that he felt like he'd been looking at her every day for months now. Maybe if he'd not grown attached to the face in the picture frame he could more easily shrug off any ideas about Andi.

How many times would he need to learn his lesson? Women weren't interested in him. Sure he could get dates, but once they got to know him, that's when the relationships ended. He couldn't keep their interest.

Vance took a long, hot shower, reflecting that there weren't too many things in life that felt as good when a person was stressed. Afterward, feeling refreshed, he dressed and set up an office in the living room instead of going to Uncle Vance's small office. He wanted to be available in case one of the workmen—who was he kidding?—in case Andi needed him. Of course, she could always find him. But staying visible gave him more opportunity to interact with her. He squeezed his eyes. He really was a desperate geek.

Nestled comfortably on the sofa with his laptop open on his lap, Vance focused on the data from the small disk Tom had given him. Peter had landed a big government contract for data mining of the specialized sort—to identify and track possible terrorist suspects and activities. It was all about predicting what might happen. Vance had spent a year writing and testing the algorithm—a real breakthrough for the project and for the company.

Then why was he staring at a tweaked version of his algorithm—a program that shouldn't be floating around on a disk or especially ending up on the floor of the company foyer? Vance scratched a nonexistent itch on his jaw. What was going on here? Had Peter given the go-ahead for others on their team of programmers to work on it, and if so, why hadn't he told Vance, or why weren't they working together on it? He should be part of that decision.

If he asked Peter what was going on, the guy would block him from the system to make sure Vance got his vacation time, and he'd have to listen to a lecture.

Vance weaved his fingers through his still-damp hair. An errant thought wrestled to get in and finally won. Peter hadn't been upfront with him on a few other occasions. Disturbing. There was the slight possibility he wouldn't get the truth if he asked.

Working on secret projects cast shadows in all directions. What if there was something underhanded going on? The algorithm belonged to Vance, or at least the company, and not just anyone should have hands on it. He needed to know if it was being used for some other purpose and why and by whom.

Was he paranoid? Maybe. But he didn't need Boolean logic to know he shouldn't see his algorithm on a disk lying on the floor. Vance would find out what was going on, *then* he would ask Peter.

He'd do a data run, a small test sampling, the kind his laptop—a micro-processing computer—could handle in comparison to the supercomputers in the dinosaur pen at work. For that, he needed test data—something he might not have access to except at ANND.

"First things first."

"Excuse me?"

The words startled him. He looked up to find Andi's sister standing over him. Too caught up in his thoughts, he'd not noticed her. He quickly averted the screen.

"You were talking to yourself." Her smile was like Andi's.

"Elisa, leave Mr. Young alone. Can't you see he's working?" Andi strode over and looked down at him. "I'm sorry. She wasn't feeling well, and I didn't want to leave her at home alone."

"No problem." Vance snickered. "Make yourself at home, Elisa."

"What's so funny?"

"The thought occurred to me that this place might protect us from a nuclear blast, but not from a cold virus."

Andi gave him an odd look. "She's not sick like that."

"Well, even if she is, she's welcome to make herself at home, raid the refrigerator or pantry for junk food."

"Really?" Elisa perked up.

Andi cocked her brow. "That's all right. I had intended for her to work with me."

"But I thought she wasn't feeling well."

Andi frowned. "I—"

"She's punishing me." Elisa slipped past her sister and meandered toward the exit.

Andi looked at him apologetically. "I'm sorry about this. She won't interfere with your work, or mine for that matter."

"There's nothing to apologize for." What was going on with Andi and her sister? "Is there anything I can do to help?"

"It's that obvious?"

Vance set the laptop on the coffee table and stood up to look directly into Andi's soft blue eyes. "Nah. Just the usual family drama when adult and teenage worlds collide."

"I guess you're right."

Women liked men who were sensitive, understanding. "It helps to talk about your problems. I'm a good listener."

"Thanks for your offer, but it's not your problem." She sighed, her guard up again. "You have work to do. So do I." She gave him a flat smile and followed Elisa out.

Vance plopped against the sofa back. She put on a tough veneer but he'd seen a glimpse of the softness inside. Why did he have to be curious about this woman?

five

At the end of the day, Andi stood with Lars in the tunnel junction outside of the equipment room. "The electrician should be here on Thursday. Hopefully he'll get the power on in there so we can begin work."

"Karl will be back in the morning, but I've got another job," Lars said.

"I understand. There's not enough work left in the other room for all of us at this point. Just the trim. Can you ask Karl to bring the pump so we can get that water out tomorrow? Then we can seal the leaks."

Lars tilted his head. "You betcha."

"In the meantime, I'm going to explore." Andi rattled her flashlight for Lars's benefit.

"Be careful." He nodded and left.

With Lars and Karl gone for the day, she was free to conduct her search, even though it was mostly in the dark. Nothing could pull Vance away from his computer so she needn't worry about him. She'd put Elisa to work with the Shop-Vac in the room that was near completion.

After opening the blast door, Andi switched on the flashlight, shining it around the large equipment room. Every time she read the letter, she became more convinced that Vance Erickson had hired her to renovate the place so she could find what her grandfather had hidden decades before. Why anyone would go to so much trouble she didn't know.

Hidden in the underground launch center was something of value meant for her grandmother, and Andi intended to discover it. Like everything else in her life, she had to work hard for it, earn it.

She took a step down into an inch of water. A slow drip

joined the echo of her footsteps as she explored. Why hadn't Mr. E just told her what to look for? Good grief. What if one of the other workers had found it and said nothing?

Yet another thing she'd never know. All she had to go on was the letter she'd discovered in her grandmother's things, written by Mr. E. At least Andi could have asked him about it if she'd found it before he'd died.

She wasn't sure how the new owner would take to the news that she was searching for something that belonged to her family but was hidden on his property, and until she knew him well enough, she probably wouldn't tell him. For that matter, would she want to know him that well? He might be cute with his charming grin and searching gaze, but he was a geek in anybody's world—consumed by things like computers and telescopes. She'd already been discarded by his type—no sense in setting herself up for that again.

For the time being, she'd keep things to herself. She sure hoped Mr. E knew what he was doing when he'd given this place to his nephew. At the moment, it didn't appear that he did. Vance Young wasn't keen on living underground.

Though she was excited at the challenge—at the opportunity she'd been given to complete the missile site, after all—the thought of renovating this room suddenly overwhelmed her. What if something went wrong? What if the younger Vance changed his mind? She knew from experience things could change overnight.

Get a grip. She drew in a deep breath and plodded through the water, shining the flashlight around and wishing she'd taken a look at the specs again. Where would her grandfather, then a young deputy flight commander, have hidden something?

The missileers who'd worked there had a lot of time on their hands even while they stayed in a state of alertness. The first time she'd been inside, she'd seen artwork painted on the blast door by what Grandma had called America's Underground Air Force. Andi couldn't imagine the pressure of being part of a missile crew, waiting for the call. One turn of the launch key could end millions of lives.

Nor could she imagine the boredom that must have accompanied the hours of waiting for a call they hoped never to get. Her grandfather had plenty of time to hide something. The fact that he'd concealed it in the nerve center of a missile launch control center told Andi he'd meant for it to stay buried, which piqued her curiosity even more.

If only she knew what she was looking for. Chances were the item was long gone. Her grandfather hadn't worked here in decades, and the place had sat decommissioned for at least ten years.

A sense of failure slammed her. She hated admitting it, but her search could very well be a lost cause. Hope started to slip through her fingers. She sucked in a breath. Nothing she hated more than watching people give up. While she had this opportunity, she would do her best. For her grandparents and Mr. E's sake, she'd search the base, and she'd wait to tell the younger Vance when the time was right.

Andi climbed to the top of a ladder and shined the light, studying the walls, looking for any sort of variance. She ran her right hand over the smooth surface while holding the flashlight with her left hand, leaning as far as possible before she'd have to move the ladder. Without more light this could take forever, and once the power was on, Lars and Karl would be working. How could she conduct a search without telling them? She hated secrets.

"What are you doing?"

Caught. Her heart pounded. The flashlight fell from her hand.

"Watch out!"

Her foot slipped on the rung but she gripped the ladder, halting her fall. Having regained her balance, Andi pressed her head against the ladder and took a deep, calming breath. She looked over at the figure standing in the doorway, light pouring in.

"Are you all right?" Vance made his way to the ladder.

"Why'd you have to scare me like that?"

He lifted his palms in surrender. "That wasn't my intention." He picked up the flashlight and shined it around. "But your reaction does make a person wonder what you were doing."

Andi began the climb down. His vague accusation made her bristle. "You startled me, how was I supposed to react?"

Vance handed her the flashlight as she stepped into the water. "I'm going up for some fresh air, thought you might like to join me."

"You did?" Andi was relieved he didn't pursue his line of questioning. But why would he think she'd want to join him? "Can't you see I'm working?"

"In the dark?"

"What else would I be doing in here?"

"I don't know. That's why I asked."

Andi paused, flustered. Vance didn't know what was hidden, did he? For the first time, she considered the possibility. Mr. E could have told him all about it—could even have asked him to look for the treasure.

"Yeah, I think fresh air would be good after all."

"So, what were you doing in here?"

Andi shined the flashlight in his face and watched him squint, but he didn't back down. "You hired me to finish Ground Zero. I'm checking things out to make sure I know what to do. The electrician will be here in a couple of days. What's with all the questions?"

Vance grinned. He was entirely too attractive. Andi stiffened, deflecting the effect he had on her.

"It wasn't a challenge, just a simple question. I'm curious about your work. That's all." He shrugged, then walked away.

Andi felt ridiculous. Her reaction would put him on alert. Still, even if she hadn't been on a search, she would have bristled at his question. It was like asking if she knew what she was doing at her own business.

Almost at the exit, he turned to look at her. "You coming?"

"Sure."

Andi followed, already regretting she'd agreed to go up with him. She was attracted to him, and she shouldn't be. What was it about this guy? He stood at the door like he needed to hold it open for her, waiting. She avoided his gaze as she moved passed. He smelled good.

Andi tightened her ponytail, nice and snug—one painful way to snatch her thoughts from the young Vance's charms. An uneducated girl like her would never fit into his world.

She'd been through that before and didn't need a second lesson.

At least she was that smart.

❧

Wearing dirty jeans and a smudged T-shirt, Andi finally looked the part of a contractor. Well, except for her curvaceous yet slim figure, which Vance attempted to ignore—he experienced a total malfunction there. Still, her lack of enthusiasm caused him to second-guess inviting her up with him. Feeling the effects of being closed in like an animal, he'd needed the break. Pleasant and distracting conversation was more in keeping with his plan, not her peculiar brand of hostility.

Her crew was gone already, yet she remained behind. Andi the enigma was a Rubik's Cube personified, which made her all the more appealing to Vance, as long as he could get her to dump the brick wall act. Rocking from heel to toe as he waited for her to step into the elevator first, he grinned as she swept past, ponytail swinging.

As soon as Vance stepped onto the elevator, his pulse increased, and to think he'd managed to control his panic inside the Ground Zero capsule. Admittedly, Ground Zero wasn't nearly as small as the elevator. A distraction from that fact would be good about now. But if he hoped for conversation, he was out of luck. Except for his heavier than normal breathing, an uncomfortable silence swallowed them.

Rubbing his neck to ease his anxiety, he decided he'd definitely made a mistake. He wasn't a great conversationalist, and if she wasn't going to meet him halfway, what was the point?

Finally, she sighed. It was something at least.

"You know, if the elevator bothers you that much, we could have taken the stairs."

The elevator door opened. Vance held it for her. "What gave me away?"

Andi shrugged and stepped through. "Your uncle, remember? He had a fear of small spaces. Acted just like you're acting now. All nervous and breathless. Opened and closed his fists a lot."

Vance looked at his hands, not realizing he'd done that. "Yeah, makes me feel cagey and nervous, especially when they're in motion. It's not quite a phobia, but still, it helps to focus on something else."

Once they stepped into the fresh air the sunshine hurt his eyes. He shaded them with his hand. "I need to get out more."

Andi laughed, making Vance think of the soothing tones of a wind chime.

She stood next to him, scanning the lone prairie that stretched for miles. "Haven't you brought your telescope outside yet?"

They strolled away from the complex, held back from the endless grasslands by the chain-link fence surrounding the missile site. "I haven't had a chance."

"Oh, come on. What's so important it takes up all your time?"

Vance leaned his head to one side and eyed her. "You serious?"

"That's right. You're a computer whiz. You spend all your time in cyberspace, while you miss what's going on around you."

Ouch. Vance covered his heart, acting mortally wounded. "You've exposed my virtual identity as a cyber-spy."

Andi's mouth dropped open, then she closed it and laughed.

"How have you figured me out in such a short time?" Before they'd even had a proper dinner date, too.

She hung her head and kicked at the ground, then peered

up at him. "I'm sorry. That wasn't nice of me. I'm sure what you do is very important. And I hope you're not really a cyber-spy."

Vance grinned, soaking up her attention. "Is that because you're afraid I'd have to kill you?" Or because she actually cared?

She nodded.

"I don't spend all my time on the computer, you know? I do have that one hobby."

"The stars, yeah. Just another kind of space, if you ask me."

How he'd love the chance to change her mind about that. "Listen, I do have a reason for bringing you out into the daylight."

"Go ahead."

"I was thinking of adding on some sort of an aboveground building."

"So you can look at the stars? I thought you weren't staying."

He cocked his head. He wasn't sure why he was exploring this, but he surveyed the area. "Have you noticed it gets cold at night around here?"

"Where'd you say you were from?"

"Texas."

Eyes teasing, she smirked. "To North Dakotans, it doesn't get that cold at night in the summer. Are you saying it doesn't get cold in Texas?"

"Not like this, no. In the summer it can be ninety degrees at ten o'clock at night."

"Can't imagine that. How long have you lived here?"

"A year."

"And you're not accustomed to our climate yet?" She cocked her head with a questioning gaze.

"Are *you*?"

"I grew up here." She laughed, then flashed him a hundred-watt smile.

Her smile sent a jolt through Vance. "So, tell me what you

know about this missile site. Do you know why my uncle would want this place for his home? It boggled my mind when I saw this instead of the mansion I expected."

"Well, considering it's farmland, maybe you should have at least expected a farmhouse."

"True, but then I didn't get that either."

Andi jabbed her hands into her jeans, a thoughtful expression in her eyes as she looked at something beyond him. A gust of wind lifted a few strands of hair from her ponytail.

What would she look like with her mass of tresses hanging down across her shoulders?

"My sister and I lived on a nearby farm when we were kids. We'd ride our bikes a few miles up the road to watch the airmen play football. But this site and I. . .we go back much further."

They strolled on for a few more moments until the fence prevented them from going farther. Still, Andi said nothing.

Vance broke the silence. "Do I get to know the rest?"

She glanced at the ground and grinned, tucking her stray hair behind an ear. "I don't know where to begin. Besides, to a guy like you, this stuff is probably boring."

"Hey, I asked, didn't I? I want to know." He started walking along the fence line.

"It's the decommissioned missile sites. This all meant something to my parents, to the folks who lived here. It's like they were a part of something bigger than themselves."

"I understand."

"My grandfather was in the air force and worked at this very site."

Vance stopped. Was it mere coincidence that she was renovating this site? He'd never been a believer in coincidence, not with the Creator of the universe running things. Andi the builder now posed an even bigger puzzle.

She looked at him with warm eyes, drawing him in. "And when Dad was still alive, we explored the base after its decommissioning. Funny, we found a carpeted concrete door in the building that was standing at the time. I always wondered what was hidden behind it." A soft sigh escaped. "I've said too much. I need to get back to Ground Zero now."

What had he said to shut her down? "The workday is over, isn't it?"

"Yeah, it is. I've got to find Elisa, then head home."

Vance couldn't stand the thought of going underground again. At least not yet. "I'm going to town to get some more groceries."

She walked backward as she spoke. "Didn't I show you the food storage room? Your uncle stocked it just in case."

"In case of what? A nuclear meltdown?"

"Yeah, something like that. He was funny that way."

"I gather." Vance thought of the freeze-dried food. "I discovered the survival food. All those meals ready to eat. Not interested, thank you very much."

Andi snickered. "You're more interested in muscle drinks and candy bars." She turned her back to him, then entered the stairwell.

"They're energy drinks," he said, but she'd already disappeared into the abyss of his eccentric uncle's missile site.

He could have enough trouble on his hands at ANND Systems. Why was he borrowing more by attempting to get involved with a woman by the same name?

Vance headed for his car, then to the grocery store to get some more salsa for his chips—another procrastination technique he'd developed called restocking the condiments.

six

With a couple of hours of daylight remaining, Vance pulled through the gate and drove up the road to the old missile base. Gravel crunched as he neared the building housing the elevator entrance. He shut off the ignition. A garage might be nice, especially in the winter.

Would the lack of one scare away a potential buyer? He hadn't exactly had time to do research on missile sites converted to homes and how well they sell. On that, he'd given Andi his complete trust, hoping he wasn't just another poor sap for a pretty face. But wasn't every guy?

Vance dragged himself from the car and grabbed the two grocery sacks from the back seat, a box of Ding Dongs sticking from the top of one, and headed down under. He entered the living room, his eyes adjusting to the fluorescents. He set the bags on the counter just as his stomach growled, and grabbed a frozen burrito. Microwaves were a product of God's mercy.

After eating dinner, he opened a bag of chips and plopped onto the sofa, the scent of Andi's perfume in the air, a reminder of what he was missing. What he'd always missed, and what he would always miss—a girlfriend. A woman's attention. Companionship. This place was the epitome of his life. Dark. Lonely. Boring.

Was this the plight of all computer geeks? His brother Matt was happily married, his wife expecting a child.

Vance blew out a breath. Hope yet remained.

The laptop sat on the coffee table where he'd left it open, applications running, and looked back expectantly. For once, he was tired of staring at his computer, but he had work to do, and procrastinating wasn't getting him anywhere. Hard to imagine.

It was just that. . .he was fried. Having to use his so-called vacation, which should have been for rest and recuperation, to work on this. . . Well, he counted it as severe loss.

After running test data all day, he'd needed fresh air. Now it was time to get down to real business. What exactly was that second algorithm producing?

Though he wasn't a data analyst, he could easily compare sample data output from both programs. The second data set produced by his government-contracted algorithm gone rogue appeared to produce a dissimilar data set. The records he'd flagged as the "bad guys" in his original algorithm weren't being flagged as often in the second.

Serious bogosity was happening here—a sham he might even call mission creep: his proprietary algorithm was being used for an entirely different purpose.

It reminded him of when he'd watched two of his colleagues fired from the Texas-based company. They'd agreed to write the company's proprietary software for someone else, in essence, selling company secrets.

But what happened when it was government secrets?

The sensation of being boxed into a small place came over him. An adrenaline rush sent sweat to his palms. His pulse raced.

Only one thought coursed through his burned-out circuits—someone wanted to produce output that was a less-than-accurate prediction of terrorists and their activities.

Could Peter be in on this? And if so, who had lined his pockets? The only reason Vance knew about it was due to a lost disk. Nothing was a coincidence.

"Okay, Lord, You wanted me to see this. I get it. Now what?" What should he do about it?

Both hands on his head, he squeezed. Despite today's adept computer forensics, Vance could potentially go down with the mission creepers, if they were caught. How could he prove he wasn't involved? Especially since Peter was a long-time friend—even though he'd changed a lot. And if Peter—assuming he was involved—was willing to go this far, might he actually try to set Vance up?

The last thing Vance should do was touch this—but his fingerprints were already all over it. His impulse was to do something now. But that's what he'd done when he'd joined ANND Systems. He'd listened to Peter's persuasion, rather than praying first. No. This time he'd pray for direction.

❧

Construction noise stirred Vance awake the next morning. He'd lain awake most of the night, his thoughts in turmoil, then finally fallen asleep in the early morning hours. Rubbing his eyes, he sat up, sure Andi had a meager opinion of him for sleeping late and forgetting to let her in as per the agreed upon protocol. She'd shown him the intercom, but he never heard her calling. He should tell her to dispense with the protocol since it wasn't working anyway.

After pulling on jeans, he headed to the kitchen where he poured a cup of coffee, compliments of the auto brew. He squeezed his eyes as the dark liquid slid down his throat. It would give him the kick he needed. After the first cup, he added fillers. Sugar, vanilla syrup, milk. That was more like it.

He hadn't exactly gotten an earful from God last night, but he'd come up with a plan. He'd write a viral worm or some other slow-to-discover interference for their project until he could gather enough information to make a rational statement to the authorities.

Trading his algorithm out for the imposter was the only difficulty.

Cup of sweet coffee in hand, he propped his back against the kitchen side of the island in an obvious leave-me-alone-I'm-thinking manner.

"You really should take better care of yourself," Andi suggested, her voice sounding lighthearted.

Couldn't she read his mind? Didn't she know he had to concentrate on his own problems?

Conceding the error of his thought, he turned around.

"What are you talking about?"

Though his question had sounded much too brusque, Andi didn't appear to notice. Leaning over the island on her elbows, she indicated the junk food he'd left out last night. "Let's see, Ding Dongs, Ho Hos, potato chips of every variety. What sort of diet is that?"

Vance watched her, confused by her unusually friendly demeanor. "Well, it gets me through. I need those sudden bursts of energy." He couldn't seem to inject any warmth into his tone this morning.

"That's what you call brain food, yeah?"

Andi playful and teasing? Why couldn't she act like this when he was in the mood to enjoy it? He frowned, studying the woman who looked similar to the photo on his desk. Andi Nielsen was nothing like he'd imagined the woman in the photo would be. Andi might bait him with her momentary charm, then an instant later her defenses would go back up, secreting her away behind guarded walls.

Was she a Christian? He didn't see a cross hanging from her neck, or any action to indicate one way or the other. With what he was about to do, he had to wonder if he was a Christian himself. Trusting God had been easy enough while things were going smoothly at his job. While life was good. But when life became volatile, that's where the true test of faith came in—how much muscle did he really have when it came to his faith?

He had a feeling he was about to find out.

Andi cleared her throat, causing him to realize he hadn't responded to her question about his brain food.

"Well, I can see you're one of those people who needs coffee before they become human."

"I've got a lot on my mind today." Guilt threaded his conscience. What was the matter with him? The woman was actually paying attention. "Like your favorite mantra, I've got work to do."

"Then you'll need one of these for that brain of yours." She pulled out a Hostess cupcake, unwrapped it, and stuck it out to him. Her hundred-watt smile burned away his irritation.

A grin broke through his frown, spreading until he laughed. How could he not? "Give me that."

He grabbed the chocolate gooey-goodness and stuffed part of it into his mouth.

"There, that's better. I've done my job." She smiled again, then flipped her ponytail as she snapped around and waltzed away.

Enchanted by her spell, Vance was unable to do anything except gape.

Andi the builder had somehow wiped away his tension, using her strange magic. She was unpredictable. He weighed the trait, deciding he liked that about her, and finished off the cupcake and coffee. As he began work on his blindsiding tactic, he hoped he could be unpredictable as well.

He hoped he hadn't made the discovery too late.

❧

After picking Elisa up from school, Andi headed back to Ground Zero. Best not only to drop her troubled sister off, but to pick her up as well. That way she could stave off concern over Elisa getting into trouble. At least while she was working.

They'd spent the morning pumping out the water in the equipment building. Guy Landers had stopped in to do a quick electrical check afterward. He'd told her he'd discovered the problem right off, when she was leaving to get Elisa. Arriving at Ground Zero, she noticed Guy's truck was gone now. She and Elisa rode the elevator down.

This morning she'd learned she'd won a bid on a job for Nielsen Remodeling. Things were finally looking up, putting her in a good mood, and for some reason, she found herself wanting to share the news with Vance. Since he'd not been in the greatest of moods, she kept the news to herself. Instead, she'd tried to encourage him, lighten things up, surprising herself. As she exited the elevator, she wondered how he was feeling now. Andi marched straight to the equipment room, the blast door propped open, and peered inside. The lights were on, lifting her spirits even higher.

She stepped through the door and looked around the large room—almost as big as a two-story house. The diesel generator as well as other equipment had been removed. All that remained were the four shock absorbers in case of a bomb blast. Though she grew up hearing stories about the Cold War era, it was difficult to imagine living with that fear, even though there were still plenty of armed missile sites around the country, especially in North Dakota.

"So this was why you were anxious to get back." Elisa stepped into the room behind her.

"Yeah, I wanted to see if the electrician got the power working. We pumped the water out so he could work." Andi motioned for Elisa to come all the way in.

"The place is a mess."

"You think?" Andi teased, happy Elisa took an interest, no matter how small. "It feels good when you transform a mess into something beautiful."

"So, why did I have to come? Why can't you just drop me off at the Rhubarb Festival? It started today, you know."

Andi kept her focus on the room so she wouldn't react. Did Elisa honestly think with her attitude that Andi would drop her off for a little fun? She'd been having a little too much fun for months now. Hence, summer school.

"I wanted to check the power. But starting tomorrow, I'm going to put you to work so you can learn responsibility."

"I've got homework, you know."

This coming from a person who was hard-pressed to even attend school? Andi eyed her sister, soon to become a woman. She wanted Elisa to have every opportunity and planned to try a different tactic. Scolding her would only drive her further away.

"We'll figure out how to make this work."

"I doubt it." Elisa turned on her heel and trotted out.

Andi sighed. She saw great potential in Elisa. If only her

sister would see the same. Though Andi might listen to her own advice. Ever since Jorgen dumped her because she wasn't as educated—would no longer fit into the life he wanted— she'd looked at the world differently, feeling anything but adequate. No one could ever accuse Andi of not trying, but now Elisa was the one with opportunities ahead of her, and Andi wouldn't let her throw them away.

Elisa was right about one thing though. This room was a mess. Once Ground Zero sold, Vance would pay her the balance of her fee plus some, and that was enough motivation to wash away her fears.

She closed her eyes and imagined discovering what her grandfather had hidden. Was it a slice of history? Or was it something valuable in terms of cold, hard cash?

Guilt began dropping on her like splotches of paint. She'd almost told Vance about her search the other day when she'd shared about her grandfather working at the military base, but she'd been afraid of how he might react. She didn't know him well enough. Would she ever?

Then he'd acted differently toward her this morning. She'd had to coax out of him the grin she liked. Did it have anything to do with the remodeling? She hoped not.

"Hey there." Vance leaned through the open doorway and smiled.

Seeing Vance, Andi straightened. "Hi."

He strolled the rest of the way into the room. "I wanted to apologize for my behavior this morning."

"Oh, you're fine. We all have our good days and bad days." And lately, she'd had her share of the latter.

"It's just that there's a problem at my company. I need to be there to work on it, but I can't exactly work on it there." He laughed and shoved a hand through his hair. "I'm not making any sense, am I?"

Andi laughed. "For a smart guy, no, you're not. But I'm sure it has more to do with my ability to understand than it does with you." Why had she said that?

A pained expression crossed his face. "You're wrong, actually. You're a beautiful and intelligent woman. On the other hand, I'm not so good at communicating."

Andi felt herself blush at his compliment. She wished she could believe him, and averted her gaze. He was being so. . . honest, and she was being so. . .not. More guilt splotches.

"I'd like to know more about my uncle. You worked with him, knew him for a while. What can you tell me about him?"

What was he playing at? Did he know about her search? She studied him. The need to tell the truth chiseled at her. "Since you asked, there is something I have to tell—"

"Can we go already?" Elisa stood in the doorway, arms crossed. "I'm tired and hungry. You didn't even let me get a snack."

What are you, five? Andi didn't want to argue in front of Vance. Her shoulders fell. "I'm sorry, I have to go. We can talk later."

She stomped after Elisa into the elevator, swathed in guilt paint splotches because she'd just used her sister as an excuse to avoid telling Vance the truth, and was ready to throw out her earlier resolve not to lecture or scold Elisa. "Did you have to be so rude? I was in the middle of a conversation."

When she received no response she glanced at her sister. That explained it. She was plugged into music.

Just as well. Drained, Andi didn't have the energy to talk to the teenager at the moment. Once outside, they headed for the truck.

"Hey, wait up," Vance called.

Andi turned to see him walking toward her, out of breath. He must have taken the stairs. She admired his lithe form, wondering how he kept in shape with the way he ate.

"Yeah? What's up?"

"I don't feel like eating dinner alone tonight, especially in the dungeon. How about I take you and Elisa somewhere? Where's a good place to eat?"

Andi stood speechless.

Elisa leaned out of the truck. "The Rhubarb Festival. They have food there."

Talk about selective hearing. "Elisa," Andi hissed. She hadn't even accepted the invitation yet.

"Come on, Andi. We can make it a business meeting, discuss the work you're doing." He pulled his glasses off and hung them from the corner of his lip—a mannerism that was beginning to grow on her.

Why did she always have to like smart guys?

seven

Vance held his breath. Would she agree? He wanted a replay of the Andi he'd seen this morning—lively and flirtatious, especially after the day he'd had. He wanted to see a flash of her hundred-watt smile.

Instead, she cocked her head. "You're the boss," she said, then climbed into her old pickup.

"Stellarific." Vance grinned, though her words didn't hold much encouragement. Still, it was hard to keep a guy down amid the prospect of having dinner—even at a rhubarb festival—in the company of a beautiful woman. Add to that, coming above ground into the real world for a change was almost like watching a meteor impact on Jupiter—a rare, celebratory event even for astronomy geeks.

Truck started and rumbling, Andi rolled down the window and leaned out. "The festival should have a lot of your kind of food, though mostly rhubarb-related, including pies, a carnival, and competitions between the longest stalk and the largest leaf. What more could you want?"

"Rhubarb, huh?" He'd eaten strawberry-rhubarb pie once. Made him sick.

"I don't suppose you know where the Rhubarb Festival is, do you?"

"I've been out of the dungeon and around the block a few times, but can't say that I do."

"Follow me."

"I'm right behind you." Vance pulled his keys out of his pocket and locked the entrance to Ground Zero.

He climbed into his car as Andi turned onto the main road and sped away like she was running from the law. One thing about this part of North Dakota—it was so flat you could see someone coming for miles. He chuckled as he climbed into his car and followed Andi from a distance for several miles and then into town.

He teased her, pulling next to her when the road allowed, and waved. Only Elisa responded. Waiting behind Andi's truck at a red light, he noticed Andi watching him through her rearview mirror.

He'd told her it could be a business dinner—a small twist of the truth. During his day of writing slightly malicious code to slow the misuse of his algorithm, Andi had permeated his thoughts. When he needed to concentrate most, he couldn't shake her smile or her earlier playfulness, though it had lasted all of fifteen seconds. As far as talk of remodeling the missile site, whatever it took to keep her company. Maybe he was only focused on her because she was his primary human contact throughout the day.

Nah. There was more to it than that.

Vance followed her into a parking lot filled with cars. People headed toward what looked like a pavilion-enclosed farmer's market and a small carnival. He waited as Andi and Elisa got out of their truck. Andi gave a tight smile, giving him the impression she'd rather be anywhere else. Or had she and Elisa been at it again?

"How long does this festival last?" he asked.

"Through the weekend. Today's the first day," Elisa said, as they headed toward the pavilion.

There was a small entrance fee of three dollars a person. Vance paid for all three of them despite Andi's protests. They visited several booths featuring various rhubarb recipes, jams and jellies, bread and cookies, and surprisingly, pork roast, stir-fries, and potpies.

Andi bought two slices of pie, one each for her and Elisa, and offered Vance a bite of hers.

The memory of the last time he'd eaten anything rhubarb prickled. "Shouldn't we eat dinner first?"

Andi worked to swallow her mouthful of pie. "I thought

you were the king of junk food?"

Vance enjoyed watching Andi stuff her face with pie. "Once in a while, I get hungry for real food."

Music boomed from the nearby carnival. Elisa handed Vance her unfinished pie. "Here, you can have this."

Vance tossed it in the garbage can next to him.

"Hey, sis, I see some friends. I'm going to hang out."

Irritation flashed in Andi's eyes. "Oh no you don't."

Elisa glared, then looked at Vance and softened. "But I want to go on the rides."

"We're here because Vance wanted dinner, remember? Some of the restaurants offer sample meals made from rhubarb. Let's walk across the street to the corner of Main and Houser. Otto's has steaks."

Vance grinned, his mouth watering at the thought of prime rib. "Can I get that without rhubarb?"

Andi laughed and the smile Vance liked almost peeked through. Oh yeah, she was definitely loosening up. Once inside Otto's, a hostess showed them to a booth where Andi and Elisa took their seats opposite each other. There was an awkward moment when he needed to decide where to sit.

Finally, he slid next to Elisa, facing Andi. "This way I can see your pretty face."

"Go, Andi. Vance thinks you're pretty," Elisa said.

Rather than killing her sister with a glare, as Vance would have expected, Andi kept her eyes on the menu, though a light shade of pink rose in her cheeks.

Andi shy and embarrassed because of him? Was he delusional that a girl like her could like a guy like him? Or could he relish the twist of heat in his stomach?

The waiter brought their drinks and they ordered. Andi took a sip of her water with lemon. Taking her time, she shared about growing up in the area. In her voice, he heard a sense of pride mingled with past hurts.

"Tell me, how did you end up in North Dakota all the way from Texas?" she asked.

He would have loved to hear more about her, but apparently she was ready to turn the topic to him.

Funny, he couldn't run from thoughts of ANND or Peter even at a Rhubarb Festival. "My college roommate and I had a competition to see who would start his own company first. Four years later, I got a call to work for him in Fargo—that was last year. I think maybe he just wanted to rub my face in it, but I was tired of working as one of hundreds of droids in a large Texas company. Plus, he offered me the opportunity of a lifetime."

Peter had plenty of talented programmers but had wanted Vance to join him. Better to be a big fish in a small pond, Vance's dad always said.

"So what do you do exactly?" Andi asked.

"Let me guess. It has to be something related to computers." Elisa had her back to the wall, sitting sideways in the booth.

Vance laughed. "Why do you say that?"

Their waiter brought their food and set plates before each of them.

Elisa tore a chicken strip in half and dipped it into rhubarb and horseradish sauce. "You just have that look about you."

Vance glanced at Andi, trying to read her. Andi chewed her food while bearing a friendly smirk.

"So, you, too, huh?"

Vance thought he'd seen a subtle nod, but Andi just smiled. Elisa laughed. "Andi's last boyfriend was a geek."

Andi scoured her sister with her gaze, then she looked at Vance. Fortunately her expression softened. "You never did answer my question. What do you do?"

Vance savored a bite of his medium-rare prime rib. "You know, they really do have some of the best steak in North Dakota. I'll give you that."

"Yeah, I agree. What do you do?" Andi wasn't going to let it go.

He couldn't exactly tell them all the secret stuff. "I work for a data mining company. You were right, too." He glanced at

Elisa. "I'm a programmer. I like to call it software engineer—sounds better."

Elisa leaned closer. "What's data mining?"

"Leave the man alone, would you? Let him tell us what he will."

Now she takes that stance. Well this was it. Once he told her everything, she'd write him off. But then again he was leaving, wasn't he?

"In Texas, I worked for one of the largest database computing software firms in the world. We developed software to manage large amounts of data, which required super computers. If you think about it, everything we do in this technological age generates data. Data mining, in the simplest of terms, is looking for hidden patterns in the data."

"But why would you want to do that? What do you do with the information?"

"Predict the future," he said, then took another bite of steak, ignoring the baked potato, and chewed.

Elisa laughed. "You're kidding, right?"

"Not entirely. Patterns in the data can reveal future trends. Behavior."

Andi's eyes grew wide and she lowered her fork slowly to her plate. "Like when I receive a catalogue in the mail that I didn't ask for, it's because they decided I'm a potential customer."

Vance nodded his head in a vague motion. "Yes and no. It's more likely you answered a questionnaire somewhere or bought a product that's related to that catalogue—transaction-based data. Still, it's all about the data."

Vance took a sip of his tea.

Andi played with her chicken Caesar salad. "So, in the company you work for now, what kind of data mining do you do? What are you looking for?"

Vance nearly spewed his tea. That wasn't exactly the sort of question he wanted to answer at the moment. He wiped his mouth with a napkin and composed himself, feeling trapped. "Mostly manufacturing applications. Some government applications as well." There. He'd answered without giving too much away.

Elisa leaned closer. "I want to hear about the government stuff. That sounds so exciting. What do they want to know? Who will be the next president?"

Stellar. If he kept talking, they'd have him telling them about the confidential contract and the algorithm he'd written. He'd never thought of himself in a cloak-and-dagger situation, but maybe that's exactly what he was in.

"Who would have thought Fargo would be a place for something like that." Andi laid her napkin on her plate.

"As a matter of fact, Fargo-Moorehead is home to several high-tech companies."

Andi's eyes took on that glazed look so familiar to Vance. Disappointment invaded like a virus. Though he'd expected it eventually, it still hurt. He'd be better off with a protective wall like Andi's.

"Let's talk about something else," he said.

❧

When Vance's eyes took on a distant look, she could tell he was bored with the conversation, even though it was about him. She didn't know enough to ask intelligent questions.

"I'll be right back." She excused herself and headed to the restroom.

In front of the mirror she tried to compose herself, push away the emotions. Listening to Vance talk about his job and his life in Fargo brought images of Jorgen to mind. Vance was no different than Jorgen. Educated. Brilliant. Lived in the city.

When would she get over how much he'd hurt her?

They'd dated through high school, then Jorgen had gone to college ahead of her and she was able to join him for a short period of time until her grandmother died. She'd had to return to take care of Elisa. He no longer had room for her in his life after that. Once he landed a job with a high-tech firm in Fargo he had big plans that didn't include an uneducated wife. She wasn't good enough. Never would be. Who was she kidding? She'd started the business to pay the bills and care for her sister, but she'd also wanted to make something of herself.

No matter how hard she worked, life worked against her. God seemed to bless others, while Andi stood on the sidelines. She finally had a glimmer of hope, at least for her business. But was it enough? Though Vance had brought her the hope, she resented people like him—people who were handed things on a silver platter. People who were able to fulfill their dreams without working hard for them.

Andi released a breath of pent-up jealousy, sagging as she washed her hands. No matter how hard she tried, she was beaten down at every turn, and Jorgen's breakup had almost done her in. But her attitude was wrong. She couldn't blame Vance Young.

She stared at the mirror again, making certain her face appeared free of the turmoil she felt inside. Vance was her client and to let her mind think of him as anything else went beyond professional. It was ridiculous. Still, she couldn't fight the sense that there was something more between them—somehow she had to annihilate the idea.

When she returned to the table, Elisa was trying to talk Vance into tasting the sampling of rhubarb jam. Andi slid into her seat as she watched, wanting to forget about the pain she felt over Jorgen and simply enjoy the faces Vance made.

"You're like a little kid who won't try something new," she teased.

"Who said I haven't tried it? I have, and I remember what it did to my stomach."

Andi peered at him. "It could have been bad rhubarb or bad eggs."

Before Vance could answer, the waiter returned and asked if they wanted dessert. Both Andi and Vance said no, but Elisa piped up. "I do."

Andi shook her head. "You don't need dessert. We had pie, remember?"

"Look, I ordered a small plate so I could save room."

Andi sighed. "Oh, all right. I'll have coffee since I've got to wait for you anyway."

Vance ordered coffee as well. "So, it's my turn to ask a question."

Andi laughed. "I can't imagine what you could possibly ask me that would be of any interest."

That encouraged a snort from Elisa. "And that's the truth."

Hurt but not surprised, Andi stared at her sister. Elisa smiled and looked down. "I'm only teasing, sis." Then to Vance, "She's very interesting. You'll see."

Embarrassed again, Andi said, "All right, that's enough."

"I know you were my uncle's contractor for Ground Zero, but I get the sense that you knew him as much more."

"What makes you say that?"

Andi looked into Vance's sharp eyes. She saw kindness there. Part of her wanted to know him better, much better. Again, she reminded herself it was out of the question.

"You've said a few things here and there. But when you say his name, you speak it with a warm familiarity."

He noticed that? The sensitive way he said the words squeezed her chest. Her heart warmed, sending a soft smile across her lips as she wrapped her hand around her coffee cup.

"I'll prove it to you. Come on, say his name."

"What?" Andi laughed. "You're not kidding, are you?" She cleared her throat. "Mr. Erickson."

"See? You feel something when you say his name."

She felt it all right. A blush up her neck and cheeks at the way Vance could tell how she felt. Her pulse raced under his intense stare. "He was a good man, though a little strange. I think you would have liked him a lot. If you'd had the chance to spend time with him."

"Like you did." Vance worked to fold his napkin into some sort of origami creature.

This guy was astute, able to read people. She had to squash

her growing schoolgirl crush on him—yeah, might as well admit it—before he read that, too. He'd figure out her secret hidden at the missile base.

Sooner or later.

"Your uncle knew my grandparents. He bought the farmland and missile site when it became available several years ago after my grandfather died. Seemed like he was around a lot, spending time with my grandmother. After she died and I had to quit school. . ." Andi hadn't meant to reveal that information. A knot formed in her throat.

"Andi." His voice low, he reached over to place his hand over hers. "You had to quit school? I'm so sorry."

Electricity surged up her arm. Andi stared at his hand, then slowly lifted her gaze to his. Tenderness, understanding, and longing were all wrapped together in one searching look.

It scared her. He scared her. She was in no way ready to be vulnerable again.

Gut it up. If she didn't harden herself now, it might be too late. "Thanks, but it's okay." She pulled her hand from his and continued her story. "He approached me to do the work and over time I got to know him better. It surprised me to learn he was wealthy. Made me wonder why he stuck around here."

"So you're not against getting to know the people you work with." He appeared to contemplate his words as though thinking out loud.

She couldn't go there. Not now. Not with him. "Your uncle Vance had the inside story on my grandparents. Had been friends with both of them when they were younger. You betcha, I wanted to hear about them."

Vance smiled. "Really?"

"Yeah." Andi nodded. "You see, he'd had a thing for my grandmother. But she was married to my grandfather, of course." *The letter. Tell him about the letter.* Like Vance, she, too, fidgeted with her napkin but nothing so elaborate as an origami space ship.

Vance pushed against his seat back, appearing surprised.

"That is completely stellar and shocking news. It explains a lot, really. You're working on the missile site where your grandfather was an airman. I had a feeling you were more than a contractor to my uncle—more like a granddaughter."

Elisa snickered from her corner. "Andi thinks he only hired her because—"

Andi kicked her under the table. "We'd better go. Elisa has school in the morning." She looked for the check but saw nothing.

Vance held it up and grinned. "You're not getting this. Now go. I've got it. You can get it next time."

Andi frowned, though a warmth spread through her. He was getting under her skin way too fast. He was exactly the kind of man she didn't want to allow in. She resolved there wouldn't be a next time.

Deep inside—*sigh*—she really wanted there to be.

eight

For the next week, Andi worked with her crew in the equipment building, preparing load-bearing walls for additional floor space in the form of a loft. One of Andi's friends agreed to give Elisa a ride from school each day so Andi wouldn't need to stop work. And when she did, she made sure to avoid Vance, though he seemed to be caught up in a project, albeit computer-related, of his own.

Once, she caught a glimpse of his somber expression and it worried her more than she had a right to be. She'd itched to drop next to him on the sofa to see what bothered him and imagined listening to him explain his work in what would sound like a foreign language to her. Then, all her insecurities would come crashing down. Why couldn't she just get over what Jorgen had done to her? Why did she believe he was right about her?

Again, she reminded herself, Vance was her client, nothing more, and she intended to keep her distance.

Quitting for the day, Lars and Karl said their good-byes, then took the elevator up. Andi should stop, too, but she wanted to spend a few minutes searching for the elusive item her grandfather hid decades before. The closer she came to finishing this job, the more her hopes sank that she'd ever recover it or that it had even remained undisturbed.

Tired all the way to her bones, her muscles ached and so did her head. As she pondered what to do next, Elisa's laughter drifted through the tunnel.

That was it, then. After gathering her tools into her tool bag, she headed down the tunnel to get Elisa. Soft voices replaced the laughter. Andi peered through the door to see her sister mesmerized, hanging on every word Vance uttered.

Andi's breath caught in her throat. She lowered her tool bag to the floor.

Arms folded, she straddled the blast door frame and leaned against it, watching, listening. Her sister was actually interested in the conversation. Did Elisa only act the rebellious teenager while with her? The truth hurt. But then again, that would mean there was more than enough hope for her sister. For them.

Vance pointed out various parts of his telescope, explaining them. His eyes shone with love for the hobby. Funny thing was, so did her sister's. He'd extracted Elisa from her self-inflicted shell of a bad attitude. Amazing. Another crack in Andi's defenses. It was one thing to harden herself when his tactics were aimed at her, but getting her sister excited about astronomy—why would she put a stop to that?

She observed them, unnoticed from her perch.

"Oh yeah, star clusters, swirling galaxies, nebulae are all there to show us how big God is. . ."

Andi became lost in her own thoughts while listening to his soothing voice and watching Elisa's vivid expression and shining eyes. She'd not done a good job of raising her sister these last couple of years. Regret clung to her.

Still, Vance. . .he'd changed things, stirring life into her sister in only a few days. Stirring something else into Andi. If only she could bury her heart much deeper, like the launch control center was buried in the ground with shock absorbers to protect against attacks. She almost laughed at the image.

As though she'd laughed out loud and given herself away, Vance looked up from the telescope, directly into her eyes, pinning her with the intensity of his gaze. Without moving, he stared for what seemed far too long. She could live in the warmth of his hazel-eyed gaze forever. Wanting to shake free, she stepped all the way into the room. That did the trick.

Elisa's demeanor returned to her normal flippancy, hammering the nail of disappointment into Andi. By stepping into the room, she'd destroyed the magic.

"Don't mind me. I still have work to do," she lied.

 za

Vance witnessed Elisa's wall go up the instant she realized her sister had caught her interest in astronomy. And Andi was quick to recover from what looked like disappointment by sliding a hard protective shell over her face before she left.

What is it with these women? He wasn't a therapist, but if he were to salvage the light he'd seen in both of them, he'd have to work fast. "I'll show you the stars tonight, if you'd like."

Elisa's eyes brightened again. "You will?"

"Sure." Vance looked at his watch. "It's almost six now. Would nine-thirty work?"

Andi peeked through the doorway again, this time a smile cracking open the armor. Vance would have winked but didn't want to risk losing Elisa's enthusiasm again.

Suddenly, Elisa frowned. "I doubt Andi will let me."

"Since when has that ever stopped you?" Andi came to stand next to them.

"Vance wants to show me the stars."

Uh-oh. The way she said it. . .

Vance realized that Elisa might have misinterpreted his intentions. "And you, too, Andi, if you're interested."

He held his breath, waiting for her answer.

She looked thoughtful, took her time—he'd bet to torture him—then, "Yeah, I'd like that very much." She pulled Elisa to her in a hug. "We'd like it very much. Thanks."

The look in her eyes sent radiant heat rushing through him—a stellar eruption on his star chart. Well, at least he'd discovered one way to breach her walls. But with the discovery came a disturbing uncertainty. Just what did he think he was doing?

He squashed it. No point in disrupting the joy fest.

Elisa relaxed in Andi's embrace. At least he'd been wrong that Elisa's fascination was more with him than the stars. He almost chuckled at the momentary delusion.

"I'll see you back here at dark?"

Smile beaming, Andi released Elisa. "That sounds fine.

We'd better grab some dinner."

"Listen, I'd invite you to eat—"

Andi held up her hand and laughed. "We need something of real sustenance. Not the junk food you manage to survive on. Thanks, but no."

Elisa snapped her fingers. "Hey, I know. Why don't you let my sister cook for you?"

A subtle frown crossed Andi's face.

Vance shook his head, hoping to spare her. "I have a few things to do. But thanks for the invitation."

"Maybe some other time." Tool bag slung over her shoulder, Andi waved and tugged Elisa behind her.

He watched them head out the blast door—a sight he dreaded every night. Andi had a way of livening up the place. Granted, it was mostly the construction noise that kept him company, but since they'd moved into the equipment building, he couldn't hear as much of it.

Smiling, he rummaged through the freezer in search of a microwave meal. Strange he preferred them instead of the survival food in the storage closet. Was there really much difference?

Who cares? In a few hours he'd be staring at the stars with Andi Nielsen. It was every geek's dream, or at least this geek's. And he fairly glowed inside at the idea of sparking an interest in a troubled teen, and even better that it helped Andi.

Maybe she'd come to appreciate him. Hating to get his hopes up, he sighed.

He placed a Mexican dinner in the microwave. What was he thinking, allowing any attachment to the woman? His time here would end soon enough, and then he'd be like every other jerk and leave. But he couldn't help himself. He'd seen something—no matter how small—in her eyes that encouraged him to try. Something he'd never seen before, not even in Janice.

An hour before Andi and Elisa were to arrive, Vance was nervous as a schoolboy. He couldn't remember the last time he'd been able to share his love for the stars with someone.

Nor could he imagine anyone he'd rather share it with. A seed of doubt pricked at him. Did Andi really want to look at the stars? Or had she agreed only to encourage her sister's interest? He'd been so caught up in the idea of stargazing that he hadn't considered the possibility.

But he refused to let it dampen his spirits. He slathered himself with mosquito repellent. If there was one thing he'd learned, you needed armor against the onslaught of mosquitoes in North Dakota. The cold of summer nights bothered him more than it seemed to affect the mosquitoes. After repellent, he pulled a fleece sweatshirt over long sleeves, then donned a ball cap and a vest with plenty of pockets. As he prepared for the night sky, he prayed he could open up a world of wonder for both Andi and her sister.

Once he found the perfect spot for stargazing he set up his telescope, then rolled out a blanket on the ground and waited. Vance glanced at his watch. Nine forty-five. He frowned. What if something came up and they couldn't make it? He reclined on the blanket and stared up into the sky like he used to do when he was a kid, imagining himself soaring through outer space, through the stars, wishing he could be a Jedi knight. North Dakota was certainly flat enough that a person could block all other images out. No light pollution whatsoever out here. Perfect.

"You look comfy." Andi's face appeared in his line of vision. He jumped up.

"Sorry we're late." She glanced back at Elisa, who jogged toward them.

"No problem. Everything's ready."

With a strange grin, Andi scanned him from head to toe with her flashlight. "What *are* you wearing?" She burst out laughing.

Vance spread out his arms and looked to see what she found so funny.

"You're swathed in designer outerwear." Andi circled him, looking him over. Embarrassed, Vance tugged off the vest, allowing himself a laugh as well. "When you shop in a Dallas sports store, gearing up for the North Dakota climate, this is what they tell you to wear."

Andi laughed heartily at that.

"Let's just say I wanted to be prepared."

"I've learned something about you." She cuffed his cap. "You like to shop."

Feeling defensive, Vance added, "There's not much else to do in a city that has more square footage of shopping than Manhattan."

"Uh-huh." Andi collapsed on the blanket. "So show us the stars, city boy."

Elisa giggled.

And there it was, the playful Andi that Vance had hoped to see again for over a week now. "There's a lot you can see without my telescope. As long as you have dark skies. That's key."

Elisa stood near the telescope. "What about a mountaintop? Wouldn't that be best?"

"Well, I don't see many of those around here." He pointed at the sky. "Can you identify any constellations?"

"Um, no."

"Look. There's Libra."

"Well, what about something more exciting? Everyone knows about constellations."

"Coming right up. Let me explain a few things first. I don't want you to be disappointed at what you see. This won't be like those pictures from the Hubble."

"What's the Hubble?"

Vance stifled the sigh. What did they teach these kids in school? "It's a giant telescope that orbits earth, which allows it to view the universe without interference from earth's atmosphere. But you can't see those types of images from a small telescope like mine." No matter how expensive it was.

"Hey, don't apologize," Andi offered.

"Still there's an advantage. The stars are like diamonds and, well. . .you'll have to see for yourself."

Vance looked through the eyepiece and adjusted it. "I'm looking at Jupiter right now. Actually, you can see it with the naked eye. But with a telescope, you can see the moons. Or at least a couple of them tonight." Vance stepped aside, allowing Elisa access to the telescope.

Elisa peered through the eyepiece. "That's cool. It doesn't look like it does in those science book pictures. It looks more like. . .a whole world!" Excitement emanated from her voice.

"I've always wanted to know how stars get their names." From the blanket, Andi gazed upward, looking thoughtful. . . and beautiful as. . .*a glimmering star*. . .

The small light that flickered inside of him when she was around began glowing brighter. But it wouldn't do to appear like some goggle-eyed schoolboy. "IAU. International Astronomical Union. They use the Greek letters, naming stars according to their brightness and constellations where they reside. For instance, Alpha Centauri."

"Let me guess. The first star in the Centaurus constellation?" Andi asked.

Vance cut a glance her way, surprised at her quick response. "Yep, it's the brightest. You're a smart one, but then I never doubted that."

Andi rose from the blanket and moved next to Elisa, nudging her. "Okay, it's my turn to look now."

"Wait." Vance adjusted the telescope and peered through the eyepiece, tapping it gently. "This is a globular cluster."

"A what?" both women asked.

For the next few minutes, Vance enjoyed answering their questions, sharing his love of the stars.

Eventually, all three of them reclined on the blanket and stared at the night sky—diamond-laden black velvet. Vance couldn't remember when he'd been happier. Why did he have to have the trouble with his job?

"Since you enjoy the wide open sky, no wonder you don't like living underground." Andi sounded relaxed, though sadness remained in her voice. "Tell me, when did you first become interested in the stars?"

Vance had hoped she would ask. "For as long as I can remember, I've loved to look at the night sky. It makes me realize how small I am compared to the universe. And to think that the Creator of this universe cares about us, cares about me even though I'm tiny in comparison. He cares about the smallest sparrow."

An uncomfortable quiet filled the air, contrasting the previous relaxed atmosphere. Vance pushed past the growing anxiety that he'd ruined the mood by simply bringing God into it. But how could he not? "There's a star that's 650 times the diameter of our sun. In other words, if it was our sun, its mass would encompass all the planets out to the orbit of Mars. Imagine that!"

"What's it called?"

"Betelgeuse."

"Beetlejuice? Like the movie?" Andi rolled on her side and propped on her elbow.

"Yeah, it's hard to comprehend. Like standing deep in a large cavern. You can't see how large it is," Elisa said, almost reverently.

"Back to God. I'm not so sure that the Creator of the universe really cares about us like that, I mean every little detail of our life. How could He?" Andi asked.

"That's just it. The universe shows how awesome and big He is. And yet, He's able to care for even the smallest in His creation. It's mind-bending."

Andi sat up and began picking up their things. "I can't buy that."

"You're leaving already?" To Vance, they'd only just started. He enjoyed the deep thoughts about God that always seemed to result from staring at the stars. He stood. How could he be sorry for talking about God?

Andi nodded, sadness in her eyes. "Remember, it's a school night. We should get going."

Vance folded the blanket, attempting to shove aside the pain that seeped too deep for him to say a word in response.

nine

As they drove down the dark highway, Andi could feel her sister's tension.

"What was that about?" Elisa sounded close to tears.

"What?"

"It was just getting good and you jumped up to leave. It was. . .weird."

"It's a school night. You knew we couldn't stay long."

"Who cares about school? I learned a lot more tonight than I ever have in school."

Andi sighed. "I don't want to get into an argument."

Bright headlights beamed toward them as a lone car passed. Andi focused on the road since the other driver hadn't dimmed his lights. She wasn't sure why she'd had the urge to leave. Maybe the conversation was getting too serious.

Once back at home, Andi listened to her phone messages. "Elisa, you have a message from Todd. Who is he?"

Elisa came out of the bathroom, brushing her teeth, eyes wide. She ran back in and returned, having rinsed out her mouth. "Todd called? What did he say?"

"Something about going out tonight." Andi wished she hadn't told Elisa.

"Are you serious?" Elisa grabbed the phone from Andi.

"What do you think you're doing? You're not going anywhere, and you're not calling boys." Grandma had drilled that rule into Andi, but Andi hadn't often obeyed. She could see Elisa wasn't much different. "Besides, it's after ten. It's rude to call people so late."

"Just because you can't keep a boyfriend, doesn't mean you have to keep me from having one."

Andi's planted her hands on her hips. "Excuse me?"

"You heard me. Just because Jorgen dumped you, you don't think you're good enough for anyone. You're jealous of me. You don't want me to be good enough either."

Andi was almost too incensed for words, as fury and hurt stabbed her insides. "What happened with him has nothing to do with this. Or with you."

"Doesn't it? I see that Vance has eyes for you, but you won't let him get close. You don't want anyone to get close to me either. That's why you won't let me have fun anymore. You watch me like I'm your prisoner. I wish I didn't live here with you." Tears filled Elisa's eyes and she rushed away from Andi, slamming the bedroom door.

Andi dragged herself to the kitchen table and slid into a chair. Numb with pain, she put her head in her hands. How dare her sister speak to her that way. She'd lost Jorgen because she'd left school, and she'd left school for Elisa.

But...

Part of Elisa's accusation was true. Jorgen had hurt Andi more than by simply breaking off their relationship—he'd made her feel like she wasn't good enough, nor would she ever be. For some reason, she'd taken Jorgen's proclamation over her life to heart, and she wouldn't give someone else the chance to hurt her like that. Ever again.

Elisa had seen right to the heart of the matter. A cold draft wafted over Andi, and she rubbed her arms. It was one thing to carry that burden, but to make Elisa carry it, too?

For Elisa's sake, Andi had given up her own dreams. Why couldn't Elisa see that part of the equation? Elisa had the chance to make something of herself, and she wouldn't have to quit school for anyone or any reason.

Guilt throbbed inside. Could Andi be forcing her own dreams on Elisa? Or was she punishing her? Lost in thought, Andi rose from the kitchen chair, then prepared for bed, though she knew she wouldn't sleep. Instead, she laid her head on her pillow, wide awake.

Vance had spoken of the Creator of the universe, caring

for people and all the details of their lives. But she didn't feel like He cared. At least not about her. Without any help from God, she took care of herself and Elisa. She protected them from people who had the ability to destroy their lives.

People like Jorgen who'd given her up for superficial reasons. People like Vance. Elisa's words filtered through her thoughts. *"Vance has eyes for you."*

She thought she'd kept the door to her heart—a blast door—tightly sealed. But somehow Vance Young had shaken it loose. She'd have to slam it shut again—the thought bringing an ache to her heart.

How did Vance feel? Was he lonely, too, shut up in the darkness of the underground capsule? If she closed the door on possibilities, all she'd have would be the chilling prospect of a lonely future.

But Vance wasn't lonely—he had God. She sensed that for Vance, looking at the stars brought him closer to God.

"God of the universe, if You really do care about the little things in my life, show me. Help me get over this pain."

And please help me find the treasure my grandfather hid.

꙳

Vance spent the next week amid the distant sounds of construction and renovation, hammering on his keyboard and testing a program to render the rogue algorithm he'd discovered ineffective. It would take them—whoever they were—time to discover what had happened, then even more time to fix things. In turn, Vance would have time to learn what exactly was going on, and hopefully he'd have concrete evidence to present to the authorities—evidence that didn't lead to him as the principal architect and instigator.

The quandary he'd yet to resolve was how and where to install the new algorithm.

Thankfully, his concentration on the problem took his mind off Andi. She'd come and gone every day without much interaction with him—a simple hello if he saw her in the morning and, if he were lucky, a good-bye at the end of the day.

She'd distanced herself even further from him the night they'd looked at the stars. Any hopes she'd have an interest in him beyond their business relationship had disappeared like a Mars space probe. Should he give up altogether? A more important question loomed. Their paths had crossed, but their lives were largely perpendicular—why would he allow himself feelings for her when he planned to sell Ground Zero? Planned to leave? It was part of their agreement. Not like he could back out of that.

He had to admit—he had second thoughts about leaving. He credited Andi with that. A somber realization struck him. Could he stop his growing feelings for her even if he tried?

His thoughts went back to the contentment he'd felt the night they'd looked at the stars together. The night sky sans light pollution on the lonesome prairie had given way to an extraordinary stargazing experience like nothing he'd known before. He'd been able to share that with Andi and Elisa. Though they seemed as enamored with the stars as Vance, neither of them had spoken to him about that night.

Probably for the best.

He forced his attention back to his computer screen. The landline phone rang, the interruption annoying him as he glanced at the clock. Four o'clock already? No one ever called on the thing.

"Vance here."

"Can you please give my sister a message?" Elisa's voice sounded shaky.

"What, no 'hello, Vance'?"

"She forgot to pick me up from school. She insisted on doing that today so she can keep me in her own private prison. Just tell her not to worry about me, I got a ride." She hung up.

Vance whistled. Where did Elisa find the energy to be so livid? He scratched his chin, then headed for the fridge, grabbing a soda to fuel his thoughts as he considered Andi. She'd find out soon enough, of course, that Elisa had found a ride home. Still, that wasn't like Andi. She tried way too hard to prove herself a responsible guardian for Elisa. Too bad Elisa couldn't see how much Andi loved her.

Vance blew out a long breath. The sound of construction stopped awhile ago. Why hadn't he noticed? He decided to go above ground to see if she was there along with the crew who usually quit for the day about now. Just to be sure.

Taking the stairs like he'd done every day that week, he noticed a great improvement in his stamina. He wasn't nearly as breathless as he stepped into the sunlight. He shielded his eyes, though the sun had long passed its blinding zenith by this time of day. Karl, Lars, and a new man Vance hadn't noticed before were loading items into the back of their trucks.

"Hey, why do you bother taking that stuff home every night only to bring it back the next day?" Vance asked.

Chuckling, Lars exchanged a look with his brother. "There's plenty that remains underground, in case you haven't noticed."

"Yeah, besides that, my wife's got me reworking the kitchen cabinets," Karl said.

"So, you finish up here only to have to work at home."

"If it makes the missus happy, it's worth it." Karl winked.

The new sub backed up and drove away onto the main road.

Vance noticed Andi's truck was still there. "Say, have you seen the boss today?"

Karl raised an eyebrow. "Haven't seen her in a couple of hours. Frankly, I thought she was talking to you."

Lars laughed and stared at Vance, with one of those knowing smiles—a subtle insinuation. Apparently the brothers thought Vance and Andi had something romantic in the works. Maybe they knew something he didn't, though not likely.

"I haven't seen her all day," Vance said.

The brothers grew serious and shared a glance.

"We'd better go check on her," Lars said.

"So, are you really worried about her?" Vance hurried after

them. "You don't think something could have happened, do you? Her sister called. She was supposed to pick her up."

Vance joined them on the elevator.

"There are a couple of places that a person wouldn't want to fall into."

"What?" Vance's gut tightened as he looked from one brother to the other. "What places?"

"No point in borrowing trouble." Karl shrugged.

"Yeah, she's probably looking around by herself like she always does after we leave."

"Looking around? For what?" How did they know she looked around after they left if they were gone? Odd.

Neither brother answered, but Vance didn't miss their shared glance.

While they waited for the doors to open, the thought that Andi could be hurt somewhere on the missile launch center crept over Vance. He shoved it away. Like Karl said, no point in borrowing trouble. But if something had happened to her...

His concerns over his job and the tricky game he played with the algorithm meant nothing to him. He had to find Andi, make sure she was all right. She already meant way too much to him. Never mind that she'd built a barrier he couldn't seem to scale. Never mind that it was obvious she and God weren't on good terms.

At the moment, he cared about nothing except finding her.

ten

Andi wanted to say a few distasteful words she'd heard from construction crews but bit her lip instead. After the guys had gone up, she'd climbed into an air plenum, looking for her grandfather's hidden prize. The air plenum had been secured with screws, which she'd heartily dismantled to allow herself entry. Then she'd heard a slow scraping followed by a heavy thud. At the time, intent on her search, she'd thought nothing of it. But later, when she'd tried to back out of the space, it suddenly dawned on her. Something had fallen—probably sheetrock—blocking her escape.

After several unsuccessful attempts at pushing away the object that held her captive, she gave up. If they found her—no, *when* they found her—she'd never live this down.

Though embarrassment crashed against her, there was no way around it—she'd have to call for help.

Andi yelled, feeling as though her cries didn't go much beyond the walls imprisoning her. Unfortunately, the only chance she had of being heard would be if someone were in the equipment building capsule.

"Oh no." Andi pressed her forehead against the wall. She'd missed picking up Elisa. Hope lay in that disruption—that is, if Elisa cared that Andi hadn't shown up to get her.

Andi wished she could at least sit or lie down. Even though it was an air plenum, the space was too small for her to do much but stand. The air became stuffy, her body sticky with sweat. She didn't want to stay here all night.

After minutes ticked into an hour, her humiliation gave way to panic.

A nervous laugh escaped, precluding a whimper. She thought of Vance's reaction if he were stuck in this small space. But she couldn't imagine him wedging himself into such a precarious position.

"Andi. . .Andi?" Vance's voice echoed from somewhere nearby.

"In here! Vance, I'm in here!"

A few seconds later, she heard Vance groan, then heave. Again, then several times more she heard his efforts accompanied with panting. Andi pushed the wall plate she'd dismantled as relief flowed through her. The plate gave way. Vance's face appeared in her line of vision, as he tugged the wall out of her path.

She smiled, defying the torrent of embarrassment and relief entwining her, and stepped out of the compartment. "Oh, thank—" Shaky legs gave way as her knees buckled under her.

"Andi!" Vance swept her against him, steadying her. "Are you all right?" His words were breathy, laced with concern.

She allowed herself a moment, relishing his embrace. All comfort and strength, his heart beat rapidly. He felt so good.

Breathing a sigh, she became aware she'd stayed too long and stepped free.

"Yes, I think so." She stood as tall as she could and faced her humiliation. She'd shown herself weak, practically collapsing into his arms. What sort of ninny was she?

"Looks like all that sheetrock fell over and wedged you into that space." Vance peered into where she'd been trapped. "What on earth were you doing in there?"

This was the part where Andi should tell him she was searching for something her grandfather supposedly hid. But sharing that information on the heels of what just happened might give Vance all the reason he needed to shut her down, keeping her from searching.

"Well, what do you think? I need to know what is behind every cavity, every nook and cranny, every hidden space in order to make this an efficient living area." There. Her answer had been confident because it was true. Under most circumstances. She stared back, looking into his searching gaze, glad he knew nothing about construction.

Or did he?

He smiled, but wariness lurked in his eyes. "I'm just glad you're all right. But let your crew do that sort of thing for you next time, will you?"

Funny. He hadn't made her feel like an idiot for getting stuck. On the contrary, he appeared concerned. Very concerned. And she'd worked hard this past week to avoid him and his God talk. Now she wondered why. Being with him made her feel good inside. Though he was brilliant, he never made her feel ignorant, or less than him. Never spoke to her in a condescending way.

Holding out his hand, he said, "If you're ready, I'll escort you up top."

She laughed as she took it. "Is that to make sure I leave?"

His gaze lingered before he replied. "I never like to see you leave."

What did he mean?

"Well, if you don't mind, I want to use your restroom and wash my hands. I feel grimy. Oh, and I need to call Elisa."

"You can thank her. She called to say she'd found a way home, but she wasn't happy that you weren't there to pick her up."

"And that's when you became concerned?"

Vance nodded.

Andi's heart warmed. She realized they were still holding hands.

"So you found her!" Karl and Lars stepped into the room, beaming with relieved smiles. Their gaze flitted to Andi and Vance, holding hands. She quickly released his, but not fast enough.

Lars chuckled. "Well, looks like everything is under control down here. We'd better head home."

After Andi refreshed herself she headed up top, leaving Vance to his computer. From there, she called Elisa.

She got no answer and huffed. Climbing into her truck, she

noticed Vance standing there, watching. "Are you checking on me again?"

"I thought I might."

How she loved his Texas accent and wished she had an excuse to stay longer. But Elisa was waiting.

Once at home, Andi walked into the house. "Elisa?"

A quiet and empty house greeted her.

❧

How had Andi gotten herself into that predicament? Though relieved, Vance remained concerned for her well-being as she continued work on the missile site. But then, was there any line of work that was safe? As his thoughts returned to his own problems, he recognized that he was putting himself into a precarious position, too.

Vance munched on a bag of sour cream potato chips, then washed them down with a cola. He'd remotely searched the ANND Systems computers for all versions of his algorithm, finding nothing out of the ordinary. The one thing he had going for him was that he'd known Peter a very long time. That was to his partner's disadvantage. No wonder he'd wanted Vance away. Vance guessed that Peter was running a parallel system, within the mainframe—a system that Vance wouldn't know to look for unless, of course, he had a reason.

Should he do it, or should he not? The moral dilemma of the day.

He crumpled the empty bag of potato chips and shot for the garbage can across the room. Missed. His aim was lousy these days, in more ways than one. He'd created the new program, now what did he do with it?

Stellar.

Vance had always prided himself on seeing things as either black or white. Something was either right or it was wrong. But he'd entered a situation—partly of his own making—in which things were blurred, morphing into a dull gray. If a parallel system were running a rogue version of Vance's algorithm, then he had to know about it, he had to stop it.

There was only one way to find out and that was by logging on to Peter's account. If said system existed, then Peter was certainly in on it. Vance should have done this to begin with. But he'd put it off, not wanting to face reality.

But D-day was upon him. With a heavy heart Vance released a long, slow breath.

Several weeks ago while in Peter's office, Vance had noticed Peter's last password. It had been written on a Post-it note and stuck on the inside edge of the desk. Vance hadn't intended to see it, but he couldn't miss it, and once he'd seen it, it was forever written in his memory. The guy had changed it by now—but it told Vance everything he needed to know. If he'd learned anything about his former college roommate, he knew how he selected passwords. The sticky pad told Vance he hadn't changed his method.

Peter used acronyms based on activities he enjoyed. That, plus four numbers tacked on the end. They were always the same four numbers—5624. That was the problem with passwords. They had to be something a person could remember, so switching the numbers around made no sense. But add them to a new word and you had a strong password. At least against cyber attacks.

Vance made a list of Peter's activities and from those created acronyms, then tagged Peter's four numbers at the end. Like any fail-safe system, ANND allowed three attempts. Satisfied that he'd included as many acronyms as possible, Vance sat back and closed his eyes, relaxing. He wanted to pray for God's help, but he didn't feel right about asking God in on his somewhat uncouth activity. That thought alone should tell him to stop.

Vance pulled up the login for ANND Systems and with nervous fingers entered in his first attempt.

Unsuccessful.

A rush of moisture slammed his palms.

He entered the second password.

Unsuccessful.

Heart pounding, he slumped against the sofa back. He wasn't wired for covert activities.

Closing his eyes, he remembered his last conversation with Peter in the boardroom, with Carolyn hanging close to Peter, practically clinging to him. Peter had dated several women in the office—ANND had no policy against interoffice romance, resulting in at least two married couples. Carolyn was his latest. No one seemed concerned about harassment. Natasha, Sybil, Angela, Vespa, and Carolyn. NSAVC. Vance sat up. Could that be it?

He wondered, though, if Carolyn's initial should be included or not. The guess was as good as any. He typed in NSAVC5624. Almost too many letters. He swallowed and, despite his hesitation, sent up a silent prayer, then pressed the login button.

Welcome, Peter Lundgren.

"Yes." Vance pumped his arm.

Because he was after only one thing, he avoided looking at anything else on Peter's account. He scrolled through files to systems manager and opened it. Two systems appeared. Vance opened the one he'd been unaware of, searching for his algorithm.

There. A sick feeling hit the middle of his stomach. He ignored it, putting his mind to quickly creating a new username and password that would give him access to the parallel system. He then logged out of Peter's account. The less time he spent on Peter's account the less likely someone would notice the unauthorized access.

Using his newly created account, Vance logged in again. What he was about to do would eventually be discovered. He hoped his plan worked.

The phone rang. Vance kept his eyes on the screen while the program loaded, watching for any glitches. "Vance here."

"It's Andi."

The nervous edge in her voice put Vance on alert. "What is it?"

"Elisa's gone."

eleven

"What do you mean?" Vance asked.

This was awkward. It wasn't any of his concern. Really. But Andi had already called Shawna next door. She hadn't seen her sister. But Elisa *had* called and spoken to Vance. Maybe she'd told Vance something.

Andi tried to calm her voice. "She wasn't at home when I got here. I can't locate her at any of the usual places. What exactly did she say when she called?"

"Give me a sec."

Andi paced her kitchen, waiting for his answer. She sprayed air freshener around the stale-smelling room, then knocked over a cup, spilling coffee.

"Just that she was getting a ride home and not to worry about her."

"That's all?"

"Yeah, but she was pretty incensed. . .oh wait, she did say something about your keeping her in prison."

Andi huffed. "Leave it to her to put a spin on everything."

"Listen, Andi. What can I do to help?"

"I. . .uh. . ." What could he do? "I just needed to know if she'd told you she was going somewhere. I'm sure she's fine."

"I'm coming over. I can help you look."

She cleared her throat. "That's not necessary. I didn't want to bother you but had hoped you might know something."

"I probably have your address written down somewhere, but what is it again?"

"Vance. . ." She hesitated, realizing she'd carried a small twinge of hope. Just being with him lifted her spirit. And that's exactly why she had to avoid him. "You don't have to do that."

"I need to get out for some air. Besides, I care about your sister."

What about me? The unwelcome thought irked her.

Still, bringing Vance into the equation would defuse an explosive situation, that is, once she found Elisa. Her sister liked him, opened up to him. Ready to detonate, Andi steadied her voice. "Four fifty-five Glenwood."

"See you in a few."

Andi cleaned up the spilled coffee, cleared the counters, and loaded the dishwasher, but her mind was far from these tasks. She and her sister hadn't spoken much to each other since their argument a few days before—the night they'd gone stargazing with Vance.

"You watch me like I'm your prisoner. I wish I didn't live here with you."

Elisa's words bombarded her. At the time, Andi had taken them for an idle threat. But what if it wasn't?

Gazing out the kitchen window, Andi thought about the possibility. Had Elisa run away? It was clear that Elisa was completely miserable, but wasn't that the way of things? Andi wasn't all that happy either, but at Elisa's age, kids were pretty self-absorbed.

Shaking her head, she sighed. She wouldn't put it past Elisa to pull a stunt like this, considering everything else she'd done. Andi hung her head over the sink, fighting back tears. Once again, God wasn't there for her, for them.

Wouldn't it be nice if she could simply wish upon a star—one of the brightest shimmering in the sky like she'd seen the other night—and have her wish answered? Why couldn't God work like a wishing star?

She had to be strong and fix this problem—as usual, on her own. Having a talent for fixing things, she'd started her business for that very reason. Unfortunately, that talent didn't extend to family problems or she'd have resolved hers long ago. But she had to try.

Now she wished she'd not allowed Vance to come. Rather

than wait for him, she could be driving around town, looking for Elisa. She listened to the messages on the house phone and cell phone voice mail one more time while she glanced around for a note Elisa might have left.

Her room! If Elisa had run away, she'd have taken a bag of clothes. Things remaining in place would go a long way to drive the worry from Andi's mind. She opened Elisa's door and flipped on the light. The bed was askew, nothing new there. Clothes spilled from the too full closet. Andi relaxed a little.

A sudden pang of regret for their bad fortune in losing family and being on their own pummeled her. Elisa was probably safe somewhere, but the remote thought that she wasn't unsettled Andi. She began picking up the clutter. A surge of love ran through her. She wanted to do better. Had to.

Lord, please bring her home safely, and help me to be a better sister and guardian. I'm asking for Elisa, not for myself.

She'd added the last part to be sure God heard her. He had a soft spot for children, didn't He? Grandma had made sure she got to Sunday school at least some of the time. Though Elisa was probably closer to an adult now than a child, Andi remembered something about Jesus' wanting the little children near Him.

A knock on the door jolted her. Elisa? Andi fairly ran from the room. Elisa would have come through the door without knocking, though.

Unless she'd forgotten her key.

Hands in pockets, Vance stood on the porch with a muted grin.

"Hi there." At seeing him, Andi tugged her hair back into her usual ponytail.

He sent her an odd look, resulting in flutters to her insides. "Hey. Any luck finding her?"

Andi frowned. "Nope. Come on in."

Vance meandered through the small foyer, following Andi into the living room. "What's the plan then?"

Andi rubbed her forehead. "You know, I feel ridiculous having you come all this way. I should have just driven around town. She could be anywhere that kids hang out."

"She doesn't have a cell phone?"

Andi swallowed and looked at her hands. "It seems such a small thing now. But no. . . I didn't want to spend the money, and we live in such a small town, it didn't seem necessary." Number one on her list to do better.

"Who've you called?"

"The parents of her friends and even the few friends whose cell numbers I have before calling you. No one has seen her." Now that she'd said the words out loud. . . Andi sank to the couch.

Vance sat next to her. "Don't panic. You stay here to answer the phone and wait for Elisa. I'll drive around town."

She eyed him, wary yet hopeful. "You'd. . .do that?"

"Of course."

"But I can't just sit here."

"Of course you can. And I'll do more. I'll pray."

Andi hoped his prayers would do more good than hers. "Thanks."

Though she appreciated his words, she shook her head and looked away. Why was she letting herself get worked up? If they hadn't had that stupid argument. . .

❧

Vance walked to the door. "Stay calm. She's all right."

At least until Andi gets her hands on her. Then Andi would explode, of that Vance had no doubt. He closed the door, leaving Andi sitting on the sofa, looking forlorn. He jumped in his car and backed from the drive of the small ranch house.

"Lord, You have Elisa in the palm of Your hands, so just keep her safe. Let me find her. Please."

As Vance drove down Main Street, it occurred to him that maybe God had sent him all the way to North Dakota to help this family. An arrogant thought, at that. But he cared about them both—Elisa and Andi. . .well, Andi made his insides feel too strange for comfort, but in a good way. And if there weren't any coincidences, then what else could he think? Still, he had to tread carefully. He had every intention of leaving once his long vacation was up. And go where? He didn't know that yet, but one problem at a time. One thing he knew as a software engineer—structure was everything. First things first.

Tonight's problem apparently had to do with a lost teenager. First he'd tackled the local fast food joints. Dairy Queen, Burger King, McDonald's, and the local taco place. He smiled. Dairy Queen was a Texas-born company, but apparently Taco Bell execs—out of San Antonio—hadn't gotten their claws into this small town in North Dakota yet.

Vance drove into the shopping center parking lot, looking at the young people coming in and out of the store, some loitering, then to the nearby coffee kiosk. On a hunch, he drove through the kiosk window and ordered an iced caramel macchiato with an extra shot.

"Say, do you know Elisa Nielsen?"

The kid shook his head. "Sorry."

Vance frowned. The town was bigger than he thought. "Where do kids go in this town to hang out?"

"You got me. I'm here all the time."

Vance tipped the guy. "Keep up the good work, then."

His chugged the sugary, caffeine-loaded drink, hoping to fire his neurons. The last thing he wanted was to go home empty-handed to Andi.

Home? He blew out a breath. What was he thinking?

Elisa had talked about some guy from school that she liked, saying he was smart. Vance leaned his head against the seat and squeezed his eyes. What was his name again? Todd. Todd something. Had Andi called his house? He wasn't sure she even knew about the boy. Elisa always clammed up about him when Andi walked through the room. The guy had a name similar to an actor's. That's all Vance could remember.

Using his smart phone, he scanned the Internet for actors.

Tom Cruise! That's it. He dialed information and called all three Crews families, asking for Todd. Once he found the correct residence he asked for Elisa. She answered, cautious rebellion in her voice. Vance wanted to put her at ease—a big brother, on her side. On his way there he phoned Andi to let her know he'd found Elisa and that she'd been studying. He hoped it was enough to defuse the bomb.

When Vance pulled up to the curb next to the Crews home, Elisa, carrying a couple of textbooks, came out of the house but turned to speak to a boy in the doorway. Vance waited patiently, thinking about how vulnerable Andi was where her sister was concerned. What could he say to Elisa without causing more strain between the two?

Elisa finally opened the door to his car. Her smile, as she stepped in, was tight. "So, Andi sent *you*. . . ." She looked out the passenger window. "Too busy to pick me up herself," she mumbled.

Vance heard the hurt she carried. Never finding himself in this position before, he was surprised at how quickly a lecture formed in his mind. *Careful now.* He would try to handle this differently than Andi because lectures weren't getting her anywhere with Elisa. He turned onto Main Street, heading back to Andi and Elisa's home.

"Actually, your sister had no idea where you were."

"Figures."

Vance needed to find something else to talk about. He peered at the books on her lap. "Geometry and biology. Two of my favorites. You mentioned Todd made good grades. Is he tutoring you?"

Elisa relaxed. "Something like that. I want to do better. We only have a couple more weeks of summer school."

Vance turned left onto Glenwood. "Good girl."

"I have tests coming up. It'd be nice to surprise Andi with good grades for a change."

After pulling into the driveway, Vance shifted into PARK

and with a wide grin tilted his head at Elisa. "That's the best news I've heard all day."

She smiled in return and pulled on the door handle. The door clicked but didn't open.

"Wait."

Elisa looked at him, curiosity in her expression.

"I need to prepare you. Andi had an accident today."

Elisa's eyes widened. "What? Is she all right?"

He hadn't meant to word it that way, but her reaction told him she loved her sister. *Good.* "She's fine. But she got stuck behind a wall. Nobody knew where she was." For the first time since looking for Andi, Vance recalled the brothers' comment about her searching for something, and Vance's initial suspicion when he asked her why she'd climbed into the small space.

He scratched his chin. Something to consider, but later. Much later.

For a moment, Elisa's eyes appeared to tear up. "Don't tell me. She was trapped and that's why she couldn't pick me up."

Nodding, Vance put his hand on her shoulder and squeezed. "That's right, but it was your phone call that alerted me to a possible problem. We found her, thankfully. Then she came home and couldn't find you."

Vance was certain that's why Andi's nerves were on edge, contributing to her overreaction at not finding Elisa at home.

Elisa stared out the windshield, where drops of rain began to play on the glass. With a thick voice, she said, "I'm in trouble now."

Vance almost chuckled. She would have been in trouble anyway, but knowing that her sister had been trapped had opened a part of Elisa's heart to see.

"Look, I'm no psychoanalyst, but I'm thinking she'll just be glad to see you."

Hands on hips, Andi stood in the doorway, looking anything but patient as she watched them sit in the car. Vance and Elisa stepped from the car. Elisa hurried to Andi and hugged her.

Andi wrapped her arms around her sister in return, her gaze finding Vance's, gratitude shining in her beautiful blue eyes.

She said, "Thank you," without putting voice to the words.

His heart skipped a beat, Elisa's words echoing in his mind. *"I'm in trouble now."*

twelve

Releasing her bear-hug on Elisa, Andi waved to Vance, disappointed to see him go as he backed from the drive. He reminded her of a handsome prince who'd stepped from a fairy-tale book, though he couldn't be real. Nor was she a beautiful princess.

But more than a prince, he seemed to be an answer to her prayers—prayers she had no faith to pray. Joy and happiness swirled inside, emotions she hadn't felt in years. It was as if he'd uncovered a hidden treasure inside her she'd not known was there.

"Um, shouldn't we have invited him in or something?" Elisa swiped her eyes.

Elisa crying? Andi had feared she'd fall into lecturing again, which would then digress into the usual argument. But with Elisa's apparent change in attitude, how could she be angry?

"I suspect he's giving us some time to ourselves." She wished he'd stayed but wasn't about to chase him down.

Elisa followed Andi into the house. "Vance told me what happened today." Elisa hugged her again. "You need to be careful."

Andi couldn't believe what she was seeing and hearing. "Who are you and what have you done with my sister?"

The question elicited a laugh from Elisa. "Stop it. You know I love you. You're my sister." After setting her textbooks on the coffee table, Elisa meandered into the kitchen and lifted the lid on the saucepan, sniffing the Hamburger Helper Andi had thrown together earlier. "Glad I ate at Todd's."

Andi sighed. "I thought you'd run away." There, she'd said it, the words laced with regret rather than fear and anger.

"What? Why would you think that?"

103

"Our argument. Don't you remember the words you said to me?"

Elisa peered into the refrigerator, blowing a loose curl from her face. "I know what I said. I didn't mean it."

Andi pulled a box of French vanilla cake mix from the cabinet, intending to make Elisa's favorite. "I'm sorry for everything that's happened between us, and I want you to know that I'm going to try to do better. I hope you know that I love you."

After pulling out a soda and popping the top, Elisa slurped from the opening. "I'm as much to blame as you. I know that now."

Pouring the mix into the blender along with eggs, oil, and water, Andi focused on the task, afraid she'd say the wrong thing like she always did. Still, she couldn't help herself. "Can I ask what's changed?"

Elisa stiffened, knitting her brows. Thankfully, though, she soon relaxed, the hint of a grin at the left corner of her mouth. "Todd." Her eyes fairly shone when she said his name. "He's changed things."

Oh no. "Aha." Boys would come and go, Andi knew from her own painful experience. This wasn't good, but what could she say that wouldn't further alienate Elisa?

"And Vance, too. He knows so much and he loves learning."

Until that moment, Andi hadn't realized how much Vance had influenced her sister. With cake batter blending in the mixer, Andi chewed her lip, wishing she'd had more of a hand in Elisa's much-improved attitude.

"That's where I was tonight, studying. Todd talked to me about my attitude."

Andi cocked a brow, disbelieving. "How old is this guy?"

Elisa giggled. "He's a senior, but I think you'd like him, sis. He. . uh. . .invited me to church. Invited us."

"He what?" Might Todd actually be a good thing for Elisa?

Andi poured the batter into a pan and stuck it into the oven. She and Elisa chatted for a while longer until she'd pulled the cake from the oven to cool. This had been a long and rough day. She'd spread strawberry icing over the cake in the morning. After Elisa headed to bed, Andi did the same, thankful the day had ended better than she thought.

As Andi readied for bed that night, brushing her hair from the tight ponytail she wore every day, she considered the changes in her life. When she'd had to quit school after their grandmother's death to care for Elisa, Jorgen had ended their relationship. Mr. E had been the only person to help her out of the pit, and she'd been on a downward spiral ever since his death. Until Vance showed up. The younger version of the elder—wavy hair and glasses and a brain the size of the North Dakota Badlands—had set off warning sirens in her head.

Despite her best efforts to guard against his charms, he was making inroads into her heart. But was that intentional on his part, considering he would be leaving soon?

Elisa had not been immune to him either. Still, Andi was happy with the changes she'd seen in her sister, and if that were to Vance's credit, she was all for it.

Andi had been fighting for so long to hang on to what little she had left, she was afraid to trust what appeared to be good things happening in her life.

A simple thing like trust—why was it so hard?

❧

The lights automatically flipped on as soon as Vance walked through the blast door to the Ground Zero living room. He didn't even remember the drive home, his mind on continuous replay of Andi's face as she thanked him, her eyes glowing with gratitude. He was practically floating. Janice had never made him float.

The emotional high was lost as soon as he plopped on the sofa and looked at his laptop. The problem with ANND rushed toward him like a meteoric fireball. He pressed his head into the sofa back and groaned. Hadn't he done enough for one day? Saving a damsel in distress, loading an interference program, and finding the whereabouts of a lost teenager? He couldn't solve all the problems of the world in one day.

Exhausted, he went to bed, leaving the lights on. The only time he thought about buying night lights was when he wanted to sleep, never when he was in town.

The next morning he woke with a start, feeling as though someone had nudged him awake. He sat up on his elbows and squinted. No sounds of construction awaited him. What time was it anyway? He looked at the small clock next to the bed. Eight o'clock.

Great. He'd overslept. Still. . .this was supposed to be his vacation. He scratched his head. He wouldn't hear Andi and crew because they were at the far end of the underground complex in a completely different capsule on the other side of the blast door.

Dread kept him in bed for fifteen more minutes. Did he really have to face this day? Or could he ignore the fact that he'd hacked into Peter's parallel system and replaced the rogue program with another? He jerked upright. What if it was all on the up-and-up? Government-approved and contracted? Who was he to say it wasn't? Did he have oatmeal for brains?

After a good night's sleep he suddenly had a new perspective? Hadn't he slept on it before making the decision? *God in heaven, help me.*

Growling his displeasure, Vance jumped from bed and sprinted into the living room in his sweats, eager to put a stop to his crazy and irrational nonsense about somehow being able to save his reputation, and save ANND from running the wrong program.

An e-mail from Peter awaited him.

Sweet streaming malware! Had the guy discovered his intrusion already? The program he'd loaded shouldn't have been caught yet—in only a matter of hours. Pulse raging in his ears, Vance opened the e-mail and read.

They'd hit a snag and needed his help. What snag? Everything was working perfectly when he'd left, though the fact that they were still in beta testing had disturbed him. In the e-mail, Peter suggested that there wasn't any need for Vance to come all the way back from Cancun—he could make the fix remotely. The adrenaline rush subsided, relief washing it away, then. . .Vance saw Peter's sign off.

Show your face here and you're dead.

Oh man. What did that mean? Peter was kidding, of course. Under normal circumstances. But this was anything but normal. Was there a hidden threat within the e-mail? What had he gotten himself into?

Peter had spent the better part of a year courting Bob Sitze, one of his government contacts, which made Vance more than a little nervous about calling Bob regarding his discovery. Considering most everyone at ANND resented Vance because Peter brought him on as his star programmer, Vance was hesitant to trust anyone else.

Oh man. The situation was anything but stellar. *Just calm down.* Vance logged into the system and took a look at the data Peter called to his attention. Nothing to do with Vance's hacking last night. But. . .

This just gets better every minute.

Specific systems were offline for security purposes. Peter should know Vance could only make a full diagnostic sweep with in-office-only access.

Great solar masses.

Peter had just told him he was dead if he showed his face. How in the world did Peter expect him to resolve this otherwise, especially from Cancun? Except if Vance had kept his plans to go there, he would have been back by now. He'd just have go to the office after hours and hope—no, pray—that no one else was there.

Vance stood and stretched, taking several long and much-needed breaths. Oxygen would go a long way to get his mind going. If he didn't have this mess to clean up, how he'd enjoy seeing Andi this morning. At least he had one thing to look forward to.

He closed his eyes as he finished up a long stretch and imagined her sweet face, still wary. . .but sweet.

"Good morning."

He opened his eyes to a vision. Andi stood in the doorway, her dazzling smile nearly bowling him over. Fumbling for words, he could only smile in return. His day had just soared to five stars from the negative end on the how's-your-day rating system.

She meandered into the kitchen and looked at him across the island. "I see you haven't had your morning coffee."

Vance laughed. "You offering to pour me a cup?"

Two mugs in her hands, she grinned. "I was hoping to steal a cup for myself, too. That all right with you?"

"As long as you're pouring, I see no problem with that."

Pressing her lips into a playful grin, she filled both cups. "You'd better watch out if you don't want this coffee in your face."

Vance threw his hands up in surrender and moved to the island. "Okay, I give. I don't want to start my day out on the wrong side of you."

She giggled and handed him the coffee-filled mug. "Got a late start this morning."

As Vance took it from her, his fingers brushed hers, sending a charge through him. Spooning into his coffee the usual fillers, he couldn't help the smile playing on his lips as he considered how she made him feel all gooey inside, like the space-time continuum had folded and he was in the crease.

"Listen, I wanted to thank you for what you did."

"It was nothing. Elisa is a good kid. She's got a great head on her shoulders." Vance took a sip of his coffee. "Just like her sister."

She stared into her cup. Was that a blush creeping over her face? Hmm. Pretty. He liked this side of her.

"Elisa's out of school today. I almost played hooky from work, but then that wouldn't be a good example for her, would it?"

Vance opened his mouth to reply that she should have spent the time with her sister but then. . .an idea slammed him.

thirteen

"Are we there yet?" Sitting in the back, Elisa pulled on the front passenger seat.

Andi giggled. "You sound like a little kid." She enjoyed watching the landscape go by. "This was a great idea, Vance."

Staring ahead at the road, he flashed her a quick grin—a look she was becoming insanely attached to.

"It's been awhile since I've been to Fargo," she said. Unwanted memories of being together with Jorgen at North Dakota State University drifted through her mind.

"Unfortunately, I don't think it's been long enough for me."

Andi gave him a side glance. "Really. Are you saying you're growing attached to Ground Zero?"

Vance didn't answer at first. "You know, it has kind of grown on me. But I think that might have more to do with the company I'm keeping while there."

Andi's pulse jumped. Before she could react she felt the familiar pressure on the seatback.

"Thanks, Vance, we like you, too." Elisa laughed, then plopped back.

"This trip will be great for Elisa," Andi said. Elisa would be able to see there's a world of opportunity waiting for her—a world beyond the small town of Herndon.

"So what do you want to be when you grow up, Elisa?" Vance asked.

For the next couple of hours, they talked about every topic they could think of, and sometimes drove in comfortable silence. Andi couldn't remember when she'd been so happy, so relaxed.

But that was the problem. She feared getting too close, and yet here she was like a meteor drawn by the gravitational pull of a planet called Vance—he even had her thinking in astronomical terms. If she didn't watch out, she'd end up crashing. And this time, she suspected she wouldn't be the only one hurt. Elisa looked to Vance like he was a big brother.

She'd been more than surprised when he'd invited her and Elisa to go with him to Fargo. Stunned had been more like it, and then one quick, impulsive decision and she'd found herself agreeing to go. And still, she felt good about it.

Besides, she'd told herself, it was for Elisa. She and Elisa needed some time together to have fun. What better place than the largest city in North Dakota?

As Andi watched the North Dakota wheat and sunflower fields go by, she almost dozed. Finally, the traffic on the highway increased as a mass of buildings and houses took shape in the distance. Anticipation filled the car.

They drove down Broadway, then past Main, the heart of Fargo.

"That's the second tallest building in Fargo." Vance pointed as he drove through a green light. "That's where I work."

"Uff da. Can we go there?" Elisa asked.

Vance grinned. "It's a bit complicated. My partner warned me not to come in while I'm on vacation. I'm not going in until after hours."

Andi detected a subtle unease in his tone. "We won't get to see where you work then?"

"You just saw it." Vance laughed. "That building is where I work."

"I understand." She hoped she hadn't sounded as disappointed as she felt. It's not like she expected the grand tour.

"Look, I'd love to take you inside so you can see the big computers. But maybe next time, all right?" He glanced at her and winked.

She responded with a nod.

"And here we are." Vance pulled into the Radisson Hotel parking. "This is the tallest building in Fargo."

Vance had arranged for their stay in Fargo, but she doubted she could afford this. "Isn't there another hotel? Maybe even a motel?"

"Don't worry, I'm getting this. I invited you, remember?"

"But—"

"Don't. Now, let's get you checked in and while you're unpacking, I need to run by my apartment. I'll be back to pick you up in an hour and take you to a late lunch."

She stood tall and smiled. "Sounds good." They'd just have to eat cheap.

Maybe this wasn't such a great idea.

Panic swelled. Andi had imagined them walking around town, exploring sights, but because it wasn't something they did often, she hadn't considered that it might cost more than she had in her bank account at the moment, especially with what Vance had in mind. They could have a conflict of interest. She so did not want to ruin the day.

Vance grabbed their bags while Elisa skipped into the lobby, sending a tender pang through Andi. No, this was the right thing. They both needed to get away, even if only for a couple of days.

Once Andi and Elisa settled into their hotel room, Elisa was all smiles, then suddenly frowned. "I still wish we could have invited Todd."

"You know why we couldn't." This was Vance's idea and he didn't invite Todd. Nor was this a romantic getaway weekend.

"Can I call Todd?"

Andi wasn't sure why Elisa bothered to ask. "You know the answer to that as well."

"Where are we going? What are we going to do?" Elisa plopped on the bed. "I'm hungry."

Andi stared at herself in the mirror. "If I didn't know better, I'd say you were eight years old."

For that, she received a pillow in the back of the head, messing up her ponytail. "Now look what you did." She tugged the elastic band free. "I'll have to redo it."

"Ah, come on, sis. Don't you think it's time for you to let your hair down?" Elisa smiled into the mirror from behind Andi.

Andi gave her the look as she brushed her hair out. It fell across her shoulders with a golden sheen, and for the first time in a long time, she thought she might actually be pretty. But only a little.

She'd not taken the time to look at herself like this in much too long. She ran her hand over her cheek. Maybe she should have worn makeup like some girls did.

"Well, you don't have to listen to me, but I think you look beautiful with your hair down. Why not just leave it like that?"

Andi looked in the mirror at her sister, unconvinced. "You think?"

"I think."

Someone knocked on the door and before Andi could do a thing about her hair, Elisa opened it, revealing a dashing man who leaned against the frame with his hands in his pockets. He was much too handsome for this plain-looking small-town girl.

He whistled. "I like the new do."

Heat rose up her body and neck, then spread into her cheeks. Andi tried to focus, a difficult task, her head swimming as it was. "Thanks, but it's nothing special."

Vance remained in the doorway.

"You coming in?" Elisa asked.

"Nah. I'm hungry." Vance stared at Andi, something akin to longing in his eyes. "Let's go eat."

Andi grabbed her purse, fumbling and feeling strangely like her friendship with Vance had just climbed another rung on the ladder, all because she'd let her hair down. She hadn't intended to send him a signal, had she?

As she strolled past him through the door, the scent of his cologne made her dizzy. She hadn't noticed his wearing it in the car.

❧

Vance felt like he was floating in a no-gravity zone. Andi's hair. . .wowser. He'd known she was beautiful, but this. . . He cleared his throat as he turned into the restaurant parking lot, then parked. "Emilio's is my favorite Italian restaurant."

Racing around the car, Vance made sure to open the door for the ladies before they got out. Andi smiled as she stepped from the car and pulled her hair back like she was about to imprison it again.

Vance touched her hand, stopping her. "Please, don't."

Andi stared into his eyes, searching. "I'm not accustomed to wearing it down. I feel. . .funny."

"But you look. . ." *Scrumptious.* "Drop-dead gorgeous. You wouldn't want to deny a guy, would you?" Though Vance enjoyed teasing her, he wondered if he were going too far. Andi might feel compelled to be nice to him simply because she wanted—no, he knew she needed—the contract to finish Ground Zero. On that thought the anticipation of an enjoyable couple of days with her deflated.

Andi frowned, stepping out of the way as he shut the car door.

But maybe deflating was exactly what he needed. Besides, he had a purpose in coming to Fargo and needed to remain focused on that. Why had he invited her again?

As if he were in a trance, Vance remained next to the car, unmoving, as he watched her stroll toward the restaurant.

She flipped her hair off her shoulder and turned back to look at him, smiling. "You coming?"

Throat suddenly dry, Vance swallowed. He knew exactly why he'd invited her along. And at the moment, thinking about the work he'd come for was the last thing on his mind—the beautiful woman before him a huge distraction.

They enjoyed lunch together; the pleasant banter between the three of them couldn't have been more fun. Andi and Elisa were getting along better than he'd ever seen them.

"The last time I was in Fargo was to visit my boyfriend.

Well, he's my ex-boyfriend now." Andi sipped her tea.

"What happened?"

"Long-distance relationships don't work. That and I had to quit school, so he didn't think I was his equal since I don't have a college degree."

"I'm sorry to hear that, Andi. The guy must be an idiot, so I don't think his degree did anything for him."

His words brought the smile back to her face.

"Why'd you go and bring that up, sis? Jorgen is a dope for letting you go. Right, Vance?"

He nodded his agreement but a frown crept into his smile, his mood. He wondered the same—why had she brought it up? The topic shone a searchlight on his heart and on their situation. Why was he entertaining the idea of a relationship with her if he had no plans to stay in Herndon? It wasn't fair to her. To either of them.

Elisa stared into her soda and played with the straw.

Vance resolved to enjoy the weekend. They were here. "Come on. We've got lots more to see."

"Really? This isn't Dallas," Andi said.

"Maybe not, but I know where there's good shopping."

Andi giggled as they left the restaurant and smacked him with her bag.

"Ouch. What's in that thing?"

"You *are* a strange one, Vance Young. I always pictured people in Texas wearing cowboy hats and Wranglers. But you. . .you're anything but a cowboy."

"Why, thank ya', ma'am." He tipped his imaginary hat. "You experience a lot more of that in Houston than in Dallas. But in Houston, a city with millions of people, you have to run in the right crowds to see anyone dressed in Wranglers and a cowboy hat."

Vance opened the car door for the two women. Andi thanked him. He climbed into the driver's side, noticing Andi digging through her purse. Just like he didn't fit her idea of a Texan, he never imagined this side of her. At Ground Zero, she was all business and tried to put on that tough construction contractor appearance. But today, in her peach and lace knit shirt and pastel slacks, she was. . .soft.

All woman.

Vance sighed as he put the key into the ignition.

"What next?"

"Well, there's the zoo or a museum or"—Vance glanced back at Elisa—"the mall."

"The mall!" Elisa screamed.

He shared a knowing smile with Andi. She held his gaze, then her eyes drifted over his face as though looking at him for the first time. A pleasant sensation filled his chest.

"You didn't think we came all this way for you, did you?" Andi laughed.

Vance chuckled, too, as he drove out of the parking lot. He let her words put him in his place. Of course, they hadn't come with him to simply be in his company.

If he had any brains he would keep his distance.

fourteen

Sitting at the restaurant during dinner that evening, Andi felt slap-happy. "I never knew a person could cram so much into one day." She yawned and quickly covered her mouth.

Vance watched her and chuckled but seemed distracted. "You're tired. We'll call it a night."

"Ah, I thought we were going to see that movie." Elisa chewed on a straw.

"No, Vance is right. He still has to work. Besides, hours at the mall and then the zoo. . .what more could you want?"

"A movie?"

Vance grinned at Elisa. "There's always tomorrow. But your sister is right. I've got to do the work I came here to do."

"But it's late."

He grinned, toying with his glass of water. "I planned to go in after hours."

"Why?"

How Vance could frown and grin at the same time, Andi didn't know. "Enough with the questions." Still, she wondered what he was up to.

The dinner bill already paid, she stood. Vance drove them back to the hotel, quiet and distracted. She knew he must have been thinking about the work ahead of him.

He pulled into the hotel parking lot rather than under the passenger drop-off.

"What are you doing? You don't have to escort us inside."

"I know."

Andi was glad when he came around to open her door. She could get accustomed to this, but that was the problem. They walked into the foyer where the registration desk was lined with people checking in.

"Must be hosting a conference," Vance mumbled as he strode toward the elevator and punched the button.

Was he going to escort them all the way to their room?

The elevator door opened, and Elisa stepped in. Unsure if Vance would follow them, Andi paused and looked up into his eyes. "Thanks for today. It was a great time for Elisa. She needed that."

"And what about you?" In his eyes, she saw. . .what? Yearning?

Vance brushed his fingers down her cheek—she closed her eyes, melting at his touch. A quick gentle stroke, it was over too soon. And with it, she'd revealed far too much to him.

Others flowed onto the elevator, pressing her to say good-bye.

"I'll pick you up in the morning." Vance's eyes flashed, now seemingly filled with regret.

She nodded and stepped into the elevator just as the door whooshed closed, shutting her in and leaving him on the other side. Wariness crept back into her heart.

That night, Andi and Elisa each lay in their separate full-sized beds, giggling and talking like schoolgirls. Of course, Elisa still *was* a schoolgirl, albeit a freshman. It felt good to have some time for girl talk. They'd both enjoyed Vance's company today, but sometimes it seemed as if they were competing for his attention. Still, Elisa apparently missed Todd.

The girl sounded like she was in love. Andi knew the feeling well, but she also knew it was just that—only a feeling. And much of the time, at Elisa's age, it didn't last, leaving at least one, or both, people with a broken heart. Elisa wasn't inclined to listen to Andi on the topic. What teenager would be? When you had the feeling, it was like a drug and you couldn't get enough. No one could tell you that you weren't in love.

Andi sighed, listening to Elisa talk about Todd, wishing she could feel the same about love and be free to chatter on about it without fear. Andi huffed and rolled on her side.

"What's with all the sighing over there, sis?"

"Was I sighing? I'm sorry. I'm listening."

"So, is that how you feel about Vance?"

"Elisa!" Andi had probably revealed more about her emotions with that outburst than anything. She calmed herself. "Vance isn't my boyfriend. He's a client and has now become a friend. That's all."

She felt she owed him for all he'd done to bring Elisa around. That was it, wasn't it?

"I've been telling you all my secrets. Don't you think you should be as honest with me?"

How did she feel about Vance? Didn't he make her stomach flutter and her heart pound? She couldn't wait to see him again and missed him when he wasn't around. "Okay, I'll admit that he's sort of cute."

Elisa giggled in reply. There. Andi'd shared a secret. The last thing she wanted was to have Elisa close off to her again. Maybe if Dad or even Grandma had lived, this would be a normal interaction. But with Andi playing the parent, a barrier had been thrown up between them.

"Why don't you admit more than that? Maybe you should be honest with yourself, Andi." Elisa turned on her side and propped up on her elbow, facing Andi. "You know, he's not like Jorgen."

"I know." Andi's voice fairly croaked.

"But, since we're being honest, I'm worried for you. I hadn't thought about it before, but with Vance bringing us here and showing us where he works. . ."

"He lives and works here. From the sounds of it, that's not going to change."

"So, in that way, maybe he is like Jorgen."

Andi rolled away from her sister and squeezed her eyes to stop the sudden pain behind them, knowing tears might follow. How did the conversation end with Elisa lecturing Andi about love?

"Today was a good day, Elisa. I don't want to ruin it with talk of Jorgen again."

❧

The alarm clock sounded, waking Vance. He sat up in bed,

disoriented at first. After dropping Andi and Elisa off at their hotel, he'd taken a short nap, wanting his mind to be clear for the work he had to do during the night hours. As he shuffled around his apartment, getting dressed and grabbing an energy drink from the fridge, he thought about Ground Zero—the last place he'd ever want to live. But. . .

He actually missed the dungeon.

A chuckle escaped. *Who'da thunk?* The underground launch facility and bomb shelter—because that's what it was, a bomb shelter, too. In a word, the place was zany. He stood tall and put his hands on his hips, looking around his living room.

In a word. Boring.

Vance grabbed his keys and headed to ANND Systems. Sitting in the garage-enclosed parking lot, he decided to wait until after midnight when Tom's shift would begin. Vance wanted to probe Tom about the disk he'd found and given to Vance, believing he'd dropped it.

Someone else must have been in that night. Would Tom be willing to share that information?

At 11:45, Vance only had fifteen more minutes to wait. In fact, he'd give it another thirty to be sure the other guy was gone, though Vance had come on legitimate business—Peter had requested his help, after all.

He leaned his head against the seat, thinking of the day spent with Andi. All day watching her smile. All day listening to her musical laughter.

Oh, how he loved her response when he touched her cheek. And he wanted to do so much more than touch her cheek—he wanted to kiss her. But the place, the moment wasn't right.

He pounded the steering wheel. *Idiot.* What did people do when they found themselves falling for someone in an impossible situation? He'd already put in a call to his old boss in Texas. They wanted him back. His family wanted him back.

In Texas.

More than anything, he'd wanted to be part of running a company, and Peter's offer had seemed the answer. He shook his head. His vacation was meant to clear his mind, help him to know what he needed to do next. Where he needed to go.

Instead, all he could think about was Andi Nielsen, and she didn't fit into any of his plans. Feet planted firmly in North Dakota soil, she'd left college to care for her younger sister. She wasn't likely to pull up her roots, leaving North Dakota or the small town where they lived any time soon. Nor would Elisa want to leave. She had a boyfriend.

Vance rubbed his eyes and sent up a silent prayer. Somehow, he had to focus on ANND, and the work he needed to accomplish once inside. It could take hours to look at the data. Could he finish this task tonight?

Working on the legitimate program was the least of his worries. He'd panicked earlier today, and rightly so. Tonight he would attempt to discover if he'd overreacted about the rogue program that had practically fallen into his lap—the whole thing made no sense, especially considering there was no such thing as a coincidence. On the other hand, if Peter were involved in something illegal, working on what Vance had termed the mission creep project, then Vance needed to find something concrete with which to contact the authorities.

Finally, the digital clock in the car read 12:45. Adrenaline surged through him. He wasn't cut out for this. But. . .

It was time.

Lord, I think You've led me down this road. . . . Help me to find what You need for me to see.

Carrying his soft briefcase into the lobby, with phony confidence Vance looked up and smiled at. . .who was this? It wasn't Tom. Heart hammering, Vance went through the security measures, then signed his name at the desk under the scrutinizing eyes of the new guy who looked young and—thankfully—inexperienced.

Vance averted his eyes, certain they were bloodshot. No point encouraging the man in trivial conversation. Vance's athletic shoes squeaked as he crept across the cream-colored marble tiles and wiped his sweaty palms against his jeans. The sound echoed through the huge, silent foyer. Another fifteen feet to the elevator corridors and he'd be out from under the security guard's scrutiny.

His jaw itched. After punching the button to retrieve the elevator, he scratched his chin and tried to inspect his appearance in the reflective doors. With the way he looked, it was a wonder Andi paid him any attention. The weight of his job had pressed against him heavily and it showed.

"Mr. Young?" the security guy blurted from the foyer.

Vance couldn't exactly pretend he didn't hear, considering they were the only two in the foyer, maybe even the building, at nearly one a.m. Maybe the elevator would accommodate his need to get away.

The guy stood directly behind him, staring at him in the reflection.

No such luck.

"Mr. Young."

Déjà vu. Vance turned to face him. "Hey, where's Tom tonight?"

"Tom? Oh, you mean the other night security guard. I don't think he works here anymore."

"Oh, sorry to hear that." *Stellar.* Vance turned to face the elevator again. He needed to talk to Tom about the disk.

"It says you're on vacation."

It as in the computer. Vance fought the urge to run his hand down his face, revealing his anxiety. "Uh, yeah. I am, but Mr. Lundgren called me in to work out a problem." The elevator doors swooshed open, and Vance stepped in. "Hope it doesn't take too long. I'm ready to get back to my time off."

The security guard looked confused and unsure about pressing his authority. "I hear you." He nodded, and the doors shut in his face.

Again, that eerie feeling crept over him that this was all a replay. Minutes later, Vance sat at the four-faced plasma screen in the dinosaur pen. Once he was logged in he began scanning the results of Peter's last data test—the one he'd cited had problems that weren't there when Vance left. They'd made sure of that before Vance walked out the doors. So why problems now?

Though ANND Systems would crunch large amounts of data and spit out the results as defined by the government contract, the government had its own people to analyze the results. Apparently the data was jumbled and unreadable. Vance folded his arms across his chest and leaned back in the chair.

A simple operator error stared back at him.

Anyone could have corrected this. Peter had wanted Vance to do it. Why? Vance made the correction, stood, and took a deep breath, unsure about what to do next. How could he find out what was truly going on without reading Peter's e-mails?—a serious breach of ethical convention, something he'd already done to a point when he'd planted the program in the parallel system.

Should Vance leave the disk he'd discovered for the proper authorities? Would they know he'd not played a role in it if it were in fact part of a criminal act? That was his greatest fear—Peter's government contacts knew him much better than they knew Vance.

Wishing the whole thing would go away on its own, he left the computer processing room for his office. There, on his desk, stood the photograph. He lifted it, peering at the woman in the picture who reminded him so much of Andi. Or was it the other way around?

If he didn't believe in coincidence. . .

He stared at the picture, his heart torn. "Lord, show me what to do about Andi."

Both of them.

fifteen

The next day, Andi and Elisa waited in the lobby for Vance.

"I don't understand why we can't stay one more day." Elisa slouched in a plush chair.

"I have no ide—"

"Ready for breakfast?"

How did Vance come in without them seeing? Andi stood to greet him. He looked as if he hadn't slept at all. "Good morning."

Nor had he shaved, looking a little scruffy. Andi liked his rough appearance.

"Let me take your bags." Vance grabbed them, ignoring the bellhop, and strolled through the revolving doors.

As Andi sat down in the car, she noticed for the first time this weekend that Vance hadn't opened her door. She looked out the passenger window, releasing a slow sigh. The romance she'd imagined with Vance was ending before it even started. Just as well.

As they headed out of town, they made small talk. Passing all the pancake houses only heightened the rumble Andi was beginning to feel in her stomach. She thought he'd said something about breakfast. They hadn't eaten the continental breakfast. She wanted to mention it to Vance but he was clearly distracted. Something obviously bothered him. Andi hoped it wasn't her.

"So, what's wrong with you?" she asked. He was anything but warm and friendly. "Haven't had your morning coffee?"

He shot a grin in her direction but kept his focus on the road as he accelerated. "You know me too well already."

For Elisa's sake, she would remind him about breakfast. She opened her mouth to speak, shutting it as he pulled into a restaurant parking lot just outside of town. "Why are you in such a hurry to get out of town?"

They strolled into the small coffee house. "Would you believe me if I told you I miss Ground Zero?"

She laughed at his unexpected comment. "Nope."

They ordered coffee and pancakes. Vance rubbed his temples and stared out the big windows. Andi wanted to ask him what was going on but figured he would have volunteered the information if he felt like sharing. So, she and Elisa talked about Todd, engaging Vance once in a while. His mind was clearly far from them as he took a long gulp of his black coffee.

Black coffee?

"You didn't sleep last night, did you?" she pressed.

He set his mug down and leaned against folded arms. "I worked most of the night, not so unusual really. But I'm exhausted today. Sorry, I'm not in a great mood."

"But we sure had fun yesterday, didn't we?" Elisa offered.

Vance grinned. "Sure."

Andi relaxed against her seat, confused.

He finished his coffee, then asked for a double shot.

"Doesn't so much caffeine give you palpitations?"

"Maybe. Right now I need to be alert." Something in his expression softened. He reached across the booth and took her hand. "I need to deliver the two of you safely home."

Andi enjoyed the effect his touch had on her. Her thoughts from the previous night's girl talk crept into her mind—

When you had the feeling, it was like a drug and you couldn't get enough. No one could tell you that you weren't in love.

A girl could be smart, be strong. But when it came to matters of the heart. . . Even though she knew better than to allow her guard down, she had no control over the way he made her feel. And now, she wished he'd stare out the window again, think about something else rather than give her the look he was giving her.

She slipped her hand from his.

He looked out the window again. Good. Things were better this way.

Weren't they?

❧

Vance concentrated on driving and kept watch in the rearview mirror, wishing he could explain to Andi all that he was going through. But he couldn't even explain it to himself. At the moment he had too much on his mind to carry on a meaningful conversation. And women liked meaningful conversations, sensitive men. In that regard, he was sure he was blowing it with her. She tried to present herself as tough with a hard exterior, but he'd seen her soft side. She wanted what every woman wanted.

The problem was, Vance wasn't sure he could give that to her.

But maybe she wasn't part of God's plan for him. How could she be? He wasn't even sure she was a Christian. Every time he brought up God she couldn't get away fast enough. Then why did thoughts of a life without her sit wrong with him?

He risked a glimpse her way, noticing her dull expression—so different from her glowing demeanor yesterday. Without giving himself too much credit, he believed he was the cause of it.

He looked in the rearview mirror again.

That car. Unless he was being paranoid, he'd seen that car in town near the hotel, near their breakfast stop, too. Elisa needed a rest stop, so he pulled in at the next one, all the while cautious of the suspicious car. Probably nothing. The ladies returned from the restroom, and Vance drove back onto the highway, never seeing the car pass them. Where had it gone?

After ten minutes or so, he noticed the car in his rearview mirror again, though far enough behind that he could be imagining things. He'd made a huge mistake going into ANND Systems. The more he thought about it, the more he suspected that Peter knew Vance never went to Cancun, after all. Had the whole problem with the data been a ruse to bring him in? And, if so, why? If Peter had wanted to know where he was, all he had to do was ask, unless he was up to no good.

What sort of man was Vance to bring Andi and Elisa into possible danger?

Vance finally exited the highway for Herndon. He drove the long way around town to Andi's house, making sure he didn't see the suspicious car. After several stops and a wrong turn, Vance believed it was safe.

"Did you forget how to get to my house?" Andi asked, her voice sweet, yet laced with concern.

He shook his head. "No, I could never forget that." Grinning, he wanted to reassure her, especially after the way he'd acted this morning.

"Then what are you doing?"

"Just hate that our time together is ending." *She's going to think I'm an idiot, if she didn't already.*

A breathy laugh escaped Andi. "You're funny." But Vance saw her cheeks redden before she turned her face away.

Vance looked in the mirror again.

Blowing out a breath, he wasn't sure they'd even been followed. He rubbed his hand over his face, too exhausted to tell if he was only being paranoid.

Finally, he turned into Andi's driveway. While tugging their luggage from the trunk, he watched for the suspicious car. But it never showed. Relieved, he toted the luggage into the house and set it in the living room.

"Would you like something to drink? You're probably thirsty." Elisa offered him a cola.

"Sure, thanks." He took it and popped the top.

Andi came out from the hallway and smiled, looking nervous.

Vance toasted her with his soda. "Well, I'd better get going. See you on Monday?"

"Yeah, of course. But. . .can we talk?" She motioned for him to step outside onto the porch. Elisa smiled and disappeared down the hallway.

Vance took a sip. "What's up?"

"I just wanted to thank you. This meant so much to Elisa, to me. She really needed to get away. We had a good long sisterly talk. It seems like years since we've done that." Andi looked up into his face.

Her crystal blue eyes sparkled like a not-too-distant glittering star, and though her guarded wariness remained, something else took prominence in her gaze. Something big. Huge. Six hundred fifty times the size of the sun.

Searching the depths of her eyes—what he saw in them. . . Admiration. Longing.

He almost took a step back.

Was he. . . ? No, it couldn't happen. He was a geek. She was a non-geek. Never the two shall meet.

But was he finally. . .disarming Andi?

Had it been a game to him all along because he never believed it would really happen? "I. . .uh." Vance shook his head, snapping himself out of the daze.

Andi giggled and gave him a strange look. "Say, Elisa brought up having a picnic tomorrow. Want to come?"

"How about church first? I've tried the one just on the edge of town. Community Fellowship something. Ten o'clock. You want me to pick you up?"

Andi hesitated, her warm smile fading a little. Vance's heart thudded, expecting to be disappointed and hoping he wouldn't be. But he couldn't go further, shouldn't have gone this far, without knowing where she stood with God.

"Sure. Elisa said something about Todd inviting us as well. Who knows, maybe he goes to the same church. It's a small town, after all."

She lingered, and he couldn't help himself. Wanting to see and feel her response again, he traced a finger gently down her soft cheek, then cupped her chin and. . .she closed her eyes, leaning into it.

Her lips parted gently and Vance was there to meet their soft sweetness. He started to wrap his arms around her, bring her against him nice and tight.

Oh man. Wait! They were standing on her porch in broad daylight with Elisa probably peeking through the living room curtains. *Slow down. Way down.*

He gently pulled away and opened his eyes to meet hers. Again, he saw more emotion there than he should ever deserve. Girls didn't fall for him. Not like this. And they were lying if they said so. He knew that from experience.

Apprehension engulfed him. He sucked in a breath. Andi noticed him tense, then hurt flashed across her face.

"Come here." He grabbed her hand and tugged her to him in a hug. No way would he let her throw up the blast door to her heart again. He kissed the top of her head, smelling the scent of sweet watermelon in her hair.

Lord, I could stay here forever.

I think. . .I think I love her. Help me.

sixteen

After grabbing a few groceries at the local store, Vance drove out of town on the lonely road to Ground Zero, oblivious to his surroundings, not caring about the car that had supposedly followed them. Somehow, he'd dug himself into a lot of trouble the last few weeks. And not just with his company. ANND Systems was about to blow up.

Not even a bomb shelter could protect him.

The scent of Andi's hair, the feel of her lips, had an intoxicating effect on him, making focusing on his company problems almost impossible. A myriad of confusing thoughts and emotions battled to overwhelm him.

What was he thinking? Why had he let things go this far? Andi was a vibrant and beautiful woman. The last thing she needed in her life was a computer geek, especially one that had no intentions of staying in Fargo or at Ground Zero or in North Dakota where the winters were as frigid as absolute zero.

He'd been through enough rejection himself. Usually things never got this far and he hadn't worried that they would. Had he simply answered the challenge she presented with her hard shell? He hated thinking he could do such a thing, but there it was. Or was it because he'd seen her every day before he'd even arrived at Ground Zero by means of the photograph on his desk?

Maybe love was a black hole. You couldn't keep from getting sucked into the vortex of its gravitational field no matter how hard you tried—nothing, not even light could resist a black hole. The only problem was—it was a one-way trip. Once you fell in, there was no way out.

Stellarific. Despite the heaviness in his heart, he laughed.

He was probably the only guy in the universe to compare love to a black hole. But it was somehow comforting. And, if it were true, then he could stop blaming himself for letting it happen.

Her smile, though guarded, had been the gravity that tugged him ever closer and even now he was falling deeper and deeper.

He'd never had a chance.

Turning onto the main drive that would lead him to the launch facility, the heaviness lifted a little. He wouldn't blame himself for falling for Andi, but there was still a problem—what did he do now?

Two explosive situations waited for him to act, but he had no idea how to proceed. After climbing out of the car he walked to the entrance, his legs dragging. He'd planned to use his vacation time to pray and contemplate his future. Because of distractions, he'd done little of either since coming here. But now, circumstances forced him into having that serious talk with God.

Before entering the underground quarters, he glanced up at the sun high in the sky. It would be hours before he could look at the stars—when he seemed to hear God the best. He grinned. Tomorrow he'd pick up Andi and Elisa for church. A small prick in his heart told him there was hope in that—a small thing really—but huge in God's kingdom. Vance held on to that as he descended into his temporary home nestled deep underground.

&a.

It had been so long since Andi had attended church, she wasn't sure what to wear. Elisa, who went to worship services with friends on occasion, assured her that nice slacks were acceptable. Andi was glad because she didn't own a decent dress and couldn't find one pair of pantyhose in her drawer.

Nervous didn't describe how she felt this morning. She'd come very near to calling Vance and canceling. Turned out that Community Christian Fellowship was the same church

Todd and his family attended. Andi would attend for Elisa. A Christian family in Elisa's life was a good thing. Never mind that Andi had her own reservations about God.

After dressing she looked in the mirror, then began brushing her hair back into a ponytail.

"Uh uh." Elisa stood in the doorway. "Wear it down again."

Andi sighed. Her sister was right. Vance hadn't been able to take his eyes off her, at least before he'd gone into work on Friday night. She put her fingers to her lips and closed her eyes, remembering his kiss.

"It was nice, huh?"

Andi's eyes flew open. "What do you mean?"

Elisa giggled. "I knew he would kiss you."

"You spied on us?"

Elisa shrugged. "Just wanted to make sure it happened. If you had pushed him away, I would have given you a lecture. I want to see things work out between the two of you."

It felt nice having more sisterly talk.

A knock at the door drew her up tall. She sucked in a gasp. "He's here already?"

While Elisa went to answer the door, Andi opened the bottom drawer of her dresser and pulled out her grandmother's Bible. At least she'd kept it.

In the car on the way to church, Vance and Andi settled into their comfortable banter. When she placed the Bible on the seat between them, she rested her hand on it. Vance covered her hand with his.

Warmth flooded her. She smiled but then looked out the passenger seat window. What was she going to do? She cared deeply for him, maybe even loved him. Couldn't resist his charms, either way.

They drove into the church parking lot and headed for the front doors of the small church. Vance opened the door for Elisa and Andi. She tried to hide her dread.

He lifted her hand to his lips. "Relax. There's nothing to be afraid of."

Though his words comforted her, panic continued to fill her. As they marched up the steps she saw Gladys from the florist shop, who then introduced her family. There was Paul the concrete sub. His wife and boys welcomed her. Cordial, they made her feel comfortable, like she belonged.

There were many more people that she knew, growing up in the small town, and some she was more than surprised to see at church, knowing a bit of their background. A couple walked in ahead of her and Vance. Shame washed over her when she remembered being envious of them—how they'd said God had blessed them. The thought brought back her initial resentment toward Vance and the fact he'd been given the launch facility though he'd not been aware it even existed.

Why had God forgotten her? A knot formed in her throat. This wasn't the way she wanted to start her morning at church—filled with anger and resentment.

As they took a seat on the third pew from the back next to Todd and his family, the trepidation returned. Andi stared at her hands as though to still their shaking with a look. The service began with an opening prayer, announcements, and then music, the first song about God's love. A wave of emotion rolled over Andi. Tears threatened.

No, not here. Please. She quieted her emotions, hardening her heart. It had been far too long since she'd been in church, felt God's presence. It surprised her that she could even sense Him today. The congregation sang through more hymns and newer songs she'd not heard before. She decided she liked them.

Apparently more than familiar with the music, Vance sang along without missing a note, his voice strong and melodic. The praise and worship music moved her in a way she hadn't experienced before, and she wasn't certain what she thought about that. When it came time for Pastor Howel to present his sermon, he stood at the pulpit.

He spoke of being content in all things. "Paul says in Philippians, 'I am not saying this because I am in need, for

I have learned to be content whatever the circumstances. I know what it is to be in need, and I know what it is to have plenty. I have learned the secret of being content in any and every situation, whether well fed or hungry, whether living in plenty or in want. I can do everything through him who gives me strength.'"

Andi hung on his every word, sure that the sermon was meant for her alone. She'd been anything but content these last few years, blaming God for all the unfortunate things in her life. All the wrong done to her while He appeared to *bless* others. A drop of moisture touched her hand. Another tear slid down her cheek.

At some point, she'd become disillusioned with God. Yet Paul suffered and he was glad to do it. He was a prisoner of Christ.

It dawned on Andi—God didn't exist to answer her wants.

The pastor went on, " 'Delight yourself in the Lord and he will give you the desires of your heart.'"

As she listened, she understood that she'd had it all wrong. All backward. If she delighted herself in Him—His desires would become her desires.

The idea was unsettling.

After the service ended, Vance took Andi and Elisa to their home to change and grab the fried chicken they'd cooked the previous afternoon for the picnic. They were to meet him back at Ground Zero.

Before Vance left, he reached for her hand. "You all right? You seem distant since church."

"I'm fine." Regardless of feeling disturbed at the pastor's words, she smiled, wanting nothing more than to spend a pleasant afternoon with Vance.

"Good." The way he looked at her, she was sure he was thinking about their kiss.

Things had changed between them and there was no going back. At least for her. She wondered how it would feel to work on Ground Zero with him always present. That is, until he left. Would he leave now? He hadn't exactly declared his love.

Once she and Elisa arrived at Vance's place, they pulled the picnic basket from the truck and, along with Vance, walked across the flat plains to the far side of the property—at least twenty-five acres—through the sparse oak trees.

A light breeze and the cool of the shade made for an enjoyable picnic. They ate the fried chicken and potato salad, relaxing in each other's company. Andi leaned against a tree, comfortable enough to take a nap but listening to Vance and Elisa discuss science and the universe. He explained his love of creation science, piquing Elisa's interest in the topic.

What a miracle it was that he'd drawn Elisa from her shell. More than any of her other desires, hadn't Andi wanted the best for Elisa?

She closed her eyes as she listened to them along with the breeze through the trees, no longer wanting to deny that God had, in fact, been working in her life. Why had she denied it for so long? Denied Him?

"It's such a nice day, I want to take a walk," she said. When Vance and Elisa made to stand, she stopped them. "Oh no, I mean alone."

Vance frowned. "You sure?"

She nodded with a smile to ease the worried look on Vance's face. Once she was far enough away, Andi poured her heart out to God, all her hurts, heartaches, unforgiveness, and everything until she was spent.

"Now, Lord, You take it from here. This is all I have to give You. My heart." Andi began a slow stroll back to the copse of trees where she'd left Elisa and Vance, knowing her sister was in good hands. "Thank you for sending him."

Still, fear of being hurt stood in her way. Vance rose when he saw her approach. His gaze searched her face, then her eyes. He must have seen their redness but didn't say anything.

Sure You sent him, Lord, but did You send him for me? I'm not good enough for him.

Vance took her hand and pulled her to him like he'd done yesterday on her porch. He whispered into her ear, "Oh, Andi, there's so much I want to tell you."

Elisa began packing away the picnic items. Andi moved to help, but Vance wouldn't release her. He tugged her hand, urging her to come with him. Once they'd walked a bit, Vance turned her to face him, then brushed her cheek—his usual way.

He closed the distance between them, kissing her thoroughly. Her knees grew weak. She tugged free from him.

Worry laced his expression. "What's wrong?"

"I. . .I don't know if I'm good enough for you."

He shook his head. "What do you mean? Of course you are."

Well, she'd started it, might as well finish, since she was all about confessions today. "I don't have a college education. You're brilliant. I'm—"

"Stop." He pulled her close to him, her face near his chest where she could hear his heart beating. "You're smart, beautiful, independent, an entrepreneur. Should I keep going?"

Enjoying the comfort of being in his arms, Andi could only reply with an "um-hmm."

"Forget about that idiot you were with before. He doesn't define who you are."

"Hey, guys, sorry to interrupt, but I told Todd I'd be home by five. He's supposed to call. Look, I've packed the picnic up. Ready to go?" Elisa shaded her eyes against the late afternoon sun.

Sweet potato casserole. Elisa had the worst timing for someone who wanted to see things work out between Andi and Vance.

As they strolled lazily back to the missile base, another kind of guilt began growing inside Andi. With everything going on the last few days, she'd forgotten about her search within the walls of the underground missile site. They'd come so far and things between them were different. How would Vance react to the news? How would he feel about her waiting until now to tell him?

Oh, how she wished she'd just told him at the beginning. Maybe together they could have discovered the hidden treasure.

She licked her lips and slipped her hand from his. He would certainly notice her sweaty palm. "I have something I need—"

"Get down!" Vance's agitated whisper scared her.

They all dropped flat against the grass. "What is it?"

"Shh." He squinted, searching the launch facility, still a few acres away from them.

Andi followed his gaze, seeing another car parked next to theirs.

"Vance, you're scaring me. What's going on?" Fear coursed through Andi at his reaction. And if they were trying to hide, the flat prairie wasn't a good place, though maybe the grass was cover enough.

She angled her head to study him.

What did she really know about him?

Lord, guard my heart.

seventeen

"Heads down." Vance made sure Andi and Elisa pressed their heads flat against the earth. He watched two men climb into the car—the same car that had followed them from Fargo.

Idiot. He never should have gone into Fargo, to ANND Systems. The ruse was up. Peter must have caught Vance's unauthorized upload, seen him log into his account, something. What were the chances?

"Lord in heaven, help me," he whispered, not realizing he'd done so aloud.

"Vance, please. You have to tell me what's going on."

"They're gone." Elisa stood and dusted the dirt and grass away. "What was that about, anyway?"

His plans had backfired. "It's complicated." He stood and helped Andi to her feet.

Vance trotted toward Ground Zero, then realizing he was alone, turned around to see Andi hadn't moved.

"I'm not going anywhere until you tell me who those men were. Why didn't you want them to see you?"

How could he explain? He strode back to Andi and tried to tug her to him, while Elisa walked on ahead, still carrying the picnic basket. "I'll explain things, I promise. But not in front of Elisa. For now, can you trust me?"

Andi searched his eyes, a frown forming. "I don't know, Vance. This is all so. . .strange." She started after her sister. "Let's be real here. I don't know you that well. I have to think of Elisa right now."

"You're right, you do." Vance kept pace with her, head down, contemplating. He hadn't realized what he was getting into, nor had it occurred to him that he would drag others into the problem. He'd never considered himself in any danger—especially the physical kind.

Until now.

He didn't want Andi and her sister in harm's way. He stopped walking and, thankfully, so did Andi. He took her hands in his again. "Believe me when I say I don't know who those men were."

"How can I believe you? You didn't want them to see you. Clearly, you know them."

"I thought someone was following us from Fargo. That was the car."

Andi stared at him. "What? Why didn't you say anything before? What's going on?"

He wanted to brush his hand down her cheek. Kiss her. Go back to the last few hours. "I don't know enough to explain. There's something very wrong at my company. I think I dug too deep, hit a nerve, and those men have followed me."

Andi's eyes widened. She covered her mouth. "Oh, Vance, please be careful."

"I'll do my best. In the meantime, I need to get you and Elisa out of here. Take her home and lock the doors."

Andi tugged her cell phone from her pocket. "Let's call the police."

"And tell them what? For all we know, they could have knocked on the door, gotten no answer, and left. I need to check inside to see if anything was taken."

"Tell them about your company troubles. Tell them what you told me." She pressed the phone out to him.

Vance scanned the flat prairie behind her. "And risk the bad guys getting away? No, I need something solid to give the authorities. I was trying to get more information before I called them. But apparently, I've been found out."

"I see." Andi began punching numbers.

Vance stopped her. "Andi, I'll call them. I promise. This doesn't involve you or Elisa. Go home." The words came out too brusque. But he needed her safe.

Hurt filled her eyes. "You don't want my help? Fine."

She stuck her phone back in her pocket, lifted her chin, and strode away

"Andi." Vance kept up with her quickened pace to her truck. "You were the one who told me you needed to think of Elisa. I'm asking you to do that. I'm trying to protect both of you."

Once she reached her truck, Andi turned to face him. "Right, and I also said I don't really know you. You could *be* trouble. Those guys could have been government agents for all I know."

What? "Well, that's just. . ." Vance threw his hands up and walked away. Women.

If his brusque manner would make her leave, get her to safety, it was for the best. He didn't have time to explain or argue. He'd have to find a way to make it up to her later.

Hopefully, there would be a later.

Pain lashed at Vance's heart as the sound of gravel crackled under Andi's tires, taking her away from Ground Zero. He wasn't sure how he expected her to act. The circumstances were unfamiliar to him as well.

As for the two men, the elevator wouldn't work without the key or communication from underground, allowing them in. As far as he could tell, they hadn't penetrated the facility, nor the stairs.

He descended into Ground Zero with as much caution as he could muster. The closest he'd ever come to acting the part of hero was in video games. He wasn't trained in police work of any sort. Then why was he slinking around in ANND's systems, trying to gather evidence to prove his innocence while proving others guilty?

It had become painfully clear that he'd made a huge mistake. He'd look around the place, then make the call and hope—no, pray—the police would listen to him, hear him out before Peter was brought to the table to distort the facts.

What choice did he have now? He was in over his head.

First Vance looked at his laptop and other electronics—the most likely places they'd search if they'd found a way in. He blew out a breath, satisfied they'd not gained entry. Still, they'd followed him. They'd be back. He checked his e-mail to see if Peter had left him a message.

Nothing.

Making good on his promise to call the authorities was the only logical next step. He had to admit he was scared. What kind of people were these men? He'd never learned whom Peter had gotten involved with—but with big dollars involved and anti-government activity, they had to be dangerous.

Vance dialed information. Call waiting indicated another call coming in. Andi's number. He abandoned his other call to answer.

"Vance. The men—they have us. . ." Andi's voice was breathy and filled with fear. "They've got Elisa. . .and me."

&

The tough guy grabbed the phone from Andi, tugging some of her hair with it. "Ouch." She glared at him. The larger of the two men, he had red hair and looked like a bodybuilder.

Elisa sat on the sofa, petrified. Andi wanted to comfort her sister. Later she'd scold her for answering the door when she'd warned her not to. But Elisa had insisted it was Todd.

Andi could hear Vance yelling her name over the phone.

She attempted to rush to Elisa. The bodybuilder grabbed her upper arm and squeezed. Hard. Tears rushed to her eyes.

He raised the phone to his face and spoke to Vance. "You have twenty-four hours to reverse what you've done to the Nitro Project."

Vance's voice boomed over the phone. "I need more time."

"If you want to see your friends again, that's all you have." He ended the call, then shoved Andi to the sofa. She righted herself and wrapped her arms around Elisa, who whimpered.

"I'm so, so sorry, sis. I should have listened to you."

"Shh. Everything is going to be fine." *Vance is going to get us out of this.* A knot formed in Andi's throat. She wasn't sure she believed her own words, but she had to remain strong.

But this wasn't a part of her normal life, this. . .was a

tragedy. She wished she had called the police herself after all.

"What are you going to do with us?" Elisa asked.

Andi went rigid and squeezed Elisa, hoping her question didn't elicit a violent response. The men ignored her.

"What's to drink around here?" the shorter of the two said. Looking slim and agile, he had dark hair and wore a black suit. He moved out of sight and into the kitchen. Andi heard the refrigerator door open and shut, followed by the sound of a soda top *pop* and the resulting *fizz*. He reappeared, drinking the soda and looking around the room.

Andi squirmed with irritation at his audacity. Breaking into her home, kidnapping them, and stealing a cola. Who were these guys? An idea began to form. She might know little about them, but. . .she cocked her head, watching the cola guzzler. . .neither did the men know anything about her.

They didn't know about the sledgehammer leaning against the wall in the corner, or the nail gun on the bookshelf, or any of the other various tools lying around the house that could easily transform into a weapon. Andi's home was a never-ending remodeling project. Potential weapons surrounded them everywhere. If given the opportunity, a good shot of air freshener right in the eyes could give Andi and Elisa the chance they needed to escape.

Andi would wait for the right moment. With her newfound faith and trust in God, she sent up a silent prayer for a chance to get away. A shudder rolled over her body at the thought of using her tools in a violent way.

She chewed on her lip. It might be too risky to try anything. She had to think of Elisa. *Oh, Vance. Please give them what they want.*

She'd give anything if she hadn't left him in a huff. It had merely been a ploy to try and make him call the police. The maneuver had bombed.

"I have to go to the bathroom, sis," Elisa whispered. "Will they let us go?"

Andi shrugged. "Let me ask, okay?"

"Say, are we allowed to use the restroom?"

Slim nodded to his partner in crime. "See to it."

After Elisa looked at Andi, then between the two men, she cautiously rose and walked to the restroom, the bodybuilder following. Would he go in with her sister? The best Andi could hope for was they could remain comfortable on the sofa. That this wouldn't be any more difficult for them. And, of course, that they would be released soon, without harm.

Get real. They had seen the men's faces. How could they let them go free? No, she couldn't wait for this to play out in her favor. Somehow, they'd have to escape.

The bathroom window. Andi perked up and looked in that direction. Maybe Elisa would climb through and get help.

Lord, please let Elisa—

Bodybuilder appeared in the hallway, shoving Elisa ahead of him. "She tried to escape through the window."

"All right, that's it." Slim set down his soda. "We tried to be nice, but now we're going to have to tie you up."

"I thought we were taking them to—"

Slim shot him a warning glare.

Andi's spirits sagged even lower. "No, please. She's just a kid. She didn't know any better. It won't happen again. I promise."

"Yeah, well, as far as I know, you put her up to it." Slim looked around the room. "Aha. Just what I needed." He found the duct tape resting on the side table. "You're a regular handywoman, aren't you?"

Andi turned her face away from him, hoping he wouldn't discover her tools, potential weapons, lying around and remove them. Still, she or Elisa wouldn't have a chance to escape if they were tied up. And if the men took them to an unknown location? She'd heard you should never let someone take you away. Fight as hard as you could. But these two guys seemed to fill her living room with their presence. How could she fight them to escape?

The men wrapped Andi and Elisa's ankles, then their

wrists behind them with duct tape. To her dismay, they taped their mouths shut.

"Now, back the car into the garage," Slim said to Bodybuilder.

The next few minutes played before Andi like her worst nightmare. She and Elisa were lowered into the deep trunk of a car, sprawled precariously side-by-side, then Bodybuilder, smirking before he shut the trunk, blanketed them in darkness.

Do not panic. Elisa is counting on you. Andi reasoned that the men couldn't take them too far or else she and Elisa would run out of air, though she had no clue how long that would take. It seemed surreal. As soon as she falls for someone and asks God to come into her life, bad guys kidnap them.

She sensed the car traveling at a moderate speed, then stopping frequently. They were driving through downtown, no doubt there. If she concentrated, she might be able to make out where they were being taken. This was her town, after all. She counted at least five stops, then felt a right turn, a few more miles, then a left turn onto a bumpy road. The old, abandoned Garrison warehouse? That would make sense, but it made too much sense. Too predictable. Still, these men were counting on a quick job, which didn't give her much time to come up with a plan if she hoped to save them.

When the trunk opened, Andi and Elisa were tugged out and set on their feet. When her eyes adjusted, she saw the dim lighting of the old warehouse, just as she'd thought. The men had obviously searched for an abandoned location to keep Andi and Elisa while pressuring Vance.

Still wrapped in duct tape, they were made to sit in chairs positioned back-to-back, then secured again with more duct tape.

"Nobody can hear you scream here." With an evil grin, Bodybuilder ripped the tape from Andi's mouth.

Pain seared her lips, but she made no sound, not wanting to give Bodybuilder any satisfaction. From behind, she heard Elisa's yelp as the tape was removed.

For what felt like hours, Andi exhausted herself trying

to come up with a possible escape. But she had long since realized that the chance had passed when they were tied up. If they were ever set free, for even a second, it would be better to die trying than to remain here. She leaned her head against the chair back, wondering what Elisa was thinking. She'd heard that people's lives passed before their eyes as they were about to die. Instead she tried hard to avoid thinking through the events of her life.

But it didn't hurt to think about the future, did it? Would she ever discover what her grandfather had hidden? Would she even get another chance to look? And what about a future with Vance? Images of his handsome face paraded through her mind. A door slammed, seeming to shake the entire warehouse. *Good gravy.* That's all they needed was for the old building to come crashing down on them.

"Elisa, what happened?"

"One of the men left."

Facing the wall, Andi couldn't see which one. She lowered her voice. "Who's still here?"

"I don't know his name."

Andi huffed. Frustrated, she tried to kick herself, which only shook both chairs.

"Psst. Andi," Elisa whispered, almost too softly.

"Yeah."

"My hands are free."

Andi let the words soak in. "You. . . What?"

"My nail clippers, I tugged them from my back pocket. Took me a couple of hours, but I cut enough of the duct tape. . ."

"Okay, okay. Shhh. Let me think."

Elisa remained quiet.

"I need to know which one is still here. The big one or the small one?" Andi asked.

"The one who looks like a bodyguard left."

Good. They had to act now. "We have to hurry. Clip my wrists, then I'll get my ankles, since he can't see me as well as he can see you."

Andi remained as still as a statue in the chair, patiently waiting while Elisa clipped her wrists free. The trick with duct tape was to avoid the ripping sound it made.

Elisa stiffened, signaling to Andi something was up. Footsteps resounded in the warehouse. A pause, then a door shut, sounding more like a door to a room inside the warehouse. Possibly a bathroom or an office.

"Hurry, Andi."

She clipped and ripped the tape around her ankles with lightning speed and helped Elisa do the same. They ran out the door, hoping they wouldn't run directly into Bodybuilder.

"Quick. Over here." Andi tugged Elisa behind some bushes. Though sunset was upon them, they could still be spotted in the dusk.

"What are we going to do now?" Elisa's voice trembled. "We can't outrun him, can we?"

Okay, Lord. I really need Your help now like never before.

The railroad tracks. That was it. "Come on, we'll follow the tracks."

Andi began jogging next to them.

"But wait, isn't town that way?" Elisa pointed in the opposite direction.

"Yeah, and that's exactly why we're heading this way." Once Slim discovered their escape, he was sure to look for them running toward town. "Besides, Freya Emerson lives down here. We can call for help and borrow her car."

In the dimming light of day, Andi saw Elisa's smile and something else.

Respect.

She and Elisa followed the tracks for a half a mile, then jogged down a dirt road for another half a mile to Freya's century-old farmhouse. Out of breath, Andi knocked on the woman's door, knowing they'd wake her. Freya went to bed at six in the evening and got up every morning at four.

Once Freya invited them in, Andi quickly explained their

predicament. Freya offered her car and cell phone—a Jitterbug.

"Thank you, Freya. We've got to run now. Please call the police and send them to Mr. Erickson's old missile site." She hugged Freya. "And take care of yourself."

"You're not going to the missile site, are you?" Freya crinkled her brow.

"I've got to warn Vance." Andi feared too much time had passed, her only hope being that Bodybuilder hadn't made it back to the warehouse with the car yet.

"Honey, just call him." Freya indicated her cell phone.

Andi opened the screen door and didn't answer until she was on the other side of it. "I will, don't worry."

Fearing they'd already upset poor Freya's schedule, Andi allowed Elisa to come with her. Andi started the car and screeched from the drive, sending dirt and gravel flying.

"Why don't we go to the police station?"

"We have to make sure Vance is okay, too!" The words came out too loud and forced. "Please, just call him and tell him we're free, to get out of there."

"But. . .but. . ."

"Just do it." Andi took a deep, calming breath. "Look, you get ahold of him, and we won't go to the missile site, okay?"

Andi relayed Mr. E's number as she swerved off the dirt road and onto a busy street.

The way she was driving, she might have a cruiser on her tail any minute, which was good. Wasn't it?

eighteen

Nitro Project? Deep in his gut, Vance had hoped he'd made a mistake. That his fears he'd stumbled onto something nefarious were unfounded. He cradled his head in his hands. "Lord, forgive me. I made all these decisions without really asking You, waiting on Your answer. Thinking I knew how to fix things. Now I'm in deep. Please protect Andi and Elisa, show me what to do."

He stared at the corrected code he'd written, but it only presented another dilemma. If he delivered as requested, would he see Andi and Elisa safe? He'd need assurance before he uploaded. Despite his eagerness, he needed to pray for direction, for the right words before he made the call to let them know his conditions.

Lord, help me. Their lives are at stake. What do I say?

Impatience needled.

Footsteps in the tunnel alerted him to intruders, though how would they have gotten in? Vance bolted from the sofa, adrenaline pumping through him. His heart drummed, his palms grew moist.

Andi appeared in the doorway. *How—*

"Vance!" She ran to him.

He caught her up in his arms, squeezing like he'd never let her go, his face in the crook of her neck, breathing in her scent of watermelon and vowing to keep her with him always.

Vance released Andi and gripped her upper arms. "What happened? Are you all right?"

"I'm fine. We escaped and called the police. Called you, too, but you didn't answer."

"What? You know I'd have answered had it been you or

the kidnappers." Vance skimmed the caller ID. "Only a Freya somebody called. I don't have time to talk to someone I don't know."

"That was me. I borrowed her phone."

Idiot. "Oh, Andi. I'm so sorry."

"It doesn't matter. The police should be here soon."

Elisa dashed through the blast door, panic written across her face. "They're not the only ones. I thought to hit the lockdown button, but it's too late. The elevator's moving."

"A bomb shelter won't be much protection from the kidnappers unless we're locked in." Vance began pacing.

"Maybe it's the police," Andi offered

"I'm thinking the police would have hailed us first on the intercom," Vance said. "We can't take the chance. Come on."

He jammed his laptop into its soft case and slung it over his shoulder, then tugged both women behind him to the equipment building. They stepped through the blast door that was propped to remain open.

"Why are you going in here?"

"You got lost in here before. Let's do it again." Vance managed a grin.

"I know where we can hide. First, let's close the blast door. They won't be able to sneak up on us this way." Door secured, she located a place in the wall—a panel she easily removed.

She found a flashlight next to a ladder and signaled for Elisa to climb inside the wall. Though Vance believed it could prevent the bad guys from finding them, he hoped they wouldn't get stuck if things went wrong. Next, Andi squeezed into the small space.

She reached her hand out to Vance. "Come on, hurry."

Vance stepped in, keeping his back to the opening. He took her face in his hands and looked into her eyes. "In case. . . things don't work out. . ."

"Don't." Andi's eyes filled with moisture. "For Elisa," she whispered.

"I want to tell you what an amazing woman you are."

"Vance, what are you doing?"

Though it seemed like the wrong time, if they were discovered, it could very well be his last opportunity. Vance pressed his lips against hers, soaking in her goodness, her beauty, her essence, remembering her. Aware that Elisa was watching, he ended the kiss.

"I never did tell you how impressed I was with all you've done, remodeling this launch facility. It doesn't look anything like the old military site it was—I know, I looked up the original images."

She sucked in a breath. "Thanks. Now will you come inside before they see us?"

He'd done everything he could to share how he felt about her and try to give her confidence in herself and her work. Now he knew what he had to do.

Slowly shaking his head, he said, "I'm not coming in. I know how to end this. You wait here until the police come."

Andi grabbed his arm, pleading in her eyes. "Don't do this. . ."

Vance freed himself from her grip and put the panel back in place, securing it with enough screws to keep it in position. He exited the equipment building, closing the blast door behind him. That should give the women enough warning if someone entered the room.

He'd never been in a position like this—where he was literally trusting God with his life. But regardless of what happened to him, it was important that Andi and Elisa were safe. The police would be here soon. The goons Peter had sent had every reason to get rid of Vance because he could talk. And he would talk if he made it out alive. At this point, only God could save him.

He entered the living room and immediately felt the barrel of a gun against his neck. He lifted his hands in surrender. "Easy. I have the program. If you kill me, I can't give it to you."

A large, bulking man stepped from behind him, still

pointing the gun. "Bring it then. We don't have time to wait. The police are probably on their way. You're coming with us."

A shorter man stepped beside him. "You take him. I'll find the women. They're around here somewhere."

"But what about the police?"

"You want those women describing us? They'll be insurance in case the program doesn't work."

Vance's heart sank. So, this was it. . .

&

Andi kept strong for Elisa, refusing to give in to fear. In fact, she held on to the anger she felt at Vance for wanting to play hero. He could have stayed hidden with them until the police arrived. She wished she could come up with her own plan. Andi pressed her fists against the walls, frustrated. She had planned to explore this space at the right time, searching for her grandfather's secret. But now, all her thoughts were on Vance. She prayed for him. Hard. Harder than she'd ever prayed for anything in her life.

His life was in danger. Their lives were in danger, too, but he'd gone to face the bad guys alone. To protect them.

She couldn't keep up the anger long, though.

He'd said all those things to her in case something went wrong and he would never see her again. The words had been sincere, from the deepest part of his heart. She'd allowed herself to see everything through his eyes, and because of that, she realized, maybe she was good enough, after all.

Good enough for a brilliant man like Vance. Allowing her hands to slide down the wall behind her, she felt a slight variance.

Gasp. Could it be? She turned her attention to the place where she'd felt the inconsistency and examined it with the flashlight. A four-way cut had been made in the metal sheeting. There was definitely something different here. Her heart fluttered.

"Elisa," she whispered, "I think this is it. This is where Grandpa hid. . .whatever."

"Why do you care about that now?" Some of Elisa's resentment returned.

"I wasn't looking for it, but I think this is it."

Elisa moved to her side. "Well, aren't you going to open it?"

Andi ran her hand over it. "To think those guys were so bored down here, they'd go to this much trouble."

"Yeah, either that or Grandpa really wanted it hidden."

"He could have dug a hole in a field somewhere."

"But this would have been torture for someone who wanted to find it but couldn't get inside—it being a military launch control center."

Thoughts of Vance accosted Andi. "I can't do it. I can't open this without Vance. He has to be here."

"You love him, don't you?"

Andi gave a slight nod. "Yeah, I think I do."

"Have you even told him about the letter?"

"What's he going to think when I do?" What was taking the police so long? "You have to stay here, Elisa. I'm going to find out what's happening."

"No, don't leave me. Vance told you to stay here."

"And I'm telling you to stay. Something could have happened to Vance. Maybe the police are here but don't know where we are." She hated saying the words but had to admit them. Why else hadn't anyone come to let them out?

Oh, Vance. Except for Elisa, Andi had lost everyone dear to her. She wouldn't lose Vance, too.

Vance had loosely secured the screws into the panel— enough to keep it in place, but not tight. Andi easily popped them out from her side, climbed out, then secured the panel back to hide Elisa. Noticing the same mallet she'd once used to threaten Vance resting against the wall, she grabbed it to use as a weapon. As quietly as possible, she opened the blast door, all the while believing this was probably a mistake. But she couldn't wait any longer. What if Vance needed her help?

Things couldn't end this way. She wouldn't let them.

She crept through the tunnel connectors and past the

elevator and stairwell. Before entering the tunnel she listened for voices. Footsteps. Anything. She heard. . .

Breathing.

She screamed. A hand clamped over her mouth, stifling it.

nineteen

"Don't be afraid. I'm working undercover," the man whispered, then released her. "Where's your sister. Is she all right?"

Andi turned to face the slimmer of the two kidnappers. She held the mallet high. "You!" She eyed him, still suspicious and unwilling to give away Elisa's hiding place. "How do I know you're telling the truth?"

He raised his hands as though she were holding a gun rather than a mallet. "If you don't believe me, let's go above ground where they're apprehending the assailant as we speak."

"What about Vance?"

"Your boyfriend is safe."

Andi's hand began to shake. She needed to see for herself. In the meantime, Elisa would remain hidden. "Let's go, then."

Once Andi exited the elevator into the night, she witnessed flashing lights, cars, and suited men along with police everywhere. The lights blinded her as she searched through the commotion for Vance. Looking behind as she moved forward, she stumbled into someone.

"Andi!" Vance embraced her with his strength, comforting her. All the words he'd said before he left to find the bad guys came gushing back to her. Though she thought he'd been sincere, doubt crept in. Were the words only prompted by the distress of their dangerous predicament?

A man spoke to Vance. "Mr. Young, we've confiscated your computer and will need you to come with us to give us a statement."

Andi pulled from his arms to listen.

Vance nodded, his expression grim. "Right now?"

"I'm afraid so."

"Give me a sec, okay?"

The man looked from Vance to Andi. "Sure thing." He left them alone.

"What's going on? What was this all about? Are you in trouble?"

"Hold off on the hundred questions." Vance kissed her forehead. "It's complicated. I can't tell you the details, Andi. It's all. . ."

"Classified?" She searched his face.

"Something like that." He grinned.

She loved his grin and wasn't sure what she was going to do when he left. Elisa either. She gasped. "Elisa!"

Vance's eyes grew wide. "Is she okay?"

"Yeah, probably still hiding. I need to go find her."

Vance grabbed her hand. "And I have to go give them a statement."

She frowned, unsure what to say.

"Don't worry, I'm not a criminal."

"So, you won't be here when I get back with Elisa?" She could only manage a small smile.

"I don't know. They'll question you, too, I'm sure."

Andi sighed, for some reason afraid she wouldn't see Vance again.

He brought his face near and kissed her, allowing his lips to linger. All too soon he released her.

"Go get Elisa. She has to be worried," he said, a huskiness in his voice. "I'll call you when I'm done."

❧

Late that night, Vance climbed into bed, exhausted from the day's ordeal. He'd phoned Andi to let her know he was home. *Home.* When had he started thinking of this place as his home? She'd listened as he'd droned on about feeling betrayed, at being used by Peter, someone he thought he could trust—the whole thing gut-wrenching.

He'd come here with only one decision to make—now, one decision had multiplied exponentially into many.

Peter had been trying to double his money—a 1.5

million-dollar contract with the government—but deliver a substandard product for a limited time, all funded by a counter-intelligence ring, with Vance set up to take the fall if the high-tech crime was discovered. Though Peter claimed he didn't know the identity of the buyer, he'd accepted funds to produce software that would give false negatives—hence, slowing the entire process.

Tom, an FBI agent, had worked undercover as a security guard for the company, planting the disk with Vance, hoping to produce a series of events that would expose the crime ring. Then Vance reacted to what he saw on the disk and uploaded a counterprogram. Peter saw the program and called Vance in to fix a bogus problem, knowing full well he wasn't in Cancun, so that Vance could be followed. The girls were in the wrong place at the wrong time—Peter used that to his advantage, calling the shots to force Vance to restore the Nitro Project, but what he didn't know was one of the kidnappers was an undercover agent.

Vance lay in stunned silence, considering the events of the previous few weeks, disheartened that Peter was in trouble and would be for a very long time.

With Peter out of the picture, Vance considered what would happen to ANND Systems. If Vance were vice president of something—once everything was sorted out—could he run the company his own way? Not like this, not in the wake of his long-time friend's ruin.

Vance rolled over, stuffing the pillow over his head.

"Why'd you do it, Peter?" Bad enough he'd engaged in criminal activity, but to drag Vance into it, putting him in place to take the fall if they were caught? He thought he'd known Peter much better. It hurt, but along with that came anger.

How could a person trust anyone? Vance flipped on his side. He was so tired.

Then there was the missile base. He'd never intended to stay, but he'd grown comfortable here. His apartment back in

Fargo felt lonely and stale without Andi, a key ingredient to his happiness.

Andi.

What was he going to do?

twenty

Andi parked her car next to Lars's and Karl's trucks. She grabbed the letter from the passenger seat and stared at it, wishing that she'd already told Vance everything.

After listening to him share how Peter had betrayed him, and all the anger and pain in his voice. . . Andi released a sob.

They'd come so far, and she believed he cared for her. It was a big risk on her part, trusting him after all she'd gone through with Jorgen. Still, she was willing to take a chance. Vance was different.

But she'd kept a big secret from him. Granted, she'd not done anything criminal like his friend and partner, but the timing couldn't be worse for this news to come on the heels of Peter's treachery. Holding the letter in her hand made her feel like she was about to drop a bomb. Another bomb—like the one she'd dropped on Jorgen when she explained she had to quit school and move back home. That situation was entirely different, she admitted, because she had no control over her grandmother's death and the resulting need to care for Elisa.

But this. . . She'd known all along there was something hidden on the property and she'd kept it from Vance, even after they'd grown close, though that development was fairly new.

Andi leaned her forehead against the steering wheel, wishing she could put it off for another day. But that thinking was what got her into this trouble to begin with.

At least she had the Lord. He would never leave her nor forsake her. No matter Vance's reaction. Squeezing her eyes, she sent up a silent prayer. *Lord, help me explain this. Help him to understand and to forgive me.*

Andi stepped from her truck and headed into the dungeon,

as Vance called it. Did he still feel that way?

More importantly, would he stay or would he go? All she wanted was to see him grin, languish in his arms, and relish his kiss. *Wow, could he kiss.*

Yet, how could that happen with what she had to tell him? Gloomy thoughts encircled her. As soon as Andi stepped through the blast door, Vance stood in her path, grinning.

Why'd he have to be so cute?

His grin quickly turned to a frown as he took one step forward. "What's wrong?"

Andi bit her lip, trudged to the sofa, and sank. "There's something you need to see." No matter how hard she tried, she couldn't bring herself to smile. Not even for him.

He moved to sit next to her, his brows knitted. "Hey, whatever it is, I'm sure it can't be that bad."

Maybe in light of what he'd just been through, no. She smiled a little, soaking in his encouragement. But he had no idea what he was saying. Taking a deep breath, she handed over the wrinkled, coffee-stained letter she'd found after her grandmother died.

He looked at the letter, then into her eyes. "What's this?"

"Just read it. Then I'll explain."

&

Vance stared at the letter. Andi acted strangely, worrying him. Holding the letter, he read the contents.

My dearest Lenora,

I'm sure you've known my feelings for you for a very long time. Before you and Harold married, I dreamed of the same happening for you and me. I won't pretend that it didn't hurt when Harold took you from me, but I'm happy you had a long and good life together. He treated you well. I was sorry to hear of his passing.

I'm writing to let you know that I've purchased property near town. Harold hid something that belonged to you on the missile site. I hope one day soon to give it to you, and that you'll allow me to call on you when I move back to town. For old time's sake.

Love,
Vance Erickson

Vance tugged off his glasses and pinched the bridge of his nose, thinking. What did this mean? He looked at Andi, who had her head down. "I'm guessing Lenora is your grandmother?"

She allowed her eyes to drift to his, a flicker of pain there. "Yes. Your uncle had a thing for my grandmother. I told you that already."

Vance dropped the letter to the coffee table and stood. "You said you'd explain once I finished the letter."

"Yeah, well." She cleared her throat. "I found the letter in my grandmother's things after she died. Honestly, after your uncle died, too. It says there's something hidden here. I decided that maybe that's the whole reason he hired me. I started a business because I was desperate, then your uncle came to the rescue."

Vance put up his hand. "Wait a minute. You're telling me you think he hired you to find this. . .whatever it is?"

Andi nodded.

Vance plodded to the kitchen and grabbed an energy drink. He was going to need some brainpower this morning—something he'd completely exhausted over the last few weeks. He rubbed the cool can against his temple.

"Vance?" Andi's voice was soft and nervous.

"Give me a minute." He hoped he didn't sound harsh, he didn't mean it that way, but he had to think. Peter had lied to him, hidden things, too. What was it with people?

He downed the drink, swishing some of it around in his mouth, and stared at his reflection in the microwave. He was a geek. Why shouldn't Andi use him? Just like Janice.

"Vance, I should have told you sooner. I'm so sorry."

He'd had his suspicions recently, that she was keeping

something from him, though he didn't know what. He laughed and shook his head.

At himself, at his company, at Peter, then finally at the situation. After everything he'd gone through, culminating yesterday, this was by far the hardest.

Lord, give me the faith to believe, to trust again. Vance took a deep breath and turned to face Andi, hoping to find the answer to his prayer in her eyes, and in them he saw sorrow and regret. Raw anguish took the place of Andi's usual superficial, impossible-to-crack veneer.

Janice had never been sorry. Nor had he seen love in her eyes like he saw in Andi's. The kind of love every guy dreamed of seeing in a girl's eyes. He released a breath, overpowered by the emotions streaming through him. Andi had finally let down her guard, and for that Vance was thankful.

It was all worth it. He slid around the island, enjoying the questioning look on her face, and took her hand in his. It felt good. Right.

Thank You, Lord.

Andi stared at his hand and then up into his face, taken aback.

"I know it took a lot for you to tell me this. So, did you find it?"

Her mouth dropped open. Vance grinned, wishing she would close it so he could plant a fat kiss on her lips.

"I. . .uh, no. Yeah, I mean. I think I found where it might be hidden while we were hiding in the equipment building. I wanted to wait for you."

"You *waited* for me?"

Nodding, she smiled for the first time since she'd arrived.

"Okay, before we go on this treasure hunt, there is something I want to make clear. My uncle was eccentric, yes, but he was a good businessman, and he had the money to show for it. I think he hired you because he believed in you, Andi. Believed you could create this." Vance motioned to indicate the entire room.

Andi cracked a half-grin. "Maybe."

It might take some time to convince her. "One more thing. . . Whatever we find, it's yours. My uncle wanted your grandmother to have it. Don't think I want it just because it's on my property, okay?"

Her face brightened. "You've been good enough about this whole thing, I. . .I want you to keep it."

"Nope, I insist. It's yours."

They laughed together and then made their way to the equipment building where they found Karl and Lars replacing the entire section of the wall.

Andi gasped. "Oh no. Guys, wait."

They both looked up at the same time.

"Can you take a break? There's something behind that wall I need to look at."

Karl shrugged and Lars followed him over to their ice chest where they grabbed some water.

Andi found the place and began removing the wall.

"What do you think is hidden there?"

Without stopping her work, she replied, "For some reason, I always thought—no, hoped—that it would be something of value. Maybe even money. But now"—she looked at him—"I think I was completely wrong. What do you think?"

Vance watched her closely. She probably needed the money and wanted it to be money so badly—she put her hope in it. "I couldn't say. After reading the letter, I didn't picture money."

A section of the wall removed, Vance peered into the hole with Andi.

twenty-one

Andi held her breath as they slid a small box from the space between the walls. "Definitely not money."

Though she smiled up at Vance, she knew he could see her disappointment. She was an idiot to believe it might be something to help her and Elisa. In a moment that should have been exciting, she sagged, her spirits deflated.

Andi held the box out to Vance. "Will you do the honors?"

"I told you it was yours. You open it."

She opened the box to see a folded missive. "It's a letter."

"There's more." Vance lifted a smaller box and handed it to Andi.

It looked an awful lot like. . . "A ring box," she whispered. Andi opened the top to see a diamond ring and gasped. "It's beautiful."

"Are you going to read the letter?" Vance held the folded paper out to her. "Or do you want me to?"

Andi frowned. "I have a feeling I'm not going to like what it says."

Vance chuckled. "Ah, Andi, where's your sense of adventure? All this ancient history between two lovers—your grandmother, my great-uncle. It's fascinating."

"Adventurous, yes, fascinating, no." Andi slipped the ring from the box and onto the third finger on her left hand—it fit perfectly—admiring it and considering what it would feel like to be a married woman. To wear such a huge rock on her hand.

Before she realized what she'd done, she caught Vance staring at her, smiling. Her heart thudded. She quickly tugged it off and slipped it back in the box.

Vance cleared his throat as if to signal he wanted her

attention off the ring and on the letter. "Looks like it's a confession from your grandfather, Harold. He stole the ring from my uncle Vance and hid it on the missile site when he discovered Vance was about to propose to Lenora. In the meantime, he proposed to her himself, beating my uncle to the proverbial punch—your grandmother."

Andi nearly dropped the box. "Oh, Vance. I don't know what to say, I'm so sorry!"

"Why are you apologizing? All the involved parties have now passed to the afterlife. But. . .your grandmother loved two people?"

Andi shook her head, confused. "I don't know. There has to be something more, some other reason she would have married my grandfather if she loved your uncle. Unless your uncle was mistaken about her feelings."

"Could be many reasons. Maybe she didn't know of my uncle's love, or didn't think he was the right man, or her parents didn't approve. Who knows? But sounds like your grandfather felt guilty and wrote this confession to go with the ring. Must have been a serious rivalry between the two of them to win her hand."

"I wonder if he secretly hoped the ring would be discovered one day."

"And I wonder when and how my uncle learned it was hidden here."

"I'm guessing my grandfather told him he'd hidden it here, knowing there wasn't a thing Mr. E could do with it secreted away in the nerve center of a launch control facility, until, of course, he purchased it once it was decommissioned."

Andi sighed as thoughts of all the times these last few years—before Mr. E or her grandmother had died—they'd spent together. They'd seemed to enjoy each other's company, and near the end, she'd seen Mr. E kissing her grandmother. Just as things had begun to warm up, her grandmother had died.

"I still can't believe my grandfather would do such a thing."

He stole the ring from Mr. E, effectively stealing the woman he loved. *And I was about to do the same—steal the hidden treasure from his nephew.* Though only a ring, Andi had hoped and believed it was much more.

The disappointment was a direct hit to her heart, and she'd done it to herself. "Look, I know what you said, but I can't keep this." She handed the ring to Vance. "It was your uncle's, stolen by my grandfather. My grandmother didn't deserve to have it, or a second chance with your uncle."

Andi rushed from Vance toward the blast door exit.

"Andi, wait!"

Tears blurring her vision, she turned to face him, walking backward and shaking her head. "Later, Vance. . .just, later."

๛

The microwave dinged, signaling Vance that his lunch was ready.

Another day, another burrito. Man, he used to love these things, but now as he stared at it, he realized even a burrito couldn't restore his appetite. He set the plate on the kitchen island. Thanks to Andi, he wasn't hungry. That wasn't fair. He couldn't blame her. She had nothing to do with the problems at his company or with Peter. Vance assumed she needed some time to sort things out. He'd give her that.

The Lord knew they both needed it.

Adding to Vance's stack of decisions to make, a man had left a message sometime in the middle of the chaos regarding purchasing the missile site. He'd heard Vance wanted to sell. Vance hadn't made that a secret.

If he left now, he'd leave Andi. He needed more time to get to know her, to find out how she felt about him, if they were right for each other, to know what to do.

But staying had never been part of his plan. His intention had been to think about whether to stay or leave ANND Systems, but in his heart he'd decided a long time ago he was leaving. His family wanted him back in Texas. He was happier there. His dad's words came back to him. *"Sometimes a person thought he knew what he wanted and when he got it, he discovered how wrong he was."*

The box with the ring rested inches from his plate, the lid open, revealing the diamond shimmering like a distant quasar through the lens of the Hubble space telescope. Either that or, if you looked at it just right, an entire galaxy.

Vance's appetite suddenly returned, so he sat at the counter, eating and thinking. It was all unreal—his uncle bought the missile site to search for a ring a man had stolen from him decades before, hiding it away so he could propose to the woman he loved, stealing her, too. Then his uncle hired Andi, the granddaughter of the guy who stole and hid the ring, to renovate the place and gave the property to his nephew when he died—a nephew who fell in love with the granddaughter while she was renovating. Uncle Vance couldn't possibly have known.

Real life is stranger than fiction. He'd heard that old saying plenty of times. There wasn't any denying its truth. But Vance believed the Creator of the universe held all things together and worked all things for good for those who love Him.

Vance dropped his fork. He knew what to do.

twenty-two

Elisa walked through the front door after school. "So glad this is the last week of summer school." She looked at Andi. "Sis, is everything okay? Why aren't you at work?"

Andi had told Elisa she could stay home today to rest from yesterday's drama, but she'd wanted to go to school. Probably to see Todd. "I gave myself the day off."

"But I thought you were going to work after you dropped me off?"

"I did."

Elisa threw her backpack on the chair and sat next to Andi. "Did you tell him?"

"Yeah, and we found a box and opened it."

Elisa's eyes widened. "You did? What was in it?" Her excitement dampened. "Oh wait, I guess it wasn't that great or you wouldn't be sitting here depressed."

"I'm not depressed."

"Are we sisters? You always want me to talk to you. The same goes for me."

Andi took a sip of her coffee. "I placed so much importance on finding what was hidden, even believing it would be something to help us financially, that I hid the fact that I was searching for something from Vance."

"How did he react when you told him?"

"You know, I think he was upset at first, but that didn't last long. He helped me open the box. It was a ring." Andi explained about the letter and that she'd followed in her grandfather's footsteps.

"You did no such thing. You told Vance. You gave him the ring."

"It's not only that." Andi's eyes teared up. She groaned and shoved herself from the couch, hating that she'd let down her guard. None of this would have happened, she wouldn't be feeling this way if she'd guarded her heart.

"Well?"

"Someone contacted me, asking about the missile site property. They want to buy. I gave him Vance's number."

"That would mean we get our money, wouldn't it? Isn't Vance going to share some of those profits with you for the work?"

"Technically, we're not finished." Andi set her coffee cup on the kitchen table.

"Oh, I get it. If Vance sells, then he's. . ."

"Gone." That old familiar pang hit her in the chest. When would she ever learn?

"Andi, you can't know that."

"Can't I? He's always made it clear he was leaving. There isn't anything for him here."

For the rest of the day, Andi sat on the sofa, watching mindless television shows—something she usually had no time for. But it was therapy of a sort, giving her a rest from the burdens of her heart and mind.

Close to bedtime, someone rang the doorbell. Andi knew she looked horrid but didn't care. "You get it," she whispered to Elisa. "Probably Todd."

Elisa peeked out the curtains. "Nope, it's Vance. You get it." She ran to her bedroom.

Andi sighed, not ready for this conversation or confrontation. She wasn't sure which. She finger-combed her hair to make sure her ponytail was in place and took a deep breath to quiet her heart. *More like harden.*

The doorbell sounded again. Andi opened it to see a nervous smile spread across Vance's face. As always, he looked adorable with his crooked grin.

"I was beginning to think you weren't going to open the door."

Andi didn't know how to feel, her heart pounding loudly

in her ears. "Are you going to sell the site to that guy?"

"Wha— Can I come in first?"

"Oh, sure." Andi stood aside, allowing him into the living room.

They stood there, quiet and awkward. If Andi weren't so down, she would have laughed.

Another nervous chuckle escaped Vance. What was going through his mind?

"This isn't going like I imagined."

Andi angled her head. "What isn't going?"

"Can we go outside?"

"What for?"

Vance must have known that taking her hand gently in his held magical powers over her because he did just that.

"Trust me. This will go much better outside."

Andi couldn't help but smile and follow him.

"Let's take a walk." He held her hand.

Feeling more relaxed than she had all afternoon, Andi tried to enjoy the time with Vance, knowing she might not have much left.

They continued walking until they were in the field near her neighborhood. "Here. This will work. I can see the stars and still see your face."

"Vance, what's going on?"

"My uncle meant for you to have this ring, Andi." He opened the box, revealing the diamond ring.

Andi gasped, uncertain she ever wanted to see the ring again. "I thought we'd already been over this. It belongs to you."

"And I'm giving it to you."

Andi shook her head and pulled away, but Vance tugged her close and kissed her lightly. Keeping his face near hers, he said, "Once you let your guard down and let me in, I realized you're all I ever wanted. Andi Nielsen, will you marry me?"

Stunned with his proposal, her knees wobbled. She nodded.

He grinned. "Is that a yes?"

"Yes." She swallowed, barely able to speak the word. "Yes!" Louder now.

"You've just made me the happiest man in the universe."

Vance smiled, brighter than she'd ever seen—his smile shining like two colliding galaxies.

epilogue

An unusual wedding, indeed, Andi thought.

Under the night sky—the stars glittering like diamonds and the heavens a clear reminder that God held the universe together, even as He held their hearts together—Andi said her wedding vows. Vance at her side, she never dreamed she could be this happy and content. God had remodeled her heart even as she had remodeled the missile site.

"I now pronounce you man and wife. You may kiss the bride."

Andi closed her eyes and accepted her husband's kiss. *Her husband.* The words made her feel like she was floating.

When they finished, they turned to face the small crowd—including Vance's family members from Texas who were willing to brave the mosquitoes on a cool North Dakota summer evening so Andi and Vance could have their wedding under the stars.

"Introducing Mr. and Mrs. Vance Young."

Andi and her new husband hurried down the aisle between the folding chairs, arms linked.

They rushed back to their home across the field at the missile site, where they would host a reception for their guests. They'd agreed to live there for a year, while Vance worked as a contract programmer and prayed about starting his own company. Elisa would stay with Freya Emerson for a couple of weeks to give the newlyweds time alone, then she'd move into her new room at Ground Zero.

He lifted Andi in his arms, swept her into the elevator, and continued to hold her until they'd crossed over the blast door threshold. He set her gently on her feet, then pulled a gift—wrapped in white with a silver bow—from the side table and

171

handed his present to her.

She giggled as she took it. "What's this?"

"I wanted to give you something special." He winked.

If there was one thing she loved, it was a man who could make her weak in the knees with a simple wink. Oh, how she loved him. She carefully ripped open the paper to reveal a certificate and gasped. "You. . .named a star after me?"

"And why not? You're my shining star." He tugged her to him and kissed her on the top of the head. "You should know it's only a novelty gesture. The only thing I could officially name after you through the International Astronomical Union was an asteroid. I didn't think a mere asteroid was a good fit for my beautiful Andi."

"You are amazing. I love that you'd want to name a star after me, and I love you." She stared up into his eyes expectantly.

"You know, the wedding under the stars was memorable, exceptional even. I'm glad we did it." He nuzzled her neck. "But now I'm hoping the guests won't stay too long."

Andi smiled her agreement.

A Letter To Our Readers

Dear Reader:

In order that we might better contribute to your reading enjoyment, we would appreciate your taking a few minutes to respond to the following questions. We welcome your comments and read each form and letter we receive. When completed, please return to the following:

Fiction Editor
Heartsong Presents
PO Box 719
Uhrichsville, Ohio 44683

1. Did you enjoy reading *Disarming Andi* by Elizabeth Goddard?
   ❑ Very much! I would like to see more books by this author!
   ❑ Moderately. I would have enjoyed it more if

   _____

   _____

   _____

2. Are you a member of **Heartsong Presents**? ❑ Yes ❑ No
   If no, where did you purchase this book? _____

   _____

3. How would you rate, on a scale from 1 (poor) to 5 (superior), the cover design? _____

4. On a scale from 1 (poor) to 10 (superior), please rate the following elements.

   ____ Heroine   ____ Plot
   ____ Hero   ____ Inspirational theme
   ____ Setting   ____ Secondary characters

5. These characters were special because? _____

_____

_____

6. How has this book inspired your life? _____

_____

_____

7. What settings would you like to see covered in future
   Heartsong Presents books? _____

_____

_____

8. What are some inspirational themes you would like to see
   treated in future books? _____

_____

_____

9. Would you be interested in reading other **Heartsong
   Presents** titles? ❑ Yes ❑ No

10. Please check your age range:
   ❑ Under 18   ❑ 18-24
   ❑ 25-34   ❑ 35-45
   ❑ 46-55   ❑ Over 55

Name _____

Occupation _____

Address _____

City, State, Zip_____

E-mail _____

COWGIRL AT HEART

Revenge turns to romance and redemption in Sady Grove, Arkansas.

Contemporary, paperback, 320 pages, 5³⁄₁₆" x 8"

Please send me _____ copies of *Cowgirl at Heart*. I am enclosing $10.99 for each. (Please add $4.00 to cover postage and handling per order. OH add 7% tax. If outside the U.S. please call 740-922-7280 for shipping charges.)

Name _____

Address _____

City, State, Zip _____

To place a credit card order, call 1-740-922-7280.
Send to: Heartsong Presents Readers' Service, PO Box 721, Uhrichsville, OH 44683